An
IMPROBABLE
PAIRING

An

IMPROBABLE
PAIRING

GARY DICKSON

GREENLEAF
BOOK GROUP PRESS

Published by Greenleaf Book Group Press
Austin, Texas
www.gbgpress.com

Distributed by Greenleaf Book Group

For ordering information or special discounts for bulk purchases, please contact Greenleaf Book Group at PO Box 91869, Austin, TX 78709, 512.891.6100.

Design and composition by Greenleaf Book Group and Kim Lance
Cover design by Greenleaf Book Group and Kim Lance
Cover credits: woman © Thinkstock / iStock Collection / NejroN
orchids © Thinkstock / iStock Collection / Nik_Merkulov
Paris © Thinkstock / iStock Collection / elenavolkova
Author photo by Susan Collins

Publisher's Cataloging-in-Publication data is available.

Print ISBN: 978-1-62634-579-9

eBook ISBN: 978-1-62634-580-5

Part of the Tree Neutral® program, which offsets the number of trees consumed in the production and printing of this book by taking proactive steps, such as planting trees in direct proportion to the number of trees used: www.treeneutral.com

TreeNeutral

Printed in the United States of America on acid-free paper

18 19 20 21 22 23 24   10 9 8 7 6 5 4 3 2 1

First Edition

"*An Improbable Pairing* is an entertaining romp through Europe's high society of the 1960s, featuring a lovable young American rogue who aspires to love above his station and the countess who possesses the wit and charm to conquer him. Upon opening this book, you might feel you've stumbled into a Technicolor world starring a young Paul Newman and Audrey Hepburn, their romance blossoming amid the sparkling sights of Europe. Grab a box of popcorn and enjoy!"

—**Robert M. Eversz,** author of *Shooting Elvis*

"For traveled citizens of the world, Gary Dickson's *An Improbable Pairing* is a look back on glory enjoyed by the lucky few in a manner all his—experienced young and clearly owned. Reminiscent of Hemingway, Fitzgerald, and Ford Maddox Ford—with nods to Elliot's poetic sense and bright flashes of Henry James—a young American encounters Old World and an older woman with a modern ethic. To add some intriguing tang to this classic, coming-of-age romance, stir in the author's encyclopedic love of fine cuisine, fashion, fine wines, great architecture, and beautiful women. All of this adds up to a compelling travelogue of culture and a complicated love. Eyes, ears, and all senses wide open and on high alert."

—**Gregory J. Furman,** founder and chairman of The Luxury Marketing Council

"*An Improbable Pairing*, set in Paris and Geneva in the 1960s, is a delightful and architecturally cinematic romantic romp, about lovers you actually root for, written with tenderness and wit by a certifiable bon vivant. I absolutely adored it. I had so much fun. My heart was in my mouth up to the last minute. A page turner."

—**Shelley Bonus,** writer, astronomical historian, lecturer and session director of the Mt. Wilson Observatory 60-inch Telescope

To my wife, Susie, my very own countess

"Sometimes things become possible if we want them bad enough."

—T. S. Eliot

ACKNOWLEDGEMENTS

I WISH TO RECOGNIZE AND THANK THE FOLLOWING INDI-viduals and places for their sometimes unknown but certain contribution to my experience and knowledge as an author. And there are many others, though unnamed: friends, foes, and acquaintances who have unconsciously added to my perception of life and the world:

- **Susan Dickson**: My wife, who has patiently watched my successes and failures but always remained the same: steadfast, loving, and supportive.

- **Nadine Juton**: Literature professor at the Alliance Française, Los Angeles, whose casual suggestion, *"have you ever written anything?"* was the spark that launched my writing career.

- **Mark Friedman, PhD**: Confidante, teacher, and friend with whom I've had an on-going conversation of some forty years, bridging all manner of subjects from existentialism, to politics, to the finer points of a good Meursault.

- **Shelley Bonus**: Astronomer, teacher, writer, and bon vivant. A cheerleader of enormous talent.

- **Lynn Hightower**: Writing mentor at UCLA who critiqued but encouraged me in the beginning.

- **Robert Eversz**: Coach extraordinaire, teacher, cataloguer of all tips associated with writing. A kindred spirit of enormous empathy and a blend of encouragement and suggestion.

- **Jane Friedman**: The oracle at Delphi of the publishing world. Generous, thorough, encyclopedic.

- **Université de Lausanne**: A formative force in my youth and an influential memory in my present.

- **Paris**: I'll always have Paris. It's been pertinent and informative at every stage of my life.

H OW DIFFERENT SCOTT'S LIFE WOULD HAVE BEEN HAD
he been attracted to the young girl, the one more his age,
who was standing at the railing of the ship, rather than her
companion, the beautiful woman wearing a soft gray suit, her hair blond
and straight, a cashmere scarf of a crystalline blue that matched her
aquamarine eyes draped casually across her shoulders. It was she who
drew his attention. Her posture and bearing suggested a sophisticated,
long-standing confidence, and Scott was transfixed by her beauty.

He, like these two women and most of the other transatlantic passengers, had moved to the starboard side of the liner in anticipation
of an imminent departure. Peering down from the navigation deck, he
was determined to get a better look. Cutting a path through the throng,
Scott circled the deck before squeezing between two of the ship's life-
boats to gain an unobstructed view of his new interest. But by then, the
mysterious woman in gray had slipped from sight. Given her impeccable style, Scott guessed she was on her way to first class. He was in cabin
(second class)—recommended as more fun by a friend of his father.

The woman's younger companion, however, remained where she
had been, leaning against the railing. Based on her fair complexion,
reddish-blond hair, and slight frame, Scott thought her English, no
doubt. A child (from their resemblance, probably the young woman's sister) and a stern-looking woman, whom Scott imagined a
nanny, joined her. Distracted from his observations by the noise of

the crowd, Scott looked beyond the trio of women, searching for his parents among those bidding passengers farewell on Pier 86, some eighty feet below.

The day was August 30, 1963, and Scott was sailing from New York to the ports of Le Havre and Southampton aboard the SS *United States*, the fastest and most modern luxury liner afloat. In the late afternoon sun, the ship cast long shadows across the crowd below as the crew prepared to sail with the evening tide.

Though the crowd stood elbow to elbow, Scott quickly spotted his parents and waved. Mother's impeccable silhouette had caught his eye immediately, dressed as she was in her usual Celine finery; Sarah Stoddard dabbed at her eyes time and again with a white handkerchief, while his father, Edward, stood by displaying his usual steely demeanor.

Scott was headed to graduate school at the University of Geneva to study international relations. His mother thought Switzerland too far; his father considered studying abroad too extravagant. The Stoddards agreed, however, on one thing: their vision for Scott's future—a quick degree abroad before returning to get a law degree from a prestigious American university. His assignment was clear.

The ship's company jerked, startled by the two six-second blasts from the vessel's giant foghorns, which announced that the SS *United States* was soon departing.

Spurred on by the captain's megaphoned instructions from the top of the bridge, the crew scurried about on the starboard side loosening the brawny hemp ropes from the dock's massive cleats and then throwing them into the water. The twin diesel engines roared to life and, as soon as the last line was undone, the tide pulled the ship away from the dock. In seconds, Scott felt separated from everything he had known.

Dutifully waving until his parents disappeared into the mist, Scott remained at his post long after the other passengers had retreated. He watched the receding pier as the ship passed the Statue of Liberty and then exited the Hudson channel into the open Atlantic.

A noticeable lump hung in the young man's throat, and a shiver— either cold or emotion—rippled across his tall, muscled frame. Though the other passengers saw a young man, brown hair ruffled by the breeze, hands jammed into his coat's pockets, inwardly, Scott cheered—he was free: free to do whatever he wanted, free to be whomever he would be. And free from the almost constant supervision of his parents.

NPACKING IN HIS CABIN, SCOTT DISCOVERED HIS activity sheet. Intrigued, he noted there was a dance in the ballroom following dinner. His thoughts wandered to the blond woman he'd spied on deck; he felt certain he would not see her there. She would be a world away, behind many secured passageways and doors, luxuriating in the grandeur of first class, which he would only be able to experience by paging through the ship's brochure. But perhaps the young English girl, her friend, would be in attendance. Determined to make an impression, Scott dressed in an elegant dark navy suit, blue-and-white striped silk tie, and a crisp poplin white shirt, lightly starched. A last check in his mirror revealed fashionably styled dark brown hair, cropped in the day's popular Kennedy cut; a pocket square, peeping out just the right amount; and a tie with one perfect, single Windsor knot. All was in order.

Scott made his way along the ship's passages to the dining room. It was customary that passengers were assigned to tables for the duration of the voyage. He sighed as he exchanged handshakes, for Scott's assigned companions consisted of five other male passengers: two business types (who spoke no English) and three young students returning to their English boarding school. Scott was not interested in the company of these men. Impatiently, he watched the entrance for more diverting diners.

There. Scott spied the glint of reddish-blond hair. The young woman, her sister, and the nanny proceeded to the front, near the captain's table where the second in command (the executive officer, subbing for the captain) was seated with his invited guests. The young woman, too, had dressed carefully for dinner, and her attire suggested a real interest in the after-dinner dance. A black dress, with empire waistline and spaghetti straps, smartly accentuated her slender frame. Black high heels and a white pearl choker perfected her ensemble. Smiling and conversing with everyone at the table (especially one of the young officers seated across from her), she appeared to be in a very gay mood.

Dinner ended. Scott, along with almost everyone else, migrated to the lounge, where he stationed himself at the bar. Situated near the entrance, Scott was strategically positioned to observe all comings and goings. When the young Englishwoman did enter, she was not alone. Though her sister and the nanny had disappeared, four other girls were in tow. Scott knew from experience that separating her from her friends could be a challenge. Approaching two girls to ask one for a dance was chancy. With five girls, any potential suitor would have to pass muster with all to be considered by one. Grimly, he remembered the many debutante balls and cotillions he had attended since his teens—the very life he was trying to escape by leaving Charleston. Under the circumstances, he knew he must swim with the tide. Ah, well; perhaps he'd find an interesting diversion.

The music was continuous, the combo orchestra showing off its range of songs, from Bobby Vinton's *Blue Velvet* to Peter, Paul, and Mary's *Blowin' in the Wind*. The girls, animated, talked and giggled. Scott finished his drink, summoned his courage and, with good posture and a winning smile, approached them as confidently as possible.

"Good evening, Miss," he said. "I'm Scott. That dress looks like it wants to dance. Shall we?"

"That's a very brash beginning, but you're an American, so I forgive you. I'm Millie."

"That's a lovely name, but it doesn't answer the question. Would you like to dance?"

"Yes, Miss Millie Summersmith accepts with pleasure the kind invitation to dance."

"Well, we had better hurry. This song will be over if we continue to banter."

"Is there something wrong with bantering, Mr. . . what did you say your name was?"

"Scott. Scott Stoddard."

As they made their way to the dance floor, he could see the other men's envious glances and was glad he'd moved quickly. Millie's dress suited her well. Her smile was genuine, and her pale green eyes glistened in the room's soft light.

For the first few moments they were quiet, patiently learning each other's moves. As they eased into the rhythm of unconsciously following and leading, he said, "Summersmith; that's English, isn't it?"

"Are you always a master of the obvious?"

"I'm not always anything, but I was right about the dress."

For the next two dances, Millie made sure she and Scott got to know each other. She: nineteen, parents divorced, her father living in New York, her mother in London. That summer, the three of them stayed in New York, on Long Island. Scott had correctly surmised that the younger girl was her sister (Tillie) and the older woman, her sister's nanny. Millie made it clear that Miss Bannister was Tillie's nanny, not hers, letting Scott know by the subjects broached—and so many other, subtle ways—that she was a young sophisticate.

Scott volunteered that, at twenty-two, he was traveling to Geneva to earn his master's degree. Millie laughed. His first trip to Europe! She'd been going back and forth between Europe and the States from an early age. She teased him about his American accent; his good-humored rebuttal—"You're the one with the accent, Millie."

As they laughed, a well-dressed, tall (though not quite as tall as Scott), and handsome-enough guy tapped him on the shoulder to ask, "May I cut in?"

Millie answered, "Sorry, not now." The rejected suitor quickly turned to pursue another dance partner.

"He looked eager," Scott said.

"Eagerness is too common a trait."

"Then I will try to keep it in check."

When they stopped dancing, Millie asked, "Want to have some fun?"

"I thought we were."

"They have more fun in first class," she said knowingly.

"I bet they do."

"Let's go! I know someone there, a friend of my mother's."

Millie rejoined her companions' table, retrieving her evening bag and saying something to her girlfriends, who convulsed with nervous laughter. Scott wondered—was it him or their destination that prompted giggles?

three

THROUGH THE LAUNDRY ROOM, STARTLING WORKERS busy with the sheets and towels turning over and over in vast steamy vats, Scott and Millie hurried through the labyrinth below decks. Millie led them to a double steel door; when opened, the passageway revealed still another, a revolving door, to negotiate. Finally, they entered the ballroom.

Scott gaped: crystal chandeliers, mahogany paneling, etched and stained glass, and an imposing, serpentine bar created a scene of opulent elegance. The full orchestra, an animated crowd, and champagne-fueled revelry—this was how he'd imagined evenings on the *Titanic* or parties described in *The Great Gatsby*. Luxury was front and center.

"We made it," Millie said. "Let's find Desirée."

She was leading him across the ballroom when Scott spotted Millie's companion, the beautiful woman he'd admired during boarding. Weaving through the tables and dancers, they approached her table in the corner of the ballroom. A party of two men in black tie and two women wearing ball gowns, their jewelry ablaze, were gathered there. The men rose as Millie approached the table. They all seemed to know Millie.

"Millie, my darling," Scott's mystery woman said.

"Yes, *c'est moi*, up from second class," Millie said.

"I don't understand why your father insists on putting you down there."

"He says not to spoil us. Desirée, please let me introduce you to my friend, Scott Stoddard, an American. Scott, the Countess de Rovere."

The countess extended her hand. Scott took it gently and looked directly into her eyes. "*Enchanté*, Countess."

As the formalities of introduction and small talk progressed, Scott noticed the countess spoke with confidence and ease in both French and English. From what he discerned, she and her friends had spent late July and August in the Hamptons and were now returning to their respective residences in Europe. As they spoke, he marveled at her gestures, how her beautiful hands accentuated conversation; it was like watching a skilled conductor lead a symphonic orchestra. He'd never experienced any woman like her.

The countess held court. Seated at the head of the table, the others were arrayed around her. As befits the star of the show, her attire was stunning. She wore a sheath embroidered with pearls and sparkling embellishments. A silver band gathered her blond hair in a sophisticated updo while allowing copious beautiful tresses to tumble out in seemingly random—though surely planned—fashion. A delicately braided silk cord circled her neck and, suspended from it, a sapphire and diamond brooch nestled at her décolletage.

Aware that most Americans were known to gush a little too quickly, Scott spent most of the time at the countess's table listening and sipping the free-flowing champagne. When he spoke, it was sparingly and with brevity, mainly answering any questions directed his way.

At one point, he asked Millie to dance. When he pulled her close (and then a little closer), she didn't resist. He knew they made a handsome couple on the dance floor. Once they returned to the table, the questions began. Their dancing together had been noticed, and now, out of their respect to Millie, the countess and her companions were protectively interested in finding out just who this American fellow was.

"Mr. Stoddard are you going to Europe for business or pleasure?" the countess asked.

"Neither. I'm entering a graduate program at the University of Geneva in international relations," Scott replied.

"Well, you must be very smart,"

"Thank you; I have a lot of people fooled."

"The countess lives part of the year in her home near Geneva," Millie interjected.

"If you have any problems or need any help," the countess said, "I would be glad to try to assist you."

"You're too nice," Scott said, "but I couldn't impose on you."

"Not at all. Geneva can be a difficult place. Perhaps you should take my number just in case."

Take her number? Of course he would.

"Desirée knows everyone in Geneva," Millie said. "You must call."

Around midnight, Millie announced it was time to go. Scott addressed each person, following the correct and expected protocol of "good evenings" and "pleasure to meet yous." In parting, the countess turned to Millie. "Why don't you and Mr. Stoddard join me tomorrow night for dinner? We have some catching up to do, and we can't have you languishing down there. Your mother would never forgive me."

"We'd love to, wouldn't we Scott?"

"Certainly," he said, marveling at his good fortune. Things couldn't be more perfect.

They found their way back without incident, and Scott delivered Millie to her cabin on the upper decks. He wondered: was her sister's nanny lying in wait for Millie's return? As Millie deftly unlocked the door, she said, "I'll see you tomorrow" and gave him a kiss on the cheek, slightly grazing his lips in passing.

Scott walked to his stateroom and considered the evening. He recognized that Millie was the more age-appropriate romantic interest of the two women he'd met. She was perfect, lovely in every way, but he couldn't get his mind off the countess. Dare he even think of a liaison with this more sophisticated, wiser, worldlier woman? Well, he was; the thought filled his mind. The Countess de Rovere was unaccompanied. She hadn't been wearing a wedding ring; maybe she'd never married; perhaps she was divorced. Scott mulled over their encounter. Was there any reason to believe she could have anything more than a casual interest in him? Whether anything more was possible, his hopeful imagination thought perhaps she'd reveal more of herself at tomorrow night's dinner.

Scott's anticipation at seeing the countess again was building. But there was Millie; how could he give the countess the attention he so wanted and encourage any trace of reciprocity with his dinner date present? The countess would surely find any impoliteness crass. Balancing his attention between two sophisticated women, both of whom were attuned to the maneuvers of men, would be like walking a tightrope.

four

THE NEXT EVENING, MILLIE DIDN'T DISAPPOINT. DRESSing beyond her years, she wore a sexy flapper-styled dress with white fringe, lace, and beads. Obviously skilled in cosmetics, Mille had dramatically accentuated her eyes and lengthened her eyelashes with mascara. The reddest possible lipstick completed her outfit. The night before, Scott had been the only man in first class without a tux. Having never anticipated a foray out of steerage, he hadn't packed his own for the crossing; his tux, along with the rest of his stuff, would be shipped once he'd found a place in Geneva. Though he'd felt uncomfortably underdressed for first class and the countess, his charcoal suit would have to do.

Tonight, they took a more direct path through the ship, and Millie filled him in on the countess as they walked.

"I think Desirée approves of you, and she doesn't like just anybody," Millie said.

"Why, because she included me in the dinner invitation?"

"No, because she said, pointedly, that I should hang on to *that*, the *that* meaning you."

"Well I hope you do," Scott said. "So, what's her story?"

Millie's mother had known Desirée's mother, Françoise de Bellecourt, who was descended from a long French line. Desirée had married and then divorced an Italian count, who came from a Venetian shipping family, after a short and childless marriage. Something to do with the count's gambling debts, Millie supposed. She didn't reveal Desirée's age, and Scott didn't ask, though he wanted to know. He guessed she was somewhere between twenty-eight and thirty.

Fifteen minutes after nine, the countess appeared in the first-class dining room doorway. The ship's personnel, falling all over themselves, guided her to the captain's table where the countess took her seat. Scott had seen her now for the third time, and he was struck, once again, by her elegance. The Countess de Rovere wore a North African caftan of white silk and gold thread. The loose folds hung from her five-foot, seven-inch silhouette, draping her body, revealing nothing, yet suggesting everything. A single gold ring and hammered bangle cuff completed her look. Scott, momentarily mesmerized by the countess's grace and sexuality, had to mind his manners. He didn't want Millie to see him surveying the countess, or worse, staring with too much interest.

After a settling-in period of a few minutes, the countess turned to Scott and asked, "Do you have friends in Geneva?"

"No, I don't know anyone."

"Well, that's not quite true. You know me. Do you have a place to live?"

"I'm going to rent an apartment."

"It would be best to rent something in the old town, near the university, but of course it's more expensive," she said.

"Convenience has a price," Scott said.

Was she being cordial because he was a newcomer or was there something else?, Scott wondered. Now and then, it seemed Desirée's aquamarine eyes were revealing more than the casualness she affected in conversation. But he couldn't be sure. And Scott knew that the slightest indiscretion would end his budding friendship with Millie and dismantle any beginnings of a relationship with the countess. No; if a move was to be made, the countess must be the one to act. Scott realized how highly improbable this scenario was, but, if he could wait patiently enough, there was still time to find out. A woman like Desirée—beautiful, single, and wealthy—would, without a doubt, have an army of suitors.

Millie's voice broke into his thoughts: "Scott, you seem to be somewhere else," she said in an accusing tone.

"Oh yes; sorry. I was just thinking."

"About what?"

"Nothing really."

"Come now, can't we know just the tiniest hint of what took you so far away?" the countess asked.

Scott felt a certain heat in his cheeks, which he knew were turning red. He told himself to relax, to breathe, but on reflection, he wasn't totally displeased his interest had been revealed; that reverie and resulting blush had exposed Scott's preoccupation. Perhaps this gave the countess the tip she was looking for. He imagined that Desirée liked having the upper hand, and he wasn't ready to give her any more clues to confirm her suspicions. Not at this time, anyway. Scott guessed the countess could be the kind of woman who wanted to subject every man and was probably driven mad by those she couldn't immediately ensnare. *I'd love to drive her mad*, he thought.

"Forgive me," Scott responded. "I was reveling in my extraordinary fortune at having dinner with the two most beautiful women on the ship."

"Flattery will go a long way with the distaff set, Mr. Stoddard," the countess laughed.

"It's only flattery when it's not true," he replied.

On that note, their repartee ended, and conversation turned to plans for Europe. When the ship reached England, Scott learned that Millie and her sister, like most of the ship's company, would disembark in Southampton. They'd be picked up and chauffeured to their mother's summer home in Somerset, where the girls would enjoy the last few warm days before returning to London. The countess, however, would leave the ship at the first port of call, Le Havre, France, on the Normandy coast, early in the morning before it crossed the channel northward to Southampton. She'd proceed to Paris, where she would visit her mother, and then on to Florence, where she'd stay until the end of October. Although Scott didn't say, he was scheduled for a few days in both London and Paris, a kind of young man's grand tour, before arriving in Geneva.

THE NEXT TWO EVENINGS AFFORDED NO MORE VISITS TO FIRST class. Scott was disappointed. He had hoped to dine with the countess again, and the lack of invitation could mean she wasn't interested or that Millie had prevented any more threesome evenings. But this didn't stop him from thinking about Desirée. It made him obsess even more.

Still, Scott enjoyed the dinners and dancing with Millie, who always dressed in something a little too sexy or mature for her age. For a nineteen-year-old, she seemed very much of the world. Scott recognized that she knew much more than he did, which caused some anxious moments. She'd already been everywhere. Though Millie wasn't snooty (at least, with Scott), she could drop little teasers at will, such as, "Oh, at Christmas, we always go to Badrutt's in St. Moritz. The *après-ski* is marvelous there."

Scott was familiar with St. Moritz, but what was Badrutt's? He knew better than to ask. That worldliness, he reasoned, resulted in his unease around Millie. And if the younger Millie was a challenge, Scott could well imagine what spending stretches of time with the more sophisticated countess would be like. He'd always been considered smart; everything he attempted looked easy. "Lucky Scott," his friends in school had called him. But these two women were making him realize just how very far behind he was. Scott was determined to catch up.

That, however, was exactly the sort of distraction Scott didn't need right then. University would require all his concentration. And in truth, wasn't he getting ahead of himself with this preoccupation with the countess? Other than the mild (and brief) flirtation at dinner, she'd given no indication she'd wanted anything more than to charm him. Perhaps Desirée acted the same way with every man she met.

AFTER FOUR DAYS TOGETHER, IT WAS OBVIOUS MILLIE AND
Scott liked each other (though Scott could have liked her even more if
thoughts of the countess had not been lurking in his head). The young
people explored the ship and enjoyed activities, finding plenty to talk
and laugh about. They sought each other out for dinner and dancing.
On the sixth morning, the ship was scheduled to arrive in Southampton, some ninety miles southwest of London, and that made the last
night on board difficult. There is always a sadness associated with shipboard farewells—and they are particularly rough when all parties know
a next meeting will likely never occur. Not wanting to admit reality,
Millie and Scott promised to keep in touch. Scott grasped at the idea
of visiting London during the school year. It was one of many little
plots hatched during their last evening, schemes designed to assuage
their melancholy: their shipboard acquaintance would terminate when
the ship docked.

five

S COTT SET HIS ALARM TO RING BEFORE DAWN. THE NEXT morning, the SS *United States* was docking in Le Havre, and those passengers heading to Paris and other points would disembark. Among them would be the countess. He wanted one last look.

A light fog enveloped the ship. At six in the morning, only a few passengers filed down the gangway to the dock. Hidden in a dark doorway, Scott waited and watched the deck; he knew Desirée would not be among the early group, and it was essential that he spot her before she spotted him. He didn't want his interest known before he was ready. . . and before he knew hers.

Scott glimpsed her sleeve, peeking out from a cabin doorway, first. The vicuna coat, a broad gold cuff encircling a wrist, and a dark brown, kid leather glove—they could only be hers. Desirée appeared in full view, and he was again taken with her beauty: that serene face, her confident posture, and those crystal blue eyes. Encircling her neck was a yellow print Hermes scarf; a chocolate felt fedora completed the countess's travel ensemble. As Desirée headed down the deck, Scott walked in the opposite direction until he reached the stairs to the sports deck. Stopping, he watched her disembark from the ship's bow.

The countess stepped off the gangway and onto the dock and then inexplicably and unexpectedly, she turned. Her gaze traveled up the side of the ship and across the deck, suggesting that she was looking for something—or, Scott hoped, for someone. He thought he detected the slightest hint of disappointment inch across Desirée's face before she turned away, got in the waiting limousine, and was gone.

Scott reflected on this fleeting vignette for days: what had it meant? He wondered—should he have waved and acknowledged her? Why hadn't he reacted? Did Desirée's wandering glance mean what he hoped, or was it simply happenstance? Shaking his head, he thought *I have to get over her right away*. His infatuation with this woman couldn't interfere with his plans for school.

THAT LAST MORNING WAS NO BETTER THAN THE NIGHT before. Passengers were impatiently waiting to get off the ship, and Millie and Scott had the dreaded anticipation of another final fare- well. And then it was Tillie's and Miss Bannister's turn, with Millie and Scott not far behind. As they reached terra firma, Scott spied a large black Rolls Royce, the uniformed chauffeur motioning excitedly. Though the liner provided the short transfer to the London-bound train, Millie and her entourage were going some hundred and fifty miles west of London to their holiday home.

Millie gave Scott a tight embrace, a decidedly more-than-friendly kiss on the lips, and said, "It was wonderful. We had ever so much fun. Please come to London soon. Please write." And then, with a low sigh, "We had a great time, didn't we?"

"We did. An excellent time."

Millie settled into the back seat of the Rolls, extending her hand from the rear window in her signature wave. Scott knew this goodbye was likely final. No matter the promises made or sweet words said to lessen its blow, they'd enjoyed a shipboard dalliance and nothing more. He wasn't looking for an attachment with any future. But Scott knew that, if an opportunity for a liaison with the countess somehow arose, that would be an animal of a different stripe. The countess was a spe- cies all her own.

FTER A FEW DAYS IN LONDON, SCOTT LEFT FOR PARIS and checked into the George V, one of the city's great luxury establishments. He arrived in the early afternoon, the ideal time to ensure his room would be ready without delay. Entering the grand lobby, he recognized that these were not the staid colors and furnishings of conservative London. Generous use of marble and gold, wrought iron with filigree, imposing Corinthian columns, giant cascading arrangements of fresh flowers, and Aubusson rugs—a more Versailles approach to decoration—welcomed Scott; this sumptuous space resembled a palace more than a hotel. Shown to his southern-facing room on the fourth floor, Scott took in the view. There, across the Seine, about a mile away, was the top of the Eiffel Tower. He was definitely in Paris.

The porter, placing Scott's luggage on mahogany racks, offered to open the cases: should he call the maid to put monsieur's affairs in order? Scott declined, and the porter left. Alone, Scott surveyed the room. He smiled at the platter of chocolate truffles and the bottle of Moët & Chandon chilling in the silver ice bucket. As he sipped his champagne, Scott read the hotel director's welcome note and mentally thanked his father's friends who had recommended this mansion of luxury; they definitely knew their way around.

It was a long shot, but that same afternoon, Scott called Andre Bourdonnais, a feature writer for Paris' leading newspaper, *Le Figaro,* and friend of a friend, who unexpectedly invited him to lunch the very next day at Époque, a brasserie just a short walk from the George V.

Scott strolled down the Champs-Élysées, enjoying the sights of Paris. There, at the top end of the eight-lane boulevard, was the Arc de Triomphe; at the other end, some two kilometers away, he could see the Place de la Concorde. It was late September, and the large plane trees were beginning to show the effects of cooler nights; some were losing a few of their huge leaves of gold.

Upon his arrival at Époque, the maître d' informed Scott that Monsieur Bourdonnais had already been seated. As he was escorted to the table, Scott spotted his host waving at him. Another man was also at the table, and Andre introduced Leon Cardin, one of his coworkers who was a sports reporter.

The men exchanged a few pleasantries; Andre and Leon asked where Scott was staying and how long he would be in Paris. They were very interested in the SS *United States*—with its speed, the ship had become a transatlantic rival to the SS *France,* the country's flagship liner. They encouraged him to stay longer than a couple of days; there was so much to see. And the two writers indicated how impressed they were about his acceptance into the University of Geneva's graduate program.

Lunch turned into a two-hour feast of *choucroute*: various pork sausages in casings of different shapes and sizes, fresh sauerkraut, boiled potatoes, a hot grainy mustard, and lots of Alsatian draft beer from large, extremely cold, wooden barrels. Andre ordered for Scott, and the young American was glad he had. In the most French of ways, they discussed, argued, and dismissed each other's opinions of the food being consumed.

"Leon, you know the frankfurters are good here but better at Chez Julien," Andre said.

"You are completely wrong," Leon retorted. "These frankfurters have a thin casing, so the interior is more succulent and seasoned to perfection. I think you may be losing your palate or perhaps your mind. But the sauerkraut is better at Chez Julien."

"No, no, the sauerkraut is better here," Andre said. "They use too much juniper at Julien."

"It's not the juniper you taste," Leon said. "It's the combination of peppercorns and bay leaf."

"Bay leaf in sauerkraut? It's better in a stew," Andre said.

And the conversation continued, each man with his particular preference for a restaurant, dish, and preparation specifics.

Scott didn't know whether he would regret it, but he asked anyway: "On the ship, I had occasion to meet a woman whom I believe lives part of the year here, in Paris: the Countess de Rovere—"

"You met the Countess de Rovere on the ship?" Andre asked.

"Yes, it was quite by coincidence," Scott said. "She's very beautiful and quite nice, too."

"My dear boy, you are a master of understatement," Andre said. "Why do you think every eligible male in France and Italy chases her?"

"Oh, I guessed she would be very popular. Everyone seemed to like her."

"Do we detect a little hint of infatuation?" Leon asked slyly.

"Yes, my friend; you don't start modestly, I see," Andre said.

Scott was sure his feelings showed, but Andre and Leon relented when he changed the subject. He liked them both. Andre was a generous host. The two seemed so French or, at least, French as Scott imagined it in Gallic stereotypes. Andre's copious thatch of coarse hair had just the right amount of gray at the edges, and his bushy black eyebrows danced in unison with the conversation's ebb and flow. Leon, fair in complexion, was more studied in response, but, with a minimum of inspiration, primed to convulse in genuine laughter, Andre's co-conspirator in joviality and camaraderie.

The two Parisians spoke with amazing speed. Dependent on the conversation, their speech was often laced with a salty French slang. Scott lamented his basic book-learned proficiency and how hard this casual street argot would be to adopt. Andre's sage advice: acquire a French lover.

By the time dessert was ordered, the men had retreated into a kind of half French, half English that admirably fit their personalities and professions as observers and arbiters of culture. It seemed to Scott that Andre and Leon knew how to find joy in the simplest of pleasures.

As lunch came to an end, Scott thanked them for their hospitality. Andre assured him that he was welcome to call him on his next trip to Paris, which he hoped would be soon.

As Scott walked back to the hotel, he thought about the countess and her vaunted desirability. Depressed, Scott realized his worst fears had been confirmed—he'd probably made a fool of himself. Andre and Leon surely thought him presumptuous to even dream that a young, inexperienced man such as himself would have a chance with the countess. And yet . . . Scott remembered that the countess would be visiting her mother in Paris. Her mother probably lived in the 7th, 8th, or 16th arrondissement. The George V, Scott's hotel, was situated in the 8th arrondissement; could the countess be wandering about nearby? Scott scoffed at these foolish notions; such a coincidental meeting was unlikely to materialize.

No, he told himself; wait. They'd both be in Geneva at the end of October. But Scott couldn't seek her out without a reason. Perhaps he would call upon the countess to ostensibly notify her that he'd found an apartment. Scott was certain he needed to stay in touch, to be available should the countess choose to make the first romantic move. Scott laughed wryly; to think his mother often accused him of being impatient. Little did she know his patience depended on the prize.

seven

H IS BRIEF VISIT AT ITS END, SCOTT TOOK A TAXI TO
Gare de Lyon, Paris' train station for all southern destina-
tions. From there, he'd head to Geneva and school. Over-
burdened with two large train cases and several pieces of hand luggage,
he hailed a porter; between the two of them, they found the right
platform, and Scott boarded the train.

Scott sat alone in his first-class compartment, waiting for the train
to depart. The conductor shouted instructions in a stentorian voice and
slammed the carriage doors shut. The train lurched and then moved
forward, steadily gaining speed.

The door to his compartment was pushed open (and not too
daintily, either). A young woman entered, dragging a kind of duffel
bag behind her. She wore a loose-fitting, light grey turtleneck with a
cowl collar; corduroy pants in a distinctive mustard color; and beautiful boots of delicate black calfskin. Her unblemished olive skin bore
no makeup, and her long black hair was pulled into an easy ponytail.
Though pretty, the young woman wore an unpleasant scowl, appearing
intent on settling in her side of the large compartment without the
slightest acknowledgment of Scott's existence. Her aloofness hinted at
an exotic origin and dramatized her almond-shaped eyes.

The trip to Geneva, around six hours, was a long time to ignore
someone three feet away. The young woman managed it exceptionally
well until the outskirts of Dijon, the halfway point. The conductor,
making his rounds, alerted passengers that the dining car was open.

Scott, having not understood the conductor quite so well, simply followed her to the dining car. Though the young woman requested a table for one, the maître d' seated them at the same table.

"Would you prefer if I sat in the bar?" Scott asked in his schoolbook French.

She flinched, shifting in her seat, frowning, negotiating with herself. Did he mean to make her uncomfortable?

"No, please sit down," she replied in flawless English.

"It's no problem; I can sit elsewhere if you like."

"No, really. I'm sorry. I've just been thinking."

"Must be something serious. War and peace? You've been thinking for the last three hours."

She laughed. "Several days, actually."

They ordered, she a *fines herbes* omelet and he scrambled eggs and fresh fruit. Silent again, the young woman pushed her food around the plate without eating much of anything. Occasionally, she blotted the corners of her eyes and shifted her disinterested gaze to the passing scenery.

"I don't mean to pry, but you seem upset," Scott asked. "Want to talk about it?"

She sighed and drew up her shoulders and let them fall back into place in a world-weary shrug. "I don't know you."

"All the better," he said. "I don't know you either. Plus, I'm an expert."

"An expert?"

"Sure. I'm a man, I've been in love, and I've been cheated on."

"How did you know I had man troubles?" she asked, curiously.

"I told you I was an expert. Besides, what else could take days to consider?"

As their conversation progressed, the young woman's mood lightened considerably. Moving back to their compartment, they caromed through the swaying train, Scott opened the doors to each connecting car. On the way, the young woman—Solange—told him about her man trouble. Solange was French and Persian; her boyfriend had been from a highly respected French family. They'd been seeing each other for a year when his parents decided the couple was becoming too serious and demanded the relationship end. Either their son lost the girl or forfeited his funds. In a fortnight, while Solange was in Deauville with family, her boyfriend had found a new, more acceptable girl, one who would not trigger his disinheritance. When Solange returned, he informed her they were through.

At first, Solange couldn't believe what he was saying, but the young man didn't leave any margin for hope or negotiation. Though he'd couched his termination of their relationship in less pecuniary terms, Solange and those close to the situation were clear on the whys of his actions: money. Her solution was to flee Paris for Geneva, where her mother lived part of the year.

Though Scott suspected the boyfriend's parents had perhaps had a more socially acceptable young woman in mind, Solange didn't—and couldn't—seem to grasp that her mixed ethnicity might have been at least part of the parents' rejection.

Scott, however, was from the Southern part of the United States and familiar with discrimination. Charleston was certainly not Paris or Geneva, and this was his first introduction to European discriminatory practices, biases that he would come to learn were based more on ethnicity and nationality than on skin color. He could see from Solange's mix of sorrow and anger that this discrimination, if it were indeed that, had exacted a bitter toll. He felt her pain; prejudice was one of the reasons he had left the South for school in Europe.

Sitting next to her, unable to read her face, Scott sensed Solange didn't really want advice. Besides, it was probably too soon for him to offer any. Scott restrained himself during each embarrassing stretch of silence; sometimes giving another person time to regroup, he reasoned, was the best help one could offer.

After what Scott was certain was a supreme effort at composure, Solange finally asked him about himself. Under the circumstances, he gave an abridged version. As he talked, she began to relax again, even laughing at some of Scott's lively recounting of Parisian predicaments: getting lost one afternoon in the small streets of the 5th arrondissement and ordering what he thought to be veal (veal kidneys; he'd managed to choke it down nonetheless). He could have gone on and on.

When Scott turned the conversation to her life, Solange responded openly. She was perpetually traveling to the best places in France, Switzerland, and Italy. There was no mention of school or a job; her long-range plans extended at most to a few months hence and, even then, to where the snow might be best in February.

The longer they spoke, the more Scott began to think of Solange as the French version of Millie, or as the younger countess. This pleasure-filled, upper-class lifestyle—one lacking in work- and achievement-oriented goals—was foreign to Scott. Of course, he was aware of the differences between European and American cultures. These three European women were preoccupied with the best ways to enjoy a life of leisure, luxury, and entertainment. Edward and Sarah Stoddard, although well off, would never have permitted their son a life of such idle luxury. Self-made, Scott's parents embodied a pragmatic approach to life; they had agreed to fund his studies in Geneva only after demanding clear benchmarks of achievement. The understanding: these standards would need to be maintained for Scott's financial support to continue.

The two young travelers grew so intent on their conversation and getting to know each other that, when the conductor announced their upcoming arrival in Geneva, they were surprised. So soon? On the spur of the moment, Solange offered Scott a lift; his hotel, she explained, was on the way to her home on the Rive Gauche, Geneva's left bank. Her mother would be at the station to meet her, Solange said, and an additional passenger would be no trouble at all.

When the train pulled into the station, Solange wrestled her duffle bag from the compartment while Scott signaled a porter to help with their bags. Together, they exited the bustling terminal, and Scott was glad to have Solange's guidance. Businessmen bustled by in crisp suits; conversations in a cacophony of languages buffeted his ears; bicyclists whizzed by, their baskets filled with fresh fruit, French baguettes, and flowers. Close to the station entrance, Scott spotted a silver Mercedes parked at the curb; next to it waited a chic woman, whom he immediately identified as Solange's mother. Dressed in a dark blue gabardine skirt and white silk blouse, yards of gold chains encircling her neck, and matching caramel calfskin pumps and handbag, this elegant creature was clearly the French branch of Solange's family tree. Though he'd been in Paris only a short time, Scott had keenly noticed how French women of every age seemed to project an air of nonchalant sophistication.

Solange greeted her mother affectionately. "*Maman!*" she exclaimed.

"*Salut ma cherie.*" Mother and daughter embraced before turning to Scott.

"Scott Stoddard, let me introduce my mother, Madame Pahlavi," said Solange. Scott swallowed hard. Pahlavi? From newspapers, Scott recognized the Persian royal name—the shah of Iran was Moham-mad Reza Shah Pahlavi. Iran's Pahlavis were a very large family, full of multiple generations and many branches, and knowing what he did of Solange's life, the shared surname couldn't be coincidence. Scott bent over the woman's proffered hand and stammered, "It is my pleasure, Madame."

"Maman, Mr. Stoddard is a student and new to Geneva," said Solange. "He was so kind to me on the train. May we give him a lift? He's staying at the Beau Rivage."

"Of course," Madame Pahlavi said graciously. "It's no trouble." She gestured toward the driver, who loaded the luggage into the car. Within minutes, they were pulling away from the station.

"Mr. Stoddard, do you have a place to live while at the university?" Madame asked.

"No, but someone mentioned the old town," Scott said.

"Yes; definitely the old town, because you will be going to class in the buildings there, and parking is difficult," Solange said.

"But the landlords know this. When they find out you're American, the price might go up." Madame Pahlavi advised. "The landlords know they don't need to negotiate. Nevertheless, when you find something you like, take it."

Taking the young American under their wing, the women chattered genially about Geneva until reaching Scott's hotel. Before he made his goodbyes, Solange wrote down their Geneva address and telephone number, recommended a number of restaurants, and extracted Scott's promise to stay in touch.

eight

N<small>O CHAMPAGNE AND TRUFFLES ON SILVER AWAITED</small> Scott at the Beau Rivage. His room was musty, filled with antique furniture, and decorated in chintz. But rather than sharing a communal shower down the hallway, he had been given one of the rooms with an en suite bath. The hotel, though luxuriously old, fit within his student's budget. And there was a beautiful view of Lake Geneva.

In the days after arriving, he registered at the university and tried to find a furnished apartment that was convenient to school. As Madame Pahlavi and Solange had warned, housing—particularly furnished apartments in Geneva's old town—was in short supply. Scott's unfamiliarity with the city made apartment locations doubly difficult to decipher.

Thankfully, the young American made friends easily. He'd struck up a conversation with the hotel concierge, an Italian named Fausto who had learned his English from GIs. Fausto was immensely helpful in making appointments and, after a few weeks and many wild goose chases and dead ends, Scott finally found a suitable walkup. Located on the third floor of an apartment building in the oldest quarter, near his classes, it was perfect. He masked his pleasure, happy to have remembered Madame Pahlavi's advice and worn the less expensive and more rumpled of his suits for the interview. The landlord, who considered himself rather crafty, mentally sized up Scott's financial status. Shuffling around, he hesitated, then re-started, shuffled some more, and finally offered, "Six hundred Swiss francs." Inwardly, Scott smiled; he was certain the landlord had imagined this was the highest figure Scott would pay.

Without hesitation, he answered, "Unfortunately, six hundred francs is a little more than my budget." He thanked the man, sadly said goodbye, and turned to leave.

Before Scott had reached the door, the landlord countered: "What about five twenty, including utilities?"

"Five hundred, with utilities, is what I had in mind," Scott said.

"Okay, we agree," the landlord said. "We have a deal."

Scott took the plunge and signed a twelve-month lease. Though the school year lasted nine months, and that amount of time would have been ideal, most landlords had already figured that out. Fortunately (and what the landlord didn't know) was that the apartment rent was less than ten percent of Scott's monthly allowance. That number was the happy result of Edward Stoddard's unintended generosity and a favorable exchange rate. Scott's father had arrived at a monthly stipend through conversations with friends who'd lived in Europe; in an uncharacteristic error, however, neither Mr. Stoddard nor his acquaintances had taken into account the difference in the current exchange rate versus that of the past. It hadn't taken Scott long to realize that, for a student without the usual responsibilities of family and taxes, he was quite well off, even if he had been an executive.

The apartment consisted of a foyer, small bedroom with an adjacent bathroom, spacious living room, and a small kitchen area. Furnishings were sparse: a dining table *à deux*, couch, coffee table, bed and nightstand, and bookcase. For student quarters, the accommodations weren't horrible, but he couldn't imagine entertaining someone like the Countess de Rovere in this spartan room. Ever mindful of his means, Scott wanted to preserve his funds. Rather than spend on a more luxurious apartment, he wanted to enjoy some of the other pleasures he'd imagined and coveted: travel, fine clothes, gourmet dining, and nightclubs.

As soon as the telephone service was activated in his apartment, Scott bit the bullet and called his parents. His mother answered, and he settled in for a chat.

"Your father and I had hoped you would call sooner," she said reprovingly. "It's been two weeks since we've spoken with you."

She asked about the courses he'd be taking, whether he'd made any friends, and if he were homesick. Cut from the same sturdy cloth as her husband, Sarah Stoddard expected definitive answers. To please his mother, Scott often embellished his replies.

When Scott reminded her that he'd only just arrived, and it would be another few weeks before classes began, his mother professed surprise and brooded that perhaps he had left for Europe too soon. Scott quickly reminded her that Geneva was so completely foreign and new that any amount of familiarity he could achieve before the business of school was underway would be helpful. He regaled her with a few well-chosen stories and reminded his mother of tasks he'd need to accomplish, which smoothed her ruffled feathers. By the time mother and son had hung up, Mrs. Stoddard was congratulating herself on such excellent planning.

There was one piece of planning Scott hadn't shared with his mother. In those idle days, before moving to his new apartment and beginning his studies, Scott considered asking Fausto about the Countess de Rovere. The Beau Rivage's concierge had so many connections throughout the city; if he didn't already know of her, Fausto would likely have ways of finding out. But Scott was torn: yes, he wanted to know more about the countess, but he also dreaded what he might learn. In the end, he decided not to give in to his obsessive curiosity. Besides, he remembered, she wasn't returning to Geneva until the end of October. And then what? If he called to tell her he had arranged for an apartment, what next? The first call had to count;

he had to have a plausible, practical reason for an overture. If it didn't exist, how could he follow with a second call? At this point, Scott wasn't comfortable revealing his interest or such vulnerability. He would have to wait.

nine

THE MAIN BRANCH OF CREDIT SUISSE WAS NOT HARD TO find. Located in a granite and marble building at a prominent intersection in the center of Geneva's financial district, the bank was an imposing structure. Scott admired the architecture before scaling the seven granite steps leading to the entrance. Inside was no less grand. Large skylights, supported by vaulted arches and stout pillars, soared some three floors above. Bank tellers, poised behind sturdy wire and iron dividers, sat to the right-hand side of the hall; on the left, administrative personnel occupied dark, sculptured wooden desks positioned outside executive offices. On both sides, customers conducted business, and their muffled whispers—more normally in keeping with a library than a business enterprise—made the space seem uncharacteristically quiet.

Scott was at Credit Suisse on business. He questioned a passing employee, who directed him to the desk of Monsieur Richard Toth. Ensconced behind a burnished nameplate, Toth was brusquely speaking on the telephone; he motioned for Scott to take a seat in a square leather chair where Scott waited respectfully until Toth had finished his call. Being Swiss, Toth was not interested in pleasantries, and getting to the point without much idleness was a Swiss specialty. Scott expressed his desire to open an account whereby his father could direct monthly funds from the United States.

"This will require completing several forms," the banker replied tersely.

Scott sighed; everything in Switzerland seemed to require a brace of forms. Over the next thirty minutes, Toth asked questions, and Scott provided answers or documents (and in some cases, both). Meticulously, Toth filled in the forms, somehow managing never to veer outside the lines of any box irrespective of required length. No response—whether about his age, address, student status, or any other personal information—caused even the slightest change of expression until this question: "What is the sum that you will be expecting each month?"

"At the current exchange rate, around five thousand Swiss francs," Scott answered.

He couldn't pinpoint exactly which came first, the lift of the eyebrows or clearing of the throat, but for the first time, the banker appeared fazed. He recovered nicely, however, moving to the final questions: "A local contact is required. Do you know someone in Geneva? Can you provide that person's telephone number?"

Scott knew two people in the city (three, if one counted Madame Pahlavi). Frowning slightly, he asked, "Under what circumstances might this contact be called?"

"It is for an emergency only. And, sometimes, if there is an overdraft. But that hardly seems likely."

Scott reflected for a moment. The request had caught him unaware, and he vacillated between the only two personal connections he possessed in Geneva: Solange Pahlavi and the Countess de Rovere. Likely, neither woman would ever know he'd listed her as his local contact. With this unsteady reassurance, Scott's mind was made up, and he replied, "The person I know best in Geneva—though I don't know her all that well—is the Countess de Rovere."

Toth became very still and regarded Scott with a controlled expression for several heartbeats before rising to his feet. "One moment, please. I'll be right back."

In a few minutes, the banker had returned, accompanied by a very distinguished, slightly older man who was wearing a much better suit. Scott rose as Toth said, "Monsieur Stoddard, I wanted to introduce you to Andre Amiguey, a vice president of the bank."

Scott mused. A vice president? Brought in to meet a twenty-two-year-old American student opening a new account? This would've been strange even in Charleston.

"We're very pleased to have you as a new client," Amiguey said. "If there is anything—anything at all—I can do. *Et voila*, my card," he said with a flourish.

His new checkbook and the vice president's business card in hand, Scott was escorted to the door with all the ceremony reserved for royalty. He guessed that the countess must also be an account holder.

I N THOSE FREE DAYS BEFORE HIS UNIVERSITY STUDIES began, Scott explored life in Geneva. Most evenings, he would go out to dinner and invariably end up in one of the many bars catering to the city's diverse group of foreigners: diplomats attached to the nearby United Nations headquarters, exchange students, the international press contingent, a substantial number of businessmen from across the globe seeking investment funds from the Saudis' advisors and Swiss bankers. Among that group were the playboys and royals who crowded the cosmopolitan scene.

At the end of his second week in Geneva, Scott entered the Bar Napoleon. That evening wasn't his first visit to the small, cozy establishment; he had visited a few times previously. The main attraction was Nadine. Between mixing drinks and greeting regulars in one of five or six different languages (the most important being English), the middle-aged, sassy brunette bartender could be counted on to spare Scott a few words. He'd found it was nice to have someone to talk to once in a while.

While at the bar, Scott observed a small group at a nearby table drinking, laughing, and flirting. The five—two men and three women—were enjoying the kind of evening Scott wished for himself. As he watched, one of the men acted with all the familiarity of a regular; he continually smiled and laughed and teased the girls, including Nadine. Scott nursed his drink, surreptitiously trying to listen in on their lively conversation, but the sultry music of Sylvie Vartan and

Johnny Hallyday was strong competition. That, and their spirited repartee in rapid-fire slang outstripped Scott's schoolbook French. Scott
finished his drink and, with a gesture, asked Nadine for the check.
When she couldn't change his hundred-franc note, Nadine quickly
turned to a regular patron, the man Scott had been watching, to see if
he could break it. He could. And that's how Scott met Jean.

A better birddog could not be had. Their chance meeting began
a friendship that introduced Scott into the good life outside Geneva's student sphere. Jean's father was a real *Genevois*. Handsome in
his mother's Gallic way, Jean had almost black eyes, dark shiny hair,
an athletic build, and the most mischievous smile imaginable. By day,
he worked in a Swiss import-export company. Most nights, Jean was
partying into the wee hours.

Jean was a friend when Scott really needed one, and they became
inseparable. They met for lunch, and then dinner, and then beyond.
Suddenly, Scott had access to the private clubs and discotheques
frequented by Geneva's beautiful people, including the famous Le
Cinquante-huit (Club 58). Jean was extemporaneous and full of big
ideas, and Scott became an accomplice to those plans. One Tuesday
evening, he suggested they spend the weekend in Paris. "We'll leave
on Thursday, right after lunch," Jean said. (Apparently, Jean's weekends
began early.)

Though the two friends didn't stay any place resembling the George
V, Scott learned that top-rated hotels weren't a requirement for enjoying Paris. A lot of fun could be had in the 5th arrondissement, the
student quarter. Jean's mother had an apartment in Paris, but he never
stayed there, much preferring the chic bistros and nightlife in the city
he knew so well.

Regine's was Jean's favorite haunt. Scott met a few of Jean's friends
there, and one girl, Daphne, stood out. With her tousled, honeyed curls;
plump lips; ample bust and great figure; and head-to-toe Parisian style,
Scott couldn't help but be captivated. At only twenty-three, she was
the most coquette of creatures. Daphne teased—she touched Scott
often, grazing his arm lightly but purposefully. She turned her head,
tossed her curls, her every action the epitome of seduction. Whenever

Jean nuzzled up to Daphne, she laughed and somehow still eluded his advances. God, she was murderous.

Scott watched Daphne all night. In some ways, it was so achingly pleasant. Nothing about Daphne's flirtation was premeditated. She didn't need to think about what to do; her quintessential charm and the power she exerted over her male companions was completely simple and natural. How had she acquired this feminine mystique? Scott couldn't tell whether Daphne was a current or former flame, but it was clear Jean was under her spell as much as he—perhaps more so. Understanding that Scott was Jean's good friend and how taken the young man was with her, Daphne tempered her impossibly quick French. She asked a few easy, little questions. She treated him like a teddy bear, which, surprisingly, didn't feel all that bad.

Late that night, when the party had broken up, Daphne accompanied them to the hotel. She disappeared into Jean's room. The next morning, Scott looked for her at breakfast, but she didn't appear, and Jean didn't offer any details.

OVER THE DAYS AND NIGHTS OF THAT HEADY WEEKEND, JEAN taught Scott to love Paris. But Scott knew that, once the school term began, classroom responsibilities would crowd out the extended lunches, late dinners, and into-the-wee-hours discotheque dates that had strayed into his first weeks in Geneva. Graduate-level academics had rigorous reading and research demands, activities that were not entirely compatible with late nights and the resulting foggy mornings. Was there room enough in Scott's life for Geneva's pleasures and scholarly pursuits? Though it might take a while, he was confident he'd find the right balance between his newfound friends, social diversions, and schoolwork.

eleven

ONE AFTERNOON, SOLANGE CALLED. SHE HAD RETURNED from Florence, where she and her mother had been pampered houseguests, moving from one family friend's villa to the next, for a month.

"You must have had a fabulous trip," Scott said enviously.

"We go every year at the same time," replied Solange, in a rather blasé tone. "My mother has more fun in Florence than I do, and a month is longer than I'd like to be there. She has her friends—the writers, musicians, and poets—the interesting people—and I'm left to hobnob with immature Italian *nobili*. Oh, they can be so boring and self-centered; all they care to do is play *tombola*, and drink until the wee hours of the morning. Do you know the game, tombola?"

"No—sounds Italian."

Solange laughed lightly. "No, silly. It's a very old Neapolitan game, like bingo. The young men love it because the wagering is fast and furious; one can lose or win vast amounts of lira in a flash. They were drinking so much and losing so much and screaming at the top of their voices—I thought I was at a horse race." Scott heard an exasperated sigh. "One night is interesting, but every night? Tombola gets old."

"That doesn't sound like you."

"It isn't me at all. Listen, I'm not calling only to say hello; I need an escort to a charity benefit. It's for the Geneva Opera and is being given at a beautiful home on the lake, and it would be an opportunity for you to meet some real Genevois."

"That sounds amazing, but why me?"

Scott could practically see the mischievous gleam in Solange's beautiful almond eyes as she responded: "You're handsome, no one knows you, and everyone will wonder where I found you."

AN OVERSIZED, OFFICIAL-LOOKING ENVELOPE APPEARED IN Scott's apartment mailbox on the following Saturday. As he trudged up the three flights of steps, he turned the envelope over to see the name of the sender: Grand Théâtre de Genève. The invitation, no doubt. Opening the embossed envelope, a stiff card fell out. Scott glanced at its text—a list of names, the opera's benefactors, many of which he recognized as ambassadors, consuls, and aristocrats, seemingly ranked by the largesse of their financial donations. Turning his attention to the invitation itself, he scanned the engraved page. There, centered in an elaborate script, were the heart-stopping words: "The Countess de Rovere and the Committee for the Geneva Opera Gala request the pleasure of your company. . . ." At the bottom of the page, the gala's address: the countess's home. He read it again to make sure he'd read correctly the first time.

What an unexpected bit of serendipity! Scott's heart was pounding —he would see the countess again—next week—at her home. There was no need to make that unsolicited call he'd been dreading. But one dread was quickly replaced by another: what if she didn't remember him? Something new to worry about.

THE NIGHT OF THE GALA, SCOTT TOOK A TAXI TO THE PAHLAVI residence. The three-story French Normandy building of limestone, with its floor-to-ceiling windows and balconies enclosed with black wrought iron, was everything he'd expected Solange's home to be. The butler greeted him at the door, led him to the second floor grand salon, where he left Scott to wait for Solange. As part of the host committee, Madame Pahlavi had already left for the event.

Left to his own devices, Scott admired the elegant and eclectic décor of the apartment. Colors and fabrics gave hints of the Middle East; urns of Persian design were placed here and there; all mingled with French antiques. Large leather divans and ottomans were grouped to allow for friendly conversation.

Scott remembered Solange's corduroys and turtleneck from the train and wondered what transformation would occur this evening. He didn't have long to wait; the *click, click* of heels on the circular marble stairway signaled her arrival.

Solange had accentuated her exotic olive skin and dark eyes with a scarlet silk dress. The modest length was offset by its plunging back. A necklace of cabochon rubies, their deep red enhanced by the white brilliance of diamonds, commanded an admiring appraisal. The sheer size and clarity of the stones in the pendant had the look of a family heirloom. Her lustrous dark hair was formally, though simply, coiffed to expose the cabochon ruby studs in each ear lobe. The transformation from bohemian traveler to socialite bombshell quite took Scott's breath away.

"You're stunning this evening," he said.

Solange smiled as she gave a slow pirouette, basking in his admiring gaze. "You're handsome yourself in that tux. Very svelte."

The evening was pleasant, and so Solange dismissed the driver. Her red, two-seater Mercedes roadster would be ever so much more fun, she said, and asked if Scott wanted to drive. He slipped behind the wheel with pleasure. She directed him along the lake. Their destination wasn't far away—a half hour drive or less.

"I was surprised when I realized the event is at Countess de Roverc's home," Scott said. "It's such a coincidence. I met her on the ship coming over from the United States."

"You know Desirée?" Solange said.

"Yes. We've been introduced and had dinner on board together, but we are not such friends that I could call her Desirée."

Solange cut a glance at Scott. "Everyone loves her."

"I'm not so sure she will remember me," he said.

"I'm sure she'll remember you. She rarely forgets anything, particularly handsome men."

Scott blushed at the compliment. "Yes," he said depreciatingly, "That's why she may not remember me."

They arrived at the front turnaround, and Scott reluctantly relinquished the roadster to the valet. As they approached the entrance, Scott wished it weren't quite so dark. He would have liked to have been able to see more of the grounds and exterior of the house. What he could see, however, was immaculately clipped, manicured, and raked. The gardens spoke of constant care from a crew of groundskeepers; everything was in its place.

The white two-story stucco and stone home with its exposed timbers was impressively large, and it gleamed in the moonlight. Stone drives, patios, and terraces surrounded the house. Across the lake in the distance, evening lights flickered, lending a magical feel to the night.

As Scott, Solange, and the rest of the attendees entered the foyer, they were welcomed by ladies of the sponsor corps. That evening, these women from Geneva's social elite passed furs and coats to waiting check attendants. Solange was immediately recognized, and her graceful introductions accorded Scott a tentative acceptance. By this time, Scott had grown accustomed to being a person of interest, and being reduced to "the young American student" didn't bother him nearly as much as when he'd first arrived in Switzerland—though he still thought it hilarious.

Once greeted, they wandered into the home's main entertaining rooms. Scott was accustomed to his parents' comfortable, well-appointed home, but this was a new level of splendor. Decorated in what looked like museum-worthy antiques, Scott admired the golden-hued honey color and implacably French, hand-rubbed, high polish that identifies furniture of the highest quality. Fresh flower arrangements—anthuriums, calla lilies, birds of paradise, and amaryllis—enhanced the soft greens, blues, golds, and lilacs of the silk upholstery and drapes. Murano glass sculptures and antique silver graced bookshelves and tables. Pausing at the fireplace, Scott stared; was there any doubt that the painting hanging there was an original Cézanne?

Solange was on a hunt for her mother, who was somewhere among the ladies of the sponsor corps. Their systematic search took the couple through the crowd and into distant, less crowded rooms. But instead of finding Madame Pahlavi, Scott and Solange found (or, rather, were found by) none other than the palatial home's owner, the Countess de Rovere.

"Solange, my dear," exclaimed the countess gracefully. "I was just asking your mother where you were. And now, I see you with my travel acquaintance, Mr. Stoddard. How are you Mr. Stoddard?" She gave Scott a cool appraisal before adding, "It would appear you are doing very well."

She was more beautiful than he remembered. That didn't help, because Scott couldn't take his eyes off her.

Her mane of blond hair was pulled up, but small, fine wisps lurked here and there about her neck, tantalizing Scott. Her clear translucent blue eyes, high cheekbones, and patrician profile were all accentuated by flawless makeup. The cobalt blue of her sheath—Dior, no doubt—defined her seductive silhouette; the sapphires and diamonds the countess wore were almost dull against her shining beauty. The moment Scott saw her, all other women in the room dimmed in comparison. She was the belle of the ball. And she'd remembered his name.

Scott felt Solange watching him; he knew the countess was waiting for a reply and cursed himself for not responding more quickly. He shook himself free of her spell.

"Thank you, Countess," he said, bowing over her proffered hand. "It is a pleasure to see you again. You are correct; I am quite well." Looking up into her eyes, he dared to say more. "Solange, whom I met on the train from Paris, was kind enough to extend tonight's invitation. I had thought you might still be in Italy, so discovering you here is an unexpected pleasure."

Madame Pahlavi materialized from across the room, and Solange turned to the countess, briefly touching her arm. "Oh, Desirée, Scott; excuse me for a moment. I see Maman." In a flash of scarlet, she'd left Scott alone with the countess.

There was a slight pause before the countess inquired, "Were you able to find an apartment in the old town?"

"Yes, I did. Simple student quarters"—he laughed ruefully—"nothing like your magnificent home."

The countess smiled, and Scott, feeling encouraged, pressed on. "I wanted to thank you for the lovely dinner we had on board ship, but I didn't see you again until the morning we docked at Le Havre."

A slight, puzzled frown crossed her lovely brow. "You saw me? But I remember. . . I left very early, around six in the morning."

Scott felt a momentary panic and scrambled to explain: "Yes, I know it was early, but something woke me up. I was roaming the upper decks when I saw you. Vicuna coat and brown fedora, right?"

The frown shifted into a small, knowing smile. "Why, Mr. Stoddard—you remember my traveling ensemble after all this time," she replied coyly. "However, I'm sure I didn't see you."

Scott met the countess's gaze. He paused for just a heartbeat before replying, "For a minute, I thought you'd looked up, but I didn't want to shout your name."

"You should have."

The expression in her eyes revealed that his confession pleased her. She knew he'd purposefully lurked in the shadows, hidden. Not for a moment did she believe he'd been awake that morning and present on deck for any other reason than to have one final glimpse of her.

The countess plucked a flute of champagne from a passing waiter's tray. A small sip and then she said, "I invited you and Millie to join me at my table again that last night on board." She gave Scott's reaction an appraising glance. "She told me you'd been invited by friends elsewhere."

Scott raised an eyebrow. "Millie's clever," he said. "I don't remember any invitation."

Her laugh rang out as she raised her glass in a mock toast. "To Millie. Obviously, I underestimated the girl. I see now she must have had a different agenda."

"Quite different. Different from mine as well," he added.

For a moment, it was as though everything in the room had gone still. Scott held his breath, waiting, as his reply hung between them. Suddenly, Solange and Madame Pahlavi were there, and the subtle tension was broken.

"Scott, it's so nice to see you again," Solange's mother said. "Solange tells me that you know Desirée." The two friends quickly kissed one another's cheeks and exchanged pleasantries, giving Scott a moment to admire the trio of fashionable women surrounding him. Like Solange's scarlet dress, Madame Pahlavi's burnt-orange velvet sheath with three-quarter sleeves complimented her perfectly. She was a very beautiful woman and would've been stunning even without the long strand of large, perfect pearls that accentuated her décolleté. But neither she nor her daughter were in league with the countess. Few, he thought, were.

"Yes, dear—we met on the ship, and I offered to help if he needed anything in Geneva."

"The countess doesn't make that offer every day," Madame Pahlavi said, leaning conspiratorially toward Scott, her eyes wide. "She can be of enormous help."

The women's conversation turned elsewhere, and Scott breathed a small sigh of frustration. Every time he and the countess were together in the same room, he was in the company of another woman. First Millie, now Solange. He couldn't be rude and ignore his date (nor did he want to; he genuinely enjoyed both Millie's and Solange's company), but every fiber of his being wished to engage further with the countess. Were his feelings obvious? He feared that, like Millie, Solange would sense his disappointment.

The rest of the evening went as Scott thought most of these grand affairs should. He stood at Solange's side, shifting from foot to foot while carefully balancing a drink and canapé, which he nibbled in small bites that allowed intelligible speech about nothing of substance. The night dissolved in a crowd of self-important people, who wouldn't remember him, his face, or his name tomorrow.

Scott's mind wandered often to the countess. He imagined that her social calendar entailed gatherings such as this on a frequent basis. Was she so involved with Geneva society, he wondered? Or was sponsoring and hosting various benefits a matter of reciprocity, with attendance and participation de rigueur for those events she herself hadn't hosted?

He'd already had a taste of this lifestyle at home in Charleston. His parents' circle (and later, the university's social circle) had pushed

Scott into traditions and sensibilities that his more modern inclina-
tions found utterly tiresome. *Those debutant balls*, he thought disdain-
fully; *nothing more than some society-minded mothers drafting eligible
young men to provide the proper accoutrement for their little beauties'
coming-out.* He found even the most practiced participants' conversation boring and the accompanying rituals outdated and arcane.
However, this had been his mother's world, and he loved her too
much to disappoint.

Scott didn't see much of the countess for the rest of the evening. Their small exchange filled his mind, and he mulled over every
phrase. Clearly his interest had pleased her, but Scott doubted he
could anticipate much of anything more. Nevertheless, it didn't stop
his consideration of "what if?" What if he did follow up and call the
countess? What if she accepted his overtures? As he glanced around
at Geneva's most influential people enjoying the countess's hospitality, he was certain his interests would ultimately be set aside in
deference to hers.

As the evening wound down, Solange suggested they find Desirée
to thank her, but she was nowhere to be seen. Madame Pahlavi had left
earlier, so they resorted to leaving their expression of thanks with one of
the hostesses (who, Scott thought ruefully, might or might not remember to pass it along to the countess). Another opportunity missed.

On the drive home, Solange noted, "You know Desirée is a little
miffed because you haven't called her."

"Why do you say that?"

"She told my mother she thought you had better manners."

"I'm surprised. Did she say anything else?"

"She said you were quite intelligent, a very good dancer, and never
at a loss for words."

"I don't remember dancing with her."

Scott was surprised at the countess's compliments and delighted to
learn he had not played the game as she'd expected. And she'd tipped
her hand; of course, Scott would've remembered a dance with the
countess. No; that first evening, she'd watched him dance with Millie.

As Scott contemplated Madame Pahlavi's revelations, Solange

became uncharacteristically quiet. She, like Millie, was becoming suspicious of the coquetry developing between the countess and her American friend.

Solange shifted in the roadster's leather seat and studied Scott's profile. Nonchalantly, she dropped a shocker. "Have you ever considered that the countess might be interested in you?"

Scott kept his eyes firmly on the road. "No, why would she be?"

"You may be a good dancer," she said, laughingly, "but you're a terrible liar."

Scott didn't protest. Denial would only reveal the strength of his attraction for the countess. It wasn't that he felt guilty—other than friendship, Solange had never indicated any interest in him. He liked Solange, and under other circumstances, he could have been interested in her romantically. In Scott's experience, turning a friend into a lover could be very difficult. It was, he thought, equally as difficult to turn a love interest into a friend. A relationship's beginning had a lot to do with its ending.

But now, his friend had told him the countess was miffed. He decided to wait even longer before attempting to see her. If Scott called now, after the countess's comments to Madame Pahlavi, he'd be playing into her more experienced hands. Besides, classes at the university were starting on Monday. He needed to concentrate on what was important and not go chasing after some fantasy.

twelve

SCOTT WAS THE ONLY AMERICAN IN THE CLASS OF twenty students. And whether through paranoia or perspective, it seemed that the entire class—split about seventy/thirty percent male to female—collectively wondered what he was doing there. He was asking himself the same question.

This group of graduate students was a competitive crowd, one perhaps unwilling—or unable—to easily accept a foreigner in their midst. That they were already separated into small groups indicated earlier familiarity, and Scott carefully considered his options for developing study partners and companions. In assessing the possibilities, his eyes came to rest on a statuesque woman talking with two classmates. Sitting at the other end of the room, Scott couldn't discern the nature of their conversation because her voice was soft, mannerisms and facial expressions restrained. The other man and woman listened to her intently, without interruption, fixated on her dark, expressive eyes and puffy lips.

When the professor entered, everyone who wasn't already seated quickly channeled themselves into the pew-like benches. Influenced by a spartan, no-nonsense Calvinist tradition, the classroom was furnished with rough benches and desks hewn from Alpine evergreens. The *docteur* ascended his pulpit-like platform, so students were compelled to gaze reverentially upward at him; for the next few months, he would be their master. Switzerland has few universities and, therefore, limited professorial positions for any one subject or category;

Scott's professors seemed to have had tenure since the Ice Age. Most were much older than Scott's professors in the United States, and it was obvious that whatever the course, it had been given many times before in the same manner, down to the same bibliography, inflections, and analysis.

The Swiss, watchmakers and bankers at heart, are precise and detailed. Predictably, Scott's courses were thorough and exacting, concentrating on the finer points of fact and displaying an ample skepticism of any overanalysis. From the beginning, it was clear that his classmates were brilliant, the crème de la crème. All spoke at least three languages fluently, whereas Scott, with no previous European travel and only classroom conversation, struggled to keep up with lectures. His ego deflated, he knew he was at a disadvantage. The Swiss educational administration categorizes students at an early age as to their abilities and intellectual capacities. Some go to trade school; the academic stars go to the university and land in the Faculté des Lettres—more precisely, in courses connected to the international program. What luck that he should fall in with this precocious and seemingly xenophobic group of geniuses!

At Northwestern, Scott's original studies had concentrated on a science- and math-based education. But he'd become enamored with history, particularly French and Italian history, and so he'd switched from pre-med to a liberal arts degree. Thanks to that earlier focus, Scott was sure he knew more about calculus, chemistry, and physics, but while his French had been good enough to gain admission to the program, it was still not where it needed to be—and he was intimidated. His classmates seemed determined to make it difficult for him to integrate; they scarcely pretended he might belong in their club. As a result, Scott attended the lectures, most of the time lying low and trying to be the most inconspicuous of students. His intent was to imitate a piece of furniture.

Agrarian Policies and Outcomes in the Soviet Union began, with Professor Blicht launching into his lecture with certitude. As the old docteur droned on, expounding theories, Scott's attention wandered to the young woman, the animated conversationalist. Lost in admiring her flawless complexion, it took Scott a minute to realize the professor had called on him. Not knowing the desired student's name, he had simply pointed.

With every eye in the classroom turned his way, Scott's first inclination was to faint. He stammered some unintelligible reply, which was suddenly and quite unexpectedly supported and expanded on by that same young woman, who was sitting next to him. The lecture resumed, and Scott breathed a sigh of relief.

When class ended, Scott thanked his savior and asked if he could buy her a coffee. At first, she refused, saying it wasn't necessary (and she was right; a simple "thank you" was all the situation required). Scott had other motives, though; he hoped saying yes to coffee could then be leveraged into getting to know this popular classmate. Plus, she clearly grasped the course material in ways that Scott didn't. And nothing could hide the fact that, even dressing like a demure Catholic schoolgirl, she was very, very pretty.

The two students walked the short distance to one of the cafés near the university. In typical Swiss fashion, each ordered a café au lait; beyond that, she didn't speak. Scott saw he'd need to talk for two.

Her name was Marlyse Richter. Scott ventured an observation: "Our classmates are a little cool. At least, they are to me."

"They will need time to warm up to you," she said.

"Will I live that long?" he asked with a rakish grin.

She laughed but didn't answer.

The next day, Marlyse wasn't in any of his classes, but she appeared in the following morning's class, and they sat next to each other. Scott didn't want to spook her, so he decided to take "becoming more acquainted" relatively slowly. After class, he asked Marlyse if she would like to have dinner one evening. Yes, she responded, though she didn't want to stay out too late. Scott wasn't sure what that meant exactly, but he responded with an enthusiastic "Great!"

The following Friday, they met at Les Armures, known for its fondue and Swiss specialties. The rustic restaurant, painted in old town's ubiquitous yellow ivory, with hewn wooden beams and straight-backed booths and tables, was dimly lit by iron chandeliers and small candles on each table that softened the ambiance. Pink tablecloths, substantial china and silverware, paneled walls festooned with taxidermy deer, antelope, boar, and fish comprised traditional décor. Opposite the bar was a large fireplace. Marlyse and Scott had a cozy table nestled near the hearth.

Scott broke the ice. "I'm glad you could come this evening," he said.

"Normally, I don't go out with foreigners," Marlyse responded, practically pursing those resplendent lips.

"Why not?"

"Well, foreign students are here today and gone tomorrow. Most are just looking to pass time. Most are not serious."

Scott could see that any levelheaded response would not get very far, so he made a playful argument instead. "I think you've found me out right away. I came here from the United States, signed up for a two- to three-year program at the university, rented an apartment for a year, have had all my stuff shipped to Geneva, and I'm going to buy a car. But you're right; I'll probably be gone by the end of next week." He threw up his hands in mock surrender. "Should we say goodbye now?"

To his relief, Marlyse looked amused. "All right, you've made your point," she said. "Are you always this difficult?"

"Yes, and sometimes even more difficult."

"Well, let me warn you; Swiss professors don't like to be argued with."

"Never met one who did, Swiss or otherwise."

"*Touché.* I think I see now why they let you into the university. Tell me, Scott—are you used to getting your way?"

"It depends."

"I won't ask on what."

From that point on, Marlyse was much better company. He began to see the relaxed, conversational side he'd noticed in class. She chattered about her life. Marlyse was from a village near Basel, where her parents owned a small *auberge.* There was a division of labor; her mother managed the inn. The attached restaurant, run by her father, belonged to the Chaîne des Rôtisseurs (Scott knew enough about good food and fine dining to be impressed). Marlyse had learned English at a one-year boarding school in London and a summer program at the University of Pennsylvania.

Marlyse ticked methodically through a careful list, checking off chronologically and sequentially the most pertinent facts that, though providing full disclosure, would also profile her in the best possible light. She was intensely serious, her measured voice quietly enumerating experiences and attributes—almost as if she were applying for a job. When she reached the end of her recital, it was Scott's turn. He didn't try to emulate her factual delivery but shared some stories about growing up in Charleston. He hoped he'd entertained her with enough details to be comfortable with dinner conversation.

Scott was glad she'd spoken of her father's restaurant association. His fascination with Europe extended to its food, and he was enchanted with Marlyse's running culinary commentary on the menu: Wiener schnitzel, potatoes, mixed salad, flan, and a nice Dôle (a red wine from French-speaking Switzerland). Scott ordered the veal with morel sauce, a salad, and apple strudel. The warm fire, satisfying food, and light, fruity wine helped reduce barriers, and by the end of the meal a more casual conversation was flowing.

As he paid the check, Scott took a chance. "Would you like to go dancing?" he asked.

Marlyse looked thoughtfully at her watch. "It's not too late. Okay, but where?"

"I was thinking we might go to Club 58."

"But don't you need to be a member to go there?"

"You do," he said.

Marlyse had never been to Club 58, and so to see the room, Scott took a table against the wall. They sat on a banquette; it was half past eleven o'clock on a Friday, the most important night of the week. One expected to see a lot, as the good-looking, well-dressed crowd was ready to have fun. Scott ordered a bottle of champagne. The band began playing a slow song, and so he asked Marlyse to dance. As they swayed to the music, he could detect a certain formality in her movements that was not entirely unexpected.

Marlyse was pretty, and dancing allowed Scott the chance to touch her: pressing his hand into the small of her back, holding her hand in his. Her black dress, with its simple cut, meant he could appreciate her figure and admire the slenderness of her arms. As the first song turned into a second, he pressed her closer. She didn't pull away—almost imperceptibly, she pressed back.

At the end of the evening, Scott took her home. Marlyse hesitated at the door, just long enough for him to give her a kiss, on the lips no less. She didn't push him away; happy and surprised, he guessed she'd had a good time.

THEIR NEXT OUTING WAS A LUNCH DATE. SCOTT TOOK Marlyse to the Café de la Paix; luckily, it was a beautiful day for dining al fresco. The restaurant's large terrace, tables set with yellow linens and fresh flowers, overlooked the Arve and, in the distance, Mont Blanc, Europe's highest mountain, and the Alps of France's Haute-Savoie. Scott's favorite table took advantage of the view and proximity of one of the space heaters, which took the chill off when eating outdoors. Scott noticed Marlyse's outfit; she was turned out in a knee-length tight skirt and burnt orange sweater and shawl. She'd put some thought into what she wore for lunch, and he appreciated the gesture. The demure Catholic schoolgirl uniform was taking a break.

The solicitous maître d' took their order—steamed trout, lamb chops, and a crisp white Dézaley wine—and Scott noticed Marlyse seemed a little nervous, quite unlike her mood from their last date. Perhaps that was it, Scott thought. Maybe she wasn't sure she wanted to continue the mood.

Marlyse seemed to be reading his thoughts. Smoothing her napkin, she looked down into her lap. "I may have had too much to drink the other night," she said primly.

"Did you? Why, I just thought you were having fun," he said.

"I don't want you to get the wrong idea," she said.

As Scott leaned forward to assure her he had only the rightest of ideas, he heard a familiar voice.

"*Scott, ça fait longtemps, dis donc.* Where have you been?" It was Jean. Those mischievous eyes lighted on Marlyse, and his already infectious grin widened. "Never mind," he quipped quietly in Scott's ear as the two friends shook hands. "I see where you've been."

"Let me introduce you to Marlyse Richter, a friend from school."

"Enchanté, Mademoiselle." Gesturing toward Scott, Jean said jokingly, "You need to be careful of this one. Scott, let's get together. I miss seeing you."

"I'm sorry, Jean. I'll call next week."

Marlyse's little pout told Scott that he had some explaining to do regarding Jean's teasing remarks. He explained that Jean, who knew everyone, had taken him under his wing when he'd first arrived in Geneva, introducing him around at all the clubs, showing him all the right places, including weekending in Paris. Still Marlyse was hardly satisfied. Scott found her reaction a bit mystifying. They'd had two dates (well, almost two). Perhaps Marlyse wanted him all to herself. Or maybe Marlyse was simply more at ease with the students like herself and Scott than with Jean, who came from another milieu.

thirteen

SCOTT AND MARLYSE CONTINUED TO SEE ONE ANOTHER outside of classes, enjoying meals, exploring Geneva, and becoming better acquainted. On one evening, they chose the Hotel Richemont to eat at the Gentilhomme, a bastion of elegance and fine dining. Scott had never seen Marlyse look more beautiful. Normally, she wore simple clothes and flats (what he thought of as her schoolgirl uniform), but tonight she was in heels and a figure-hugging emerald green dress. Two small jade studs pierced her earlobes, and Marlyse's simple updo accentuated the length of her bare neck. Her eyes sparkled as they talked, and Scott was captivated, watching her lush, crimson-colored lips move.

After checking their coats, they entered the hotel's bar for a quick aperitif. The bar, always crowded, was no exception that evening. Nevertheless, Scott spotted the Countess de Rovere almost immediately, at a small table, surrounded by several friends. She saw him, too, and Scott was glad that he'd overdressed—a crepe black suit, white shirt, and a silver-gray tie in a half-Windsor knot—for his dinner date with Marlyse. As usual, the countess was stunningly put together, in a fashionable Chanel dress, the black fabric's dark richness all the better to set off the requisite strand of pearls. He was achingly aware of her sophisticated beauty.

"Scott Stoddard!" the countess trilled from across the room. "Come here and say hello!"

Leading Marlyse through the throng, Scott wended their way toward the countess's entourage. He introduced the two women:

"Countess, my friend, Mademoiselle Marlyse Richter. Marlyse, may I present the Countess de Rovere."

Good evenings were exchanged, and the countess introduced her friends. "Scott, every time I see you, you are with another beautiful girl," the countess exclaimed. Marlyse cut Scott a sideways glance, and he detected the faint beginnings of a familiar pout.

Leaning close to Scott's ear, the countess whispered, "I thought you were going to call me." And then, turning back toward Scott and Marlyse, she commented, "Well, I'm in Geneva until Christmas, and then Gstaad for the ski season. You are welcome to visit me, and please—bring Mademoiselle Richter.

"Thank you, Countess. Very nice of you."

The maître d' announced their table was ready, and Scott was relieved to escape before she made any mention of his last beautiful girl, Solange. Luckily, the countess and her entourage soon lit elsewhere. One thing was for certain; he'd detected a tone of pique, and that meant he still held the worldlier woman's interest. He'd deduced correctly—the Countess de Rovere was accustomed to eagerness; she expected men to be taken by her—and his nonexistent call nettled. Yes; he couldn't appear too eager. Besides, he was with Marlyse.

After they ordered, Marlyse remained quiet. He was sure she was curious about the countess. A revealing frown showed that her thoughts were leaning toward jealousy and suspicion, and Scott fully expected an interrogation. While a compliment of sorts, the countess's teasing comment about him always being with a beautiful woman had stung Marlyse. . . just as the countess intended. She didn't miss many opportunities to score points against an opponent.

Marlyse fired the opening salvo: "You seem to know a lot of people."

"The countess is a friend of a friend I met on the ship coming over from America."

"For a friend, she seemed a little offended that you haven't called."

Ah—so Marlyse had heard. Scott chose to deny and seem oblivious. "I don't think so," he said slowly. "When she'd asked before, I told her I thought calling would be an imposition." Marlyse practically rolled her eyes at him.

"Scott, you are so naïve. Though she's older and so much more sophisticated, anyone can see she clearly has an interest in you."

"I hope she likes me. But really, I don't want to be the poor lonely foreigner who calls begging for lunch or dinner."

Again, Marlyse scoffed. "Scott, she's not worried about lunch or dinner. A woman knows," she said.

Another woman, another pointed comment about the countess's interest. Could everyone see? Scott deflected, hoping to close the conversation. "Maybe that's why I've never figured one out—a woman, I mean."

"Don't try to be funny." Marlyse fixed him with a no-nonsense stare. "Tell me; are you interested in her?"

On this dangerous ground, Scott ducked. "Now you're funny. Of course not," he lied.

Scott's carefully planned evening wasn't working out. His chance meeting with the countess and her provocative comments had driven distance between him and Marlyse. Any conversation they had was clipped, Marlyse's smile gone, and her appetite uncharacteristically lost. She denied anything was wrong, denied that she was acting differently toward him, but he could see she was jealous. And understandably so. Scott was clearly infatuated; the older, worldlier woman was intimidating; and Millie, Solange, and Marlyse had all three sensed that the countess was targeting their beau and friend. Scott groaned inwardly. Would dating a more appropriate girl—one his own age and of similar social standing—be any less complicated than calling the countess, whatever might happen? He'd thought a relationship with Marlyse would be easier to navigate, and perhaps it would've been without his feelings for the countess. Marlyse was treating him as if he hadn't any options. But Scott was going to make the call, and soon, before the countess lost interest (or patience).

After their desultory dinner and during the taxi ride back to her place, Marlyse did not relent. She pouted, cajoling Scott about his intentions regarding the countess. And Scott knew that anything he could say would worsen the situation. There was no way to logically disabuse her of suspicions about the countess's interest, and he worried that his expressions might inadvertently reveal his own unrequited passion. Therefore, he remained silent, which seemed to accommodate them both.

PUTTING THOUGHTS OF THE COUNTESS ASIDE, SCOTT WORKED hard to make amends with Marlyse. He felt bad about the ruined date and hoped to repair their relations; she was, after all, one of his few university friends. A few days later, Marlyse agreed to come to his apartment, and after her first visit, the ice was broken. They were back to their easy conversations. She then came regularly, sometimes to study in the quiet of Scott's apartment. As time passed, she'd arrive after dinner just so they could be together.

The girl who accepted that first brief kiss on her doorstep had blossomed into a more passionate young woman. Soon, those evenings of convivial togetherness included more intimate moments. In the afternoons and early evenings, Scott and Marlyse found themselves engaged in passionate make out sessions, kissing, touching—and always stopping just short of where they both wanted to end. While Scott wasn't exactly Casanova himself, he knew she was even less experienced. As Scott became surer of his desires, he sensed an ambiguity of feeling, a fear of losing control, as Marlyse contemplated the act of love.

She distanced herself, offering excuses as to why she couldn't come over. "I think I might be coming down with something," she'd say. Or, another time, "I need to study alone. I need to concentrate."

There were many excuses.

She wasn't telling him everything.

Marlyse lived in one room of a large apartment on the top floor of a pre-war building. Her landlord, Madame Giradet, was a Swiss widow of some means and little nonsense. Her temperament found expression in her ensemble: a bare face, tight perm, and brown, high-top lace-up shoes (never count on a flexible disposition from a woman who wears overly sensible shoes). Madame Giradet's colors of choice for her wardrobe were gray, dark gray, and even darker gray.

This somber woman had assumed the mantle of Marlyse's in-residence parent-away-from-home. From the beginning, Scott had had to endure Madame Giradet's lightly veiled disapproving looks and comments. His defects were based on the old woman's dislike of foreigners, and he was certain that, when he wasn't around, Marlyse was getting an earful. Heaven forbid that the American should take advantage of young Marlyse. Along with Madame Giradet's xenophobia were traces of jealousy toward the young and a general sour misanthropy.

Scott's suspicions were soon confirmed. One evening when he was picking up Marlyse, Madame Giradet invited him into her salon. "Monsieur Stoddard," she sniffed, "I believe that Marlyse's parents would want her home earlier than is your habit."

Scott smoothed the waters, politely assuring her that he'd return Marlyse in a more appropriate timeframe. But he wondered—would Madame Giradet's antipathy persuade Marlyse to stop seeing him? Or would the old biddy go so far as to intercede with Marlyse's parents?

fourteen

MARLYSE SURPRISED SCOTT BY PROPOSING THEY pick up prepared food, have dinner in the apartment, and listen to some music. He thought it a lovely idea, as he'd wanted her to hear the new Beatle's release, *Please, Please Me*, he'd picked up when passing through London.

After class, they stopped in at Manuel's, where they bought an assortment of small bites—canapés, some cheese, chocolate—and a bottle of Meursault. Back at Scott's apartment, dinner was spread out on the coffee table in the middle of the living room. Turning on the phonograph, they spread a blanket on the floor and sat, sipping wine and listening to music. The mood changed as the night wore on; playfully feeding each other canapés as Johnny Mathis crooned *Chances Are,* Scott became mesmerized by Marlyse's mouth as she savored each bite. Her sensuous enjoyment was almost like sex itself. Did she realize the effect she was having on him? Scott reached for Marlyse and held her close. He kissed her long and slow, gently probing her lips apart with his tongue until her arms encircled his neck, pulling him closer. Her body writhed against his, and Marlyse gave short, muffled moans with his every touch. This, then, was the time; this time, neither would be left wanting, and their lovemaking was urgent and satisfying. Afterward, Scott felt a serene, almost surreal exhaustion, and they stayed wrapped in each other's arms for a long time. When the record player stopped, they still didn't move. Tenderly pulling the blanket over them both, Scott cradled her in his arms, preserving the sweet feeling.

❧

OVER THE NEXT FEW DAYS, SCOTT WAS SURPRISED TO LEARN that intimacy changes everything—and not always for the better. Marlyse had become distant. After that blissful evening, a week went by before Scott saw Marlyse again, and she acted as if he'd hurt her in some way. He tried to tenderly nudge her back to a better place, but she would have none of it.

"What's wrong?" he asked gently. "Marlyse, please tell me—why are you pushing me away?"

At first, she wouldn't answer, but he held her close and waited. "We shouldn't have made love. It was wrong. Everything's happening too fast. We should've waited until we were married. Or at least engaged. I'm Catholic, you know," Marlyse said tearfully.

No amount of reminding her of their affection made any difference whatsoever. Scott saw she was suffering from a bad case of guilt and drowning in a sea of self-inflicted punishment. He'd understood she was inexperienced, but could she really have this much guilt about premarital sex? It was 1963!

Scott was floored at what came next. Marlyse said, "Maybe we need some time apart. Maybe we need to think about what we really want."

Later, when he called, Madame Giradet answered the telephone, and he could hear Marlyse in the background, whispering: "Tell him I'm not here."

Scott guessed that Marlyse was using deprivation of her presence and affection—a well-worn tactic (one Scott was using himself, with the countess)—to force him to see it her way. How could he have been so unaware? Scott berated himself for this predicament; he'd been so focused on their enjoyment of one another that he'd not realized Marlyse's more traditional feelings. She believed what they'd done was wrong, and he'd never thought they'd marry. Could she be holding back, outlandishly hoping to push Scott toward marriage, simply because they'd been to bed together?

Marlyse and Scott had had tentative plans for him to travel to Basel sometime before Christmas to spend the holidays together. Although they hadn't spoken of it, he presumed the invitation to visit her family was off. Lacking any precision of details or a direct withdrawal, his punishment seemed to stretch on indefinitely.

AS THE HOLIDAYS CREPT CLOSER, SCOTT HAD TO ATTEND TO other pressing matters. He'd signed a contract to buy an Austin-Healey, which he was to pick up in Rotterdam. The car would be available at the Dutch free port any time after the seventeenth of December, and so he needed to travel from Geneva. He and Marlyse were still at an impasse. If this were to resolve before their planned holiday, he calculated less than a week to mend their break.

For days, Scott attempted to contact Marlyse. After several unreturned telephone calls, he purchased a ticket on an overnight sleeper. When Marlyse finally called, she didn't seem as upset as she had been when they last spoke. Scott was grateful for the truce; he'd missed her. When he reminded her of his obligation to pick up his car in the Netherlands the next day, Marlyse realized he was leaving. There was a long pause, and then she emotionally wished him well; she hoped he'd have a nice Christmas. The holiday, then, was off. Scott tried again; he asked if they could get together to talk. Again, Marlyse adamantly said it was no use right now. He became resigned—their relationship was over.

When Marlyse called the next morning to say she wanted to see him off, Scott was incredulous. Why? It made no sense. He tried to persuade her not to—another goodbye would be difficult for them— but she insisted. Scott had the taxi pick her up, and they rode in silence to the train station. Waiting on the platform, she asked, "Have you thought about what I said?"

"I've thought of little else."

"So, what do you want from me, Scott? You know what I want from you."

"Marlyse, be reasonable. We can't go back and pretend that night didn't happen."

"But we could make it right. We could get engaged."

Ultimatums are a bad way to start a relationship and an even worse way to continue one. Had Marlyse orchestrated this melodramatic scene simply to work his feelings? As Scott boarded the train, he wondered—was he doing the right thing by standing fast and refusing to be manipulated? The train departed the station, and he looked back to see Marlyse standing there, emotionless except for a frown.

IN ROTTERDAM THE NEXT DAY, THE CAR PICKUP WENT WITH-out a hitch. Scott had prepaid, so it was just a matter of signing for receipt, packing his luggage, and speeding off through the low country into Belgium. His next stop, the Hotel des Marronniers in Paris' 6th arrondissement, a familiar haunt. He and Jean had stayed there several times, so he knew the neighborhood well. Dropping off his bags, Scott made his way to Le Bilboquet, a fashionable restaurant and jazz bar where young professionals relaxed after work. He stayed until late in the evening.

Paris in winter is often cold and wet and disagreeable, and it rained for several days. Scott's enjoyment was dampened; the city wasn't quite the same when alone. On the spur of the moment, he headed back to Geneva, although he knew his loneliness was sure to continue there. When he arrived at his apartment, it was clear Marlyse had used her key and his time away to clear out the few items she'd brought over. He knew what that meant.

Still hoping to repair things between them, he called Marlyse at her parents' home in Basel on Christmas Day, but their holiday wishes were perfunctory and abbreviated. There were long pauses as they searched for the right thing to say. He knew what she wanted to hear. But he couldn't say it.

The sound of a heavy sigh filled his ears. "Scott, you know it's over," Marlyse said. "I think you were only in it for the sex, anyway."

"Please, Marlyse. You want something more serious and more permanent than I can give. You're trying to make me prove how much I love you."

"We went too far," she said, unmoved.

"We're too young to get married. We're students; be practical."

She hung up.

The relationship was truly over. And given Marlyse's seriousness and temperament, she would be hurt and angry for a long time. Angry at the thought he'd led her on, which he hadn't intended to do. Angry that she had allowed herself to fall in love.

Nevertheless, Marlyse had been right to insist on the time away. Being apart from her had cleared up the ambiguity gnawing at Scott. He was acutely aware that disappointing anyone was very difficult for him—his parents had made sure of that. Marriage was a big, irreversible step. He wasn't ready, no matter how much he cared for and hated to disappoint Marlyse.

THE HOLIDAY ENDED, AND CLASSES RESUMED. SCOTT'S FIRST class was an art history course he was auditing. Next, he climbed the stone steps to the second floor of one of the oldest buildings at the university for a history course on the French Revolution. As he entered the classroom, he saw Marlyse talking and laughing with a group of her Swiss friends. She didn't acknowledge him.

He sat a few rows behind and to her left, but she never looked back—not even for a discreet glance. When the class was over, she sprang from the room, scurried down the steps, and disappeared into one of the side streets in the old town.

Scott was realistic. He hadn't anticipated a warm welcome, and, while disappointing, Marlyse's distance was expected. Deep down, however, he knew Marlyse was not one to give up. Anyone who knew her the least little bit understood how willful and determined she could be. Underneath that ingénue exterior was a woman who knew what she wanted. And he wondered if she might try again to get what she wanted from him.

fifteen

IT WAS TIME. SCOTT OPENED HIS ADDRESS BOOK TO THE page listing Countess de Rovere's name and telephone number. He was now faced with the cold reality of calling her rather than just fantasizing about it. He procrastinated awhile, hoping that some inspiration would allow him to glibly call her in high spirits. He wanted none of the doldrums he'd been experiencing after his fallout with Marlyse. Scott worried; what if she could detect something in his voice, defeat perhaps, or worse, sadness? He didn't want her to think she was a consolation prize.

Finally, he dialed her number. Two rings and the call was answered by one of her staff, who informed him the countess was away and took his number.

Later that afternoon, the telephone rang. "Monsieur Stoddard, I thought you were too busy to call," she said.

"That's over," he said.

"So, you've ended things with your beautiful young friend?" Scott felt a subtle shift in the countess's voice. "How sad for her. Or did she break your heart? No matter—what is it they say? All's fair in love and war. Perhaps you need to pick on someone your own size."

He took a sharp breath. "Are you my size, Countess? Perhaps you have some idea about how this investigation should proceed."

"Why don't you come to Gstaad for a few days? You can stay at the Palace. A change of altitude will surely do you worlds of good."

"You're not counting on oxygen deprivation to. . . ?"

"I've never found deprivation of any kind to be all that beneficial."

Scott's head swam. An invitation, from the countess—he'd imagined a few pleasantries at best. "I think you're teasing me," he replied, hesitantly.

"Oh, don't be so American," she laughed. "Can't you flirt a little bit?"

"Sadly, I seem to be out of practice."

The countess paused on the line, a long pause. Finally, she said, "Do you know the best cure for a failed affair?"

"No, but I'm sure you can advise me."

"I can. Come visit for a few days. It will help you to get away, and who knows . . ." The countess's voice trailed off seductively.

"I must warn you; I don't ski all that well."

He loved the sound of her musical laugh. "Scott, dear—we *cognoscenti* don't ski; we après-ski. Let's have a little fun."

"The Gstaad Palace," he said, falteringly. How Scott hated to remind her of his lowly student status. "That's expensive, isn't it? Perhaps I should stay elsewhere."

"Scott, are you poor?"

"I'll be there Friday afternoon," he said.

It was already Wednesday, and Scott burst into a flurry of activity. He called the Palace and reserved a room for the weekend. The next morning, he shopped at Schaffer Sports, buying all the fashionable ski gear and warm clothing he thought necessary for Gstaad: après-ski boots, cashmere sweaters, a shearling coat, fur-lined gloves, scarves, heavy socks, various hats, and thermal underwear. Though he might not ski well, at least he would look good and stay warm.

FRIDAY, WHEN HE TURNED THE KEY IN THE AUSTIN-HEALEY'S ignition and started his drive to Gstaad, Scott was close to jubilant. Was it truly possible he was on his way to the moment he'd been dreaming of and anticipating for months? Finally, he'd have time alone with the countess—the exact circumstances he'd longed for.

The car was a dream to handle, and the drive passed quickly. In roughly three hours, Scott saw the sign: "Gstaad, 1050 m. elev." Scott's American mind quickly converted meters into feet; at 3,445 feet, he'd climbed more than 2,000 feet from Geneva. It had snowed the night before, and the roadway was hard-packed, but the Austin-Healey, equipped with Pirelli snow tires, found traction, and Scott entered Gstaad in no time.

Streets, shops, and cafés were filled with skiers, vacationers, and tourists wearing the chicest sportswear in bright yellows, reds, and oranges—attention-getting colors. As he drove by the small train station, he passed the Palace's signature buttery-cream vintage Rolls-Royce waiting to ferry clients to the hotel. The next left turn sent him up a trailing narrow lane, and there was the Palace.

The Palace was an iconic structure, and Scott gaped at the story-book castle. He'd seen its façade many times on postcards, but those images gave little credit to the actual vista. A bellboy showed him to a third-floor room, one with the preferred, south-facing view overlooking the scenic village below. Snow-dusted evergreens dotted the slopes, encircling the many private chalets nestled to the east of the village.

He dropped on the sofa, before noticing an exotic flower arrangement and bottle of champagne on the coffee table. There was a handwritten note in beautiful script: "Welcome to Gstaad. Call me when you arrive."

Finding her number in the note, he telephoned. When he heard her say hello, he simply said, "I'm here."

"See, that wasn't that difficult now, was it?"

"Thanks for the flowers and the champagne. And the note."

"I thought perhaps you might change your mind and not come."

"It never occurred to me."

"This is a good beginning. You see, the altitude is already working its magic."

"Yes; as they say, I'm yours, Countess."

"A good place to be. Now, please, call me Desirée. Dinner is at eight o'clock. I'll meet you in the hotel bar at half past seven. I'll tell you about dinner when I see you—it's no fun knowing everything all at once."

"As you wish, Countess . . . ah, Desirée."

Scott arrived at the bar a few minutes early. He expected to wait; beautiful women are seldom on time. He ordered a drink, trying to appear nonchalant when everything about him was screaming in anticipation. When she swept in, it was with a flourish, effortlessly floating through the doors of the bar, swathed in gray chinchilla and gold lamé. The maître d' hurried to take her coat, and it was then she spied Scott.

Gliding toward him, Desirée was exuberance itself. Her face glowed with pleasure, and Scott admired her casually tousled but expertly coiffed hair, silver-patina lipstick, and crystal blue eyes. They embraced, and she kissed him on both cheeks like a lover, which emboldened him to hold her a little longer, with a touch more resolve, until she pulled away. "I'm so glad you came," Desirée said.

"Is it all right if I say you are stunning this evening?"

"It's more than all right. It is absolutely mandatory."

"Then I'll say it again. You are beautiful."

She tilted her head to look up at him playfully. "Does this mean you're not pining for—now, what was her name—Marianne?"

"Let's talk about *anything* else. Now, where are we going to dinner?"

"Okay, my darling. We are going to Le Chesery. You'll like it; it's definitely your style."

Scott was curious. "What is my style?" he wondered aloud.

"That's the beauty of it. Your style is my style, darling. Haven't you noticed?"

While they sipped two splits of champagne, the bar slowly filled with hotel guests and residents of Gstaad. During December, January, and February, the Palace was their social annex. Both groups shared a single defining denominator—wealth. Scott found it easy to pick out the few who knew they didn't belong by their uncomfortable body language, and he steeled himself not to show any tentativeness in Desirée's presence. A quiet, dignified manner was without doubt his best course. And, naturally, he had a leg up; anyone seen with the countess had temporary approval—at least, until other more definitive judgments could be made.

The bar, more reminiscent of a club than a ritzy hotel bar, was luxuriously homey. Fat chairs upholstered in velvet and soft leathers, intimate tables scattered, the glow of soft lights on elegant and studied accessories of silver, porcelain, and hand-painted ceramics completed the décor. Although Scott and Desirée were seated at a discreet table, the countess was constantly being spotted and buttonholed by an array of friends and acquaintances. And the curious expression on their jaded faces indicated that, while interested in being acknowledged by the countess, they were equally inquisitive as to the young American she had in tow. Of course, Desirée was coy to the point of being maddening with details of Scott's provenance.

At last they escaped, and it was a short trip down into the village for dinner. The white stucco chalet housing Le Chesery, one of Gstaad's oldest, most expensive, and best restaurants, had various rooms paneled in dark wood and featured multiple fireplaces, with nooks that afforded privacy and decorum. Le Chesery boasted one of Switzerland's most extensive wine lists, bound in a well-worn leather binder, the domains and vintages noted in detail, and the prices commensurate to their rarity. Near the hearths, large, shiny cooking and serving vessels hung from racks; everything about the décor reinforced that Le Chesery was a serious eating establishment.

Walking into the dining room with Desirée was like walking the red carpet. All eyes turned their way. She knew everyone, and everyone knew her. As Scott watched her effortlessly and gracefully greet her many admirers, he marveled; she was thoroughly lovely. There were the superficial things, the obvious—her physical beauty of face and figure, her extraordinary taste in clothes and jewelry—as well as character traits that showed refinement: her elegant and sophisticated gestures and mannerisms and an unconsciously aristocratic bearing, learned early. All completed the vision known as the Countess de Rovere.

It was not by chance they had the perfect table.

Scott ordered the Charolais tenderloin: Desirée had the brook trout, steamed, with a lemon butter sauce and *pommes vapeur*. Together, they decided on dessert: Black Forest cake, paired with the ever-flowing champagne.

Wholly absorbed in each other and the fine meal, two hours flew by. Desirée excused herself; while she was away, Scott asked for the check. The waiter left and returned with the maître d', who whispered that everything had previously been arranged.

"Is something wrong?" Desirée asked when she returned to the table.

"Yes. You embarrass me by paying for dinner without telling me."

"If I had told you, you wouldn't have let me pay. Let's not get into some crass discussion about money. After all, it's more fun to spend than to save."

"Did you think that I might've enjoyed that particular fun? I may be a student, but I'm not so poor that I can't take a beautiful woman out to dinner." Scott couldn't help feeling that his masculine pride had been wounded by the countess's generosity.

Desirée smiled sweetly at him with the practice of someone who'd had to deal with financial inequities before. "Sometimes I think about ungrateful young Americans who don't know the first thing about fun," she teased. "Oh darling; it's my treat. I invited you here, so let me enjoy this."

Scott was immediately contrite. The last thing he wanted to do was diminish Desirée's enjoyment of his company. "Look, I'm sorry. I was caught off guard. I'm not trying to ruin the evening. What's next, then?"

"If you are in the mood, we could go to the GreenGo, the discotheque in the Palace."

"I don't believe we have ever danced together," he said.

"I can tell you we haven't," Desirée said, biting her lip. "I've always had to watch you dance with someone else."

Gustav, her driver, was waiting with the car, and in five minutes, they were at the GreenGo. Lines of hopefuls (the young and not-quite-so-young, fashionable and even more fashionable) waited in the cold for their chance to be admitted to one of Europe's best discotheques. There was no line for the countess. Uniformed doormen parted the sea of people and cleared a path for her. Though the place was already jammed, Desirée and Scott were ushered to a table for two, where an ice bucket and bottle of champagne awaited their arrival.

The music was eclectic, borrowing heavily from the United States, Italy, and Brazil. Bossa nova and samba played over and over, and Scott recognized *The Girl from Ipanema*. Etched glass panels of aquarium scenes combined with the green glow of the hotel's indoor-outdoor perimeter-hugging pool were reminiscent of Jules Verne's *20,000 Leagues Under the Sea*. The crowd of beautiful French, Italian, German, and white-blond Scandinavian revelers was framed by expensive wall coverings and tiled bars and tables. The GreenGo was a beautiful place, full of beautiful people.

When the strains of the popular Italian ballad, *Sapore di Sale*, rose, Scott brought Desirée to her feet for their first dance. The lyrics, with their pleading and desire, were set to the beat of slow sex. Scott couldn't have chosen a more perfect song to take Desirée into his arms, and he clasped her hand in his. By the end of the song, his hand was at home in the small of her back while the contours of her body had gradually molded to his. Her warmth and feminine softness was bliss. From time to time, Scott pulled back to look directly into her eyes—could he read her thoughts? She returned his gaze, and he wanted desperately to be right about what he believed he saw in her eyes, a trace of something good.

The dance floor seemed to be the only place where they could be alone, and so they prolonged their embrace. One dance led to another. Whenever they returned to their table, the stream of people resumed, telling their stories and laughing at their own jokes. Scott wasn't in the mood to share the countess.

Around one o'clock, they left the discotheque. As Desirée settled into the luxurious leather of the Mercedes' rear seat, Scott leaned through the window into the car. He wasn't so inexperienced that he thought he'd be invited for a nightcap. His role was to be patient, not act his age and be so juvenile as to insult her. He could wait. She'd be the one to say "if" and "when," and Scott knew Desirée loved exercising that control. But once she did, Scott would see if he could drive her mad with passion.

"Scott, my dear I do believe you are going to kiss me!" she said.

"I was going to try," he admitted. Desirée laughed gleefully at his yearning expression, sliding just slightly out of kissable range.

"And if I let you, then what? I'm not one of those young girls you can toy with."

"Is this part of the fun you talked about earlier?"

"It's late. You can try to seduce me tomorrow."

With that, Desirée's car eased down the drive and through the parking lot and disappeared into the night.

sixteen

I   N SPITE OF THE COLD, SCOTT DECIDED TO WALK BACK TO
     the hotel; he needed to clear his head. What was he getting him-
     self into? Desirée was not Marlyse. Or Millie. As she had warned,
he would have little control over any relationship they might have.
Desirée was unquestionably beautiful, intelligent, and interesting. And
he loved their little games of repartee (and with all the self-assurance
of a twenty-two-year-old, felt he'd held his own). But Scott was pain-
fully aware of their differences. Age was only the first. She was seven
years older, a much more experienced player. Next, their social stand-
ings. Desirée was a wealthy and cultured aristocrat; Scott, the son of
a self-made businessman. And finally, culture. Desirée was European,
with a wealth of travel and other experiences that Scott had only read
about in books. Growing up in Charleston and attending university in
the Midwest hadn't prepared him for palaces, opera galas, and skiing
at Gstaad. But somehow, these things didn't seem to matter to Desirée.
She'd never been snooty to the eager American student (at least, not
in front of him)—at least not yet. She was rich, and he was a young
man on an allowance. She liked nice things. Scott wondered if he were
just Desirée's latest nice thing. Would he be satisfied with that, or did
he need more?

The sun was shining brightly at breakfast the next morning. Seated
by one of the windows in the grand dining room, Scott could view the
entire village. Fresh snow covered the landscape. Tall evergreen spruces
and chalets dotted the landscape in irregular patterns; smoke from

chimneys rose across the valley and up the slopes. A sumptuous buffet was set with every fruit imaginable and baskets of bread—brioches, croissants, toasts, and pastries—as well as dried meats, *les delices des Grisons,* various juices and yogurts, and eggs cooked on demand in any fashion. He sampled everything.

A hotel page approached him. "Monsieur Stoddard, you have a telephone call." He guided Scott to the house telephone just outside the dining room, and there was no surprise when the call came through. Desirée.

"Good morning," she said. "Did you dream about me?"

Scott laughed. "No, I didn't."

"You are so mean. Are you mad that I didn't let you give me a kiss?"

"Should I be?"

"Of course not, silly. Anticipation, I hear, is a most powerful aphrodisiac."

"I guess it's more of an aphrodisiac for the one doling out the potion."

"Touché, my darling. Remember that we are having dinner tonight at eight with a few friends here at my chalet. For lunch, I thought we could go up on the mountain, get some fresh air, and take some sun. I'll pick you up at eleven thirty. Dress warmly."

"Sounds good. Have any other plans for me?"

"None that you need to know about."

GUSTAV AND THE BIG BLACK MERCEDES PULLED UP IN FRONT. A few guests, their breath crystallizing in the cold, gathered to catch taxis. Scott came down the few steps as the doorman opened the back door on the driver's side. He slid into the backseat beside her; she turned one cheek then the other for his kiss, her lips a deep pink, her complexion flawless. A delicate scent of lavender and jasmine lingered in the air. Desirée's form-fitting lilac ski pants contrasted brightly with the rest of her white ensemble: cashmere turtleneck, scarf, fox ski jacket and hat with matching white, furry boots. She looked like a photo from the pages of French *Vogue.*

"Is this new?" she asked, touching his jacket.

"Yes, you know I must do my best to keep up with the Countess de Rovere."

"It's quite macho, my darling. It fits your style."

"It certainly fits your idea of my style."

Desirée slid her gloved hand through the crook of his arm, snuggling against him. "My dear Scott, you truly don't know how to accept a compliment."

"I'm sure it's one of my many faults."

Scott hadn't intended to sound quite so, well, petulant, but there it was. Unlinking their arms, Desirée wagged a finger at him. "I think you are a little mad about last night. Am I right?"

"Well, to use one of your French words, I thought your behavior *coquette*."

"Coquette? *Moi*?" she exclaimed in mock horror. "No one has ever even dreamt it." Her laughter died away, and Scott's clever response died on his lips when she leaned in close and whispered, "Tell me . . . do you still want to kiss me?"

"Now?" Scott couldn't break the spell of her aquamarine eyes.

"Why not?"

He glanced toward the driver before whispering, "What about Gustav?"

"Gustav is blind to matters of my heart."

Scott put his hands on either side of her face and drew it within inches of his own. They gazed into each other's eyes, and Scott thought he saw a promise in her clear blue-green gaze. He closed the gap, capturing her lips lightly with his own before fully enjoying their tender softness. As they separated, Desirée gave a little sigh, which Scott took as license to pull her close again. They kissed with more intensity and insistence, parting lips and thrusting tongues. It was no accident that she'd initiated their kisses in her car; with Gustav nearby, there was no worry that Scott's passion would exceed any limits she intended. But that promise . . . Scott could see in her eyes and feel in the receptiveness of her body that their desire would not be denied for long.

She relaxed into the leather and removed a compact from her bag.

As she studied her makeup in the mirror, she said, "I was right about anticipation." She wiped a smudge of lipstick from Scott's face.

"Are you always right?" He couldn't help but grin; he was already anticipating their next kiss.

"Had you rather I be wrong?"

"I don't know yet."

"Take your time. I'm not in a hurry."

Gustav dropped them at the entrance to the station for the cable car that would take them up to Wasserngrat, one of the midpoint stops, where they could have lunch on the terrace overlooking the slopes. It was a perfect day—brilliant sunshine, fresh powder, and not too cold. The cable car was crammed with skiers and their equipment. Scott noticed that he and Desirée were the only cognoscenti aboard and then remembered that they didn't intend to ski.

It was a short walk from the cable car station to the restaurant. Their table gave them an unrestricted view of the valley floor below while the sun, flooding across the terrace, provided unexpected warmth. The altitude made the air thin and the sunshine feel quite intense.

Scott watched Desirée all the time. He wasn't staring; it was rather an unrequited and continuing gaze, the kind of careful attention to detail he'd give a rare and beautiful piece of art. She smiled when she caught him, and her easy gesture told him she didn't mind, that she felt complimented.

His mind wandered over the events of the last few months, all the way back to the SS *United States*, when he dared not pursue Desirée directly. All those days when he failed to call, principally because of his uncertainty about her response. All those incidents where he longed for just one moment alone with her. Now, he was basking in the promise of their next kiss.

"Darling, you seem far away." Desirée broke through his thoughts. She'd been watching him, too.

"I was just thinking about the first time I saw you."

"When Millie introduced us on the ship. How is Millie?"

"I don't know anything about Millie."

He knew he would tell her whatever she asked. Basking in the sun, it felt as though they were the only two people in Eden. She said gently, "Tell me about the first time you saw me."

"I saw you long before we ever met, when you were boarding."

"Were you in love immediately?"

"Yes." Scott's mouth was dry. All those months of carefully remaining aloof, waiting for some sign of interest from Desirée, were erased with one word. "Yes."

"Yes? That's all? Tell me everything. I want to hear it."

"I'll tell you tonight. You know, anticipation. It's a good thing."

SHE SENT GUSTAV TO FETCH SCOTT FROM THE HOTEL AT seven thirty. It was only a short drive through the village across the bridge and up the hill into the private section of Gstaad, where tight restrictions forced the nouveau riche to be considerate of architectural tradition. The Swiss are firm believers that good paper makes good friends, and building laws and zoning kept these villas and chalets appearing modest, though they were the properties of Europe's rich and famous. The countess's chalet was located at the crest of one of the smaller hills, within walking distance of the village, yet protected from its neighbors by a series of fir trees. The two-story traditional wooden structure was hidden and disguised by its surroundings.

A uniformed domestic opened the door to Scott's knock before leading him to a great room to await the countess. The décor was decidedly modern. Various sectional seating, sofas, and lounges were arranged in strategic positions in relation to a large stone fireplace ablaze with a fire of crimson embers that cracked and popped. The room suggested comfort, laziness, and romantic foreplay.

Lost in anticipation, Scott admired the fire, and so Desirée caught him unaware. "Darling, you are so handsome," she said.

Taking Desirée in his arms, Scott held her for a moment. He looked into her eyes, and the next he knew, Scott found he was kissing her flush on the lips. His heart pounded—this kiss was better, more reassuring and passionate, than the others because, somehow, they meshed perfectly.

When at last they broke apart, Scott slowly turned Desirée; he wanted to take her in from every angle. She delighted in his admiration, her mischievous expression showing her pleasure. She had dressed for him, clothed in a black silk lounge pajama, piped with silver thread on the lapels and cuffs. Three rhinestone buttons decorated the bodice, and her breasts were loose and free beneath the lustrous fabric. The open back draped in a slow cascade, descending almost to the gentle curve of her lower spine.

Desirée reclined on one of the sofas and patted the seat next to her. "Here. Let me tell you who is coming tonight," she said.

"I hope you don't expect me to remember their names."

"Of course not; I just want to give you a little preview. We will be eight. You and I, that's two; Yves and Jacqueline Bertrand, he's with Paribas, the bank, and she's from a champagne family in Reims; Jon and Louise Goosens, he's director of a Dutch investment group, and she's a director of a Dutch fashion house; Rheiner Honig, a journalist from Berlin; and Arianna Strozzi, a sculptor from Florence. These are friends of mine, and they have been coming to Gstaad for years."

The Bertrands were the first to arrive, followed by Rheiner Honig. The rest were together; the Goosens had picked up the sculptor, because she didn't like to drive on the snowy roads.

Desirée had hired extra staff for the evening to tend bar and serve hors d'oeuvres. Champagne was the drink of choice for all except Honig, who preferred scotch. Desirée introduced him as a friend from Berlin; without more clarity and any attendant detail, Scott's curiosity and suspicion were aroused. Was the man truly just a friend or should he be wary of a potential rival?

"Mr. Stoddard," Yves asked once they were seated around the table, "is Geneva what you thought it would be or is it different?"

"I tried not to form any preconceptions, but in general, I would say that people have been nicer than I had been led to expect," Scott answered.

"Had you heard that the Swiss are rude or don't like foreigners?"

"I have, and it wasn't confined to the Swiss. Perhaps my informant was suspicious of everyone," Scott said.

Louise decided to try her luck. "Unless you've been many times to Europe or lived in Europe, it must be a difficult adjustment."

Scott answered with care. "I presume that any situation could prove difficult, especially if one is inflexible. I try to remain open to different ideas and customs and not be defensive about things I either don't understand or don't agree with."

"There are Europeans who don't like Americans. Maybe it's jealousy. Maybe it's, oh, who knows?" added Jacqueline.

"I hope present company excepted," Scott said. "Overall, everyone has been truly kind, and if there were some problems, I can't be sure they were not of my own making."

"But at times it must be frustrating, living in a foreign country," Yves interjected. "The language, the expense, the differences. It goes on and on. And it must have been very difficult for you being so far away from the United States in November when President Kennedy was assassinated?"

"Yes, the devastating news was sparse and incomplete regarding President Kennedy's death. My classmates told me. Because all the lines were jammed, I couldn't call home for several days. And you're right, it is frustrating at times, but when I think that I could be in law school back in the States and not enjoying the experiences I'm having here . . . well, all these challenges are insignificant compared to the benefits of living here."

Next Rheiner, the journalist, chimed in. "The Americans must be very angry with President de Gaulle for threatening to pull out of NATO."

"Each country must follow its own ideas of sovereignty. It is unequivocal that France and America will always have a special connection," Scott responded.

Dinner was superb and the conversation lively. Obviously, Desirée's guests had been intent on learning more about him. He thought the third degree went on a little too long, but deep down, he'd enjoyed the challenge.

Eventually the guests left. When Scott heard the last car pull away, he breathed deeply with relief. "I'm glad that's over."

"Don't be cross. You were perfect, my darling."

"I'm not cross, but I came here to be with you, not spar with your nosy friends."

"They're just protective. They like me best when I'm alone."

"Me too. Look, tomorrow is Sunday, and I will need to get back to Geneva in the evening."

"Tomorrow! You just arrived."

"I know, I hate to leave, but—"

"Shhh, my darling. You need a reason to stay."

Extinguishing lights as they went, Desirée led Scott back into the great room. Settling into a corner of one of the sofas facing the fireplace, they were bathed in a faint, warm glow. She nestled in his arms, pulling him into the kind of kiss that inflames passion, that lights a fire that cannot be contained.

Scott found Desirée to be a gift lightly wrapped. One gentle tug, a lift of her hips, three buttons undone, and her body was his to admire. Lying before him in the firelight, Desirée remained as still as a statue, enjoying how his eyes caressed each curve and soft place. And then she reached for him.

seventeen

W HEN SCOTT AWOKE THE NEXT MORNING, HE WAS alone in the countess's massive bed. It had been dark when they made their way upstairs, but the rosy morning light now filtering in revealed a bedroom replete with luxury—silk sheets, fur blanket, and a padded leather headboard before a huge fireplace. Scott stretched like a satisfied lion.

He quickly dressed and descended the stairs, moving through the chalet's main rooms, looking for Desirée. There was the great room, already back in order, and the dining room, where they'd spent the evening with friends. He finally found her in a room off the kitchen, reading at a table set in a bay window. She was wrapped in a cashmere white robe with canary yellow sash, the matching hair ribbon pulling her thick golden locks back from her face. Devoid of makeup, her hair in a simple ponytail, Desirée looked good in the morning.

"There you are, sleepyhead," she said.

Standing behind her chair, he circled his arms around her. She turned, and they exchanged another passionate kiss.

The door to the kitchen opened, and a woman of some girth appeared. A stout and stern-looking Swiss woman of about fifty stood before him. "Helena, this is my friend Scott Stoddard. Could you prepare Mr. Stoddard some breakfast? Scott, tell Helena what you would like."

The expression on Helena's face gave a warning, and Scott read it thus: *Don't hurt the countess.* He figured it would take some time to win her over. He hoped he had that long.

"Thank you. Just some coffee and a croissant, please," he said. Helena nodded, turned, and returned to the kitchen. There wasn't to be any wasted chatter with this one.

"My darling, you are very quiet this morning," Desirée said.

"I'm enjoying the moment."

"Like you did last night?"

"You noticed?"

"I did. Are you still off to Geneva this afternoon?"

"No, I found that reason to stay."

Beyond the light banter, Scott and Desirée didn't discuss the night before. Nor did they delve into the significance of their quick progression from acquaintances to lovers. Possibly knowing the weekend was short, they reasoned that there was no time to waste. Perhaps it was due to anticipation; their attraction, sparked back in September on the boat, had intensified so quickly because they had been unable to explore their infatuation. Scott thought it was futile to question when the answers were unknowable. What he did know—his feelings for Desirée were intense and, rather than question why and how, he would let this romance play out and see where it would go. And whether his feelings arose from satisfaction of the conquest or something more profound, only time would tell.

As they were finishing breakfast, the telephone rang, and Desirée answered. Covering the receiver, she whispered to Scott that it was Louise. "Didn't we have a good time? I'm so glad you and Jon were able to come. . . . Of course, darling. He's nice, isn't he? And so intelligent." Scott continued with his breakfast while Desirée, clearly enjoying his discomfiture at being discussed within earshot, prattled on with her friend. More small talk ensued; then, laying a hand on Scott's arm, she said in a confidential tone, "Louise, I think I'm in love. No, I know I'm in love, because I haven't been in love for a long time. But you mustn't tell anyone. Promise?" She blew a kiss toward Scott.

That was quick, Scott thought. Desirée's declaration put him on unfamiliar and dangerous ground. Of course, he was happy that she was so thrilled with him. The feeling couldn't be more mutual, but he felt a nagging anxiety. He couldn't help thinking of Marlyse—he'd have preferred the countess come to love more slowly. Could her feelings disappear as quickly as they'd arrived?

When she hung up, he said, "Desirée, I know you are not naïve. You must have another motive, because that woman will surely tell everyone who was at dinner last night that you're in love."

She smiled sweetly at him and took a sip of her coffee. "Of course, my prince; I'm counting on Louise to share not only with them, but also with many others. In fact, I would bet she's on the line now. Don't forget, I'm coquette." Scott laughed as she exaggeratedly batted her eyelashes at him. "Let's go to mass and then lunch."

"I didn't know you were religious," he said and thought silently, *There's a lot about you I don't know.*

ST. JOSEPH, GSTAAD'S CATHOLIC CHURCH, WAS A RELATIVELY small, white stucco structure with a high-pitched roof and a Byzantine steeple. Desirée and Scott sat near the front, and he passed the time by idly watching the parishioners take their seats; a mix of townspeople in their Sunday best and seasonal visitors in their casual finery filled the unforgiving pine pews. The priest, Scott learned, was an old friend of Desirée's. He'd been helpful during the time she was separated from her husband and ultimately seeking an annulment. The mass passed slowly, and Scott was happy when they finally stepped out into the crisp air and bright afternoon sunshine.

Over lunch, Desirée commented, "My darling, you are not Catholic."

"You noticed."

"But are you religious?"

"No, not at all."

"Did you ever go to church?"

"Yes, when I was a child, and up to the time I went to college. My parents and I attended a Baptist church; I was even baptized."

"Once you escaped Mommy and Daddy, you didn't go anymore?"

"That's what happened," he said. "Does my religion matter? To you, I mean."

"Of course not, I wouldn't go either, except I feel I must. Guilt remains, if taught early enough."

A debonair man approached their table. Curious as to who this interloper might be, Scott frowned at the interruption when the man spoke to Desirée in Italian. Shifting politely into French, Desirée was quick to introduce Scott to her old friend, Francesco, and include him in their conversation. Francesco was dressed impeccably, as only Italian men know how to do, and he flashed an inscrutable smile before exchanging a few pleasantries with Scott.

"What brings you to Gstaad, Francesco?" Desirée inquired. "I thought you couldn't be pried from Cortina this time of year."

"Can you imagine I became bored in Cortina?" he said. "The snow was not good, and . . . well, now I'm here." Francesco studiously kept his eyes on the countess. "I saw Louise Goosens this morning, and she mentioned they dined at your chalet only yesterday."

Arching an eyebrow, Desirée smiled up at her friend. "It's too bad I didn't know you were in town. I would have invited you." She reached across the table to cover Scott's hand with hers. "We always have room for one more." The gesture was not lost on Francesco.

"You are too kind," he said. "But you see, I only arrived late last evening."

"I'm surprised Clarissa is not with you," Desirée said with an innocent look of surprise.

"My dear Desirée, I'm sad to say that you have put your finger on why the snow is so bad in Cortina. From time to time, conditions deteriorate—the weather turns frigid and inhospitable. Very unfortunate. Relationships, too, have their moments; they come, then *poof*, they go, and we, poor souls that we are, must trudge on and make the best of it. *Così, è la vita.*" Francesco lifted his hands, palms up, in the classic gesture of complete innocence and world weariness.

"You poor boy," Desirée cooed. "Perhaps I should check with Clarissa to better understand the outlook in Cortina."

"I'm not sure conditions would be improved by such an inquiry."

"I thought as much," Desirée said. "Let us change the subject. Are you staying long?"

"Just through next weekend. I believe you know Celine Montaigne. She invited me to attend the Sleigh Ball next weekend. Are you to attend? Will Signore Stoddard accompany you?"

"Celine is a dear friend. I have known her since we were in school together at the Lycée de Paris," Desirée said. "You be nice to her." Scott noticed that Desirée had deftly sidestepped Francesco's questions regarding the ball. The handsome Italian reacted to her chastisement in mock horror: "Desirée, you embarrass me."

"Not at all, my dear Francesco. You embarrass yourself." And with that, she signaled the conversation was over. Francesco said his good-byes and sauntered off. Desirée turned her attention to her champagne as Scott contemplated the encounter; in this small, cosmopolitan society, gossip was the coin of the realm, and he had become one of the commodities of barter.

"Francesco is an old friend?" Scott asked.

"My ex-husband's best friend and business partner."

The Count de Rovere. What did Scott know of his standing with Desirée? Now was as good a time as any to ask, "Are you on good terms with your ex?"

Desirée folded her hands in her lap, straightened her shoulders, and held her chin up. "My relationship with Stefano is as good as could be expected," she said crisply. "In the end, he didn't want the annulment, but he should have thought about it before his dalliances. I knew he was a playboy—just like Francesco—but I thought I could be the center of his life. It was a mistake. My brief marriage was annulled. Is that enough history, or do you want more?" Her blue-green eyes glinted as she dared him to delve deeper.

"Just one more thing."

"What's that?"

"Is the count, Stefano, still in love with you?" How could any man put Desirée out of his mind and heart? Scott was sure he knew the answer, but it was Desirée's delivery that mattered.

"More than ever. But it is *pour rien*. Do you know this expression?"

"I believe the translation is *for nothing*."

"Literally, yes. But it really means *there's no chance*." Scott was pleased to see that, beyond a bored exasperation, Desirée was clearly unmoved by her former husband's continuing infatuation.

"Does it bother you that Francesco has already heard of us? That Louise has so quickly spread that you're in love?"

She gave him a knowing look, and he was reminded of his relative inexperience. "Do you think I want to sneak around with you, playing hide-and-seek, pretending, lying?"

"What happened to discretion?"

"Discretion is such an inconvenient and confining idea. Besides— why should you worry? You don't know any of these people." She shook her head. "It's ironic that you're the one worried about your reputation."

"Don't be ridiculous. I'm not worried about my reputation. I'm worried about yours."

"Well don't. I am the Countess de Rovere, and I have been managing my reputation quite handily for some time." Shaking off the serious tone, she lifted her glass of champagne toward Scott and gave him a sultry once-over. "And, please; tell me how can being in love with you—a handsome, young American; a fresh face on the scene; someone tall and athletic, with manners and style—how can that hurt my reputation?" She laughed in delight. "Why, you, my little mystery, can only improve it! And this reminds me; will you be my escort to the Sleigh Ball next weekend?"

Still reeling from the countess's list of compliments, Scott paused, incredulous at what he was about to say. He asked, "Do you remember that I have school?"

"Oh yes, school. But the Sleigh Ball is one of the most important events of the season. You must stay and go with me."

"What if I get up early tomorrow, go back to Geneva, attend my classes, and then come back for the weekend?"

"Let's compromise. You go back on Tuesday morning and come back Thursday afternoon."

"I better agree now, because one more back and forth, and I'll not be going back at all."

An uncomfortable silence ensued, and Scott wondered what

Desirée could be scheming. He hated to interject reality into their romance, but university was the reason he was in Geneva. Romance was not an acceptable reason to miss graduate classes. Right now, it was the Sleigh Ball—and this was just the beginning. At this pace, he would only be attending class fifty percent of the time, with even fewer hours devoted to study. He could feel the cold glare of his parents' disapproval from across the ocean, and Scott squirmed at making a choice between disappointing them or saying no to Desirée.

Desirée filled the silence with a suggestion. "Why don't I drop you off at the hotel so you can collect your things and check out? You'll stay at the chalet. Shall we plan a quiet dinner at home this evening? Helena and Gustav have Sunday evening off."

Her wish was his command; soon, Scott was checked out of the hotel and in the car heading back to the chalet. In her bedroom, Desirée threw open the closets as she busily explained where he should put this and that (in awe at the volume of clothing, he wondered just how many pairs of Bogner ski pants she had, not to mention the endless stream of cashmere turtleneck sweaters she coordinated with them). Scott placed his suitcase on a luggage rack set up for the purpose and then took her hand. Pulling her close, and then closer, he slid his other arm under her arm, embraced her, and kissed her over and over. His breath escaped in gasps of anticipation, and his hands rushed to find those places that elicited the most response. Soon they settled to the floor, renewing their passion of the night before.

LATER, THEY WENT DOWN TO THE GREAT ROOM WHERE GUS-tav had laid a fire. A match struck and inserted in a few places had flames leaping into a warming glow. Scott and Desirée reclined on cushions; she in a pink cashmere jumpsuit with silk satin slippers; he in black corduroy pants and a camel-colored silk and mohair V-neck. They were enjoying what Desirée termed an evening snack—smoked Norwegian salmon; Beluga caviar from the Caspian with toast points, trimmed of their crust; capers; diced hard-boiled egg; dollops of crème

fraîche; and a bottle of vintage Veuve Clicquot. Soft music crooned in
the background.

"Are you happy, my darling?"

"Very," he said.

"Do you love me?" she asked.

Firmly and without a moment's thought, he replied, "I love you."
Scott knew any kind of qualified response or mumbled hesitation was
not what Desirée wanted to hear. Nor was it what he wanted to give.
But he would have preferred that she hadn't asked, that she could have
waited for him to tell her on his own terms. He was certain he would
have told her he loved her.

DESIRÉE WAS ON THE PHONE AGAIN AS SCOTT STROLLED INTO
the breakfast room the next morning. She looked at him with a knowing smile, and he bent to whisper in her ear, "I love you, *mon petit chou*."
He could tell she liked the French touch by the way her eyes sparkled.
Without missing a beat, Desirée continued her conversation.

"But you won't have time for me. I know how you adore those royals. All right then; it's Wednesday for lunch. *Au revoir.*"

She hung up the phone. For a moment, she was deep in reflection.
She turned to Scott and said, "That was my mother."

"I couldn't help but overhear you're meeting her for lunch," Scott
said.

"Yes, there's no way around it. She's coming to Lausanne to see a
friend and will be in Geneva on Wednesday to catch the afternoon
train to Nice. She spends her winters in Cannes."

"It will be nice for you to spend some time with her," Scott ventured.

"No, it will not."

"You don't like your mother?" Scott, reflecting on his some-
times-strained relationship with his own mother, was more curious
than surprised.

"We like each other so much that we don't get along. We are too
much alike."

"As someone who finds you absolutely divine, knowing there's another like you sounds pleasant. Tell me—are you going to tell your mother anything about us?"

"I won't have to. Why do you think she is turning up for lunch?"

"Are you joking?" Desirée had professed her love to one person yesterday morning, and the news had traveled across countries. Scott was both impressed and appalled at the legs on society gossip. At what point would this juicy item travel across the sea to his parents' ears?

"No, my dear. The Mossad calls my mother when they are stumped."

THE BLACK MERCEDES WAS ON THE ROAD TO GENEVA early the next morning. Gustav's more direct politeness and deference revealed Scott's new status; in the spacious back seat, he and Desirée lounged under a fur throw, sipping hot chocolate from a silver thermos. The steady hum of the car's vibration slowly induced a kind of sleepy reverie. Desirée leaned against him, her head resting against Scott's shoulder, and they napped during the three-hour drive.

"Madame and monsieur. . . ." Gustav's gentle voice announced they were close to Desirée's estate, fifteen kilometers outside the city. Although Scott well remembered the opera gala, his visit to the countess's lakeside estate had occurred in the dark. Now, in the bright light of day, he could fully appreciate its grandeur. Some twenty-five acres extended from the lakeside road to the top of a long slope carved by the same Rhone glacier that, eons ago, had formed the lake's contours. At the summit, stood her large two-story home. Fruit trees, now dormant, dotted the undulating, snow-covered pastures. A concrete and pea-gravel driveway curved up through the property to a grand turnaround, which also served as a lookout over the lake. Iron-forged benches shaded by plane trees, all expertly pruned for the winter, had been strategically placed to take in the view. Scott remembered the stone walls and steep roof, generous overhanging eves, stout chimneys, and windows with inner and outer shutters, and he had a new appreciation for its thoroughly Swiss architecture. A Porsche painted in British racing green was parked in the turnaround.

When he'd last visited, throngs of guests had obscured the dark green front door (or perhaps Scott had simply been too nervous to notice the unique, antique specimen, with its impressive brass knocker). The public spaces looked much different without crowds of guests, though Scott remembered exactly where he and Desirée had exchanged their first words alone. Desirée's personal quarters on the second floor, however, were uncharted territory, and Scott ascended the stairs with a thrill. Along the south side of the house, expansive windows were positioned specifically to catch the view, and her bedroom and day room took advantage of the prime location. With a start, Scott looked at his watch and realized that he would be late to class. He quickly interrupted their leisurely tour: "Desirée, I need to go. If I leave in the next few minutes, I can still make my afternoon classes."

"Oh all right. If you give me a kiss, I'll give you the key."

"The key?"

"To my Porsche. It's my plaything."

"I thought I was."

"Are we meeting for dinner on Wednesday? Maybe by that time, I will have recovered from being with my mother."

There was no way to refuse her and no way to refuse his desire for her. Scott hadn't thought about his books in more than a week; if he didn't get away soon, it appeared this week's schoolwork was in jeopardy as well. He kissed her, then kissed her again more passionately. God, she was maddening. Breaking the embrace, she reached for the key. Placing it in his hand, she said, "We could meet tonight, after your classes," she said.

Scott bounded down the stairs and flung himself out the door. Despite his haste, he had to stop before the Porsche—it was every young man's dream car. Gustav opened the driver's side door and, as Scott climbed in, he offered a silent prayer—*God forbid anything should happen to this car while I am driving.*

Turning the key produced the unmistakable, signature sound of a Porsche engine. To an aficionado, cars like a Porsche or Ferrari and boats such as the Riva, the Italian Chris Craft, produce distinctive, sweet music to the ear, and Scott enjoyed a full thirty minutes of mechanical serenade before he parked near the university and climbed the steps to International Alliances and Unions of Southeast Asia, his Tuesday afternoon class.

Professor Blount commented on Scott's tardiness (all of two minutes) and mockingly congratulated him on attending. Any illusion Scott had entertained about professors not keeping track of his absences was dashed. They were, and his classmates enthusiastically enjoyed the docteur's public reprimand.

As he quickly slid into one of the empty seats, Scott glimpsed Marlyse on the other side of the classroom, away from the door. My God, how he had moved on! Though he still found her pretty (even prettier when she smiled), the passion he'd felt for her seemed so long ago; his time with the countess was another world, so distinctively and seductively different. Throughout the long hour, he could feel Marlyse's eyes square on his back. At the end of the lecture, she was lying in wait outside the classroom door. There would be no smiles today.

"You've been away," she said.

"Yes. Marlyse, you know I can't give you what you want. Our relationship is over. Let's not make this difficult."

"It's the countess, isn't it? You've been with that woman."

"Yes."

She burst into tears, blotting her eyes as she ran down the steps and into the street. Scott didn't follow after her. What was there to say? Better an abrupt truth than drawing out a lie.

Still, he felt guilty for the way he'd hurt Marlyse. He'd never intended to lead her on—he hadn't promised her anything, and they'd never discussed marriage. Yet now he understood that, once they'd been intimate, her religious beliefs and expectations surrounding sex had risen to a level he couldn't meet. What if he had known in advance? Would it have changed the outcome? Perhaps. But Scott couldn't undo the past, and there was no point in fretting over it; he had other things to worry about.

From this point on, Scott had to assume his professors would be very conscious of his attendance, and they'd probably begun to wonder if he were serious about his studies. He groaned at how unprepared he was, how little he'd studied, and just how loathe he was to put in the time and effort to catch up. He was one question away from being humiliated, and he shuddered to think how much Marlyse and his classmates would enjoy that.

Collecting the Porsche, Scott drove to his apartment; he needed a peaceful place to think. There, he sat on the sofa, looking ruefully at the pile of books and papers he'd abandoned days ago. How was he to manage school and Desirée? His graduate work was why he'd traveled to Geneva in the first place. The allowance his parents provided was to support his studies. And yet his mind, heart, and body were full of Desirée.

Who could he turn to for advice? No easy answer emerged, and other than Jean, he had no close friends, confidants, or advisors to give counsel (and he knew what Jean would say). And, unlike Desirée, he did care about what others thought—especially two people: Edward and Sarah Stoddard. He couldn't allow his parents to hear even a whisper of his relationship with the countess.

His mind raced, sorting out the pertinent facts, wondering how to balance desire with responsibility and guard the secret of his affair. And then there was Desirée herself—she would do as she pleased. No need to wonder.

The telephone rang, interrupting his thoughts. Glancing at his watch, he knew it would be his parents. Ever the sticklers on routine, they were calling late.

"How's school coming?" (Always his mother's first question.) "Is it as hard as you thought it would be?" she asked. "Have you made any more friends?"

"It's quite difficult," Scott said. "There's a lot to read outside class, and, of course, it's all in French." Against his better judgment, he admitted, "I've met someone new."

"But what happened to Marlyse?"

"She and I broke up a few weeks ago."

"Is this someone you met in one of your classes?" his mother asked.

"No, she's not a student. We met through a friend, on the ship coming over. She's Swiss and French. She lives just outside of Geneva."

He could practically feel his mother's frown. "Not a student? What does she do, then?"

Scott knew this was an important question. His mother would want him to be connected to someone in pursuit of an appropriate goal. For the self-made Stoddards, idleness was abhorrent. He couldn't say Desirée did nothing. "She's involved in charitable work."

There was a whispered conference, and then his father was on the line. "This girl you're seeing—she does charitable work? Is she a fundraiser, then?" his father asked.

Scott silently gave thanks; Father had made it easy to say yes.

"Well, we hope you remember why you're in Europe. Your mother and I are glad you have some friends, but Son, don't let anyone or anything interfere with your studies."

They would never run out of questions, but he had provided enough satisfactory answers that they let him go. Scott wearily hung up the phone. Why did he always need a drink after these chats? He was in the kitchen pouring a scotch when the phone rang again.

"Do you miss me?" Desirée purred. "Why don't I come into town tonight? We could have dinner."

"No, I need to study a little and . . . oh, to hell with it. What time?"

"I'll pick you up at half past seven."

He had surrendered. Had he even mounted any opposition? And this hadn't even been a battle; in the grand scheme of social obligations, one dinner was more of a skirmish. For some reason, Scott couldn't resist Desirée. Christ, he couldn't resist himself. At half past seven, he was stationed in front of his apartment building, waiting, when the Mercedes stopped in front of him, Gustav at the wheel. As Scott got into the car, something caught his eye. Was that Marlyse, down the block, hiding in the shadows? But as soon as he was in the car, Desirée reached for him and thoughts of anything else fled as she murmured in his ear, "I love you, my darling."

He kissed her neck and mouth, obeying natural reflex, as if he hadn't seen her in a week. Did Marlyse witness this embrace? He didn't care.

Desirée had made a reservation at Le Café Normand on Geneva's right bank, which was known for its fresh fish. The interior was modern, all glass and chrome and leather installation—quite different from the bucolic seaside atmosphere suggested by the restaurant's name. As usual, they were seated at one of the best tables, which meant that Desirée could see and, more importantly, be seen. They had just ordered a crisp St. Saphorin and pan-sautéed *loup de mer* when Scott's friend Jean entered the restaurant with a coterie of friends. They spotted one another, and Jean immediately came to say hello.

"Scott, do you remember me?" he said smiling. "It's your old friend, Jean." The last time the friends had crossed paths, Scott and Marlyse were just becoming a couple; in the days that followed, Scott had deserted Jean to spend time with her. Now, he was here with someone new.

"I'm sorry I haven't called," Scott said. "I'm a bad friend." When he introduced Desirée, Jean was graciousness itself. In a singular and practiced motion, he lifted Desirée's hand and kissed it. Turning his head, he winked at Scott.

Nothing escaped Desirée's attention, especially if men were involved. "It seems you two have something to discuss," Desirée said tartly. "Excuse me for a moment." She left the friends alone, making her way to the powder room.

Jean could hardly wait for her to be out of earshot. "The Countess de Rovere! *Mon Dieu*, are you dating her? Everyone wants to be with her. I'm jealous."

"We're friends, good friends," said Scott, hoping to end talk about his relationship with Desirée.

But Jean's interest couldn't be deterred. He asked how they met and how long they'd known each other. And then more questions, all in rapid succession without waiting to hear Scott's answers. Then he professed to understand why he hadn't seen Scott in so long: "I'm jealous."

Though she'd played the game and given the two young men a chance to discuss the beautiful woman at the table, Scott didn't want Desirée coming back and finding them talking about her. Hoping to hurry Jean on his way, he said, "Here she comes."

"But you're not telling me—" Desirée's return cut Jean short. "It was so nice to meet one of Scott's friends," she said. As she took her seat,

Desirée subtly indicated that Scott's friend had been dismissed; Jean realized his time was up and that he needed to rejoin his own party. He hadn't gotten all the answers nor asked all the questions he wanted. Undoubtedly, he was shocked to find Scott with Desirée. The older, more sophisticated Frenchman was not accustomed to being upstaged by a protégé; normally, Jean was the one who had the beautiful woman on his arm. Scott knew Jean's third degree was not complete and that he could expect a call from Jean in the not-too-distant future.

"Now, tell me; why is your friend unhappy with you, my prince?"

"He's not really unhappy. He's just teasing me." He told her the story about how a one-hundred-franc note had introduced him to Jean and how helpful he'd been when Scott first arrived. They were best friends; Jean showed him the real Paris, the Parisians' Paris. But recently, circumstances had caused them to drift apart.

"He asked about me, didn't he?" Desirée said with a knowing smile. When Scott nodded yes, she asked, "And what did you tell him?"

"I didn't tell him much. He talked more than I did. But don't worry; he will call me, and soon."

Dinner over, Gustav drove them back to Scott's apartment in the old town. Desirée wanted to come up, just for a minute, to see where her darling lived. He held her off, protesting that he needed to be more prepared for her visit. And he had to study. Unexpectedly, she relented, and Scott was relieved; he knew what would likely ensue if she made it up to his apartment.

The next evening, he waited for her in the lobby of Le Gentilhomme, the restaurant at the Hotel Richemont, which was often frequented by the diplomatic corps and visiting royals. It wasn't long before the Mercedes arrived, the doorman greeted her, and Desirée swept up the steps; as soon as she exited the revolving door, Scott was by her side.

Joy was a permanent part of her countenance, and it was infectious. Scott kissed her on both cheeks and held her an extra moment as they embraced. She shed her coat, a full-length Russian snow leopard, revealing a cobalt blue sheath with exaggerated shoulders and pencil waist. Her impossibly high heels clicked against the marble floor as they were guided to their table.

"How did it go with your mother today?" Scott asked.

"Like a session of the Spanish Inquisition."

"I don't see any bruises from the rack."

"Her methods don't leave visible marks."

"You may not be hungry."

"I'm starved," she said, perusing the menu. "Who could eat lunch while trying to answer all her questions?"

"If it was such an ordeal and you don't enjoy spending time with her, why did you go to lunch with your mother?"

"For the same reasons I go to church. I must."

Desirée and her mother had thrust and parried over generalities for the first part of their duel, but then the clever matriarch turned the conversation to the rumor that a young American—a much younger American—had been seen more than once with her daughter.

"What did you say?" Scott asked.

"Why, naturally, I told her I was in love. I told you; I see no need to sneak around."

"I should say you don't," Scott said wryly. Taking a sip of his martini, he quipped, "And if you're interested, I hear *The International Herald Tribune* has a special on rates. You could take out a full-page ad."

"Oh, my darling—you are so funny. I wish you could have seen her face. Of course, Maman knows she can disapprove, she can fume, and she can fuss—and I'll listen politely. But in the end, she knows I do what I want." Leaning across the table, she took Scott's hand in both of hers. "You're what I want."

"You are what I want. Well, I'm glad that's cleared up. As long as we're on the subject, what are your mother's main objections to me?"

"They're not important. My mother wants me all to herself; she doesn't like to share."

"Nor do I," Scott said. "I want you all to myself."

IT WAS BACK TO GSTAAD THAT THURSDAY. SCOTT AND
Desirée stopped for dinner at a local favorite, Sonnenhof, a quiet
gourmet restaurant in the center of the village whose wood beams
and cozy booths with comfortable lounge pillows kept regulars coming back, year after year.

Bathed in the warm glow of several fireplaces, Desirée leaned into
Scott's side. They settled into a homey meal (venison steak, red cabbage,
and *spaetzle*, a soft egg noodle specialty of German speaking Switzerland) and a full-bodied red. Scott savored the food and Desirée's softness next to him.

The next morning, they strolled through the main shopping street
of Gstaad, stopping at Maison Lorenz Bach. The luxury boutique had
been around for years, offering discerning men and women an array
of luxury goods: sweaters, jackets, scarfs and shawls, Hermes ties, a
limited collection of furs, and a boutique jewelry department featuring
Buccellati (Desirée was a fan of the Italian jeweler's cocktail rings).
The staff welcomed Desirée with such effusiveness she had to be an
important customer. Introducing Scott as her friend, she informed
the clerk that she wanted to purchase a bow tie for his tuxedo—a
nice black silk one, preferably grosgrain. The selection made, she then
inquired about cuff links.

The clerk pointed to a jewelry case containing multiple sets of
sophisticated cuff links and studs, and there was one set that drew
Desirée's attention. Two small disks of blue lapis lazuli, with diamonds

set on the outside edge, and a small gold chain: one disk became the button on one side of the cuff, the second disk on the other. They were elegant and obviously expensive.

"We'll take those, too," Desirée commanded. "Please add them to my bill and have them wrapped. It is Mr. Stoddard's birthday."

Scott started to protest, but she signaled him not to embarrass her. He waited until they were outside and a few steps away from the shop. "I can't let you do that."

"And why not?"

"The expense makes me uncomfortable. You know I can't afford these things."

"My darling, don't be provincial. Must we do only the things you can afford? Or will you be sensible and learn to enjoy the things that I can afford?" Nothing could cut him to the core so much as being labeled provincial. A little pond and small minds—the very thing he'd hoped to escape by leaving his parents and Charleston.

Could he learn to enjoy her paying his way? Time after time, Desirée had treated him. Dinners, hotels, drinks, and now clothes and jewelry. Aren't there ugly names for men who allow women to pay? Scott cringed at how provincial that thought was. He couldn't keep up with her financially (he was a student on an allowance—a generous one, but still, an allowance—and she had family money and had married into nobility) or match her sophistication (she was older, well traveled, fashionable, worldly in a way the young American could never grasp). But Scott thought he acquitted himself rather well in other areas: native intelligence, academic knowledge, and the bedroom. Yes, she was French and had had other lovers, but he knew she appreciated his abandon and stamina in the lovemaking department. They were good together, and they both knew it.

These imbalances were aspects of their relationship that Scott had to resolve before they went much further—assuming he could turn off this passion if he wanted to. He was in love; she was in love. What future could they possibly have? And how much of that future was his decision? He didn't sense any leverage where Desirée was concerned. Had he given up all power when she financed his keep? She was a countess and had been married to a powerful man; it was unlikely she was looking for liaisons with powerful men again. Scott was sure that part of his appeal was just how much power she could wield over him.

Sooner or later, he returned to the one question that continually gnawed at him: how was he going to succeed in a very difficult field of study at the university and be available to Desirée? His parents had afforded him the opportunity to go to school in Europe, but the agreed-upon quid pro quo was that studies came first. How could he ever justify giving precedence to the countess's extensive social calendar? If he managed to somehow successfully complete his degree, how would Desirée react to a lover with a career? How likely was it that any position in international business would allow the kind of freedom that being Desirée's companion would demand?

As he dressed for the ball, the glittering cuff links with their chains reminded Scott that gifts often came with a price.

THE SLEIGH BALL AT THE PALACE WAS ONE OF GSTAAD society's premiere events of the season. While some attendees, having flown in for the event itself, were staying at the hotel, others streamed in from various surrounding chalets and villas. Everyone gathered for pre-dinner cocktails in the great hall, which had been cleared for the evening of the Palace's usual hoi polloi. Champagne flowed, and canapés were passed continuously to keep the revelers' spirits high and their appetites whetted for what was to come.

The Palace's palatial ballroom was the scene following cocktail hour, and the elegantly attired guests took their seats with anticipation. The multicourse dinner featured *foie gras de Strasbourg*, roast duck from the Dordogne, various cheeses, and a floating island dessert. The best white burgundies and full-bodied reds from Bordeaux complemented each course. Over three hours, conversation flowed while waiters served and poured.

Music filled the ballroom, which had been transformed into a winter scene. The effect was of a quaint village in the Alps. Between courses, there was dancing; two bands, one traditional and one playing current pop music, alternated without break, so everyone wanting to take a turn on the floor had the right tune.

Couples (mostly married, if not exclusive) and singles (some on the prowl) filled the tables and dance floors. There were probably a hundred and fifty people, and the fashion show they presented was *tres chic*. J. Mendel furs, jewelry from Harry Winston, and family heirloom jewels (retrieved, Scott guessed by the size and quality of stones, from bank vaults) adorned many of the perfectly coiffed women, who furtively evaluated and compared one another's couture gowns from the corner of their eyes.

Scott, like the other men, was smartly outfitted in black tie. He was a handsome complement to Desirée. Dressed in a spectacular Christian Dior gown of winter white, her curves were fully and provocatively on display; a side slit ascended suggestively up one smooth leg. As Desirée moved, greeting friends and numerous admirers, the light caught the diamonds on her choker, earrings, and jewel-encrusted bodice of her dress. She could not have been more radiant.

They were seated with the Bertrands, whom Scott remembered from Desirée's dinner at the chalet, and an assortment of the countess's friends: a couple from Milan, the Soldati; the Marquis and Marquise de Valoir, from Paris; a lovely French woman, Celine Montaigne, Desirée's childhood friend; and Celine's escort, the ebullient and rakish Francesco, whom Scott had met two weeks earlier. Celine was mannerly and reserved, and Scott found her difficult to read, which worried him—he knew how important it was for her to like him.

Curious, Scott whispered to Desirée, "Why are we sitting with Francesco?"

"First, Francesco is sitting with us, and it is for Celine," Desirée said *sotto voce*. "She is so sweet and my close friend forever; I enjoy her company. And second, do we really want Francesco wondering about us from afar? *Non*. I like him wondering close at hand, where I can keep an eye on him." Placing a hand on Scott's shoulder, she both caressed and signaled a change of topic. "And you, my darling, with your new *papillon* and studs, look so continental."

"Ah, yes, my birthday present. Thank you again. You have impeccable taste."

They attempted to dance, but friends and acquaintances constantly interrupted, trapping the couple at the table with necessary introductions and ensuing chitchat. Scott's frustration grew as the night progressed. To the blasé and beautiful, he was an outsider and a difficult person to quantify. Their comments and questions indicated a judgmental curiosity about exactly who he was—well, he wouldn't help them. In the restroom, enclosed in one of the stalls, he overheard two men speculating that he was the son of an American financier. Gritting his teeth, Scott wondered: How bored were these people? And just how superficial?

When Desirée and Celine excused themselves from the table for a moment, Francesco took the opportunity to move over a few chairs until he was across the table from Scott.

"I understand you are in the international program at the university in Geneva," Francesco said. "What a prestigious program. A few years ago, I heard it was very difficult to get in."

Scott laughed depreciatingly. "I guess they'll let anyone in now," he said.

"Oh, I doubt that, Monsieur Stoddard. You seem to know what you want and how to get it. You're quite a fast worker."

"I have never been called slow."

"Don't be so quick that you get into trouble." Scott eyed Francesco, but before he could respond, the ladies returned to their seats.

"Now what are you two discussing?" Desirée asked, noting the proximity and sensing the tension between the men. "Politics? I hope not. Religion? Francesco, I hope I don't learn that you've been rude. I know you mean well, and I love you dearly, but I really can't abide rudeness." She wagged a finger impishly.

"My dear Desirée, you know me," he said. Then he related how he was asking Scott about Gstaad and congratulating him on being in the university's international program. Scott remained silent; challenging Francesco would only look boorish.

"That is very charming of you," Desirée said, clapping her hands lightly. "We just want to be nice to each other and not betray our breeding." Sensing an opportunity for escape, Francesco quickly rose; taking Celine by the arm, he guided her toward the dance floor. As they passed, Scott thought he read the slightest look of gratitude on Francesco's face.

Scott had to admire Desirée's deftness; watching her in social settings was an education. No matter the unpleasantness, she never showed temper, only resolve; her approval was gracious, and her disdain was deft. Publicly, she always seemed above the fray, what Scott thought others might read as aloof. Privately, he knew her to be warm, tender, and emotional.

"Next weekend, my darling," Desirée said, "you may get to meet my ex-husband." Now this would be a new social situation for Scott, and he wondered whether he'd be able to channel some of Desirée's grace and aloofness. She continued, "Francesco informed me that Stefano might be coming to Gstaad for the weekend." She waved a hand dismissively at the room full of people. "We know all the same people. It is a small society here."

"Lucky me. So he just suddenly decided to come up for the weekend?"

"No, not suddenly—when he heard about you, my darling."

"Somehow I'm not complimented."

"Don't be cross. I can't control his comings and goings. Since our annulment, if I'm seen with the same man twice, he can't stand it."

"Tomorrow is Sunday, and I need to get back to Geneva." Though he intended only to remind her of his commitment to school and his studies, Scott knew he sounded like a child having to share a favorite toy.

"Now you're mad, but I can't help it. I don't control Stefano."

"Let's just drop it," he said.

They didn't discuss the count anymore, but Scott continued to dwell on this new development. He felt blindsided, disturbed; even though she was divorced, he hadn't expected a jealous ex to be circling. It had been, what, three years? Furthermore, Scott hadn't anticipated an ex who was apparently still reeling from his loss and determined to win back his former wife. The count was much more sophisticated than Scott, a playboy of legendary proportion. And wealthier. Desirée sat next to Scott, glittering in diamonds, and he couldn't afford those expensive cuff links she'd so easily given him. He couldn't compete with Stefano's wealth.

Was it possible Desirée was using him to inflame Stefano's jealousy? The count was still carrying a torch, and a young, ardent lover would be such exquisite provocation. Could Desirée still be interested in Stefano and was she using Scott as a match to light passions? Or was she merely bent on torturing Stefano at Scott's expense? He hated to think she was capable of such a thing, but revenge is a strong motivation. No, Scott wouldn't consider that their tender moments were anything less than genuine. Maybe she didn't know what her unconscious motives were.

Whatever Desirée's feelings, Scott decided to refrain from showing any displeasure. There would be no pouting or petulance, as anger would be a sure sign of insecurity. The image of Marlyse frowning at the train station appeared in his mind, and Scott remembered how manipulative and small her silence and demands had seemed. He shuddered; no, he wouldn't play that game—the anxiety-ridden lover, preoccupied with fear. He had to be the picture of self-assurance, even to the point of being nonchalant when presented with Stefano. Anything less would only add to the control Desirée currently held over Scott. He wondered if she was using this episode to induce a jealous reaction from Scott rather than from her ex.

The evening passed in a blur. Once back at the chalet, their lovemaking reflected the insecurities and lack of trust Scott felt, despite his intentions to ignore the unwelcome interloper. It wasn't that he wasn't passionate—he was—but the level of intimacy that had characterized their earlier private moments wasn't present. Neither of them called attention to the difference, but Scott was certain Desirée had noticed as well. Whether they discussed it or not, something had changed. The next morning, Scott found himself in bed alone; Desirée already up and at breakfast was fast becoming their habit. He dressed and went downstairs, following the sound of her voice into the breakfast room.

On a whim, Scott said, "I have an idea. Let's go to Paris this weekend."

Desirée responded as though she'd read his thoughts and uncovered his insecurities. "My darling, at some time—either this weekend or sometime later—my ex will be around. We share too many friends, and we often find ourselves in the same places: Gstaad, Paris, Florence, or the Côte d'Azur. Is it awkward? Yes. Is it uncomfortable? Yes, again. But are we going to be provincial and run away, or are we mature, sophisticated adults?"

There was that word again, *provincial.* "Desirée, I understand, but help me, please. What do you want me to do? How do I deal with Stefano?" he begged.

"Please realize that the only way to be rid of Stefano's unwanted attention is to show him the futility of his efforts. Since our annulment three years ago, I have not had a serious relationship; because I haven't, his mind leaves open the possibility of reconciliation, no matter how futile I have pronounced our reunion. Your presence will signal a reality. Stefano doesn't really love me. He never did; I was just a prize, and when I wouldn't ignore his assignations and left him, his male ego was crushed. He refused to accept the truth. Now he wants me back, so he can enjoy his reputation and tell those sycophantic friends of his that I'm unable to live without him." She put her arms around Scott's neck and rested her head on his shoulder before continuing. The soft weight of her was reassuring; her words more so. "Stefano is playing a fantasy that can't happen. I stopped loving him years ago." She placed a hand over his heart. "I started loving you."

Scott covered her small hand with his larger one and gently asked, "What do you want me to do?"

"Act normal, and just love me. Now let's get ready and go to mass and then have lunch."

"I'll try. You know I love you, but it's difficult. Navigating your social circle, dealing with your former husband—who's a count—and knowing the right things to say, the correct way to act. . . ."

"Life is difficult, my darling," she chided. "But we must deal with it. And while you're bathing in your woe-is-me pool, remember—this is not easy for me, either. Yet I haven't hesitated. I entered this relationship withholding nothing. I introduced you to my friends, skeptical though they are. I've endured my mother's criticism and unwanted admonitions. It's not been a bed of roses. But dealing with these rough spots will be easier if you can see the situation as *ours* rather than just *yours*."

This woman—she could teach him so much about the world. Scott shook off his insecurities regarding Stefano, in awe of how gracefully Desirée navigated life's more troublesome aspects.

"You're right, and I'll do whatever I can to help your ex see the error of his ways. Shall we announce our engagement and finish him off?" Scott asked, kissing the top of her head. Desirée pulled back to give him a serious look.

"You're joking I know, but please—don't. Not about that. Let's try to get through next weekend first," she said solemnly. "I love your wit, but at the moment, it is not funny."

Scott smiled. He loved teasing her, and at the heart of his dry humor sometimes Desirée couldn't quite tell whether he was serious or not. "And what if I were serious? About marriage?" With surprise, he realized his heart was racing as he waited to hear her answer.

"I'll know when you are."

ASS BEGAN AT NOON, AND THEY ENTERED THE church with only minutes to spare. Desirée insisted on sitting in front, which meant walking down the length of the center aisle, essentially parading before all the townspeople and visitors whose seasonal turnout warmed the Catholic priest's heart while burnishing the church's collection coffers.

As the usher showed them to their pew, Desirée said to Scott, "I need to speak with Father Kohler after the service. I hope you don't mind."

As the liturgy wound its way through the ceremony—a cross between Swiss German and Latin—Scott wondered about the motive behind her meeting with the good father. True, he was an old friend, probably a counsel of some rank, and Desirée rarely did anything without a reason. So, why then, did she need to speak with Father Kohler?

AFTER THE BENEDICTION, FATHER KOHLER GREETED HIS departing parishioners on the steps of the church before joining Desirée and Scott, who were waiting for him in the foyer.

He greeted Desirée affectionately and said, "Mr. Stoddard, you are becoming a regular at St. Joseph's. We must make you a member. Countess, shall we speak in my office?"

Waiting in the car with Gustav, Scott tried not to appear impatient. Half an hour passed, and again he wondered what they could possibly be discussing. Finally, Desirée and Father Kohler appeared at the front door of the church. They lingered a moment more. Desirée, agitated, shifted from one foot to the other, her gestures uncharacteristically emphatic. Finally, she bid the cleric goodbye and strode down the steps. Gustav opened the rear car door, and she slid in next to him.

"I'm sorry we took so long," she said apologetically.

"Want to discuss it?"

"Father Kohler has asked me to help a Romanian family—their grandmother is a friend of Helena, my cook. They want to immigrate to Switzerland and need money to bribe their way out. I agreed to finance their exit, but anonymously." Desirée explained she often helped Father Kohler with problems in his parish. He was more than just her priest; after Desirée's father died, Father Kohler became an advisor and confidant. He had been close to the family since his years at the Vatican, and naturally, he had advised her during her annulment. Still, something about Desirée's delivery made Scott feel she hadn't told him everything.

"There must have been something else. You seem disturbed." He put an arm around her solicitously. "Please tell me."

He was surprised to see a faint sheen of tears in her eyes. "Yes, there was something else."

"Was it . . . did I come up in the conversation?" he asked tentatively.

"My mother called Father Kohler and asked him to please talk some sense into me." For all her brave talk about not caring what others thought, Desirée clearly cared about Father Kohler's opinion. Scott could see she was shaken. She wiped her eyes and said, "Let's not talk about it."

They rode in silence to the restaurant, where Desirée's subdued demeanor continued through lunch. It wasn't a complete calm, but the conversation (if it could be so euphemized) consisted of a series of long stretches of silence interrupted by a few perfunctory comments about the quality of the food and the changing weather.

Scott couldn't help but worry that Desirée would listen to his detractors. He hadn't even met Madame de Bellecourt, and Desirée's mother was already desperate enough to enlist the trusted family priest to help derail their romance. Did he really need to ask about the nature of the objections? Scott had to admit he'd been wrestling with those same objections himself. There was no need to press her for more details, and he hated to give them more importance by asking.

"I know what you're thinking," Desirée said, breaking the silence. "Father Kohler won't be interloping again. I hope I didn't hurt his feelings. It's not his fault; it's my mother's."

"There seem to be a lot of people interested in breaking us up," Scott observed carefully.

"Some people insist on wasting their time."

twenty-one

AT FIVE THIRTY THE NEXT MORNING, THERE WAS NO traffic, and the roads weren't icy. Scott was glad, because he did some of his best thinking behind the wheel when he could reflect without having to overly concentrate on driving.

A little over three weeks had passed since Desirée returned his call. In that short time, he'd fallen in love with this strong, mysterious, surprising, and delightful woman. A more improbable story could not be imagined, but Scott was not going to pinch himself. If it were a dream, he wanted the dream to continue. On his drive back to Geneva, he promised himself he wouldn't be the one to break the trance.

As the miles sped by, he failed to find any ideas to counter Desirée's mother's opposition or Stefano's jealousy. Resignedly, he decided that, if their relationship was to survive, it would be up to Desirée. She'd have to reject the naysayers and embrace Scott completely. He then thought of his parents. They wouldn't be pleased, but for different reasons; once they discovered Scott was neglecting his studies, the Stoddards wouldn't care one whit who or what was diverting his attention. Christ, he hated to disappoint them. He found strength remembering Desirée's words: *These rough spots will be easier if you can see the situation as* ours *rather than just* yours.

His reverie carried him into the environs of Geneva. There was just enough time to drop by his apartment, take his bags up, and check the mail before he went to class. He stopped, confused; the door to his apartment was unlocked. Scott was certain he'd locked it when he left. No one else had a key; Marlyse had returned hers, and he doubted she would have made a duplicate. Perhaps the building's concierge had entered during his absence to check on the radiator or the plumbing.

Entering, he surveyed the apartment and noticed the closet door was open. Scott's military prep school upbringing had trained him well; he never left anything out of place—doors closed, bed made, and clothes neatly folded—first, from following orders; later, out of habit and pride. Strange; he couldn't remember the last time he'd left his closet door open.

What didn't surprise him was a small stack of mail in his box, including two letters from his mother. There was her familiar handwriting on the blue engraved Crane stationery, the envelopes bulging. He would read those later, knowing already their copious contents: demands to know all about his activities, reprimands for not writing, and probing inquiries (one part caring, the other supervisory, wanting to make sure he was always on track).

The telephone rang; he thought it might be Desirée, but it was Jean. "*Bonjour* my friend! I knew you had to come back to Geneva some time. I've been calling you for over a week. Where have you been?"

"In Gstaad," Scott said.

"Uh-oh, I know what that means," Jean said. "The countess wouldn't have anything to do with Gstaad, would she?"

"Haven't you heard what happened to the curious cat?"

"I know about the cat, but my curiosity is irresistible. Can we have dinner this evening? I want to know everything."

SCOTT DECIDED TO WALK FROM HIS APARTMENT ON THE LEFT bank to Le Relais de l'Entrecôte—it was only across the bridge and up the little square not far from the train station. The moments in the fresh air gave him time to think. He arrived a little late at the bistro; though unpretentious, with wooden tables and chairs and a plank floor, it was one of the friends' favorite spots. The waiters wore traditional white and black uniforms, and they bustled among the tables covered in white linen and set with silver sterling. Oh, the food! The specialty of the house was steak in many different cuts with various sauces (Scott and Jean had agreed long ago that the maître d'hôtel sauce, a garlic butter concoction, was the best). The main attraction, however, was the golden, crunchy *pommes frites* that still tasted of potato.

Jean had taken a booth and already started a bottle of Bordeaux. As usual, he was the suave and debonair charmer, dressed in a French blue suit of impeccable cut, a blue shirt, and a Hermes tie. They embraced. It didn't take Jean long. "Okay, tell me everything."

"I'm in love with the Countess de Rovere." There; he had said it, out loud, in public, to someone other than Desirée.

Jean whistled low. "That was quick," he said.

"I know it sounds crazy, even improbable, but I've been in love with her since I first met her in September."

"Improbable?" Jean said. "More like impossible."

"What does that mean?" Scott asked. "You think it's impossible that Desirée is in love with me?"

"No, that's improbable," Jean said. "The Countess de Rovere is one of the most sought-after women in Geneva and in Paris. My mother knows her mother quite well. She attended the countess's wedding some years ago in Paris at the church of Saint Sulpice. Although I had never met her, I had thought of calling on her myself, but I presumed that she was looking for an older man. Then, you arrive on the scene, and in a few months, the two of you are seen everywhere together."

"Did I mention she's in love with me?" Scott said.

"Perfect. I'm jealous, but I'm happy for you too," Jean said. "Can I be both?"

"I hope you can, because I've never been happier."

"You told me that you had broken up with Marlyse because you thought she wanted to get married and you didn't," Jean said. "And now, you sound really serious. But you should be careful, my friend."

Jean began a rambling account, filling in many of the personal blanks that Scott had been too discreet to ask Desirée about directly. The de Roveres dated back to the Doges, the rulers of Venice, and the family was currently involved in Venetian real estate, shipping, and finance. Stefano was only tangentially involved in these holdings (more about that in a minute); he spent most of his time in the various watering holes inhabited by the rich playboys of France and Italy. Jean was unsure how Desirée had met the count but remembered reading in the tabloids that they'd had a flash romance that ended at the altar some six months later.

At the time, both families had approved of the marriage, and they held a high-mass wedding in one of Paris' oldest and most prestigious churches. The reception was held at the Allied Club in the rue de Faubourg Saint-Honoré, and it was the society event of the season. Their marriage, however, lasted a little over a year, and Jean mused that perhaps Stefano had not discussed his view that wedding vows were not to be an impediment to his *boulevardier* ways. And, as Scott knew from Desirée's own accounts, Stefano had not realized that his new wife would not stand being neglected or made the subject of derision and rumor about the status of her marriage. Stefano had forgotten that the countess, while French, was also Swiss.

When telling photographs of the count and various Italian cinema starlets began to appear in the shoddy press so addicted to gossip and innuendo, the countess was furious. One story dealt with a popular singer (a very vulgar woman by most accounts, Jean said with a knowing look). Reportedly, she and the count had abandoned the dance floor of a well-known nightclub in Venice and taken a water taxi to the Cipriani Hotel, only to be photographed as they left together, several hours later, disheveled and in an embrace suggesting something more than friendship. The article had also listed a chronology of the count's previous escapades and speculated whether the count's new wife knew of his nocturnal trysts.

Although he couldn't vouch for the rumor's validity, Jean had heard that the count was also an inveterate gambler who bet on everything from horses to baccarat—and mostly lost. The count's father had set a strict allowance; he'd paid off his son's gambling debt too many times, and people in the know said Stefano was banned from working in the family businesses. If prevailing gossip was to be trusted, the count had used Desirée's money to extricate himself from staggering debt. That, coupled with prurient tabloid stories, had provided the *coup de grace* to the relationship.

As Jean remembered, the couple had been residing in a palazzo in Venice when the countess left in the middle of the night, fleeing in her father's car to Paris and her mother's apartment in the 16th arrondissement. Everyone heard, Jean said, how furious the count was when he returned home after his all-night fling and found the palazzo abandoned—without even a note.

The count made numerous trips to Paris to try to change Desirée's mind, but she was firm. The more Stefano tried, the more humiliating the situation became; the tabloids were having a field day. Even his friends were unable to dissuade him. Finally, Stefano and a coterie of friends retreated to Rome, where he attempted to distract himself from Desirée through the usual but ineffective means.

Through various channels of influence and with the family priest's (Father Kohler, Scott recalled) intercession, Desirée had obtained an annulment. While she could have demanded and without question received a large financial settlement, everyone was surprised to hear that she'd ended the relationship and the marriage without conditions or terms pertaining to the de Rovere family trust. Well, after all, as Jean explained, Desirée was wealthy in her own right; her grandfather on her father's side had been a banker in Geneva (*ah*, thought Scott, *that explains the reaction when I opened my account*), and her father, Bertrand de Bellecourt, had inherited. Her mother, Francoise, was also from a privileged family; together, their union created a formidable fortune, and Desirée de Bellecourt was brought up in luxury. Her parents eventually parted to live separate lives, and in the early fifties, her father moved to California, where he had made another fortune in real estate. A year after the annulment, her father was dead, Desirée was heartbroken.

When the estate was settled, Desirée was left the de Bellecourt family home in Switzerland, an apartment in Paris, and a huge trust fund. Once again and despite the sordid affairs of her ex-husband, Desirée became one of society's most eligible and desirable catches. Two years had passed, and Desirée had filled her time in Geneva and Gstaad with galas and balls, hosting one must-attend event after another. There were seasonal sightings in Cap d'Antibes and Paris. But to Jean's quite extensive knowledge of gossip, though she had been seen with suitable escorts at various functions, Desirée had not been linked romantically with any one person since her annulment.

"So, my dear Scott," Jean said, "now perhaps you see why originally I thought it might be both improbable and impossible."

"Maybe my timing was right," Scott said.

"Right?" Jean said. "Dear God, more like perfect. And, if we're being honest, completely lucky. But Scott, some friendly advice. The Count de Rovere is an Italian aristocrat. His pride has been deeply offended. I'm not saying he's dangerous, but he's probably angry and vengeful, and at times, he curries a rough crowd. I'd be careful if I were you."

WHEN THEY LEFT THE RESTAURANT, THEIR FRIENDSHIP HAD been reaffirmed. Jean seemed satisfied that Scott's previous neglect was based in good reason rather than through a lack of caring. And Scott appreciated his friend's interest as solicitous, not nosy. To be frank, Jean's version of Desirée's story made him uneasy. It wasn't merely Jean's melodramatic concerns about the count; if Jean, who knew Scott as a friend, thought he was just lucky, then others might be interpreting the relationship similarly. Without money or social standing, it seemed Scott didn't really count for anything in this world. Perhaps Desirée would be influenced by what her friends thought and begin thinking of the improbability of their relationship. Though he knew her to be strong minded and independent, Scott couldn't help but reflect on how quickly Stefano had found himself on the outside of the proverbial castle, moat filled, and drawbridge up. One day, Scott feared, he might very well find himself banished, too.

When he got back to his apartment, it was late, and he forgot to give the place a thorough inspection. But the next morning, it appeared that the contents of his dresser's top drawer might have been rifled through. Scott couldn't be sure, though; in the lateness of the hour (and after a lot of wine), he might have rummaged around in that drawer without remembering. Lurking in the back of his mind was Jean's comment about Stefano, but he quickly pushed it away. *Stop it*, he told himself.

ARLYSE APPROACHED SCOTT AFTER CLASS AND asked him to have a coffee with her. They went to the café where they had first spent time together. She was dressed conservatively, Scott noticed; her gray below-the-knee skirt that flared at the bottom, white blouse, and black cardigan signaled serious intent. The place was empty, the morning rush over. Coffee mugs and croissant bits still littered some of the tables, and a smoky haze hung in the air. They chose a corner table where they could talk, ordered, and then sat in silence until Marlyse said, "I thought you were in love with me."

"Marlyse . . . when I told you I wasn't ready for marriage, you told me we were over, if you remember?" Scott said, with a defeated attitude. Why were they rehashing this?

"People sometimes say things they don't mean just to influence the other person, to make them realize what they might lose."

"Well, I believed you. I can't retrace my steps and go back to where I was."

"Then I don't think you really loved me. I think you were looking for a way out."

He couldn't deny that she might be right. "Marlyse, I never intended to hurt you. I guess I have, but I can't help it, and I can't change it. I'm sorry."

"For God's sake, Scott, I don't think you know what you want." She reflected for a moment, before asking, "Are you in love with the countess?"

"Yes, I am."

"Is she in love with you?"

"She says she is."

"Now I've heard it all. Do you have any idea who she is?" Realizing this was a rhetorical question, Scott remained silent. Marlyse continued angrily. "Forget it, Scott! You'll have your heart broken, just like you've broken mine, you bastard. I give it to the end of the ski season. Yes, by March, that should do it—that woman will have completely lost interest in you. Goodbye and good riddance!" With that, she stormed out of the café, and she didn't look back.

When Scott arrived at his last class of the day, the professor handed him a note; his student counselor would like to see him that afternoon, if possible. This couldn't be good, Scott thought; it was the end of the session, and no tests or grades had been assigned. He couldn't imagine why the counselor wanted to see him.

The university's administration offices were in one of the old town's oldest buildings. Minimalist in decoration, the three stories of granite and mortar, punctuated with large windows, halls, and stairs of stone were purely functional in appointments. Scott stopped before Dr. Eric Hochstadt's closed door, rang the buzzer, and was approved for entry by a green sign that lit up announcing, "*Entrez.*"

"Monsieur Stoddard, thank you for coming so promptly; please sit down," the counselor said, gesturing toward one of the two uncomfortable chairs in front of his desk. "It has come to my attention that, for the past two or three weeks, you have been absent from your classes quite a lot—notably each Thursday, Friday, and Monday. Although not required, attendance is beneficial to successfully navigate the courses in your field of study, and this is especially true for our foreign students." Dr. Hochstadt hardly took a breath. "You arrived here with the highest marks and recommendations, and in the beginning, you seemed to be a very serious student. After the holidays, however, this new and troubling pattern has arisen. Your professors and I were wondering why, what could be the reason? Then it became clear." As though he were presenting evidence in a trial, Dr. Hochstadt pushed a folded newspaper across his desk.

Scott was shocked—prominently displayed on the society page of the *Tribune de Genève* was a large photo of him and Desirée in a telling embrace. The caption: "Who is the mystery admirer of the Countess de Rovere at the Gstaad Palace Sleigh Ball?" Inwardly, he groaned.

"It seems we may have underestimated the full scope of your assimilative abilities, Monsieur Stoddard," Dr. Hochstadt said wryly. "We here at the university often worry about the integration of our foreign students, hoping they will find friends in Geneva, and so forth. It appears our concern here was misplaced. You seem to be managing very well on your own."

Scott listened carefully, certain Dr. Hochstadt would ultimately be positing the very question he'd been debating with himself.

"But do you think Monsieur Stoddard that your friendship with the Countess de Rovere is detracting from your studies? I ask this question not to pry but to give guidance, as your counselor."

"Yes sir, I believe it very well could," Scott answered. "As you have noted, I'm finding it difficult to be in class these days. Studying is problematic, given the choices dictated by the countess's lifestyle."

"I admire your honesty, young man, however unsettling, and I pray that this distraction is worth it."

"I hope so, too," Scott said. "It's early, so I don't know. I don't have any sort of plan; I'm playing this relationship by ear. My schooling, however, is definitely important to me."

The counselor shuffled a few papers on this desk. From the rather pointless stacking and restacking, Scott was certain he was merely taking a moment to regroup before expressing an unpleasant thought. "Monsieur Stoddard, these courses are difficult. I will be surprised if you can manage both. But I can't tell you what to do. I only hope you know the risk you're taking."

After dinner that evening, Scott decided he couldn't postpone reading his mother's letters. How could the day get any worse? The envelope with the oldest postmark, containing a four pager, was where he started reading. It was the usual communication—his mother wondered how he was doing and asked how school was coming along; had he made any friends? Was he lonely? Did he miss home? She scolded him for not writing or phoning; they had called several times at different hours two weekends ago, but he hadn't picked up.

The second letter carried some of the same questions and complaints. She'd written it only a few days ago, Scott noted. She hadn't even allowed time for a transatlantic post to reach home, he thought, shaking his head. Sighing, he picked up the last letter. This one made his jaw drop in surprise.

The Stoddards had made plans to visit Geneva during Scott's summer vacation, which was still five months away. They wanted to see for themselves where he lived and went to school. Then, he could come home during the summer and work at his father's building supply business. His mother liked to plan.

Scott dropped his head into his hands. That wouldn't work. He had no intention of leaving Desirée for the summer, under any circumstance. If his parents decided to travel to Geneva . . . he couldn't stop them.

The jangling sound of the telephone broke Scott's thoughts. "Good evening, my darling. Were you too glad to be back in class instead of being here with me?"

He told Desirée about the photo and being summoned by his counselor who'd recognized him in the *Tribune de Genève*. Desirée *tsk tsk*ed nonchalantly; paparazzi photos in society pages were like mosquitoes in summer—bothersome but completely expected.

"I know; my mother called early this morning. She had seen the same photo and some others in *Le Figaro*; it's the hot topic in Paris. Aren't you excited that everyone is wondering who you are?"

"I'm positively beside myself with glee. My professors believe I'm neglecting my studies, the counselor questions my judgement, my best friend thinks I'm an improbable suitor, my parents—they're threatening to come to Geneva to check up on me—and this weekend, I'll be cheek to jowl with your ex. Yes, I am so very excited," he said with an uncharacteristic bit of biting sarcasm.

"My prince, don't let these things trouble you. You're already a winner. You've got me."

Scott was without words. Was she really dismissing all his concerns?

"My darling, are you there? Did you hear what I just said?"

His normal reaction would have been to argue with anyone who presented such an easy solution, but Scott felt in his heart that Desirée was right. Her impossibly positive attitude was difficult to challenge, and he didn't want her to think he was petty or petulant. They would face his problems together. "Yes," he said. "You make it sound so easy. I want to trust your judgment."

"Everything is going to be fine," the countess soothed. "Now, can you be here in the early afternoon on Thursday? There's a benefit that evening for Father Kohler's church, and I need to be there, or he'll imagine we are angry with him."

twenty-three

ON THURSDAY MORNING, SCOTT ATTENDED CLASS. BY ten o'clock, he was on the road to Gstaad. The sun shone brilliantly against a blue cloudless sky, and the roads were clear. He was making good time, and the beautiful scenery was post-card-perfect. Passing through small villages, he saw trails of smoke rising from chimneys. Fanatical skiers were everywhere, carrying skis and poles on their shoulders, and heading toward the slopes, covered with fresh snow and still glazed by the overnight freeze.

Despite everything that was beautiful and right about the morning, Scott felt dread. The closer he got to Gstaad, the nearer his meeting Stefano. He had no delusions—after what Desirée and Jean had told him, Stefano would surely find a way to engage Desirée. Scott's worry was that this rejected lover might also attempt to embarrass him in some show of bravado or act of revenge. Because the count was older and a man of prominent social standing, Scott was certain they would not sink to the level of physical altercation (although the younger man would not have shrunk from a fight; he'd boxed in college and wasn't a pushover).

Desirée would not entertain or appreciate any impoliteness or bad behavior. Even so, his encounter with Stefano promised a verbal joust, employing innuendo, sarcasm, deprecation, and belittlement. Scott felt out of his depth; he'd gone from dating girls to sparring with an older woman's ex-husband. If he didn't have that social experience, he'd draw from academia and his own native intelligence. Scott had been a champion of sorts on the debate team. He understood where an opponent's weakness lay; once identified, he homed in with a killer's instinct. If he were to prevail (or even hold his own), Scott would need all his intelligence and precision to keep the count from embarrassing him in front of Desirée and triggering any feelings that he was somehow inept.

THE AUSTIN-HEALEY'S TIRES CRUNCHED AGAINST THE SNOW as Scott came to a stop in front of Desirée's chalet. Gustav rushed to unload his bag, and Helena greeted him at the door, both speaking in the most courteous and yet familiar manner. In a short time, he'd transitioned from an overnight guest, with the accompanying hesitancy and uneasy embarrassment, to an accepted fact of life. Neither seemed unhappy or disgruntled about his special link to the mistress of the house. They both adored Desirée (and she, them), so if Scott treated her well and made her happy, then he would enjoy their acceptance.

As the two bustled with his things, Desirée appeared. Standing in the doorway, she was the picture of radiance and beauty. He took in the full measure of her: long legs, slightly parted; glistening hair; the reddest of lipsticks; her sexy silhouette, clothed in powder blue from her graceful neck to her delicate ankles. Gustav and Helena passed by her, but he lingered at the car, enjoying the sight.

"Desirée," he said, approaching and taking her in his arms, squeezing her tightly against him. "I missed you." He guided her inside and closed the door.

"My darling, being apart for even a few days is too hard. We can't do this anymore," Desirée said, trembling in his arms. They held each other for a long while. Scott could've spent the rest of his life in her embrace. He loved touching Desirée and breathing her in—her reassuring firmness, her soft skin's natural scent, intensified by a concoction of jasmine and lavender. He couldn't resist kissing her moist and inviting mouth.

Breaking away, Desirée said, "Let's have lunch, and then maybe we can come back to have dessert."

"I prefer my dessert first," he said. "But I can wait."

THE ALPEN, LOCATED AT THE EDGE OF TOWN, WAS A SMALL hotel with a cozy restaurant. In typical Swiss style, a large stone fireplace dominated a room with pine floors, paneling, beams, and, in this case, pine booths with floral patterned, edelweiss cushions. Customers could enjoy their privacy, thanks to the booths' high backs, and foreigners frequented the place with regularity (the Alpen being too pricey for the frugal Swiss).

Desirée and Scott snuggled side by side, near enough to feel the warmth from the fire. They both ordered Russian-style eggs (deviled hard-boiled eggs, homemade mayonnaise, diced carrots, and little green peas) with a full-bodied white burgundy. Scott took advantage of the privacy of the booth; moments before their food arrived, he pulled her arm through his. Thus interlocked, he breathed gently on the expanse of bare neck below her ear. Desirée shivered but did not pull away, and he cautiously moved closer, nuzzling her neck and cheek against his lips.

As they ate their meal, Desirée turned uncharacteristically pensive. Scott backtracked over their preceding conversation, and when he couldn't come up with anything unsettling, he asked her if anything was wrong.

"I'm thinking of the business with the Romanian family, the one I'm helping Father Kohler with. There have been some complications; mainly, when the Romanians learned of the availability of the funds, they decided the grandmother should pay more," she said.

"Those bastards. How much more?"

"Double."

"What happened?"

"I paid it, and now she is to arrive next week in Zurich. Father Kohler has arranged for her to be driven here."

"The family and children must be ecstatic."

"They are, and they are curious as to their benefactor."

"And has Helena mentioned it to you?"

"Yes, she said that a miracle had happened."

"Is that all?"

"She had a gleam in her eye, but otherwise didn't reveal the slightest *soupçon*."

BACK AT THE CHALET, SCOTT UNPACKED HIS THINGS WHILE Desirée lay on the bed, watching. Placing the empty suitcase outside the bedroom door for Gustav to retrieve and place in storage, Scott closed the door quietly. Crawling onto the bed, he leaned over Desirée and said with a devilish grin, "Do you have any whipped cream?"

"Whipped cream?" she said, arching her eyebrows knowingly.

"Yes, I think it is time for that dessert."

She flashed a delighted smile and laughed. "Am I not sweet enough?"

NOTHING IS QUITE SO SWEET AS THE SLEEP FOLLOWING afternoon sex. Desirée napped quietly in Scott's arms; he dozed while he held her. When they roused, the lovers stayed cocooned in the luxurious bed, watching the play of light on the walls, murmuring to each other. Desirée's thoughts turned to the evening's affair, the benefit for St. Joseph, her church. "What will you wear tonight?" she inquired.

"What would you like me to wear?

"You wear a lot of black."

"You don't like black?"

"I do; it makes you look very handsome and strong. My girlfriends think so, too."

"That's nice, but I'm more interested in what you think."

"You should take the compliment. Some people I know don't think most Americans dress very well."

"Some also say that most Americans don't make love very well."

With a contented purr, Desirée snuggled close. "I know one who does."

THE BENEFIT FOR ST. JOSEPH WAS BEING HELD IN THE PARK Hotel's ballroom, and Scott and Desirée made their entrance at eight o'clock. Most of the guests had already arrived; Father Kohler was busy greeting attendees in the public rooms where the reception line was set. Scott assumed Desirée had contrived their late entry to turn heads and make an impression on those already vying for attention from the who's who.

Desirée commanded attention, even attired in a long-sleeved, demure black dress of simple proportions. Her hair was down, curled into a seductive coil of ringlets, and diamonds dazzled at her wrist and ears, brilliant against the darkness of the dress. Scott's charcoal suit, white shirt, and cobalt blue tie made the perfect complement. They were impeccably paired.

The cast of regulars—the Goosens, Bertrands, Soldatis, and Desirée's other friends Scott had met over the last few weeks—soon joined them in the ballroom. As they stood talking and drinking champagne, Francesco approached the group; with him was another man. Scott apprised the newcomer from the corner of his eye: the stranger was blond, blue-eyed, maybe five-eight, slight but handsome, and impeccably dressed in a dark suit and an Italian-knotted silk tie with snowflake motif. He walked with an entitled confidence. Scott knew instantly that this must be Stefano.

It didn't take long for Francesco and Stefano to join the small circle of friends gathered around Scott and Desirée. Though Scott was certain Desirée was aware of Stefano's presence, she ignored him. But he wasn't to be cast off so lightly.

"*Cara*, it is so nice to see you," Stefano injected ingratiatingly, forcing Desirée to recognize him in front of the group. "Are you still angry with your bad little boy?" There was an awkward moment, as everyone waited to see how she would respond.

"My dear count," she said coolly, as though greeting a casual acquaintance. "Actually, I never think of him." Scott placed a reassuring hand at the small of her back, a gesture that did not go unnoticed. Stefano glanced his way.

"And I think I know why," he said, staring at Scott. "Will you introduce Monsieur Stoddard, or should I introduce myself?"

"Why ask permission, when you'll clearly do it yourself?" She turned her back to Stefano, returning to her conversation with friends. Stefano fixed Scott with a cold stare, and Scott stood straighter. He could sense that the room was listening, curious as to how the countess's new lover would handle the situation.

"Monsieur Stoddard, I'm Count Stefano Ambrosi Saccone de Rovere."

"Pleased," Scott replied. "Scott Stoddard, as you know."

"I've heard all about you," Stefano went on. "Other than being American, people say you are quite charming."

"There are mixed reports as to charming, but I am most definitely American."

"Why don't you go back to where you belong? We would hate to see you overstay your welcome in Geneva."

"Is that a command?" Scott asked with mock innocence. "And I thought you a count, not a king." There was a slight titter from the eavesdroppers. Stefano clinched his jaw, and Scott watched the muscle jump with satisfaction.

"I think you will regret knowing me, Monsieur Stoddard," Stefano growled. "I am not easily dismissed."

Desirée, with her customary grace, found that moment to slip her arm into Scott's and announce, "Darling, I absolutely must pay my respects to Father Kohler. Shall we?"

The Stefano incident was over. At least, it was over for the evening.

twenty-four

D ESIRÉE SQUEEZED HIS ARM, LEANED CLOSE, AND said, "I think they've had quite enough for tonight, my darling. You can relax and stop showing off. I would think that the count has learned a lesson."

"Was I showing off?" he murmured in her ear. "I wasn't trying to."

"You don't have to," she said. Her simple response conveyed so much; it reassured that, as much as Stefano might antagonize him, it was Scott who shared Desirée's bed, and Scott whom she loved. Relieved, he adopted a nonchalant expression. Let others be the judge of who'd won that first round, but he knew who'd won Desirée's heart.

Desirée said good night to Father Kohler, who thanked her for her generosity, and while she made the rounds with her friends, Scott stood apart from the crowd, watching and thinking. Her remark must mean he had acquitted himself well; at least, she wasn't unhappy. That conversation with Stefano had been a performance for him—a performance for an audience of one; no one mattered but Desirée. True, he and the count were locked in a contest as old as time—the romantic in him saw two knights jousting for a lady's favor. Scott felt a bit silly; he had thought himself above such primal emotion. Having prided himself on an appreciation of intellectual and philosophical pursuits, Scott was disappointed to discover how vulnerable he was to raw jealousy. That male competitiveness didn't seem to care whether he was familiar with Aristotle or not. Being in love with the right woman had brought out the beast. Scott shook his head ruefully; he had never felt quite like this before, and he knew the truth—he was a goner.

He also knew that his love—no, his fear of losing Desirée—was a path to possessiveness. That feeling, a sucking undercurrent, would pull him into an orbit around her. He'd want to stay with her, protect her, claim her—he'd hate to leave her alone for any period of time. Where would school and the future he and his parents had planned fit (he shuddered at their disappointment)? Would he drown in Desirée?

They left the party, and Gustav made the short drive through Gstaad and up the winding drive to the Palace for dinner at the ultra-chic Grill. The black marble bar glistened; the mirrored walls reflected the lined bottles of whisky, aperitifs, and digestives. Barstools upholstered in French brocade and gold piping faced the carved, turned-edge bar, while small bar tables scattered about allowed those who were seated to enjoy views of the pool and village.

Desirée was in high spirits. Positively euphoric, she greeted some of the patrons at the bar and blew kisses to others as they proceeded to their table.

"Should we order some champagne to celebrate?" she asked.

"And we are celebrating . . . " Scott had no interest in dampening her effusive spirits, but he was flummoxed as to its cause.

"Winning!" Her eyes gleamed fiercely.

"What did we win?" he asked, genuinely curious.

"You won, because Stefano lost. He lost his composure; he lost his manners. The rude always lose. You know you won; I saw it in your eyes—and in his."

"All right, my clever little fox," Scott replied with a jaunty smile. "Let's make it Krug then." Desirée gave a conspiratorial little laugh and kissed him on the cheek. Because it would make her happy, Scott would celebrate, but he knew better than to gloat. Desirée hated any smugness at having bested someone, even her ex. They toasted his victory, but as soon as he could, Scott directed the conversation elsewhere.

≈

CHRIST, DESIRÉE'S AN EARLY RISER **WAS THE FIRST THING** SCOTT thought when he awoke, alone, in the massive bed. She was already up—and who knew what might have happened had she remained beside him? Scott had sensed a subtle shift in last night's lovemaking. From the beginning of their relationship, Desirée had been in control, but she'd gradually relinquished her director's role and finally enjoyed the delight of sheer abandon. The experience was intoxicatingly seductive, and Scott was still drunk from that new feeling of dominance, particularly in contrast to how vulnerable he felt outside the bedroom.

Passing through the kitchen, he said good morning to Helena and asked for his usual. "Of course," she replied cheerfully, and he continued to the breakfast room. There, Desirée sat at the table, radiant as usual, her hair down, a lilac robe slightly askew, and her long legs pulled up in her favorite chair. She was on the telephone. Covering the receiver, she mouthed a good morning before resuming her conversation.

"That's ridiculous," Desirée exclaimed. "As usual, he adopts a story devoid of facts. No one would believe that unless they were jealous of Scott. The one thing that you can count on from Stefano is that, in respect to me, he will always find ways to further embarrass himself." After a few more exchanges, Desirée said goodbye and hung up.

"Who was that?" Scott asked, buttering his toast.

"Louise Goosens. She was giving me a report from the count's camp."

"And?" Scott said.

"The count finds you rude, and his sensibilities are hurt."

"I'm only nice to a point. And should I mention—better his sensibilities than his nose?" Scott reflected that Jean had predicted Stefano's reaction to him.

"Louise says that he is angrier than ever."

Remembering Jean's warning, Scott hoped he wasn't underestimating the count.

The Goosens were giving a cocktail party at their chalet that evening, and Scott was not enthused. Yet another party where he would be a topic of conversation and subject for inspection. And having learned Louise was privy to the count's feelings, Stefano was almost certainly invited. The last thing Scott wanted was to deal with that pompous fool. But this social scene, with its consecutive evenings of parties and balls and unending obligations, was the fabric of Desirée's life. If he wanted to be with her—and he most certainly did—then his attitude needed adjustment. Scott knew he must accept her way of life. After all, what did he have to offer her in contrast? A walkup, one-bedroom apartment; a student's life, bookish nights, dining in small restaurants; the occasional weekend road trip to small villages in the Alps? Would he even retain that modest lifestyle, once his parents knew he had taken up with an older woman? Desirée's wealth afforded him a style and level he'd only read about, which his parents' social circle had tangentially touched. To enjoy his relationship with Desirée fully, Scott would have to set aside his insecurities and embrace her support.

At the same time, he continued arguing with himself; was he pursuing the right path? Given his desire, was there a choice? Did he honestly believe he could really resist the call of a life with Desirée? Could he chuck his love, go back to Geneva, and renew his schoolwork as if nothing had happened?

Not likely. He was in deep, and Scott decided to quit fighting the inevitable and nurture their relationship. He would be the one to change; she wouldn't and shouldn't. A massive weight seemed to lift, and Scott felt a warm happiness at the thought of a future with Desirée. Still, a small voice in his head whispered that he was throwing away his academic dreams and wasting his parents' considerable investment in his future. There was going to be a good portion of hurt and disappointment, but he couldn't change it.

THE GOOSENS' CHALET, REVE DE NEIGE, WAS VERY NEAR Desirée's chalet. A classic structure, the three-floor A-frame rose out of a small forest of Alpen spruce. The Goosens were Dutch, and the low-slung modern and minimalist furnishings reflected their northern European sensibilities. Generous fur throws and piles of soft pillows softened the otherwise straight lines of the décor, which were further warmed by a fireplace in each of the public rooms. Scott wasn't surprised to see a few abstract sculptures by Calder and Moore interspersed among original Cezanne, Modigliani, and Braque oils hanging on the walls.

Jon and Louise were among Desirée's best friends, and Scott felt he had a chance to be accepted by them. Celine Montaigne, Desirée's childhood friend, was there when they arrived. Perhaps with her, too, he would have a chance. Taking tally, Scott noted that was three down; how many to go? Thank God Celine didn't seem to be with Francesco; perhaps Stefano would not be there either. Louise was no fool, and she'd probably engineered the party by inviting the guests least likely to make a fuss. Scott reminded himself to be nice, smile, and behave modestly. Showing off wouldn't win him any more friends.

Desirée quickly got involved with a group of friends, most of whom Scott hadn't met. He whispered he was going to get them both another flute of champagne; she nodded absently, and he left her side to push through the crowd toward the bar. As he walked down the hall, he saw Celine at the other end.

"Good evening, Scott," she said. "Can I speak to you for a moment?" Leading him away from the crowd, they followed a short walkway to the breakfast room. She closed the door behind them.

"Must be something serious," Scott said.

"Serious—and none of my business," she replied gravely. "You can tell me so if you like, and I will drop the matter."

"Celine, I know you to be Desirée's close friend. Please, tell me— what is it that you need to say to me?"

"I don't know you well, but I do know Desirée is madly in love with you. So, I want to like you, too, but I'm worried; I can't be entirely sure of the sincerity of your motives." Her voice was rising and falling with each nervous tremor.

"Worried about what?"

"Desirée would kill me if she knew I had spoken to you. I'm worried that she's going to get hurt. You aren't Catholic, and that could be a problem."

"My God, Celine, I would never hurt Desirée. Let's face it; it's more likely she will hurt me. I'm no threat to her; she's quite capable of taking care of herself. Though she'd appreciate your concern, she really has no need of all the well-meaning assistance. And aren't you jumping pretty far ahead to worry that I'm not Catholic?"

"I'm sorry, I shouldn't have said anything."

"Forget it. You're just being a good friend to the woman I adore. Let's just start over."

Celine considered Scott for a long moment. "I think I just figured out why she loves you," she said thoughtfully.

He smiled at her. "I see why Desirée values your friendship—and I promise you, I will never hurt her. Now," he said brusquely, "we should get back to the party, don't you think?"

As he rejoined Desirée and handed her the glass of sparkling liquid, she said, "There must have been a long line."

"No, it wasn't that long," he said, "but ladies first, you know."

Sunday meant mass and lunch at one of the small restaurants in a village two valleys away. Scott and Desirée returned to the chalet around three in the afternoon. The impending threat of separation—whether dreaded Monday or terrible Tuesday—crept into their psyches like a nagging toothache. Despite Scott's recent resolve to embrace happiness with Desirée, that little voice continued to berate him about his studies and school responsibilities. Could he stay? In the face of pressure that he knew Desirée would put on him to stay, Scott reasoned that perhaps the time had come for a frank discussion of academic and financial issues.

"Desirée, if I'm to continue my studies, I will need to get back to Geneva by at least noon tomorrow. That way, I will miss only one class in the morning. And I can come back on Friday," Scott said.

"Are we to be weekend lovers, then?" Desirée asked. "It seems I'm always taking you away from your school, always interfering with your studies. Perhaps one day you will hate me for interrupting your school to fall in love with me."

"Don't be ridiculous. No one wants to stay more than I do."

"Look," she said, "when this began, neither you nor I thought rationally. It just happened. Had we thought about it, considered all the ramifications, then—"

"Why do you think I didn't call you for several months? I thought about all the reasons why I wasn't suitable, but from the first moment I saw you, I fell in love. You were the only one for me, and no amount of reasonable thought, no consideration of school or anything else, made a damn bit of difference. I resisted it, but in the end—"

"So why are we arguing?" she said softly. "We will find a way to be together."

twenty-five

LATER THAT EVENING, AS THEY LOUNGED ON THE SOFA in front of the fire, dreading Scott's upcoming departure, Desirée said, "Why don't we both go to Geneva? You can move whatever you need into the house and go to class from there. At least we will be together."

What could he say? Yes, this new living arrangement would allow them to spend more time together, but what Desirée was proposing wouldn't help him get any studying done. At least he would appear in class, he reasoned (and he'd hope he didn't get called on).

"Also, darling—this next weekend is the Cresta Run Ball. We'll need to leave early Thursday morning to drive to St. Moritz."

Scott's sense of Swiss geography was still developing. "St. Moritz: isn't that way over in the Graubünden canton?" She nodded. Scott took a deep breath before plunging into another difficult topic. "Desirée, something is bothering me. We need to discuss the finances of all this. I know talking about money can seem, well, unrefined but I'm sure you are aware I have a budget, albeit a nice one: an allowance from my parents, provided to support my academic studies. I have paid for a few dinners and lunches, but the big expenses—balls, dinners at the Palace, clothing, and champagne—you have graciously seen to these. Now, you propose a trip to St. Moritz, which doesn't have the reputation of being a place where the needy hang out."

Desirée brushed her hair back and straightened herself on the sofa. "We've touched on this before, my dear, since that first dinner at Le

Chesery. Yes, I have accounts at some of these nice places, and they send me a monthly bill. We both are aware that you, living on a student stipend, couldn't possibly underwrite what we are enjoying." There was a distinct silence for a time. Aware that the younger man was struggling with her greater wealth, Desirée gently said, "This is one of those rational and reasonable problems that we chose to ignore when we embarked on this relationship. Is my financial support a problem we can't overcome?"

"Of course not," he said. "But I must find a solution to my means."

"I have one," she said. Scott waited, expectantly. "It's time to discuss pocket money."

"Pocket money?" A slight flush spread across his face.

"Yes, an incidental sum that I will transfer the first of every month to your account. But we can still enjoy some of the benefits of my accounts at the hotels, restaurants, and stores, can't we?"

"But—" Desirée watched Scott's face as he struggled with his masculine pride. He'd be trading his parents' financial support for his lover's. Was he strong enough to buck conventional roles?

"No "buts", Scott. This is the most practical solution. I have enough money, and we want to be together. As I asked before, can't you learn to enjoy the things I can afford?" She looked at him expectantly, awaiting his response.

Scott couldn't argue with Desirée's logic, but his pride was at stake, as inconvenient and tiresome as that conventional upbringing was. Damn it, he'd be a kept man. Would accepting an allowance undermine his manhood and, ultimately, diminish his virility—an important concern in their relationship, no doubt. Depending on his attitude and Desirée's handling, Scott feared it was possible.

According to plan, they arrived at Desirée's house near Geneva in time for Scott to attend his afternoon classes. While he received some chastising looks from fellow students, his professors, however, said nothing (which, in its own way, was more worrisome than a direct rebuke). In the language of international relations, he had become a student without portfolio—not to be taken seriously.

After class, he stopped by the apartment, checked his mail, and packed two suitcases in preparation for the trip to St. Moritz at the end of the week.

IN THE FOLLOWING DAYS, LIFE WITH DESIRÉE SETTLED INTO a routine. Scott commuted to his classes at the university and dropped by the empty apartment to collect his mail. More letters arrived from his mother, each one more pressing, each demanding more information. He received an advisory from Credit Suisse, his bank, that 10,000 Swiss francs had been credited to his account. He wasn't shocked about the deposit; Desirée had asked for the account number so she could provide "something for incidentals," as she put it. They hadn't discussed the amount, but some incidentals! It was twice the amount he received monthly from his father. He had some ambivalent feelings about the money and its implications, his mind returning to the phrase *pocket money.*

There was another letter of unrecognizable origin. Scott examined the envelope; the return address indicated a law firm in Geneva. Inside was a letter from a Monsieur Henri du Bois, attorney at law, requesting Scott's presence at his office on Tuesday at eleven. There was a matter of some urgency and confidentiality, and the attorney admonished him to tell no one of the letter or their proposed meeting.

Who and what was behind this, Scott wondered. Desirée? He thought not. His mother and father? Unlikely but not impossible. And why was an attorney involved? They couldn't prosecute him for skipping school, could they?

INSTEAD OF GOING TO CLASS, SCOTT MADE HIS WAY TO DU Bois' office on Avenue General Guisan, a tony address in Geneva's business center, where he was shown into a conference room and immediately joined by the attorney. Du Bois brusquely turned to the business at hand.

"Mr. Stoddard, I know you were probably surprised by my letter, and I hope that you have honored my request to keep this meeting in strictest confidence. I'll get right to the point. My role in this is to make you an offer, an offer that you shouldn't refuse."

Scott had not expected this at all. Genuinely curious and thoroughly perplexed, he inquired, "An offer of what?"

"My client has instructed me to offer you the sum of 300,000 Swiss francs to end your relationship with the Countess de Rovere. If you accept, then you will not communicate—"

His reaction was immediate and forceful. "No, no, and no! I won't do it," Scott shouted, leaping to his feet.

Despite the angry young man towering over him, the attorney remained unfazed. "But Mr. Stoddard, you should take your time to think this through. Your chance of a committed relationship with the countess is a decided long shot. Your studies are suffering. Eventually, she will tire of you. Think what this sum could do for your future."

"You don't have enough money to buy me off. Tell your client to go to hell."

"There's no need for anger. It's only business." Du Bois smiled in a ruthless manner. "You must know, however, that my client will not be pleased to hear of your refusal."

Scott snorted in disgust. "Not pleased? Your innuendo is highly unethical. Should I report you to the police or the Swiss Bar Association?"

"And what would you report?"

"That first, you attempted to bribe me and second, when that failed, made a threat."

"But I haven't." The attorney was thoroughly unruffled.

"I can't imagine that you or your client would like the publicity. It would be your word against mine. And you summoned me, remember?"

"I'm not sure anyone would benefit from any publicity. "Tell me, young man, said Du Bois, poising his pen expectantly over the paper before him, "is there a larger sum you would consider?"

Without responding, Scott walked out, slamming the office door. He decided that for the moment he would keep this from Desirée. He could imagine her rage if she were to find out. The count (for surely,

Du Bois' client could be none other than Stefano) must be stupid if he thought Scott could be bought. No, Scott was not the gold digger the count assumed him to be. And he'd be insane to imagine he could win Desirée back, with or without Scott in the picture.

twenty-six

S T. MORITZ WAS SOME FIVE TO SIX HOURS AWAY, SO
Desirée and Scott got a decent hour start on Thursday. Even
with Gustav behind the wheel, a long lunch at the Baur au
Lac with one of Desirée's friends, a middle-aged woman of exiled
Russian royalty, they still arrived at the fabled Badrutt's Palace as the
sun set on the lake below the hotel. When the Badrutt brothers themselves came out to greet Desirée and assure her of the luxury of the
accommodations, Scott smiled to remember Millie's once confusing
reference to Badrutt's. Everything had been taken care of, they said;
the steamer trunks Desirée had sent by train earlier in the week for
Saturday's ball had been delivered, their contents pressed and hung in
the suite's closets.

Their suite was on the sixth floor, its large windows overlooking
the lake—a spectacular view—some three hundred meters below. In
the distance, the Engadin mountains loomed. It was already dark, but
the iced lake shimmered in the moonlight. Scott had heard that, on
weekends, horse races were held on its frozen surface.

Furnished in the French style of Louis XV, the apartment had a
large salon and an equally luxurious bedroom, with a private dressing
room for Countess de Rovere, two large closets, and a bathroom fit for
a queen. On the coffee table, placed along with a large basket of fruit
and various cheeses, was a bundle of letters addressed to Desirée.

"We've been here thirty minutes," Scott said, incredulously. "And
you've already received mail."

"Invitations, my prince. We must choose which to accept." Desirée began to work her way through the stack.

"How do you choose?" he asked.

"Carefully," she said. "I try to accept the most agreeable and refuse the most cumbersome."

"Sounds difficult."

"It takes practice."

Scott didn't offer any advice. He knew she would work it all out; she would please some and offend none. That was her way. Always conscious of other's feelings, Desirée never intentionally hurt anyone, and those she had to refuse, Scott knew, would be compensated in some other fashion to assuage their disappointment. Her sensitivity helped her anticipate the feelings of others before they even experienced them.

THE SEASON'S OPENING OF THE CRESTA RUN WAS AN EVENT not to be missed. Cresta (a sport that evolved into the skeleton event) involves men holding on to sleds and hurtling themselves down the icy track at breakneck speeds. Hosting some thirty annual races, the Cresta Run had been entertaining winter sports fans since 1884.

The Kulm Hotel, located near the Cresta Run's starting point, was the home of the British contingent of high society and sporting life in St. Moritz, and so its owner hosted the reception, essentially a pre-party for the ball that would take place the following evening. Haute couture was the uniform of the evening, and as they dressed, Scott soon learned what Desirée had packed in those pre-delivered cases. She wore Balenciaga, and her metallic silver gown, a kind of Roman toga, was created from a supple fabric that suggestively kissed her body's contours. With her blond hair cascading over a silver band, an exquisite diamond necklace and pair of chandelier earrings dazzled about her face and décolleté. All in all, Desirée was a stunner from every angle. Scott wore his tuxedo along with his birthday cuff links and studs. Before leaving the suite, they stood side by side and studied themselves in the large mirror and agreed that, as a couple, they weren't bad.

Scott couldn't keep up or remember the many persons to whom he was introduced—the marquis, the comtesse, the ambassadeur—even though Desirée gave *sotto voce* running commentary on each. Scott found some solace in the large number of people; with so many unfamiliar faces, he wasn't of interest, nor did the glittering crowd seem to notice that he didn't know anyone.

Eventually, they left the cocktail party with two other couples and returned to Badrutt's for dinner. As Desirée and Scott walked to the elevator that would take them down to the Grill, there was Millie Summersmith. Pretty as ever, and, as ever, pushing the limits with her outfit, a trendy silver mini skirt and white fur jacket. They saw each other at the same time, and Millie turned from the group she was talking with to greet Scott and the countess.

"Millie, my dear, what are you doing here?" Desirée asked, hugging and kissing her friend.

"Desirée, Scott—my word, are you two together?"

"Why yes, dear," Desirée replied. "We've just been to the reception at the Kulm." Scott couldn't help but slide a proprietary arm around her waist, and she melted into his side. Scott watched Millie's face—there was a look of momentary shock (after all, she'd kissed him when they last saw one another), but it was quickly replaced with a warm smile.

Millie recovered brilliantly: "I'm not at all surprised. I had a feeling back in September, when you two couldn't keep your eyes off each other. I presumed the hands would be next," she laughed, with a wink at Scott. "Anyway, my charming Scott is too mature for me." She turned to him flirtatiously. "Scott, you are uncharacteristically quiet."

"A wise man knows when to be silent," he quipped. Millie was a fun girl. But having spent these last weeks with the countess, she now seemed juvenile.

"Are you here with your dear mother?" Desirée inquired. "Will you tell your mother hello and that I will call her?"

"Of course," Millie said. With that, she rejoined her friends, and Scott noted, "She wasn't shocked to see us."

"She was, and she wasn't, but she behaved well," Desirée said. "It's a sign of a good education."

They joined Desirée's friends, who were already seated at the table in the restaurant. Juan Carlos de Flora and his wife, Teresa, split their time between Paris and Madrid. Juan Carlos's mother was a lady-in-waiting to the exiled Queen of Spain, Victoria Eugenie, who lived in Lausanne. She and Desirée's mother, Madame de Bellecourt, were close friends, and Madame de Bellecourt often visited Lausanne to pay court to the queen. The other couple, Jacques Deschamps and his wife, Caroline, were Parisians. He was an attorney, and she owned a chic art gallery on the rue de Faubourg Saint-Honoré. Both couples seemed to be in their mid to late thirties.

From the questions asked, Scott surmised they had been prepped to meet him; Desirée had been busy. They all seemed to know where he attended school and what he was studying. Their easy conversation revealed these to be some of her closest friends. Juan Carlos was the funniest and, apparently, he loved teasing Desirée.

"You are the talk of the Spanish court in Lausanne," Juan Carlos said to Scott. "Our mothers are talking, too—Madame de Bellecourt told my mother you have captured Desirée's heart. Well, that's how I remember it. She may have had a bit more to say, something about Cupid being careless with his darts."

"I can't imagine that I'm the talk of anything," Scott said.

"Your imagination is not in question, but we all would like to know what your magic is," Juan Carlo said.

"If there is magic, it's all Desirée's," Scott said. "I am completely under her spell and have been, from the moment I first saw her."

"I will be frank: For several years, her friends and I have been proposing very nice young men to the countess, but she has always demurred. We wondered when she would pick someone for herself. She has excellent taste, as you know, so we would never disagree with her choice," Juan Carlos said.

"Nor would I," Scott said.

Juan Carlos reached across the table and shook his hand. It was a hearty, sincere shake. The movement caught Desirée's eye, and she beamed, giving Scott an affectionate look across the table.

"Desirée, I presume we shall see you and Scott at the film festival in Cannes in May," Jacques Deschamps said. "Will you stay at your mother's place in Mougins or at the Carlton?"

"We haven't discussed it. My mother actually wants me to come for Easter, which is just a few weeks away," Desirée said. "It's early this year."

"Scott, have you met Desirée's mother yet?" Caroline Deschamps asked, with a quick glance toward Desirée.

"No, I haven't had the pleasure."

"It remains to be seen if that will be a pleasure," Desirée muttered darkly. Teresa patted Scott's hand in a soothing way. "Don't mind Desirée," she said soothingly. "Madame de Bellecourt just pretends to be difficult. It's part of the persona she projects. I'm sure she will love you, too."

This back and forth between trusted friends revealed that Desirée had much longer-term plans than Scott was privy to. It was the middle of February, and she'd just announced two projects in the works that had been unknown to him: one in March, just weeks away, and the other in May. When had Desirée planned to tell him? How many other schemes were awaiting the proper moment for disclosure? Knowing how Scott intended to maintain his studies, she might have maneuvered this unwitting group to reveal what she didn't want to broach directly. She was clever.

After dinner, they descended to the King's Club, the Badrutt's private nightclub, where champagne cost 120 Swiss francs per bottle and the décor was more Arabian Nights than Louis XV. A crowd had already gathered, but the stylish group was given a corner table, commanding a view of the dance floor.

On the dance floor, Scott was finally able to hold Desirée in his arms. He was aware of an audience; their party made no attempt to hide their interest, eager to determine if body language *en dansant* would give insight into the depth of Scott and Desirée's connection. Desirée must have sensed this, too; in her most sensual way, her arms embraced his neck, and her body, swathed in the silver lamé, seemed magnetized to his. In perfect synchrony, they followed the slow and incessant rhythms of the beat.

Taking advantage of the moment with her sole attention, Scott murmured in her ear, "Am I going with you at Easter?"

"I want you to," she said, her aquamarine eyes looking up at him.

"Does your mother know I'll be coming?"

"She suspects, I'm sure."

"When will you tell her?"

"Tomorrow. She's waiting for an answer."

"Will she like me?"

"If she will let herself."

They didn't speak any more about the upcoming visit. Scott left the matter in her hands because he knew Desirée would engineer this in her own way; all he had to do was show up and behave in a nice, intelligent, and slightly unpredictable manner. From everyone's comments, Madame de Bellecourt seemed to have already formed her opinions. With her mind made up, maybe a good strategy for dealing with Desirée's mother would be to upset and contradict her prejudgments.

THEY GOT BACK TO THE SUITE LATE, AND DESIRÉE INDICATED in little ways that she was tired; they'd had a long day, and she wasn't sure she was up for an even longer evening. Once they were in bed and the lights were out, Scott moved to caress her. At first, Desirée pulled away—she knew what he was up to. But all Scott needed to do was excite her, and any reluctance and fatigue would disappear. Little by little, her resistance waned, and she changed her mind, deciding to encourage his attentions to her body. As her breathing intensified and her first sounds of pleasure escaped, Scott knew she was glad he'd persisted. In sync, they moved together slowly, sensuously; in the end, their lovemaking was better than ever.

THE ROOM SERVICE WAITER AWAKENED THEM THE NEXT morning. He rolled in a large table set with Bernardaud china, Baccarat crystal, and Christofle silver. Fluffy scrambled eggs with truffle shavings, thick-cut crispy slices of bacon, and golden hash browns beckoned from domed sterling chafing dishes. A large cut-crystal pitcher filled with freshly squeezed orange juice, a silver wire basket of breads and morning pastries covered by a white linen napkin, coffee with warm milk, and a vase with a fresh bouquet completed breakfast. *This,* thought Scott as he belted his plush robe, *this was the life.* He took a seat, admiring the spread as sunlight filled the room.

Desirée joined him from the bedroom. She wore a chocolate brown robe covering a negligee with ivory lace, and her cheeks were still slightly pink from the stubble of his beard.

"Good morning, my darling," she said, just as the telephone rang. She answered it. "Yes, Maman; I was expecting your call. I've decided to come to Mougins for Easter, and I would like to bring my friend." Desirée listened for a few moments and then said, "It's your decision, but I think you'll like him."

She hung up the phone and gave Scott a kiss. "It's done. We're going to Mougins for Easter."

"Really?" Scott said skeptically. "It sounded more like you may have given her an ultimatum."

Desirée sighed. "My mother understands better when she's not given a choice."

twenty-seven

THREE WEEKS AND INNUMERABLE PARTIES, LUNCHES, and dinners later (and very few classes), and Scott and Desirée were on their way to Mougins for Easter. They'd take an Air France flight to Nice, where they would rent a car.

After conversation with her mother and in anticipation of their visit, Desiree had been providing Scott with more family information. Françoise de Borchgrave, the daughter of the Count and Countess de Borchgrave, had married Bertrand de Bellecourt, the son of a Swiss private banking family. They had been introduced when Bertrand was working in the family's investment office in Paris. Once wed, they'd lived in Geneva, Paris, and Mougins for some thirty years. Over time, however, the couple's interests had diverged. Finally, Desirée's devoutly Catholic parents decided to live separate lives, which allowed them to avoid the unthinkable—divorce. That was when Desirée's father moved to Los Angeles to pursue banking interests and, later, real estate investments. He had died unexpectedly of a heart attack three years ago, leaving the family home outside Geneva and an apartment in Paris to Desirée, his only child. Her mother had retained the home in Mougins and acquired her apartment in Paris on the Avenue Foch, close to Desirée's. Madame de Bellecourt was an energetic, well-connected woman who actively participated in Parisian social life; she supported many charities connected to her first love, the preservation of French historic architecture. Parisian through and through, Madame de Bellecourt was fiercely protective of Desirée, her only child.

Scott and Desirée landed at the Nice airport, where he was thrilled to collect their rented Mercedes Benz 230SL convertible. Since the car was a two-seater, a separate messenger would transport their luggage to Mougins just in time for lunch. *Bon appetit*, Scott thought.

Desirée drove. She'd taken the route many times, and the car climbed smoothly from the Mediterranean coast to the heights above Cannes. The views were magnificent in all directions, and Scott soaked in the experience. They drove through the medieval town of Mougins and continued until they passed under an arch. Spanning the narrow lane, it was inscribed with *Le Vallon de l'Oeuf*.

"The Valley of the Egg?" Scott translated. "Nice name."

"My father came up with it," Desirée explained. "He thought it funny."

She pulled the car up to the entrance of the house, which stood atop an outcrop overlooking a valley of native Mediterranean scrub flora. Fruit trees and grape vines filled the landscape on the other side of the two-story, ivory-and-white stone structure. It was classical *mas*, a particular kind of farmhouse originally built to be a self-sufficient unit (house and grounds supporting the people who lived there, generally an extended family, as well as their animals). In the past, the terrain surrounding these provincial homes was usually planted with various grains for the animals and an extensive vegetable garden, fruit orchard, and root cellar, but it was obvious that comprehensive renovations and additions had been made to the once bucolic practicality of earlier times.

The noise created by the tires rolling over the pea gravel driveway must have alerted Madame, because there she stood on the front veranda: erect, proud, and attired in Hermes. Not everyone appreciates how conservative French women of a certain milieu and age can be. Their chic dress, paucity of makeup, and restrained use of jewelry are unconsciously but assuredly assembled to communicate perfection and a no-nonsense and rigid preference for manners, etiquette, and decorum. Madame de Bellecourt was a perfect example.

A gray twill skirt trimmed in a thin band of leather; a print blouse of yellow and gray, depicting swans floating along a peaceful lake; a gold bracelet of simple anchor chain links dangling from her wrist; and a large yellow tourmaline cabochon on her left index finger all disclosed the origin of Desirée's impeccable taste. Her silver hair—every strand in place—hung straight before flipping at the ends. Removing her sunglasses, Scott saw familiar eyes of aquamarine.

Desirée led Scott up the few steps to the veranda, where she greeted, embraced, and kissed her mother, before turning to say, "Scott, please let me introduce you to my mother, Madame de Bellecourt. Maman, Scott Stoddard."

"Mr. Stoddard, welcome to Le Vallon de l'Oeuf." Madame de Bellecourt greeted him formally.

"*Enchanté,* Madame," Scott said. He was not surprised at the stiff beginning. She would undoubtedly warm up and then get around to addressing her beloved daughter's relationship. The question was, how long would it take before what was on her mind would overwhelm the dam of *politesse,* spill over, and become a torrent?

They were shown to their respective rooms. The décor was country French: comfortable, low-key, Provençal prints and colors, overstuffed chairs and wooden furniture, earthenware crockery, and watercolor landscapes. Scott chuckled at the connecting door; Madame, a staunch Catholic, may not have approved, but irrespective of her predilections, she was a realist.

At precisely one o'clock, they were summoned to the dining room. Lunch was served. At the large, well-worn farmhouse table, positioned before two sets of French doors leading out to a terrace and garden, Scott was accorded the seat of honor, to the right of Madame; Desirée sat to her left. Outside, Scott noticed there was another dining table on the terrace, under a large tree; he imagined in warmer weather, meals were taken outside under this oak. Beyond that he could see a swimming pool and pool house flanking the garden and terrace.

A servant (Scott later learned he was the husband of the cook; the couple cared for the property year-round) opened a bottle of Domaines Ott, a rosé from nearby St. Tropez, and poured each a glass. A fresh and appetizing *salade Niçoise* in a large serving dish was passed—Desirée first, Madame second, and Scott last—along with a loaf of crusty peasant bread, which they broke off portion by portion by hand, and crock of unsalted butter. Dessert was a Pears Charlotte (caramelized pears topped with a dollop of whipped cream).

Conversation at the table was a two-party affair between Desirée and her mother. Though Desirée made several attempts to integrate him into the discussion, Scott responded when necessary. But he offered nothing more than required, because he sensed Madame wasn't ready to accord him equal status in their interaction. She—not Desirée—would determine when (and even if) that would come. Nevertheless, the conversation that did transpire was very pleasant and cordial. It was a conversation that almost any mother and daughter might have about myriad subjects: Madame's ambulatory issue, since improved; upcoming schedules regarding Geneva, Paris, and Cannes; mutual friends, including the Deschamps, and others Scott hadn't met; and the status of Gustav and Father Kohler. They decided—no, Madame decided—that they would take coffee on the terrace.

Desirée excused herself as the coffee was served, and Madame de Bellecourt and Scott sat in silence. He had the distinct feeling that the dam was about ready to give way.

Madame de Bellecourt set down her cup of coffee and turned to him. *Here it comes*, he thought. He looked at her expectantly, waiting.

"Mr. Stoddard, I presume I don't need to inform you that your relationship with my daughter is very troubling and not one of which I approve," she said.

Scott knew he should tread carefully with his response. "Your opinion has, in one form or another, been communicated to me through a variety of sources," Scott said without emotion.

"Can you find even one reason for which my 'opinion' should be altered?"

"Madame, I hope your mind is not set. At present, I fear you are not prepared to hear that I love your daughter; I make her happy, which is the best reason possible for you to accept our relationship," Scott said earnestly.

"I believe that my objections would not be viewed as exceptional by any fair-minded person," Madame said. "You are young. You are American . . . need I go on?"

"With all due respect, I'm not contesting the validity of your objections. But if it turns out that your premise is faulty, then the results will be erroneous, too."

"But Mr. Stoddard, my objections are many."

"Nor am I surprised. Please; let's review your list together to see if we have collected all the reasons for which this relationship is flawed and should be abandoned as quickly as possible," Scott said. "I'm glad of the opportunity to discuss this frankly." (He wondered, though, if the next few minutes would teach him that he only thought he appreciated directness.)

Madame de Bellecourt's eye's flicked toward the doorway; Desirée might appear at any minute. "I'm not sure discussion would be beneficial," she said.

"I can assure you I will not be offended by any of your concerns. I have my own prejudices, so I understand too well and, on the contrary, feel it could be very helpful for you to know how deeply I understand your reservations."

"Then list away, Mr. Stoddard," she said, folding her hands in her lap.

"Let's see: differences in age, social status, experiences, finances, culture, and religion." Scott's eyes met hers as though to ask, *How am I doing?*

"That's quite a list, Mr. Stoddard. It seems insurmountable," she said.

"It would be, except. . . ."

"Except what?"

"Except we love each other," he said. "And I ask you to remember: You approved Desirée's union with her ex husband. I presume you gave your blessing for the very reason that their relationship lacked any of the objectionable differences you raise. But their homogeneity did not prevent the couple's dissolution, and I propose it was missing two crucial ingredients that can overcome the greatest impediments: love and respect." Scott leaned forward, looking directly into Madame de Bellecourt's eyes in a confidential manner. Without blinking, she stared back. In some fashion, they understood each other.

"Who knows what tomorrow will bring?" Scott continued. "We must live as we feel in the moment, not structuring our current lives to conform to preconceived ideas that course toward an unknowable future. Madame, I would ask you to reserve your judgment until you, like we, can see if our relationship has the wherewithal to go the distance."

Madame seemed at a loss for words, and after a moment of reflection, she took a sip of coffee. In a softer tone, she said, "Mr. Stoddard, I'm glad we could speak directly regarding my concerns, but I will also tell you that I remain unconvinced."

"I, too, like everything out in the open, and I appreciate your candor. I know how precious your daughter is to you, and I had not presumed of having the slightest chance to convince you on our first meeting. I hope you will drop your objections; it would make Desirée so very happy, and her happiness is paramount to me."

For the first time, Madame de Bellecourt smiled at Scott. "Monsieur, the issue at hand is not your intelligence or your remarkable skills of argument. But facts are facts, and you and Desirée are very dissimilar."

Desirée, with her usual, perfect timing, reappeared at that moment. "You two look quite serious," she said. "What have you been talking about?"

As Madame searched for an answer, Scott seized the moment and interjected, "Your mother and I have been discussing the importance of making organized and efficient lists." Though Desirée was puzzled, Madame appeared relieved.

That evening before dinner, Scott was alone in the great room of the house, lost among the large bookshelves, which contained an array of titles on many different subjects in several languages. He'd just selected a history about the search to find the source of the Nile when Madame entered the room. Would he like a drink? When he said yes, she inquired—was he familiar with *pastis*, a licorice-flavored French aperitif? No, Scott wasn't and, since she seemed to genuinely want to introduce it to him, he accepted a glass. She had one, as well. When Desirée joined them, she made a face and had a flute of champagne instead.

"Madame, I see you have quite a number of books in English," Scott commented. "I wouldn't have expected this."

"Those are from the house in Geneva. During the Second World War, when Desirée was nine, we sheltered Allied pilots whose planes had crash-landed. Many of the families along the lake took in these American and British pilots until the end of the war. During that period, Bertrand and I often had anywhere from six to twelve guests at one time, so we built a kind of barracks adjoining the work sheds. There was little for them to do, so Bertrand scoured Switzerland to find books in English for them to read," she explained. Glancing at the book in Scott's hands, she smiled. "I see you have found something of interest. Some of the subjects are fairly exotic, I fear."

"Madame, your family constantly amazes me. How very generous. I can see where Desirée gets her charitable impulses."

"At the time, it seemed like very little. As you know, I am French, and—not that I am complaining, mind you—it was very difficult knowing we were safe in Switzerland with such rampant privation in Paris. My family home near the Bois de Boulogne was commandeered by a general in the Wehrmacht, my parents were confined to two rooms in their own home and then later relocated to a run-down apartment in the 17th arrondissement." Madame de Bellecourt seemed far away, lost in the memory of those difficult days.

"My father had two brothers; they were in different corps, but both landed at Normandy," Scott said softly. "One entered Paris on the day of its liberation. I have seen photos of him on a tank, surrounded by several beautiful and very happy young French girls, who are smiling. He's smiling, too, by the way."

She laughed warmly. "We will never forget the Americans and what they did for France." Just as Scott began to congratulate himself on finding a chip in Desirée's mother's formidable armor, her expression hardened. "But of course, Mr. Stoddard," she said sternly, "my gratitude has its limits."

THE THREE OF THEM VENTURED INTO MOUGINS THAT EVE-
ning, choosing the restaurant Le Relais de Mougins, a one-star
Michelin establishment on the main square, for dinner. Like her
daughter, Madame de Bellecourt was well known wherever she went
and commanded the best in service. They were seated at a table for
four against the wall, and Le Relais's simple furnishings created an
atmosphere of dining in an undiscovered part of the South of France.
They shared a giant bouillabaisse and Madame insisted that Scott try
a Calvados of 1928, and the light mood at the table was a pleasant
change from lunch's tenuous air.

EASTER WAS OBSERVED WITH HIGH MASS AT THE NOON HOUR.
St. Jacques le Majeur was packed but as was the family habit, Desirée
and her mother marched to their customary front pew, Scott in tow. He
noticed that, unlike her usual practice, Desirée did not receive commu-
nion, and Scott assumed this was in deference to her mother. (She was,
according to Madame and the church, "living in sin.") Surrounded by
rituals and observing mother and daughter, Scott understood that his
Baptist upbringing and personal lack of faith would pose a significant
problem if he and Desirée ever contemplated marriage. Celine had
warned him.

⸎

SCOTT AND DESIRÉE WERE SCHEDULED TO CATCH A FLIGHT
to Geneva on Monday afternoon. Before leaving for the airport, they
ended up where the weekend had begun, on the veranda.

"Maman, it was so good of you to have us," Desirée said. "I love you
and thank you."

"I love you too, darling," she replied fondly. There was a moment
when all three enjoyed the sound of leaves rustling in the spring air,

and then Madame de Bellecourt turned to Scott. "And Mr. Stoddard, I am glad to have met you. Regarding our list making—for the present, I will take your advice and review my list to determine if it is as important as I think. Perhaps I will find a way for us to become good friends."

"Madame, nothing could make me happier," Scott said.

twenty-eight

S COTT STOPPED BY HIS APARTMENT IN GENEVA TO PICK up his mail. It was a lonely, empty place; he went by intermittently now. Moving into Desirée's house on the lake had been a gradual process. At first, he took a few changes of clothes for when he'd stay the night. Next, he gathered up his school books (those he still needed to read and the ones he was supposed to be reading) and his favorite records—the Beatles, Dusty Springfield, and Petula Clark. As Scott's things made their slow migration, Desirée made room, pushing aside things and clearing a few drawers, shelves, and racks for him. Little by little, he filled in the space until one day, there was nothing of his in the little furnished apartment he'd rented.

Scott's attendance at the university was sporadic at best, and why his interest had waned was no longer a secret. News of the American student's relationship with the countess was common knowledge among his fellow students, and he was certain his professors were probably following their comings and goings in the press, too. Ever since the Sleigh Ball in Gstaad, papers in Geneva and Paris published photographs and reports of the events they attended, such as the St. Moritz Bal de Neige, in their society sections. Scott and Desirée were often highlighted, as these reports generally concentrated on the finery of dress and jewelry and the august list of attendees at these regal events.

Those society papers also included bits of gossip. Whenever possible, the Count de Rovere added to the couple's notoriety by making pronouncements regarding Scott's motives, commentary on the countess's foolishness, and predictions on the relationship's longevity, veiling his calumny in hypothetical terms so as to never quite reach the limits of libel. All this was a world away from the cloistered academic lives of both students and professors; Scott wasn't sure if he were considered a celebrity or a pariah. Regardless, his professors didn't call on him any more than they had pre-Desirée, and when they did, Scott managed to squeeze out an acceptable, appropriate answer.

But Scott wasn't fooling anyone, least of all himself. He estimated he spent only about a third of the time he would have devoted to studying before becoming involved with Desirée. The studying he did was not his usual reading-with-focus, but rather a cursory review; there were too many interruptions for him to fully concentrate. This failure—to responsibility, to himself, to his parents—weighed on Scott's conscience. At some point, his dereliction would become clear to his parents, and a confession would be in order. They were still threatening to come to Europe (he knew the visit would happen sooner rather than later), but he kept putting them off.

Also weighing on his conscience was his failure to come clean about Desirée. He chastised himself for not confiding in them; all those phone calls, and he only once revealed his casual interest in Desirée. At this late date, announcing the seriousness of their relationship would appear suspicious. They'd assume it had happened overnight or that his intentions were less than honorable. If he told them he'd begun seeing Desirée much sooner upon his arrival in Geneva, it would beg the question: Why hadn't he told them earlier? It wouldn't matter to them, particularly to his mother, that Desirée was a countess; they would concentrate on her age and the interruption of their plans for Scott's future. And she was Catholic. While Scott was not religious, his mother maintained the family's connection to church, and it wasn't the Catholic kind. With exasperation, Scott thought, *Madame de Bellecourt did not have a franchise on objecting to their relationship—the two grand dames would probably see eye to eye on many things.*

Scott had had girlfriends and suffered through at least one serious breakup, but his blossoming relationship with Desirée was beyond anything he'd ever experienced. Handling his parents and soliciting their support would be much more complicated than navigating those past young loves. He was sure his parents wouldn't understand or approve. So, how to break the news?

A letter, not a phone call, was the best medium, Scott decided. He started breezily, talking about school, before mentioning his travels to the South of France over Easter break with his girlfriend, the one who was French and Swiss and lived in Geneva. He wrote matter-of-factly that he was awfully fond of Desirée (finally, he gave her a name).

He knew the abbreviated information would generate all the questions he wasn't eager to answer. His mother, reading the phrase "awfully fond of" and knowing how understated Scott could be in matters of the heart, would want to know everything. Could he dribble out the information in such a timeline and fashion to minimize the shock of it all? Could he describe for his parents their age differential, her title and wealth—in fact, address the exact list of objections that Madame de Bellecourt outlined—and somehow gain approval for their love?

Scott anticipated that the letter would be delivered, his mother would read it several times, and then accost his father as soon as he arrived home from work. Mrs. Stoddard would lay her opinions out in detail and persuade her husband that they needed to telephone Scott to determine exactly what was going on. Since Scott was living at Desirée's, there would be no answer when they called. They would try several times, at different hours of the day, which would ratchet their anxiety to an unacceptable level. It might even generate an immediate flight to Geneva.

That scenario simply wasn't acceptable; Scott couldn't risk that. No, he would give the letter time enough to arrive and be read, and then he would make a preemptive phone call. If his timing were right, he could eliminate that heightened anxiety and postpone the inevitable visit.

AFTER POSTING THE LETTER, SCOTT'S NEXT CHORE WAS informing Desirée of his plan (well, maybe not the entire plan, but the acceptable part of the plan).

The skies were clear, but the weather was damp and cold. Bundled up in heavy double cashmere parkas and scarves, they marveled at the two spikes, Les Dents de Midi, rising against the Alps in the south, across the lake, as they enjoyed an afternoon walk around the property.

"I wrote my parents today," Scott told her tentatively, anxious to see her reaction. "I told them about you," he said.

"Did you tell them you were in love?" Desirée asked, her eyes as calm and clear as the blue water of the lake.

Scott hedged. "I didn't put it quite like that, but my mother will decode and realize I'm serious." Desirée said nothing, leaving Scott to decipher her reaction to his "declaration."

Scott waited a week before calling his parents. With the six-hour time difference, he could call during his afternoon in Geneva, which would be before his father left for work in Charleston. His mother answered on the first ring; she sang out that Scott was on the phone, and his father picked up the other receiver. Scott was not surprised when Mr. Stoddard said gruffly, "We called several times yesterday, and there was no answer."

"I must have been out," Scott said.

Predictably, his mother homed in on the romance: "Your letter was very short. I was disappointed not to have more news. And this is the same girl, right? The fund-raiser?"

"Sorry, I've been really busy since Easter," he said. "Yes, the same one I told you about. A friend introduced us."

"You wrote that she lives nearby? Who is she?" His mother didn't let up.

"No, she lives outside Geneva, in her family's home; she did go to school, but now, as I told you, she works in charity."

"If you went away together, this girl must be more than a friend," his mother said.

"Yes, I like Desirée a lot," Scott said. "She's pretty, she's intelligent, and she's kind. She's very nice, really nice, to everyone. You'd like her, Mother," Scott said.

His mother continued to pump Scott for information, asking about school and his classes, his friends, and "the girl," but he withheld more specific details about Desirée, figuring that giving only small doses was the best path forward, in this case.

The conversation went well, and all things considered, the Stoddards' level of dissatisfaction appeared tolerable. His father listened and said little, a quiet, solid presence on the other end, a counterbalance to Scott's mother's chatty inquisition. But Scott knew that in the months to come, there would be a reckoning. Afterward, Scott felt better—at least his parents were aware that he was involved in a serious relationship. How serious was the question, but knowledge of Desirée's existence in his life was a beginning. Looking ahead to the future, Scott knew he would need to guard against outright lies and slippery truths as the Stoddards learned more of the world he inhabited with the countess.

THAT CONVERSATION WITH HIS PARENTS TRIGGERED A BOUT of conscience regarding Scott's neglect of his studies. For the first time in his life, he couldn't seem to make a coherent and disciplined study plan. Oh, Scott formulated plenty of well-intentioned schedules, but he rarely followed through, and when he did, it was in a half-hearted fashion. Exams, eight to ten months in the future, would be exhaustive; written as well as oral, these examinations were open to the public. A candidate who had not attended class or taken exacting notes, who had not read the thorough bibliography associated with each course, would find himself hard-pressed to pass.

Scott was dreading those exams. Most people would say—hell, he told himself—that to succeed in school, he had to learn to achieve more balance. Academia was a job he'd been sent to Geneva to complete, and he needed to make the proper time and opportunity, if for no other reason than his parents expected it. His negligence wasn't Desirée's doing; she was supportive when he voiced his intentions. But he found it easier and easier to fall into the ebb and flow of her lifestyle, one unencumbered by responsibility or financial concerns. One that people like his parents, people with a strong work ethic and specific goals, would frown upon.

If exams were lurking ahead, what of their relationship's longer-term prospects? Desirée and Scott had remained silent on the subject; neither had voiced any ideas about the future to the other. Scott brooded. If Desirée didn't exist, he would be at school working on his degree, as he should—at least, in theory—for hadn't Marlyse pulled him away as well? Perhaps his heart was not truly in international business. But what kind of man would he be if he ended his relationship with the countess in favor of a degree? Or to please his parents? He was starting to believe that he simply wasn't that kind of man.

twenty-nine

ON FRIDAY, SCOTT AND DESIRÉE FLEW TO PARIS TO attend a special evening to benefit the ballet at the Palais Garnier, where Desirée was a patron. A car met them at the airport and transferred them to the expensive residential area of Avenue Foch. Desirée's apartment, which had been left to her upon her father's death, occupied the entire top floor of a beautiful Haussmann palace; in the foyer, public spaces, and grand staircase, floors and walls of pristine marble gleamed. Scott delighted in the antique lift; big enough for six passengers, it consisted of a cage with brass controls and two ostrich leather seats, one on each side of the car.

The apartment itself overlooked the Foch gardens situated in the median of the grand boulevard that runs from the L'Etoile to the Bois de Boulogne. Large mirrors hung above matching chests on each side of the foyer, and ornate French doors opened onto a grand salon and dining room that seated twelve. There was a professional kitchen, a breakfast room, and three bedrooms, including Desirée's large master suite, which spanned the entire length of the building's south side. Three sets of French doors led to balconies overlooking the park next door, and fresh-cut flowers adorned every room in anticipation of Desirée's arrival.

The furnishings, an eclectic selection of period French furniture with modern touches of sculpture and paintings, made the rooms come to life. Bright fuchsia and lime green, animal prints, and bold black and white stripes harkened of Art Deco influences. Scott thought the décor reflected Desirée well—it was a home for living and entertaining, both comfortable and relaxed.

Scott gave Desirée's bedroom an admiring once-over. Decorated in a soft yellow and silver gray, he imagined many happy hours in the painted bed. Other custom-created pieces blended with the drapery, upholstery, and bed coverings. Large, carved lamps on the French consoles provided a golden glow, and a working fireplace was laid, ready for the match. Scott opened the closet and ran his hand across the soft fabric of Desirée's clothes. As usual, her effects had been sent ahead; Desirée's personal maid, Marie Claire, had already cleaned, pressed, and put away her garments from their trip. There was also a cook, Madame Tissot.

Desirée had reserved a table at Le Grand Vefour, one of the oldest and best gourmet restaurants in Paris. They were treated to a five-course meal of crab salad Louis, pike *quenelles*, a hen from Bresse, cheese selection, *mille-feuille*, and the ever-present Krug champagne. They dined slowly, trying to savor the fine food (and even better company), but Desirée had her well-wishers; the other diners stopped by to say hello, and she introduced Scott to each acquaintance. She provided no specificity, however, about their relationship. They could speculate about the handsome young man's status as they wished.

Afterward, they were driven to the St. Germain des Prés area, the 6th arrondissement, to a private club. Chez Castel was a restaurant and nightclub whose clientele were mostly French and included young royals and cinema actors. Music and dancing occurred in the intimate and close lower level (a real jewel box of luxuriously padded red velvet), and by half past eleven, when Desirée and Scott arrived, it was packed. It would remain that way until the early hours of Saturday. Scott and Desirée secured a table not too close to the small dance floor and joined in the fun.

Desirée loved to dance, and Scott liked nothing better than to take her dancing. When she moved to the music, she was at her most sensuous. Despite the crowd, the two lovers were in a beautiful bubble; her attention was focused solely on him and his on her.

It was late when they returned to the apartment, and when Desirée came to bed, Scott pretended to be asleep. He loved teasing her, particularly in their lovemaking. He knew from their dancing and the ride back in the limousine, where they had been enthusiastically entwined, that she had certain sexual expectations for the night. Quiet, she seemed to be listening to his breathing—was Scott indeed asleep? It took all his will power to remain still. Desirée sighed, turned off her light, and moved around a little, attempting to find a comfortable position, adjusting the pillow over and again. Inwardly, he laughed; she was obviously trying to wake him. Finally, Desirée gave up and turned her back. Underneath the sheet, his arm crept across the bed and encircled her waist. Gently but powerfully, he pulled her on top of him. Delighted, she laughed and wriggled against him.

"Oh, ho, my little pretender," she cooed. "That was mean to make me think you weren't interested."

"Want me to stop?"

She didn't answer.

"**Darling, let's go buy a new tuxedo.**"

These were not the first words Scott had expected to hear that morning. He cast a sleepy eye in Desirée's direction and asked, "You don't like mine?"

"No, I like yours, but you really need two. One to wear, and the other at the cleaners," she said.

That very morning, they went to Lanvin. Located in the rue de Faubourg Saint-Honoré, Paris' most fashionable shopping street, the couture shop was a bastion of style, particularly for men and women of refined and conservative taste, its fabrics, sewing, and styles quintessential French.

Under normal circumstances, Desirée explained, Scott should have a bespoke tuxedo—handmade, tailored exactly to his specifications. But they would see what was available.

Desirée instructed the clerk, precisely defining the style of tuxedo Scott required. Several beautiful suits were brought out, all the finest wool gabardine or crepe, with silk satin lapels, their cuts designed to render a man's silhouette slim and svelte. Measuring the young American, the clerk recommended a size 52 to accommodate Scott's height and breadth of shoulders and chest. Selecting a suit, he stepped into the curtained fitting room and slipped it on. Even off the rack, the tuxedo fit him perfectly. The differences between this and the well-worn garment currently at the cleaners was the difference between, well, tourist and first class. Standing a bit taller, Scott walked to the mirror. The clerk immediately made a few adjustments, marking the hem, while Desirée watched, an approving smile playing about her face.

"Very nice," she said. "This one will be fine. Can you deliver it this afternoon?"

Desirée disappeared for a few hours after lunch, going to the *coiffeur* and having her makeup perfected for the ballet ball. Scott took a walk, enjoying time in the city he'd grown to love. Funnily enough, he found himself at the George V; had it only been six months ago when he'd first arrived in Europe, already besotted with Desirée? Inwardly, he chuckled—he'd been right to wonder if she were nearby then; her Avenue Fochs apartment was only a few blocks away. How far he had come from those first days in Paris.

Back at the apartment, Scott dragged out his books. With Desirée occupied elsewhere, it was a good time to play catch-up with his source document assignments. With a grimace, he contemplated his choices; should he begin with NATO's establishment at the end of WWII, the disastrous failure of diplomacy leading up to WWI, or the Third Reich's non-aggression treaty with the Soviet Union? Scott groaned. They all seemed a little dry. To think: he had been excited about history and blow-by-blow analysis on the origin and mechanics of these treaties and agreements. Oh, how his enthusiasm had waned.

THAT EVENING, SCOTT DRESSED IN HIS NEW TUXEDO. HE MADE quite a handsome figure as he entered the salon for a drink. Desirée was still getting ready; he'd left, knowing she needed those moments alone while slipping into her dress, selecting jewelry, and checking (and rechecking) her appearance before making a grand entrance. As he sipped his scotch, he admitted that he liked it this way. Seeing her again for the first time was always a pleasure. She always surprised.

Desirée came through the salon's large double doors on a cloud of white silk and taffeta. Scott drank in the sight of her. There was the dress—sleeveless; a sheath for the skirt; its bodice gathered to a high collar, accentuating the length and grace of her neck—and matching silk stole, trimmed in white fox with a revealing slit from clasp to cleavage. Desirée's hair was pulled to a new golden height; her accessories (custom evening heels in white silk, emerald and diamond earrings, a matched bracelet of alternating rows of green and ice stones) perfection. Scott felt all breath leave his body. His heart pounded in his chest like a sledgehammer, and any words would be inadequate. He tried anyway, telling Desirée how beautiful she was and asking her to turn several times so he could appreciate all sides. She seemed to enjoy his attention to the smallest detail of her appearance.

Gustav guided the Mercedes to the drop-off point in front of the Paris opera, or more precisely, Le Palais Garnier. The Beaux Arts masterpiece was ablaze with lights; the confluence of limousines, gathering throng of ladies in their finery, escorts turned-out in black tie, and uniformed valets assisting the arriving patrons created a scene of pandemonium.

As Desirée was assisted from the car, Scott heard the screams: "It's the Countess de Rovere. Over here, the Countess de Rovere just arrived." Gawkers and autograph seekers along with a sizable contingent of paparazzi pressed toward the car. There was pushing and shoving, but Gustav broke through the sea of people, Scott and Desirée were propelled up some thirty steps by their tireless pursuers. Once in the grand hall, they took refuge from the flashbulbs and reporters' shouted questions.

Scott was flustered—it was the first time he'd experienced that kind of unwelcome attention—but Desirée smiled, unruffled. As if nothing had transpired, she immediately engaged her friends and acquaintances, introducing Scott and making idle conversation in a most agreeable manner.

As she chatted, Scott admired the interior of the building. Dramatically, the grand entrance and vestibule were constructed like a theater; the milling patrons becoming the performers. Cascading giant staircases, Italian pink marble, frescoes, a huge chandelier, red carpeting, gilded columns and other accoutrements set the scene.

Paris was Desirée's milieu. Here, she was even more in demand than in the small societies of Geneva and Gstaad. Here, there were more people to know—and the Countess de Rovere knew them all. Scott was overwhelmed; he couldn't possibly keep up with the steady flow of introductions and endless inquiries. He silently thanked Desirée for the gradual introduction she'd provided him, realizing how intentional she'd been in her selection of their first social events. Taking a deep breath, Scott reminded himself that he was practiced at this situation and got a grip.

From time to time, Scott would catch Desirée's eye, and they would exchange a knowing glance. Ah—he was pleasing her. Nothing gave him more satisfaction than knowing she wanted him. Among Paris' most celebrated citizens, however, Scott couldn't help feeling out of place, even with Desirée's encouragement. Beyond his good looks and conversational wit, and her happiness in the bedroom, what was the attraction? What did Desirée see in him? Dare he ask?

As Scott and Desirée made their way toward their seats, the president of the opera came over to make his obligatory call on Desirée before the start of the performance. He oozed all the charm and magnanimity one would expect from someone in his position.

"My dear countess, you are simply dazzling." It was as though Scott were invisible. "I must apologize for those disagreeable people when you arrived."

Desirée laughed lightly. "*Cher*, it was fun. Now I know how Mozart must have felt when he arrived at the Staatsoper in Vienna."

Soon the lights dimmed twice, signaling that the first act of *Le Nozze de Figaro* was to begin. An usher in period costume escorted Desirée and Scott to a box overlooking the stage on the mezzanine level. As they were seated, Scott noticed Desirée nodding her head to various persons in the orchestra below.

As crafty Figaro sang, the audience's attention was impressive. These were serious opera buffs. Many of them, including Desirée, understood the lyrics, not just the music and story. After the performance, this group would discuss the merits of each singer in great detail—notes hit and missed, tempo (*troppo veloce, troppo lento*), and comparisons to previous performers—at a reception at the American Embassy for the patron's committee. As he absorbed the soaring music and timeless story, it occurred to Scott that he'd underestimated Desirée's "not doing anything." He had a lot to learn—and not just about opera.

BY MID-MORNING THE NEXT DAY, DESIRÉE WAS OFF TO SEE her lawyers and accountants. Scott called his friends, Andre and Leon, to arrange lunch at their usual spot on the Champs-Élysées. He'd done so over Desirée's cautions; she'd recognized Andre's name as a major writer for *Le Figaro* and expressed her distrust of newspaper people. They were, she noted, notoriously indiscreet. Given how the tabloids—and sometimes, the legitimate press—constantly reviewed their romance, her warning wasn't necessary. Scott understood. Her separation had received a lot of scrutiny, but after a time, and following the annulment, the coverage had faded away. Scott's appearance on her arm had reignited and fanned the flame of curiosity and sensationalism regarding tales of the Countess de Rovere. Still, Andre and Leon were friends, so he headed off to lunch.

At one o'clock, when Scott walked into Époque, Andre and Leon were there, sitting almost in the same positions as they had back in September. There were embraces and some hearty backslapping and the friendly banter of seeing someone after a lengthy time apart. To commemorate their reunion, Andre insisted on ordering a bottle of champagne. What else?

"My dear Scott, we've been wondering about you. When you didn't come back to Paris, we thought about you at your school in Geneva.

And then I was reading my own paper one Monday morning after the New Year, when I saw a photo with the caption, 'Who is the young man with the Countess de Rovere?'" Andre threw his hands up in that typical French expression of disbelief. "Can you imagine my reaction? I said to myself, *I know that young man.*"

"I know it was probably a shock," Scott said, blushing.

"No. Shock? No—I felt responsible. *Moi.* If you want to improve your French, I said, get a French lover. But a countess," he said, shaking his head in wonderment. "I didn't say she had to be a countess."

Andre and Leon leaned toward Scott; he could tell they were eager to hear the whole story (how they met, their status—the inside scoop, in newspaper terms), but he couldn't do that to Desirée, no matter how friendly and playful his friends were in asking. He couldn't be the source of any information regarding the countess's private life. The known basics would have to suffice.

"The Countess de Rovere and I were introduced by a mutual friend," he told them. "She is charming and has been helpful in introducing me to people in Geneva. She's a dear friend."

Andre and Leon exchanged exasperated glances. "Of course, Scott. I think—and I'm sure Leon would agree," at this, Leon nodded vigorously, anticipating where Andre was leading the conversation—"that there is more to this 'friendship' than you are telling. Naturally, it is your business, and we must respect that." He paused, rearranging the food on his plate slightly before fixing Scott with a pointed look. "But we are curious. And, it appears, we are not alone. Leon and I brought you today's newspapers. Photos of you and the countess dominate the society pages and speculation about your attendance at the opera last night is *the* topic."

Scott glanced at the proffered papers. He and Desirée had given them a look that morning, and the crush of the crowd and flash of cameras had all come back to him. He pushed them back toward Andre and replied wearily, "I know—they follow us everywhere we go. Frankly, I can't understand the attraction. Why don't they fixate on Brigitte Bardot and Gunther Sachs, or Liz and Richard?"

"They're news all right," Leon said, "but your story has overtones of *The Prince and the Showgirl."* He quickly corrected: "Roles reversed, that is."

Scott cringed. "I'm not sure I like the analogy," he replied gruffly. Leon's comment stung. Though, he thought wryly, there were worse things than being cast as the Marilyn Monroe equivalent in an intriguing romance with European royalty.

Andre patted him on the hand and shot Leon a critical glance. Clearly the plan was not to antagonize Scott. "The paparazzi are not interested in pleasing you," Andre explained. "It's the romance—they're only interested in whether they can tantalize their readers with a fantasy." Leon added, "Just enjoy the attention while you can."

Easy for you to say, Scott thought bitterly. It wasn't fun being the brunt of jokes and innuendo, feeling as though you don't belong. Being viewed as nothing more than a handsome bangle for a wealthy woman. Everyone seemed to want a piece of him, the fantasy of his life, but no one wanted to know him. Scott's connection to Desirée—her lifestyle and social status—could possibly change many of Scott's existing relationships, most importantly the one with his parents. Some of these people would never adjust to this rarefied world and his role within its orbit; he had some lingering doubts himself. Could he eventually acclimate? And even then, would this social set allow for his friends and family? Desirée was his ticket in, but Scott feared it was a ticket that could be punched but once.

In parting, Andre and Leon pretended all was well, but no one was fooled by the platitudes exchanged among the three. Scott's reticence to reveal any real details regarding Desirée had changed the friendship; the easy camaraderie they'd enjoyed last September was gone, along with the society pages Scott had tossed in the waste bin.

Scott left in a state of gloom. He'd be reluctant to call them again, even if his relationship with Desirée didn't work out—no, he thought with a start, *particularly* if it didn't work out. For the first time, Scott felt like a roulette player who had placed all his chips, his life's savings, on one number. The realization was like a punch in the gut.

He took a long walk, attempting to clear his head and banish his bleak mood. Down the Avenue Montaigne, up the rue George V, and then retracing his steps on the Champs-Élysées to the Arc de Triomphe and Avenue Foch. By the time he reached the apartment, Desirée had returned from her meeting and was on the phone in the bedroom. He went to the salon to wait. She found him shortly; one look at his face and she frowned, concern crossing her lovely face.

"You don't look very happy, my darling. How was lunch?" she asked.

"It was fine. We had a good time."

"Scott, you are not a very good fibber," she sighed. "Something happened with your friends. Now, either you told them all about us and you have a bad conscience, or you told them so little that they were hurt and angry. Which is it?"

Was he that transparent? Desirée's intuition continued to amaze Scott. "You know me so well," he said, pulling her onto his lap. "I didn't tell them anything. They were more interested in how we're tracked by photographers than in anything about life. They'd even brought all the newspapers showing us at the opera last night." He breathed in the scent of her hair and hid his face.

"You must learn to enjoy it or ignore it," she said gently.

He sighed. "That's the same thing they said."

"They may be better friends than you think." Pausing, she looked at him carefully. "My darling, life is about choices. You must learn that the choices you make will not always result in your happiness or the happiness of others. But you must always be true to yourself. Never betray your principles," she said.

"You're right," he replied. "You're always right." Scott felt like a child. In some ways, it was very difficult being with someone so wise. All his life, people had told Scott how smart he was. He'd aced exams left and right, never making many mistakes: "Lucky Scott." And he was lucky—lucky to be in love with someone so astute and so practical but who still lived life with passion. Oh, he could learn a lot from her. Hell, he already had. Now he just had to wait and see where the little pea in this game of roulette would come to rest.

For the next two days, Desirée flitted from one Parisian fashion house to the next—Dior, Lanvin, Balenciaga, and Givenchy. Her choices had already been set aside; now came the final fittings, followed by matching all the accessories (shoes, handbags, and hats). Scott accompanied her on the first day, and he marveled at the stage production involved in every session. Each alteration was pinned in position to ensure the fit would be correct, the seamstresses precise and gentle in their movements. Turning Desirée this way and that before the three-way mirror, applying a fold here, a chalk mark and pin there, admiring her, reassuring her. They were a ballet of women in gray and white uniforms and Desirée, their prima ballerina, her perfect fit a *fait accompli*.

Scott took a taxi to the Sorbonne. Desirée had decided to visit Celine, and Scott had always wanted to see the university's beautiful library, home of one of the world's most monumental collection of books. Scott's motives, however, were not purely scholarly. He entered the grand hall and sought out the reference books for something particular: a volume that could detail qualifications needed for couples who wished to marry in the Catholic Church—couples in which one is not Catholic. Before their relationship progressed further, he wanted to understand where he stood in respect to Desirée and her church. And her family: while Desirée might not be overly devout, her mother surely was. If they were ever to marry, Madame de Bellecourt's interests must be served.

Wandering through the labyrinth of bookcases, Scott turned down one of the narrow aisles. Suddenly, a large man wearing dark glasses and a neck scarf that partially covered his face blocked his way.

"Monsieur Stoddard?" the man said.

"*Oui*," Scott answered.

The man withdrew an envelope from his pocket, stuffing it hurriedly

into Scott's hand. Surprised, Scott stared at the envelope before realizing the man had darted through the stacks; when Scott thought to
finally look up, his accoster had disappeared from sight.

How very odd. Puzzled, Scott mused: how had anyone known he
was here? Opening the envelope, he unfolded a full page torn from
Le Figaro. The heading across the top of the page was *Les Notices
Necrologiques* (the obituaries). Across its columns listing the deceased
were scrawled four ominous words: "Don't end up here."

Shaken, Scott left the library through a side exit; he didn't want
to risk his new shadow waiting for him outside the main entrance.
He didn't really know whether he should be alarmed or not. *Be rational*, Scott thought. Was this stunt a bluff designed to make him leave
Paris and Desirée? But who was behind this? While he wanted to run
through the details and seek her council, Scott intuited he couldn't
tell Desirée. He cast his mind about—was there anyone he could discuss this odd occurrence with? Not the police, he thought. Threats,
particularly anonymous threats, aren't very believable, and they would
probably dismiss this contemptuously as matters between suitors in
a love triangle. There was no doubt in Scott's mind that the note was
Stefano's doing. Angrily, he wadded the newsprint in his hand, tossing it away. *Italians*, he thought, *can be so very dramatic at times*. Only
desperation could conjure up this stunt. No, he couldn't tell Desirée.

thirty

R ETURNING TO GENEVA, THE SKI SEASON OVER, SCOTT
was finally able to concentrate on school. For a few weeks,
their extravagant lifestyle calmed; without an unceasing
onslaught of parties and social events, Desirée and Scott's routine settled into the hum of a married couple. Was it Scott's imagination or
was there was less teasing, less laughing, and less mystery? There was
less insecurity (a plus, Scott thought) but surely less sex (which he was
not happy about). Desirée was aware and, like him, not pleased.
How, he wondered, *did we get here?*

This stage was new to Scott—he'd never been with a woman in such
a domestic relationship. He found himself hashing over the problem
like a dog with a bone. Perhaps their alliance was like a ship becalmed.
Without the next party, or ball, or trip, where was the forward prog-
ress? In less than two weeks, the Cannes Film Festival was on the
schedule, and that excitement and newness, this fresh experience, had
the power to lift them from this deadly sameness: he studying, she
shopping, doing charity work, and preserving mind and body at the
Ritz spa. Always followed by dinner and sometimes lunch together.

Every relationship has its arc, much like the stages of a person's
life: birth, adolescence, young adult period, middle-ages, senior years,
and death (hopefully put off for a long time). Scott knew this—but
where did he and Desirée fall in this arc? He could hear her laughter
in his mind—*it's been mere months, darling*. He guessed they had not
advanced much further than adolescence. But how could he tell her

that things were feeling stale, that their domesticated routine had done something to his excitement? Her feelings might be irreparably hurt. She would probably believe, no matter how he explained it, that he was bored with her. How would he feel if the situation were reversed? After all, he reasoned, she was most likely having those same thoughts about him. This, he thought, was the more likely scenario: his novelty had worn off. Many of Desirée's friends had accepted Scott, and he had become something of a given. *Maybe*, he thought, *she likes the mystery man Scott, the indefatigable but tender bedroom Scott, the Scott who was more out of step and generated the most excitement, talk, and gossip, more.* How could he discuss this lack of passion without risking losing her?

Scott mulled over what to do for days. He feared avoiding the subject might yield what he feared most—losing Desirée. He worried that he'd bungle a too direct approach. He contemplated an oblique maneuver, some sort of indirect inquiry. But what would that be? Nothing seemed the right tactic. Scott was out of his league.

IT WAS A BEAUTIFUL DAY. MONT BLANC SHIMMERED IN THE distance as Scott and Desirée sat on the terrace. They'd had a light lunch, and Desirée was enjoying a coffee, but Scott needed something stronger. He poured himself a Calvados. Desirée's mother, Madame de Bellecourt, had introduced him to the distilled spirit when they'd visited at Easter; the liqueur was somewhat like Cognac, except Calvados issued from the apple. *The fruit of original sin*, Scott mused. He poured himself a stiff one. He cleared his throat and took the plunge.

"Desirée, I would like to ask you something," he said.

She turned her eyes from the gorgeous scenery and carefully set her coffee on the table. Desirée studied him for a moment; he could see her thinking. Scott felt like a snake, mesmerized by a swaying charmer.

Finally, she said, "Are you bored, my darling?"

He hadn't realized he was holding his breath until he let it out.

Well, he had not been wrong. Why had he thought he would be? From their first flirt, he'd recognized how highly sensitive she was. Over time, they'd become more and more tuned to each other's emotions.

"You're not answering me," Desirée said. "This is serious, isn't it?"

Scott came close, sitting by her on the chaise longue. She waited, still and anxious, watching his eyes.

"Desirée, love of my life, will you marry me?"

Never had he seen a more shocked look on anyone's face. For the first time since he had known her, Desirée was disconcerted and confused. Normally the picture of self-control and mistress of her surroundings, she looked positively discombobulated.

He moved in front of her, taking her trembling hands. "Darling, you're making me nervous," he said. "Say something, please."

"I'm . . . shocked," she stammered. "I had no idea you were thinking such a thing."

"Why wouldn't I? I love you. You love me, I hope. Isn't this the natural progression of a relationship?"

He watched her gather her composure. "Of course, I love you. I love you with all my heart," and Scott was happy (and relieved) to hear the conviction in her voice. "But," she said, and he cringed, "I hadn't thought we were close to making such a big decision." She ever so slightly stressed the "we."

Was she telling him *no* or *not yet*? "I'm not sure marriage is something you weigh on the scales," he replied. "It's more something you do if it feels right." Desirée, inscrutable, listened as his words poured out. "Maybe I leaped when I should've looked. You're . . ." He searched for the right word, ". . . hesitant, and that is not a good sign. Perhaps I have misunderstood; should I have waited for you to ask me? You may call me provincial, as I can't say I didn't think that would be shocking. I did. But for some reason, I thought if I asked, you might be surprised and pleased and—well, I thought you might be happy."

Tears glistened in Desirée's eyes. This was unbearable, and Scott stood, moving away from her to the balcony's edge. She followed, placing a soft hand on his arm, turning him to face her. "Oh, Scott," she breathed. "This is coming out all wrong. I do love you. I would marry you."

His head snapped up. Angrily, he retorted, "*Would?* That's conditional. Not *will* and not exactly a confidence builder. Am I just a toy?"

"Darling, I'm not trying to hurt your feelings, but really; don't we need to give things more time? You're young, and this is still new."

Pulling away, Scott's eyes blazed at her. "I think there is such a thing as giving something too much time." He searched for an example. Picking up Desirée's cup, he said, "Take coffee. Brewing the perfect cup requires fresh water, the right amount of beans ground to the proper texture, heat enough to percolate and brew, before it flows from the pot. It's best drunk at that moment in time. Waiting around doesn't improve the coffee; letting it sit once ready only makes it stale," he said. Desirée regarded him with a calm expression, and he was reminded of how young he was and how wise she could be.

Slowly and carefully, she said, "But you will admit we have some issues, wouldn't you?"

Months of self-doubt poured from Scott's mouth. He couldn't seem to stop the flow of recriminations. "Are you speaking or thinking about all the issues that both of us chose to ignore when we fell in love? The things we said to ourselves, that you told me, didn't matter? Or are these 'issues' what your mother believes? Oh, we've talked of all the ways she believes our relationship is doomed. Did you know that? Or perhaps these are the issues your friends—and, probably, my parents, the moment they discover the truth—point out as reasons our love affair cannot endure? Which 'issues' are they, Desirée? Or is it all of them?"

"Your temper is rising. When you start making lists, particularly those irrefutable lists you use so effectively with anyone who opposes you, I know you are getting angry. And that is the last thing I meant to happen. I love you, Scott. Can't you just think on that for the moment?"

His pride wounded, Scott couldn't give an inch. He challenged her: "How do we go forward if you refuse my offer of marriage?"

She sighed heavily. "But I didn't refuse," she pointed out. "I said I would marry you."

Had she really? Scott wasn't so sure that anything short of an unequivocal and enthusiastic "yes" was acceptable. Jaw clinched, he demanded, "When?"

She thought for a few minutes. "Introduce me to your parents, then I'll marry you."

Scott wasn't buying it. He'd watched Desirée deflect too many unpleasant social situations to underestimate her skill. "You're just delaying for a few months. They have nothing, I repeat, *nothing* to do with your response," he said. "I don't like this at all. Your conditional answer to my proposal undermines our feelings for each other in some unconscious but insidious way."

"Give me until the end of June to change *I would* to *I will*. Please," she begged. "It's just two short months. I do love you. And in the meantime, can't we at least talk about some of the issues you raised? I don't want to ignore them or your feelings."

"Sure, let's talk about them," Scott said. "Let's get everything out in the open."

Desirée moved close to him, pressing her body against his. She twined her arms tightly around his waist, resting her head on his chest. "Let's do that later. I have a better idea."

"And what's that?" Scott stood there, woodenly.

"There'll be no doubt I love you."

To be honest, Scott didn't feel like making love, or being held, or being reassured. He was angry, and Desirée was distracting him from the heat of that feeling. He wasn't accustomed to rejection and didn't like anyone who interfered with his focus. *You're selfish*, he heard his mother's voice whisper. He knew his anger was childish; he knew he had to overcome this selfishness if his relationship with Desirée was to last. But no matter his best intentions, Scott was hurt and, yes, angry. Reluctantly, he allowed her to lead him from the terrace.

Desirée wasn't about to let him remain in such an emotional state, and she initiated their lovemaking carefully. She was patient, knowing how bruised his feelings were. She worked her body in a naturally sexy way to reassure Scott and distract from his injured pride. She intoxicated him with her vulnerability and tenderness. Desirée was making amends, depending on their animal attraction to move them past the hard spot and overcome a potential pitfall.

thirty-one

DESIRÉE BECAME EVEN MORE ATTENTIVE AND SOLICI-
tous of Scott's feelings and moods. Their easy laughter
returned, and he teased her, especially after a passionate session, about her reaction to his proposal. Over the next several days, they
talked, anxious to define and discuss any challenges to be overcome.

Ever the debater, Scott classified their issues into two categories:
easy for him to overcome and easy for her. Take, for example, their
age difference. This was easy for Scott to overcome. He said it didn't
matter, that there wasn't that much difference; she argued the counter
view—what would happen when she was fifty and he only forty-two?
He argued closeness in age did not guarantee happiness; that love,
compatibility, humor, and character were the main components of a
good relationship. Besides, he countered, men age faster than women.
He would catch up before it became important.

The sensitive issue for him—which, actually, was two issues rolled
into one—was their financial and social differences. She was from aris-
tocracy, and he was American upper middle class. Well, she reasoned, if
she accepted him, then others would as well. And as to the finances, she
had plenty of money for them both. No matter his success in whatever
area he chose, she pointed out, Scott would probably need twenty years
to make a portion of what she'd inherited. There was something to be
said for pride of working, Scott countered, of accomplishing something
and being dutifully employed. Desirée said she understood—was there a
middle ground? She couldn't, however, pinpoint its location.

Most of her male friends had careers in law, finance, or the family business. They had balanced their careers and personal lives; Scott could do the same. Scott wasn't prepared to give up his present path. Maybe, he argued, once they were married, he could concentrate and finish his graduate degree.

⁂

AFTER THEY HAD SEEMINGLY DEALT WITH ALL OTHER REA-sons, Desirée brought up another concern over breakfast. Buttering her croissant, she said, "My darling, there is one issue we still need to talk about. I'm Catholic, and you are not."

There it was. Scott had wanted to be prepared for this moment, and here it was. "I hope you know that I would never interfere with your religion," he said.

"I do, but that's not the issue. The whole reason my mother insisted that my marriage to Stefano be annulled was so that if I married again, I could do so in the church. On this point, she is intractable. And because you are not Catholic, our marriage cannot be consecrated. It's forbidden."

"What if I found another way? What if I received a special dispensation from Rome?" he asked.

"But I don't understand. A special dispensation to become Catholic?"

"No, there's another way, but it's debatable. I was thinking we could ask Father Kohler to help us," he said.

"Scott, tell me what you're thinking, please."

"It's not well known, but the real interdiction that the Catholic Church has against non-Catholics is about Protestantism, since those denominations were protesters of the Catholic Church and its tenets," Scott said.

"I still don't see how this helps us. You were raised a Baptist; isn't that a Protestant?"

"That's just it. Yes, I'm Baptist. The Baptist denomination is commonly lumped with Protestantism, but we never protested the Catholic Church. As a result, there is a small loophole; Baptist congregants are excluded from the rule. But I'm sure that the clergy would need to be reminded of this technicality, and the appeal could only be presented by an ecclesiastical lawyer experienced in canonical law who could persuade the bishops in Rome," he explained.

"My God, Scott. How do you know this?"

"I asked you to marry me, and I knew it might be an issue," he said. "Despite evidence to the contrary, I do know how to study—when given the proper motivation."

"You're unbelievable," she said. "This is why I love you."

"And I thought it was the sex." Scott quipped lightly.

"It's that, too."

thirty-two

FATHER KOHLER WAS KEY TO SCOTT'S PLAN, AND THAT prompted Desirée. She recalled that, prior to Father Kohler's assignment in Gstaad, he had worked in the Vatican's legal department in Rome. While he was not a lawyer and had never risen to the higher echelons, he was always close to power and a very popular and trusted confidant of those who were. If Father Kohler didn't know the right person, then he would most assuredly know how to identify him.

"I could call him, explain what the problem is, and see what he says," Desirée said.

"That might be a lot to spring on him—our possible marriage and the church's arcane technicalities. Of course, before we talk to Father Kohler, we need to clear up a certain matter." He couldn't resist cutting her a sly look. "There's the problem of wording. I believe, the difference between *would* and *will*."

"Very funny." Desirée simply ignored the comment. "Do you think we should drive to Gstaad?"

Scott said, "I think we should invite him to lunch at Grappe d'Or in Lausanne. It's halfway between Gstaad and Geneva, and we could engage a driver to bring him to the restaurant and return him afterward. Besides being a convenience, our effort would immediately alert him to its importance. A personal, face-to-face meeting allows him—and us—to gauge body language and facial expressions; we'll be able to better understand how high a hill we propose to climb."

That very afternoon, Desirée called Father Kohler, and he agreed to the arrangements: Friday, lunch at one o'clock.

The night before, they made love. Scott had made sure of their intimacy; it was his barometer for the relationship. If all was well, Desirée was free and unabashed. If there was discontent, Scott would note her perceptible tinge of reticence. He was relieved that there had been no holding back; Desirée was passionate and eager for his touch. As he watched her brush her hair the next morning, he saw that she was nervous—and he was, too. But they were working together on this problem, and that gave him courage.

Arriving in Lausanne a bit early, Desirée instructed Gustav to make a detour down to Ouchy, Lausanne's lakefront. They followed the contour of the shore so she could show Scott the promenade, where large plane trees provided shade for those strolling and anyone wishing to feed the gulls and swans. Desirée pointed out a grand residence; the exiled Queen of Spain, Victoria Eugenie, lived there and, from time to time, Desirée's mother—Madame de Bellecourt—was her guest.

The appointed hour approached. Gustav guided the car through the old town to Grappe d'Or. It was not an imposing structure. Rather small, Grappe d'Or probably seated fewer than fifty. But the humble exterior was misleading. Known as the second-best restaurant in Swiss Romande, food lovers came from all around to dine; on any given day, one might find the likes of Charlie Chaplin or Vladimir Nabokov or even Vittorio Emanuele, Italy's exiled king, at their preferred tables. Wooden floors, tables and banquettes with white tablecloths, and an open grill gave a slightly rustic feel, adding warmth to the room.

The owner was stationed just inside the door. From his perch on a straight chair, he surveyed the entire restaurant, a single lift of his eyelid conveying displeasure. Most of the waiters were of the highest professional standard; busboys were often interns from Lausanne's famous École hôtelière. Besides being a convenient meeting place, Scott and Desirée loved Grappe d'Or and often stopped there on their way to or from Gstaad.

As they were being seated, Father Kohler came through the door and, in his gentle manner, greeted them. Scott ordered a dry Pouilly-Fumé as an aperitif. The good father cleared his throat; he wanted to get to the business of the meeting. "My dear countess, Monsieur Stoddard, I am happy to play the role of the patient cleric and always pleased to see you both," Father Kohler said, beaming softly at Desirée. "My weak humanity overwhelms my patience, and so I must demonstrate my curiosity—what does this meeting concern? Why bring me here?"

Desirée took the lead. "Father, you have always been there when I needed you, and we are counting on you now." She reached out for the priest's hand, taking it in both of hers, and Father Kohler covered their clasped fingers with his other hand. It was a tender moment. With a deep breath, she continued: "Scott and I are contemplating marriage."

"I am not surprised," Father Kohler said. Though his eyes were kind, he shook his head sadly. "Under the circumstances, I'm not sure what I can do. I believe Monsieur Stoddard is not Catholic. Am I correct? Of course, he could convert to Catholicism."

"Yes, but Scott believes he has found a way for the church to grant a dispensation. Converting to Catholicism, as you know, might take a year or two. We don't want to wait that long," Desirée said. She sighed heavily before continuing, "Unless, Father, it is impossible to acquire the dispensation."

"You are both lovely people and obviously very much in love, but convincing the Holy See that a special dispensation is applicable in your case would be difficult. You would need an experienced and well-connected canonical attorney."

"Precisely." Scott said. "Father Kohler, who would that man be?"

The kindly family priest chuckled. "Aha! You have led me like a lamb to slaughter. Now I understand my role. There is but one man for this mission: Monsignor Giovanni de Pita, a former papal attorney arguing canon law before the highest court within the Vatican," Father Kohler said. "Unfortunately, he is retired and living in Ravello, Italy."

"Well, is it possible to persuade him out of retirement? Or is there someone else we should contact?" Scott asked.

"Unfortunately, I know of no other person so qualified and well connected, which is paramount to your success."

"Then we must go to Ravello and persuade Monsignor de Pita," Desirée said. She raised her wine glass—"To our success!"

With that, Desirée went to work outlining a plan. Father Kohler would make their introduction to Monsignor de Pita, but she left it to his discretion as to what to confide regarding the reason. Father Kohler indicated it might take a few days to contact the monsignor—and several more phone calls to persuade him to accept the meeting. Using praise and approval, Desirée bolstered his courage, and as they parted outside the restaurant, Scott knew they had a new member on the team.

THEY WERE IN THE SALON ONE EVENING A FEW DAYS LATER, having a glass of champagne prior to going out for dinner, when Father Kohler called to relate his conversations with the monsignor. Though he only heard Desirée's half of the conversation, Scott understood the gist. After several phone calls and multiple entreaties, Monsignor de Pita had agreed to see them, but he couldn't promise anything beyond that. It was a little disappointing, but it could have been much worse. Desirée thanked Father Kohler for using his office to secure the meeting and promised she would never forget his kindness. After several additional phone calls, a date was set for the last Thursday in May; the monsignor invited them to lunch at his villa in Ravello.

There was a shift in Desirée's tone, and Scott turned his attention fully to her conversation. From the tenseness in her shoulders, Scott guessed a new topic, not one she liked, had been broached.

"No, Father; I haven't told my mother of Scott's proposal," Desirée admitted. She listened attentively for a long minute or so, and then she said, "Yes, I understand her concerns, but it is not her decision to make."

Another minute passed with Desirée listening and making small sounds of agreement. Then: "I'm sure Maman will be calling you. I believe we can agree that, when the appropriate time comes, I should be the one to apprise her of our intent."

Scott considered Desirée admiringly; she had such a gift for informing people on proper behavior without overtly instructing them on what to do.

thirty-three

S COTT AND DESIRÉE WERE SCHEDULED TO ATTEND THE
Cannes Film Festival in May. Luckily, their trip coincided with
spring recess at the university. The plan was they'd attend the
festival and then return to Geneva before flying to Naples and driving
to Ravello to meet the monsignor.

Cannes was a tradition. For many years, Desirée and any number
of her friends (particularly those from Paris) went to the international film festival. Known worldwide as a platform for the most
avant garde and controversial cinema, the festival in the South of
France was a spectacular event. Its star-packed juries and honorary
judges selected prizes for each category, the Palme d'Or being the
most prestigious award. Sometimes the subjects were not pleasant,
but the films were always viewed as art. The festival's glamour and
glitter differed from the Academy Awards; aside from the more
international crowd, a constant hum of self-publicity by the aspiring
starlets and celebrity models circulating the festival's periphery created a frenzy in the tabloids.

Cannes sits on a huge half moon bay, some thirty kilometers from
Nice. The British, seeking more temperate climes during hard English
winters, flock to the city. Writers like Fitzgerald and Hemingway found
their muse in Cannes, and nearby Cap d'Antibes was an important
residential area for the super rich.

Having sent their trunks ahead with Gustav, Scott and Desirée
flew to Cannes unencumbered. They checked into the Carlton Hotel,

cinema central for the festival, where the concierge and staff at reception greeted Desirée as a *habitué.*

Desirée loved the convenience of the hotel. Though her mother's home in Mougins was only ten kilometers away, the number of events and late-night parties made the commute—always a difficult drive under the best of circumstances—tiresome. Ever social, Desirée found mingling with the other attendees and movie people part of the fun; being in the thick of things added to the aura of the event. The only drawback was the ever-present paparazzi who staked out the hotel.

They had a beautiful suite on the third floor, overlooking La Croisette, a wide and landscaped promenade skirting the Mediterranean shore for some two kilometers. Scott surveyed their rooms with satisfaction; the décor was period French, the furniture's upholstery and draperies combined a soft cream, pastel green, and metallic gold. Three large windows led to a patio that ran the length of the suite.

Several of Desirée's friends, including Celine, had arrived the day before and were already next door at the Le Festival restaurant, the preferred hangout for Cannes regulars, Desirée and Scott joined the crowd, and he was glad to see Francesco was not there. Celine motioned for them to join her table, which included a very handsome man, whom she introduced as Dr. Albert Bonnard, a cardiologist from Paris.

During the lengthy lunch and cocktails, Celine managed to whisper to Desirée that mutual friends had introduced her to the doctor. Over the last several weeks, the two had developed a rather intense affair. Desirée seemed pleased; the way Albert and Celine looked at each other showed a clear match in the works. Her friend had never had a serious relationship, and Desirée had worried that somehow Celine would not realize her dream of love.

When Desirée went to the powder room, Celine slid close to Scott and said furtively, "Don't say anything to Desirée, but Francesco told me that Stefano is beside himself with jealousy. I don't think he's dangerous, but he may have friends who are. I'm sorry to be the one to tell you this, but I must."

"Thanks, Celine. I wouldn't worry too much; I think Stefano is more bluster than anything else." Seeing Desirée approach, Celine moved back, and Scott plastered a bland smile across his face. Inside, his guts were roiling. Celine had proven herself to be a trusted friend; she had warmed to him as he had to her; Scott was glad Desirée had a confidant like Celine in her life.

Scott made a point to chat with Dr. Bonnard. Albert was in much the same predicament Scott had found himself in at the beginning of his and Desirée's relationship. Like Scott, Albert was not from the upper reaches of French society; he was what the French would call *bourgeoisie*.

Returning to the hotel after lunch, Scott and Desirée nestled together to take a nap before the evening's events began. Encircled in Scott's arms, Desirée sighed contentedly. "Celine and Albert seemed very happy, don't you think?" she said.

"Yes, I would say very much in love and ecstatic," Scott said, knowing how pleased Desirée was for her friend. She absently ran her hand across the hair on his chest, deep in thought.

"It's a little unusual though," she mused. "Celine is such a traditionalist. I think she always saw herself marrying someone with a title and perhaps an inheritance." Scott listened intently. The women had been friends since childhood—how much of Celine's dreams mirrored Desirée's? "She wants a husband, several children, a happy home—well, maybe two homes." They laughed together before Desirée continued. "I would have thought Albert might be a little removed from what she had in mind." *Careful, Scott*, he thought. *Watch what you say next.*

"'Removed?' Desirée, dear, is that a cipher? Are you indicating that Celine would think Albert might hail from an inferior milieu?" Scott said. *What about me*, he thought. *Am I "removed" from what you had in mind?*

Her fingers continued their wandering way across his chest, stroking and playing. Scott could not see her face as she replied, "He is nice, though. I like him."

"My darling, just be happy for her. She loves him, and from those first few minutes with Albert, you can tell he adores Celine and would never hurt her. What more should she ask?" He tilted her head up so she could see he was joking. "Must her beau be a direct descendant of the Sun King?" Desirée's answering smile lit up her entire face.

"You're right," she said. "I'm sounding like my mother."

"You've told me you're a lot alike. And you also told me you often disagreed for that very reason. I've seen how naughty you can be," he said sternly, wagging a finger at her, which elicited giggles.

"I'm a bad little girl," Desirée cooed playfully. "Perhaps I should have a little spanking."

WHEN HE AWOKE LATER IN THE AFTERNOON, DESIRÉE WAS already busy with her preparations for the evening.

"Darling, could you get dressed?" she asked. Scott stretched lazily in answer, provoking a hurried rebuke. "Frederic will be here in a few minutes." Scott sighed; Frederic was the hairdresser from Alexandre de Paris who would be arriving to tame the countess's tresses. It was a good time to be away.

"If I must. Though I was hoping you'd have more time to be a bit naughty," he said seductively. She tossed a pillow his way and shooed him out.

Scott dressed quickly; he wanted to take a walk and get some fresh air, as it would be a long night. He took a last look in the mirror, adjusting his bowtie and cummerbund before shouting out to Desirée in the dressing room (mentally, he called it "the staging area") that he was going out. She didn't mind; Scott knew how important their ritual was. He'd wait for Desirée's grand entrance at the bar and enthusiastically express surprise and delight at her ensemble. It was their own personal theater.

Eventually, Scott made his way to the Carlton's beautiful mirrored bar, a large horseshoe affair. Nooks for privacy were formed with petite chairs and tables, engendering a feeling of intimacy and closeness. Enormous French doors the length and breadth of the room led to the large umbrella-shaded terrace above the Croisette and overlooking the hotel's beach club.

Scott didn't have to wait long before he saw Desirée coming down the hallway. He gave a low whistle—even before she entered the bar, it was obvious that none of the movie starlets would be upstaging Countess de Rovere. She knew from Scott's expression that he not only approved of but also understood the thematic undertones of her outfit.

Somewhere between risky and risqué, Desirée's silk chiffon jumpsuit was less than formal but totally appropriate. Made of marine blue silk and decorated in parchment white harlequin diamonds, the outfit's high waist and expert tailoring showed her long legs to their best advantage. Scott gave Frederic a mental bow, he'd worked magic with Desirée's hair by creating a tight blond twist that somehow defied gravity. Diamonds and ivory completed the picture. As he drank in the sight of her, Scott was conscious that he wasn't alone; the entire male population of the bar was transfixed by this remarkable specimen of loveliness. When she walked up to him, he was glad for her demonstrative nature. "Ah, Mademoiselle; may I buy you a drink?" he teasingly asked.

THOUGH THE FESTIVAL PAVILION, THE THEATER, WAS ONLY A block away, they wouldn't walk. The international press had been patrolling the beach and the lobby all day, snapping away at starlets, Brigitte Bardot wannabes, who stationed themselves on either side of the red carpet leading to pavilion. Flashbulbs lit the night in an incessant barrage of flickering white light. Taking the car made navigating the gauntlet of paparazzi possible, and so Gustav pulled the Mercedes as close as possible to the steps.

Dashing from the car, Scott and Desirée were practically blinded by camera flashes as they entered the theater. Groups of attendees were scattered around the foyer, holding flutes of champagne. Scott couldn't help it; he gawked. There was Sean Connery; Rex Harrison chatted with Catherine Deneuve and Roman Polanski, Warren Beatty, and Natalie Wood. Lesser known actors and actresses mingled, awaiting the screenings as almost an afterthought; most Cannes attendees were more interested in the scene itself.

Following the film, they pushed on to dinner at Chez Felix. Part entertainer, all host, Felix was in rare form; he knew just where to seat guests and exactly the right amount of flattery to use. Scott was glad to see Celine and Albert, and another couple from Paris—Jean Pierre and Simone Beaumarchais—joined the table. Jean Pierre had apparently retired at thirty-four (Scott questioned whether he had ever truly worked), and Simone was a former student at the same *lycée* Celine and Desirée had attended. The conversation quickly turned from the recently viewed film, *The Collector,* to everyone's immediate plans for the summer vacation.

Jean Pierre and Simone were bound for Sardinia in June, the best month, and they wondered whether Desirée would be there then, too.

"Not this year," Desirée replied casually. "We're going to the Amalfi Coast. Ravello, specifically." Scott fixated on his plate.

Jean Pierre breezily launched into a review. "Ah, Ravello. I know it, but I'm not sure there's enough to keep you occupied there. The concerts are generally in August. Beyond that . . ." He made a dismissive gesture with his hands. "Capris, now; I recommend Capris. It is better—better weather, more restaurants." Pausing, he turned to Scott. Observing his blasé manner, Jean Pierre looked at Desirée, who offered no comment. "Ravello . . . what don't I know about the charms of Ravello?"

Interest now piqued, the rest of the table joined the inquest. "Yes, Desirée, why are you going to Ravello, of all places?" Celine asked curiously.

"It's my idea," Scott said, swiftly rescuing the countess. "Desirée's like you; she'd much rather be in Capris, but I'm very interested in the ruins of Pompeii and some of the other archaeological digs in that area, as well as the volcano, Vesuvius. She's being quite a good sport about the whole thing." For once, Scott was glad to play the foreign student card.

"Desirée, my dear," Jean Pierre said, "I hope you know what you're getting into."

"I tell her that every day," Scott said, exchanging a secret smile with Desirée.

"I've been to Ravello several times," Albert said. "The town is an absolute gem; at one time, it was the preferred summer residence for the most patrician families of Rome. You'll like it a lot, I'm sure." The two men nodded in solidarity; Scott liked Albert and anticipated having him as a friend.

Desirée joined in the fun. "You see? I bring Scott to Cannes for the stars, and he whisks me off to Ravello for the rocks. It's a good trade, don't you think?" she quipped, and the table erupted into good-hearted laughter.

THE WEEK WAS CONSUMED WITH A BLUR OF EVENINGS PILED on evenings of the same sort: dinner until midnight followed by a trip to the casino, where they danced and talked (and danced some more) before collapsing at the hotel around three o'clock the next morning. Scott glanced at his books, tossed in the corner of the suite. He'd been naïve to bring them—ten minutes here, twenty minutes there wasn't going to do any good. He'd become thoroughly immersed with the goings on at Cannes, and frankly, he was sad to see it end. All the excitement had also distracted them from the impending meeting with Monsignor de Pita, and Scott was glad. One less preoccupation might yield benefits; the more they thought about it, the more tension mounted. What exactly, he wondered, was on the line? What if the Holy See would not yield the desired dispensation? There had been no discussion about whether Desirée would marry him outside the church, and Scott hadn't asked. He was a little afraid of the answer, and from her silence on the subject, he guessed Desirée hadn't addressed the question either.

Once the festival was over, Desirée and Scott spent time closing the house in Geneva in preparation for their trip to Ravello. Scott was sad to leave, but they would be in Paris for the last days of spring and early part of summer. He spent a few days attending class, but Scott's interest had waned. Besides, he reasoned, there were only a few weeks remaining before the end of the semester, and his focus was the meeting with Monsignor de Pita. The Stoddards were now planning to come to Europe as early as the end of June, and Desirée had promised her definitive answer before then. Scott allowed himself to hope; his plans for their future might work out after all, but it was going to be close.

thirty-four

O NCE THEY CLEARED THE OUTSKIRTS OF NAPLES, Scott and Desirée had a three-hour drive to Positano, a beautiful town on the Amalfi Coast. Remote Ravello stands at one thousand feet above the Mediterranean, located on a precipice that provides a view of the entire coastline and the Gulf of Salerno. Their destination for the day was the Pelicano, a hotel situated directly on the water.

Ravello was only a short distance from Positano, about six miles, but the road climbed almost straight up. The hotel recommended using its driver, Pietro, for the journey. Pietro would take them and wait while they had lunch with Monsignor de Pita. At the outset, Scott was a little too friendly, releasing Pietro from formality, and the driver launched a running commentary on the sights and history of the cities of Positano and Ravello. This would not ordinarily have caused concern, but the route was dangerous. Pietro sped along the narrow, two-lane road's switchbacks, hugging the cliffs as cars approached from the opposite direction, all crossing the center line and honking their horns, while gesticulating and relating intricacies of some local story of loves lost or fortunes gained.

By the grace of God (and Pietro's skill), they arrived. What with the white-knuckle drive, the morning had been tense, but Scott and Desirée had been able to avoid snapping at each other. A lot was invested in this meeting.

Ravello's Piazza Vescovado was dominated on one side by the Duomo, its cathedral; on the other side were small shops and restaurants with tables and chairs arranged around a terrace with large umbrellas. Pietro let Scott and Desirée out just off the main piazza. Their instructions were to wait. Anselmo, a guide, would meet them at a quarter before one o'clock to guide them on a ten-minute walk to the monsignor's villa. Stationing themselves on the church steps, Scott read the historical plaque while Desirée fidgeted.

Anselmo arrived just before the appointed time. He didn't speak English or French, but Desirée spoke Italian, so there was no issue. Scott followed, captivated by the sights, as Anselmo and Desirée chatted ahead. Many little alleys and lanes, the very same used in Roman times (and before), led in all directions toward villas and hotels built against the cliffs. These lichen-covered lanes were just large enough for carts, but no more. Pierced openings in walls provided access to villas, through gardens or the service entrance. Scott noted that no signs indicated who lived at these villas, nor were there any house numbers. To arrive at Monsignor de Pita's villa, a visitor would have to know where to go and navigate the labyrinth of forks and turns; they would certainly need Anselmo to find their way back to the square.

Stopping at one of the villas, Anselmo pulled the chain of an antique brass bell; a matronly woman in a black dress and headscarf opened the door. She showed the group to a large terrace half-covered by a trellis of latticework. A climbing plant with dark green leaves and tiny white flowers had been espaliered to the lattice, and Scott breathed in the heavy scent of jasmine. The trellis had been there a long time, though the furniture was more modern than one might have expected; the rattan and wicker with its sea of puffy cushions convinced one to stay awhile. Earthen planters of all shapes and sizes lined the borders and steps into a manicured garden that somehow managed to look both wild and groomed at the same time.

Monsignor de Pita, a man of approximately sixty years old (young for a prelate to have retired) came toward them. He was of slight stature, his curly hair peppered with wiry strands of silver, eyes so mahogany they doubled for black, and sun-browned skin. He was dressed in a simple pair of white cotton trousers and white linen shirt; blue espadrilles slapped softly on the terrace stones.

"*Buon giorno*, Countess de Rovere and Signore Stoddard," he said warmly. "Welcome to Ravello."

The housekeeper served a white wine from Sicily and plate of fresh raw almonds. The monsignor seemed in no hurry to get to the principal purpose of the meeting but rather questioned Scott and Desirée on their backgrounds, how they had met, what their respective families thought about the marriage. Scott was impatient—he and Desirée had discussed these ad nauseum, so far as Scott was concerned, and Monsignor de Pita was rehashing the details again.

"It is not at all unusual that parents and other family members are not enthusiastic about a marriage," Monsignor de Pita said in a diplomatic manner. Their host seemed sympathetic, but Scott thought the older man a tough read. "Priests hear almost every possible objection, including all the ones that we've enumerated—and more." He stood, gesturing toward a table set for three underneath the trellis. "Come. Let's have some lunch."

As they enjoyed bread and another bottle of wine, the monsignor related how, after many years at the Vatican, he chose to retire from canonical law while he was still in good health.

"Tell me, Monsignor de Pita, what are some of the passions that fulfill your days here in Ravello?" Desirée said.

The monsignor's face lit up at Desirée's question. "I have two that are interrelated. One is gardening (I will show you after lunch), and the other is painting. I raise exotic flowers, all kinds of orchids and the like, and then I put together arrangements and create still life paintings. And from these paintings comes a pattern; a local kiln manufactures various lines of pottery and china with these images which are sold under the name of Ravella," he said with a flourish toward the table.

Looking down at the table setting, Scott asked, "Should we presume that these settings are from your line?"

"Humbly, yes," the monsignor replied. "Do you like them?"

"They're lovely," Desirée said. "The iris and the white rose together are beautiful." Monsignor de Pita beamed with pleasure.

Lunch was a salad of mozzarella and fresh tomatoes, olive oil and basil, followed by swordfish steak cooked *a la Livornese*. Vanilla ice cream with orange sections and toasted pine nuts and coffee at a small table in the garden under one of the giant oak trees finished the afternoon. But for the gnawing reason behind their visit, Scott would have enjoyed the day immensely. Desirée was remarkably calm and compliant with the unhurried pace, and Scott had to trust that the conversation would eventually turn.

Monsignor de Pita finished his espresso with a satisfied air. "Now, let us get to the business at hand," he said. Scott and Desirée straightened in their seats and exchanged glances. "Father Kohler informed me that, in lieu of conversion, you are interested in pursuing what I believe you have termed as a 'technicality' regarding Catholics marrying non-Catholics. Countess de Rovere, you would like to marry within the church without Signore Stoddard converting to Catholicism. Am I correct?"

"I didn't know what to call it, and I wouldn't presume to be able to investigate or to interpret the rules," Scott replied, "but from the vantage of a layperson, a layperson with a purpose, we thought it worth asking someone of an expert opinion."

"I thank you for your flattery and your modesty," Monsignor de Pita replied with a slight smile. "Father Kohler had mentioned you could be rather skillful in diplomacy."

"Father Kohler has been an important person in my life for years, from my early teens," Desirée said emphatically. "I always turn to him when I need help. We so appreciate that you have agreed to consult with us on this matter."

"Have you had the time or the interest to review the possibility?" Scott asked. "Of course, we are dying to know your opinion."

"Father Kohler was always one of my closest friends. I must tell you, my initial interest stemmed uniquely from his entreaty. And yes, I have delved into the subject, only superficially at this point," the monsignor said. "Your inexperience aside, Signore Stoddard, I think that—with the right representation and brief—you might, indeed, enjoy a dispensation based on this technicality."

"This is very good news!" Desirée said, clapping her hands together joyously.

Scott's brow furrowed. "Wait a minute!" he said. "'With the right representation and the right brief'—Monsignor de Pita, are you indicating you will not represent us in this matter?"

"I wish that I could, but I am retired and reluctant to wade back into the intricacies this case would entail."

"But you must," Desirée implored. "We have no one else to turn to."

"Countess, please don't make this difficult. I do not find it easy to refuse you, particularly after seeing you two together. It is obvious that you love each other very much."

"Then what are we to do?" Desirée asked, tears glistening. "Please . . . will you reconsider?"

"I shouldn't; I fear I will only disappoint you twice." The monsignor sighed and passed a hand through his hair. "I will give you my final answer in one week."

thirty-five

DESIRÉE DID NOT LOSE A MOMENT. AS SOON AS THEY had returned to the hotel in Positano, she placed a call to Gstaad; she told Father Kohler the results of their meeting with Monsignor de Pita and her resulting disappointment, imploring the priest to speak with the monsignor and try to persuade him. Father Kohler said he would, though he thought too much pressure on his old friend would be counterproductive and a mistake.

Scott reviewed the situation over and over, wondering what incentive they could offer. Monsignor de Pita didn't appear to lack for money (nor did he seem to be overly interested in money); in any case, Father Kohler had said the monsignor had a sizable inheritance. Was the retired lawyer attached to any charity or cause that could benefit from a grateful sponsor? Father Kohler said he would find out.

Desirée and Scott were on edge, awaiting the monsignor's decision, Father Kohler's information, and Desirée's answer to Scott's proposal.

ONCE THEY'D RETURNED TO PARIS, SCOTT DISCOVERED HE wasn't able to study one whit. On many occasions, he resolved to bear down. He picked up books, sought out quiet places, all without success—his motivation had disappeared, concentration dissolved, and discipline evaporated. He was only falling further behind in his studies.

Then, there was the matter of Stefano. Although no more ominous notes had been delivered nor any intrusions into his apartment detected, Scott had a lingering sense that Stefano might be keeping tabs on him—and perhaps Desirée as well. His preoccupation simmered. Was there a chance that Stefano's threats could be more than rhetoric?

SEVERAL LONG DAYS LATER, FATHER KOHLER CALLED. HE HAD heard from Monsignor de Pita, who was making inquiries in Rome regarding a petition of dispensation. Scott and Desirée interpreted this as good news, and Father Kohler agreed. He also relayed that Monsignor de Pita was a staunch supporter of the Santabono Children's Hospital in Naples. Nevertheless, he cautioned, they would be unwise to make a financial donation as that could be interpreted as an unsolicited incentive. Perhaps, Father Kohler wisely counseled, they might act later, if it seemed appropriate.

With all the force of youth coursing through his body, Scott found these details and strategies tedious. Circumstances were making marriage a lot more complicated than necessary, and these behind-the-scenes machinations were causing Scott to become anxious and defensive. He had asked the question, damn it, but he couldn't get a straight answer.

Full of nervous energy, Scott paced the Avenue Foch apartment. He already felt inferior to Desirée, and having to wait for her response, needing to meet all her conditions, did not bolster his confidence. Petulantly, he recalled that his offer attached no conditions.

And to top off the stress from school and strain with Desirée came a letter from his mother. Among the mail forwarded from Geneva was the familiar envelope; inside, his mother had slipped a photograph clipped from *Life* magazine. Part of a collage of people arriving at Cannes was an exceptionally clear and focused shot of Scott with Desirée, dressed in the form-fitting harlequin outfit she'd worn the first night. The caption teased about the identity of the Countess de Rovere's escort. His mother had attached a note to the photo: "Call us immediately!"

There wasn't any way around it; Scott had to call. His mother answered the phone on the first ring, and his father joined on the extension only a second later. "Is this the woman you're dating?," Mr. Stoddard demanded gruffly without preamble.

"Yes," Scott replied with relief. Finally. There was no point in hiding the truth anymore. "Desirée is the Countess de Rovere, and I'm in love with her."

Scott heard his mother's sharp intake of breath at his announcement and closed his eyes, waiting for her questions.

"How old is she?"

"She's twenty-nine."

"She's too old for you. What about your school? You can't be studying much if you're going to film festivals in the South of France; you've forgotten why we sent you to Geneva."

The recriminations continued. Scott couldn't contest their reasonable concern; rather than defuse the situation, his agreement riled his parents even more. They'd expected excuses and begging for forgiveness, but Scott did none of that. Nor did he reveal that he had proposed marriage. Why? In the emotional onslaught, Scott simply couldn't add one more "disappointment." Cynically, he thought that perhaps there was no need to reveal what might not be relevant. Either Desirée would reject his proposal or the dispensation could be unattainable, and then there would be no marriage.

Finally, there was no more to say; Scott wasn't cooperating, and the Stoddards were spent, so they said goodbye.

WHEN DESIRÉE ARRIVED HOME, SCOTT GREETED HER WITH the news that, thanks to *Life*, his parents knew about their relationship.

"Were they happy about us?" she asked.

"They were happy to know more about the woman I've been seeing," he replied cautiously. "But I can't say they were happy with everything they learned," he said.

"Why not?"

"They have some of the same objections that your mother has."

Desirée gave a bitter little laugh. "Maybe my mother has more in common with your parents than she would suppose."

thirty-six

THE ALLIED CLUB, LOCATED ON THE RUE DE FAUBOURG Saint-Honoré, was one of the most prestigious clubs in Paris. Formed during the First World War by French nationals, the club's purpose was to provide a place of camaraderie for Allied officers, principally the British and Americans. Enjoying a unique location between the American and Italian embassies, the dining room overlooked the manicured French garden of evergreen shrubs and trees and the interconnected paths of pea gravel.

Madame de Bellecourt, who had returned from Mougins, invited her daughter to lunch, and Scott was certain she had not picked this venue by chance. (*After all*, he thought, *this was where Desirée and Stefano's wedding reception had been held.*) The Allied Club was a place for formal negotiations; it was rumored, that after World War I, Woodrow Wilson negotiated many of the conditions associated with the League of Nations in those very rooms. Desirée's mother had included Scott in her invitation, which he considered a good sign—she was willing to be seen in polite society with the young man known as her daughter's lover. As Scott admired the historical setting, he considered that perhaps Madame had some weighty enterprise in mind.

Ever the grand dame, Desirée's mother had commanded a generous table for four located near one of the windows and affording ample privacy. They dined on *sole meuniere* with *pommes de terre, a la vapeur*, and enjoyed a light raspberry sorbet and fresh blueberries as dessert. The lunch conversation dealt mostly with casual news of the day, upcoming travels, and consternation over household staff. (Madame's habit was not to discuss anything too serious or unpleasant during a meal to avoid any risk of indigestion.) But when the coffee was served, she straightened her posture and fell silent. Scott had a feeling she was about to address the meaning behind this meeting. Desirée reached for his hand under the table and gave it a slight squeeze.

"Monsieur Stoddard, I have been thinking about our last conversation and the re-ordering of lists," Madame de Bellecourt said gravely.

"I'm glad you have," he said. "Dare I ask what are the results of your re-ordering?"

She took a small sip of coffee before replying. "There is some improvement, but my list is not perfect nor is it where you would like it to be. I have invited you today to discuss realities." Madame de Bellecourt lifted her chin ever so slightly, and once again Scott noted the resemblance between mother and daughter. Desirée was just as resolutely posed. Madame de Bellecourt continued: "It is true; I have hoped—even prayed—that this relationship would suffer a natural demise. Not out of lack of consideration for you both. I love my daughter dearly, and I am confident that you are a fine person, but I can't help my reservations."

Mother and daughter held each other's gaze, Scott caught between the two formidable women. "This is nothing new," Desirée interjected angrily. "Why are we here? What exactly are you saying, Maman?" A flush crept up the delicate skin of her neck, and Scott felt her hand tremble in his. *Nothing good would come of an impasse*, Scott thought.

"Wait, Desirée," Scott implored. "Please allow your mother to continue. I'm sure she has more to say to us. Don't you, Madame de Bellecourt?"

The older woman nodded and took a deep breath. "You say you are in love. You've dismissed the well-meaning counsel others close to you have offered. Be that as it may," she said with a wave of her hand. "But what I can't understand or condone, Desirée, is this flagrant display for the whole world to see and gossip about. In the beginning, the precise extent of this indiscretion was confined to a few friends; it was a private matter; but now you're traveling all over Europe together."

Madame de Bellecourt's strong display of feeling shocked Scott. He was floored; the older woman was usually so in control of her emotions. She appeared near tears.

"Now, this romance is common knowledge. Have you seen what they're saying about you, Desirée? I know you both must be aware of the vulgar press coverage. After what was printed regarding Cannes, I can hardly face my friends." Madame de Bellecourt's lips trembled, threatening her composure. She was clearly on the brink of a very upsetting pronouncement. Scott steeled himself for the worst, as Desirée's mother regrouped to continue. "If you're not going to break up, my darling, then get engaged. Please. It would bring a level of propriety and decency to the situation," she said.

Desirée sat immobile, quiet; everyone at the table seemed frozen in place. Scott knew it was not his turn to speak; the moment belonged to Desirée. Madame de Bellecourt had fixed her only child with an entreating look, one that most likely mirrored Scott's expression. *Which of us*, he wondered, *is the more eager to hear Desirée's next words?*

"Maman, you surprise me," Desirée said slowly. "Only a month ago, you were opposed; just this moment, you are pushing an engagement. I don't understand."

The elegant older woman smoothed her skirt across her lap. "Desirée, my dearest; I'm a realist. More importantly, I'm practical. Faced with two choices, I'm inclined to choose the least damaging." Scott smiled; now, this was the Madame de Bellecourt he had come to know. Catching his reaction, she raised an eyebrow and addressed him directly for the first time in many long minutes.

"You're uncharacteristically quiet, Monsieur Stoddard," she observed.

"Madame, your candor has struck me dumb."

"Then I can claim a first," came the arch reply.

LUNCH ENDED WITHOUT ANY REAL RESOLUTION. NO ONE CAME away with what they wanted: Madame received no assurance regarding her suggestion, and Scott had no more of an answer. Why didn't Desirée tell her mother of his proposal?

A few days later, Father Kohler left a message for Desirée, asking her to call him as soon as possible. When she returned his call, it took a few minutes for him to get to the phone.

"Do you have news for us?" Desirée asked, Scott waiting at her side. She listened, smiled, and mouthed the words, "Good news." She asked a few questions (*though*, Scott thought, *not the same ones he would've, but he could always speak with Father Kohler himself*). Desirée thanked the family priest profusely for his assistance before hanging up.

Father Kohler had reported that Monsignor de Pita had become intrigued with the challenge, despite his initial reluctance to become involved. Once the retired lawyer felt the proverbial itch, he had to scratch. According to the monsignor, the petition was practically writing itself; his investigation provided more precedent than he could have imagined. A few more weeks of work were needed before the petition could be presented; a few weeks after that, they could expect that a decision would be handed down—mid-July, at the latest.

Scott felt a major celebration was in order, and Desirée seemed happy to accommodate. They had a gourmet dinner, drank champagne, and even went dancing, much like when they first met. Afterward, they made love.

In the quiet of the night, with Desirée asleep in his cradling arms, Scott lay alone with his thoughts. The evening had felt false, like a game they were playing. Why didn't this good news trigger a more positive response in Desirée? As the various reasons against their marriage were stripped away, why didn't she show more joy in overcoming these obstacles to their union? Had Desirée been hiding behind the reasons, knowing that they probably couldn't be overcome? Hoping she wouldn't have to give an answer to his proposal?

Scott wasn't sure he wanted to know the answers. He wouldn't ask her.

thirty-seven

ONE AFTERNOON, SCOTT AND DESIRÉE WERE ALONE IN her Avenue Fochs apartment. They sat on the terrace over the garden, Scott reading the day's newspaper. Desirée was fidgety, a little nervous. Clearly, something was on her mind, and so Scott waited patiently. Finally, she broke the quiet and said, "Scott, I see two problems remaining for us. One: you must tell your parents you've proposed . . ."

Before she could get to the second item, Scott jumped in.

"I was hoping to tell my parents that I had asked a lovely woman to be my wife and she'd accepted," he said, attempting to remain factual without whining. "I prefer not to tell them that the woman I love and asked to marry me has requested I wait until the end of June for her answer." To her credit, Desirée blushed under Scott's steady gaze.

"I know, darling; it sounds so unfair. I'm so sorry, but you must be patient. I just need that time. Trust me, please."

Folding his paper carefully, Scott struggled to keep his voice neutral. He asked, "And what's the second thing?"

"Scott, I don't want you to get angry with me—please listen before you say anything." Desirée's lips trembled as she spoke, and Scott grew very still—what in the world could this be? "Do you remember when we came back to Paris in April? It was your first time at the apartment. I went to see my lawyers—I said it was concerning taxes." He nodded; yes, he remembered the day well. Desirée looked out at the gardens, took a deep breath. "Well, that meeting wasn't about taxes," she said.

"Yes?" Scott prodded gently. "Desirée, I won't understand unless you tell me."

"I don't know how to say this," she said, still refusing to meet his gaze. What, he wondered, would cause such discomfort in Desirée that could involve a meeting with her lawyers? An idea dawned.

"Oh, now I understand," he said. "You went to your lawyers to talk about a prenuptial agreement."

She turned to him, utterly relieved yet clearly fearful of his reaction to the revelation. "Is it so terrible?"

"Which—the agreement or the secrecy?"

"Both, I guess," she said.

"Desirée, you're a wealthy woman; I expected an agreement of some sort," Scott replied thoughtfully. "But the secrecy is worse." He stood and turned away from her. "Really, Desirée, I hadn't even asked you to marry me at that point," he said.

"Well, I must protect myself. We must have been thinking about our relationship." In her voice, Scott heard Madame de Bellecourt's pragmatism. "Tell me, Scott; what do you think about an agreement?"

He faced her, throwing his hands up in the air and giving a contemptuous laugh. "Would I mind signing an agreement that might leave me at the curb if our marriage didn't work out? No, no bother. Where do I sign? Could I sign twice, to make it extra official?"

"I knew you would be angry, and I'm sorry I didn't discuss it with you."

Scott sighed. "But Desirée, I'm not angry about the prenuptial itself. I had expected to sign an agreement. I understand completely, darling. I just hope that you will be fair. What I can't stand is that you kept this from me." With that, he turned and left the terrace.

FOR SEVERAL DAYS, TENSION EXISTED BETWEEN THE LOVERS, A kind of frosty coexistence. When time came to address the prenuptial agreement, Desirée advised Scott to retain his own lawyer, one of his choosing who would best represent his interests. Scott thought, *what interests?* He was a twenty-three-year-old student living off his parents'

stipend; he had no career, no property. If that simplified matters, then he was glad of it. He considered asking Andre for a recommendation, but the wily newspaper writer might guess what it was about. Who else? Scott decided to ask the American Embassy for names of attorneys dealing in contractual law.

The Embassy was happy to oblige and referred him to James Dinsmore, an American working in a French firm. Funnily enough, Scott had already met Dinsmore at a party after one of the galas he and Desirée had attended. Many Americans, especially those linked with interests in France, had been at the swanky Theatre Montaigne event held at the United States' embassy.

That evening, Scott had found himself side by side with Dinsmore at the bar. The gentlemen were trying to get a drink and competing to see who could be the most cordial. "No, you first," Scott had said. "No, you," Dinsmore replied. Finally, they procured their glasses of champagne and enjoyed a decent, decidedly American conversation.

Pleased that his counsel would be someone he knew (however modest their connection), Scott made the appointment with Dinsmore. Once he'd explained the nature of his need, Dinsmore understood completely; he would ask Desirée's attorneys to messenger a copy of the agreement to his office for review. In addition, he proposed a fee arrangement, one that Scott thought implied a favor.

DINSMORE CALLED WHEN HE'D RECEIVED THE PRENUPTIAL and asked Scott to stop by that afternoon to review the document. When Scott arrived, Dinsmore cut right to the chase.

"You have not read this agreement, correct?" he asked.

Scott nodded his assent. "Yes; today is the first I will have seen of it." Carefully considering Dinsmore's expression, he asked, "How bad is it, James? Do I pay her alimony if we don't work out?" Scott chuckled, but Dinsmore's face didn't relax.

"I know that you want to bring a little levity to a rather unpleasant reality," the attorney said. "My job is to explain what you are signing and offer modifications where necessary. I do not see it as my function to counsel you on the fairness of the document or whether, indeed, you should sign it or not. That," Dinsmore said emphatically, "is your decision and yours alone. It would be unfair of me to influence you."

"Give me the basic terms, and I'll read it in detail later," Scott said.

"All right." The attorney picked up the hefty document, scanning its pages and consulting a legal pad of scrawled notes. "If there should be a dissolution of the marriage within the first year, you would receive a living allowance of twice the current stipend provided by the Countess de Rovere for three years hence. After your third wedding anniversary, the settlement figure doubles and is extended to seven years; and after five additional years, it doubles again and is extended to ten years (with some other arrangements, as to living requirements, etc.). Should you and the countess have a child or children, then your investiture is immediate to the five-year provision. There are no terms to determine or assign fault. The guiding principle is that, if one or both decide to end the marriage, the tenets of this agreement will dictate the terms and principles of its dissolution," he said.

Scott took a moment to reflect. He had no experience with this sort of arrangement, but he had expected nothing. After all, he was coming to the possible union with nothing. "I'm surprised. Desirée is a very generous woman," he said. "I'm flabbergasted that her attorneys didn't persuade her otherwise."

Dinsmore shrugged. "As I indicted, it is not my role to advise on issues of fairness, only issues of legality. I'll say this much, though. She must love you."

SCOTT USED THE WALK FROM DINSMORE'S OFFICE JUST OFF the rue Marbeuf back to Desirée's apartment as time to prepare. How he handled discussing the prenuptial agreement with her was important. His natural inclination was to tease, but this was not the time. Should he tell her he thought it more than fair? Perhaps, but he didn't want to go much further than that. Desirée didn't like talking or thinking about money. Scott didn't know the extent of her wealth, and she had never volunteered or even hinted at specifics. His monthly allowance, that "pocket money," had been generous, and he'd been thankful for whatever she'd provided. He would never have asked her for further details.

That the prenuptial agreement was so generous did indicate, however, that he might be on better footing with his proposal than he'd thought. If not, her lawyers would likely have recommended a more draconian tack, reasoning that if Scott protested the terms, Desirée could always up the figures. But she obviously didn't want any negotiations or arguments over money. Desirée had tried to be candid when she said she had money enough for both of them, and these generous terms were a commitment of sorts. Maybe not the *I will* Scott wanted, but a firm step in the right direction nonetheless.

He found Desirée on the terrace. She and Celine had had lunch in the Plaza Athenée's courtyard. However, she didn't want to discuss that; she was more interested in his reaction to the prenuptial agreement. Scott didn't make her wait.

"I met with my attorney, James Dinsmore," Scott said. "He reviewed the agreement in detail with me, and I agreed to everything. He's been instructed to tell your lawyers that I would sign it, as is, when the documents are available. Desirée, I thought it very fair—and that the fairness has your signature."

Clearly relieved, she gave Scott a hug and quick kiss. "Oh, darling; I'm so glad."

He returned her embrace. Holding her arms, he stepped back so that he could look her full in the face. "I want you to know that I would have signed it anyway, no matter what the terms," Scott said earnestly. She moved closer, placing her hands on either side of his face.

"I thought as much. That's why I didn't want to make it difficult."

They sealed the moment with a kiss. Scott felt happier than he had in weeks; they were moving closer to marriage. Desirée had promised she would give him her decision in a few weeks, but she wasn't being coy about her answer. The prenuptial agreement illustrated her caution; she was methodically eliminating all those problematic elements.

Only something unexpected would cause Desirée to jump ship. But what could possibly go wrong? Her mother had urged an engagement; Celine had expressed her support to Scott several times; he would sign the financial agreement; and the church would most likely grant their dispensation. As he luxuriated in their happy kiss, Scott thought that things were certainly looking up. What could go wrong?

thirty-eight

WHAT COULD GO WRONG CAME AT THE END OF THE week. All morning and afternoon, Scott had been at the Louvre; when he returned, he'd expected to find Desirée getting ready to go out to dinner. The apartment, however, was empty; the servants had left for the evening, and when he called out for Desirée, there was no answer. After a while, when she hadn't returned, he became concerned. Scott watched from the front windows, hoping to see her arrive. More time went by; becoming slightly alarmed, he called Celine. She said she hadn't heard from Desirée but would call if she did.

Odd, Scott thought, hanging up the phone. Celine hadn't expressed any worry about Desirée. Something was amiss, but what? He decided to go ahead and prepare for dinner and went upstairs to change. In the bedroom, resting against the pillows, was a pink envelope addressed to him in Desirée's perfect penmanship. The note inside read *Need some time to think. Something unexpected came up, and I've gone to Geneva. Don't come. Just give me some time, alone, please. I love you, Desirée.*

Scott's hand was shaking. He analyzed his feelings. Was it fear? No, he was furious. Why would she leave him a note like that? Why not tell him she needed time to think? This wasn't right; it was cruel. Tables turned, that's not how he would've treated Desirée. Maybe the whole idea of their relationship was a mistake. Maybe everyone was right; there were too many problems. What had he been thinking when he proposed? Was he like Marlyse, issuing an ultimatum to force

Desirée's hand? Scott was roiled with the intense emotions flooding through him. And he didn't have one friend to confide in. He sat down on the bed, overwrought—the situation was downright embarrassing. What a fool he'd been. He'd tried to solve all the conditions, and now this. Was she rethinking their relationship?

Tossing the note aside, he got up and went to the bar, where he poured a double Glenfiddich, neat. After the second one, he picked up the phone and called Desirée's Geneva number. The alcohol was erasing his inhibitions. Yes, she'd asked for him to give her alone time, but he couldn't help himself. Another drink, another call. No answer. After many calls and no answer, Scott was very drunk. He staggered to the bedroom and passed out. Around three o'clock, he roused; at first, he thought he'd had a nightmare, but there was the note, crumpled on the bed under his body. No, it was real. Too real. His mouth fuzzy, Scott weaved his way to the kitchen for water. Resting his head on the breakfast table, he reviewed each conversation from the past week, looking for some indication, any telltale sign of what had precipitated Desirée's note. Was it him? Had he said something that could have been misinterpreted? No, he couldn't find anything.

Madame Tissot's bustling woke Scott. Rumpled and hungover, the ache in his head equal to the ache in his heart, he declined the cook's offer of breakfast. Against his better judgment, he called again and again; still no answer. He hadn't expected an answer. Desirée wasn't going to pick up, that was clear, but perhaps someone else would talk to him. Celine owed him that after last evening's misdirection.

Scott quickly dressed and hurried the four blocks to Celine's and waited across the street in the park. She walked her little dog periodically, and he hoped he might catch her on the first outing of the day; he was certainly early enough. About fifteen minutes later, Celine emerged with Marcel, her little Shih Tzu, in her arms. When they reached the park, she dropped the fluffy dog in the grass, cooing softly.

Not wanting to startle or frighten his friend, Scott made some noise as he approached. He wanted to appear as though he'd been out strolling. "Good morning, Celine," he said.

She turned, and Scott saw that she wore no makeup and a scarf hid her unstyled hair. Though she obviously hadn't intended to be seen, she didn't look at all surprised at his presence. "*Bonjour,* Scott," she said. "I'm sorry."

"Please tell me what's going on," he said. "You know I was worried sick yesterday. And still, you didn't breathe a word about Desirée's plans."

"I can't," she said, her eyes beseeching him to understand. "Desirée doesn't want me to. She made me promise."

Scott wasn't about to let it go so easily. "I've always treated Desirée fairly, and you as well. Celine, I deserve some answers, don't you think?"

"Of course, you do, but it isn't like that," she said. As the morning light brightened, people began to emerge from their homes, and Scott saw their conversation was attracting attention. Self-consciously, Celine raised a hand to her face. Scooping up Marcel, she cast a look around before grabbing Scott's arm. "Oh, come in," she said.

Bustling into the apartment, Scott could tell that Celine and Albert were now living together. Though the childhood friends shared many things, Celine's taste ran to old French—large wooden furniture and heavy dark brocades—rather than the eclectic themes and colors Desirée preferred. She prepared tea, explaining that Albert had left hours earlier. Scott sat on the sofa, she on a side chair. Her cup clattered in the saucer, she was so nervous. Though Celine tried several times to speak, whatever she wanted to say wouldn't come out.

Finally, she closed her eyes wearily and said, "Can't you give her a little time, Scott?"

"I don't begrudge her the time alone. It's not knowing the reason why she needs it. Can't I help her through whatever this is, Celine? If she's in trouble, I want to share that." Celine struggled visibly with Scott's words. He could watch the conflicting emotions play across her unvarnished face.

"I can't; I promised."

With Desirée, a gentle touch often helped. He took the teacup from Celine and held her slender hands in his. They warmed to his touch; the trembling quieted. He waited before asking again, "Celine, what is it?"

She studied him intently. There was nothing for Scott to do but wait as that internal argument played out. After several long moments, Celine removed her hands and covered her face. Suddenly, she straightened up, faced Scott, and said, "She's . . . Desirée is pregnant."

"Pregnant?" Scott exclaimed. A thousand thoughts flooded him all at once. She'd left Paris without telling him? Numbly, he couldn't help but think of their parents; her mother would be furious (at first with her, and then with him) over the public embarrassment. Scott had no doubt what his mother would say. Sarah Stoddard had cautioned against this possibility, it seemed, since Scott was in puberty. A baby and not married? God, the *whole world* was going to be furious with them.

Quickly, he calculated Desirée's condition. It had to have been that warm spring afternoon just six weeks ago; he and Desirée had rented a small cabin cruiser to motor down the Seine. The idyllic float and warm afternoon; a little too much wine; a progressive and impassioned series of kisses and fondling. They'd been careless; she, thinking it safe; he, lost in lust. To be truthful, Scott realized he simply hadn't cared.

My God, he thought, *I'm only twenty-three and going to be a father.* He'd never considered the possibility of becoming a father. He and Desirée had never discussed children other than to imply they both wanted some—later.

He groaned inwardly, *Oh, Desirée!* What was she feeling? Had she gone to Geneva because she was embarrassed? Was she worried that he would be disappointed, maybe angry? Did she care about what her mother and everyone else would think? Was she sad that, contrary to some master plan, her life would change? Was she was angry at herself? Or did she blame him?

Celine sat as still as a statue, hardly breathing. "Please, Scott; I wasn't supposed to tell you. She'll tell you when she's ready. Give her some time to work through this."

"There is more to consider and no time to waste. Tell me right now—does anyone else know?"

"Her mother. That's how it all started. When she told Madame de Bellecourt that she was pregnant, her mother exploded in anger, accusing Desirée of being irresponsible and uncaring."

Now it was clear why Desirée had left so abruptly for Geneva: her mother had shamed her. It is one thing to encourage an engagement between Desirée and her Baptist lover; it was quite another to have the world see her pregnant daughter wed outside the church. Madame de Bellecourt's previous opposition to Desirée's marriage to Scott was a moot point and, while she wasn't a mean woman, she liked to have her way. Scott well knew she was probably fuming at this very moment.

And what of poor, humiliated Desirée? Scolded by her mother and embarrassed by the circumstances, she'd rushed off to Geneva, leaving Paris and Scott without explanation. It was so unlike Desirée, a complete contradiction to her normal behavior. Scott ached. How might he reconcile this predicament? Though he had a right to be angry, there was no reason to punish Desirée for leaving. Bringing attention to how much his feelings were hurt could undermine their relationship; she'd feel even more guilty and he'd be that selfish boy his mother always accused him of being. If ever a time called for empathy and understanding, this was it. *No*, he told himself, *this isn't about my feelings.*

He understood that Desirée would never be happy without her mother's support and esteem, no matter how much the two women fought or disagreed. Deep down, they loved and admired each other, but neither could seem to relinquish their continuing battle for dominance. How could Scott bring them together? What would reconcile all parties?

Breaking into his thoughts, Celine said, "Desirée is going to be so angry with me."

Her comment propelled Scott into action. Standing, he prepared to leave. "Listen, Celine," he said, putting on his coat. "Don't call her when I leave. Give me a day." There was no practical way to exact a promise from her. If Celine couldn't understand that it was in her best interests to resist the urge to call Desirée for the next twenty-four hours, then she would wish that she had when Desirée finished with her.

"What are you going to do?" Celine asked, wide-eyed.

"I'll tell you tomorrow," he said, rushing from the apartment.

thirty-nine

NINE O'CLOCK IN THE MORNING IS, UNDER NORMAL circumstances, too early for a house call, but these circumstances were anything but ordinary. Scott passed Desirée's apartment and arrived at 445 Avenue Foch, just two blocks further on. Madame de Bellecourt's mansion sat on the tree-lined boulevard, a five-story Haussmann edifice of limestone and marble as imposing as the woman who resided within. A two-meter-high fence of black hexagonal rods with gold-tipped spears encircled the property. Generous etched-glass double doors stood at the top of four steps. Inside, paintings of illustrious French generals from the Napoleonic era decorated the lobby walls, a detailed Gobelins-esque carpet stretching across the floor.

The building's concierge announced Scott's presence by telephone before ushering him to the elevator. Arriving at the fifth floor, he was greeted by a gray and white uniformed woman who showed him into the grand salon. Decorated in gold and red embroidered silks, the room of inestimable formality contained an antique clavichord; it was a royal room, a close cousin of Versailles.

Already formally dressed in a Chanel suit of soft blue with cream piping on the lapels and cuffs, Madame de Bellecourt stood waiting, a grim look on her face. Her dress and the tone of her salutation revealed that she had expected him.

"Good morning, Monsieur Stoddard," she said with a steely demeanor. "I presume your unannounced and inconveniently early visit is due to your having been informed of Desirée's situation?"

"Madame, first let me say that I owe you an apology for my considerable part in this awkward circumstance. I hope you will accept it, as it is sincere. It is completely understandable that you are angry with Desirée and me. Nevertheless, you and I, as improbable as it may sound, must work together to resolve any issues that remain as an impediment to our marriage."

"She's very upset," Madame said. "She had not planned this. I'm upset too. It's embarrassing."

Firmly facing Madame de Bellecourt, Scott squared his shoulders. "I'm elated," he said. "Surprised, but happy."

The older woman shook her head. "You can afford those sentiments because you don't fully understand the consequences. You are so young."

"Perhaps, but Desirée's not. She will be a fantastic mother, and I intend to be her equal as a husband and father. Yes, we're all in shock right now, but I am sure your reservations about our marriage will fade away when this grandchild is born. I'm asking you, begging you, to put aside your preconceptions and focus on the most important issues. Let's find a way to make this right."

"And you feel that to be what, exactly?" Madame de Bellecourt inquired icily.

"You and I and Desirée all know very well what the best course is. We must get married as soon as possible. In the long run, the exact timing of the marriage and our baby's arrival fade in importance. For all concerned, please forgive Desirée; I'm sure she is in Geneva grieving because she has disappointed you. She doesn't deserve this treatment; she's going to be a mother."

"This is not at all what I had planned," Madame asserted.

"I understand. It is not what any of us planned," Scott reiterated. While he had no desire to touch Madame de Bellecourt as he might her daughter, he moved closer. "If we leave in the next two hours, we can be in Geneva by nightfall."

Desirée's mother narrowed her eyes. "Desirée will be very unhappy that you have found out her secret," she said. "Nor will she like being surprised. She told me she needed time alone to think things through. Why should we ignore her wishes?"

"You are correct, but I predict that, after the first few moments, she will be relieved that I know her secret and bolstered by our united presence. Will you come with me, Madame?"

"You've given me no choice," she said. "I'll have Vincent bring the car around. We'll pick you up in an hour."

Jubilant, Scott hurried back to Desirée's apartment. It was just the right amount of time to put a few things together, telephone Father Kohler, and rejoin Madame de Bellecourt. The Mercedes pulled up shortly before eleven o'clock, and they left for Geneva.

SEVEN HOURS IN THE CAR LAY BEFORE SCOTT AND MADAME de Bellecourt, an eternity. They sat quietly in the back seat; although family chauffeurs traditionally could be counted on for discretion, Scott wasn't sure about Vincent. He guessed that whatever Madame was willing to discuss would indicate her trust and the degree of discretion required. When Madame asked about the state of the dispensation, the question was answered. Scott said he had called Father Kohler that very morning to determine the status of their petition, and the priest said he would contact Monsignor de Pita as soon as possible. Scott was to call back the next day.

Scott had so many questions. When and how did Desirée find out she was pregnant? Had she been to a doctor? No matter how discreet Vincent might be, Scott couldn't ask these questions of Madame de Bellecourt. She was of a more refined era. Desirée's mother probably didn't know the answers, and her daughter's delicate condition was not something she'd feel comfortable discussing with Desirée's lover in the first place. This situation was highly irregular and embarrassing, and Madame de Bellecourt was having a difficult time accepting the inconvenient circumstance. Things like this just didn't happen in the de Bellecourt family. Scott understood she might be looking to place blame, and of the two possibilities—himself and Desirée—he was by far the more likely candidate. Given the level of her anger, she probably thought it prudent to remain silent.

They silently gazed out the car windows at the passing scenery. After a few hundred kilometers, Scott said, "I love her, you know."

"I know, and Desirée loves you. If only love were all that is required."

"It's the most important thing," Scott said. Emboldened by the slight smile on her face, he added, "I hope that you will find a way to forgive both of us."

forty

SHORTLY AFTER SIX THAT EVENING, THE MERCEDES turned into the driveway of the Geneva house. Desirée, dressed in a full-skirted primrose dress with small white polka dots, her hair pulled into a casual ponytail, looked more beautiful than ever. From the car, Scott noted her surprise.

As the chauffeur scurried around to open Madame de Bellecourt's door, Desirée exclaimed, "Maman, what are you doing here?"

Scott opened his door and stood, silently regarding Desirée over the roof of the Mercedes. Was it surprise or shock that registered on her face? Maybe it was both. It didn't matter. Scott rushed toward Desirée. Taking her in his arms, he buried his face in her hair and whispered, "I love you, my darling."

"Are you angry?" she asked.

"A little, but I'm happy too."

Madame de Bellecourt followed the couple into the house. Once inside, conversation was difficult. Realizing that mother and daughter probably wanted some time alone, he excused himself to freshen up. He tried to stay away a good half-hour, taking a shower and shaving. When he returned, Desirée was alone in the salon, quietly crying.

When he sat down next to her, Desirée leaned into the firm wall of his chest. "What happened?" Scott inquired tenderly.

"We talked and apologized to each other. Maman said she was sorry she got so angry. And then she asked if she could help me plan our wedding."

"I'm glad. I talked her into coming here for that very reason, and I'm happy she found the courage," he said, smiling softly. Desirée looked up at Scott, and he knew the question in her eyes.

"Is it true, then? She said you gave her the idea, and she knew you were right. But what about you, my darling; what are you feeling?"

Scott listened to the sounds of the house for a few minutes, deciding what he wanted to say. "At first, I was angry—more about your leaving like you did. When I found out about the pregnancy; well, it does take two, you know." He gazed at her fondly and was relieved to see a small, answering smile to his little joke. "I understand how it all happened, and I am not unhappy with our solution. I've always wanted to marry you, and it only follows that you would be the mother of our children. It all just arrived a little earlier than expected," Scott said.

There was a sobbing embrace, and reassurances flowed between them, each affirming to the other their love and respect.

With dusk, a slight chill permeated the air, and Desirée and Scott retired to the great room, where a fire smoldered in the hearth. Secure in his arms, Desirée rested her head against his chest; Scott massaged the back of her neck, whispering over and over that he loved her. He kissed her cheeks, her forehead, and then her mouth, never releasing her from the pressure of his embrace.

"My darling," he said, "tell me. Tell me everything."

Desirée sighed. "When I missed my period, I panicked; you know I'm always on schedule, like a Swiss train. I knew I was pregnant before going to the doctor because I felt different," she said, stroking her still flat belly. "And the doctor confirmed it; I'm pregnant. Then I thought of you, and us, and all the plans we had made. You're so young; you might not be ready to be a papa. And I worried—I'm almost thirty—is this too old? I felt responsible, and I couldn't face the idea of telling you. And my mother was so angry; I couldn't disagree with her judgment that I'd acted irresponsibly. With that swirling in my head, I just simply and regrettably ran away. Truly, though, I only needed to get away to think."

In the glow of the fire, Desirée's hair gleamed like liquid gold. Scott stroked its fine softness absently. Under his soothing caress, Desirée opened her heart to him.

"I can't say that I'm ready, but in truth is one ever ready to become a mother? I'm beginning to cherish the idea, and I wonder—will it be a boy or a girl? I'm thinking of baby clothes, and nursery décor, and what I should eat. I'm fast becoming an expectant mother."

Scott kissed her head. "Sweetheart, you are completely wonderful. I love you even more than ever, if that's possible," he said. "You and your mother need to plan the wedding quickly, so it takes place in the least amount of time possible." Pulling back, he lifted her chin so their eyes met. "Desirée, you haven't asked me how I found out."

"I'd told two people: Maman and Celine. I knew you would seek Celine out, and I knew she wouldn't be able to resist telling you if pressed."

"You're right," Scott said. "I begged her. Has she called you since I saw her?"

"No; she's so sweet and is probably much too frightened to call."

"Celine is a good friend—to both of us. Maybe you should call her," Scott said. "She could use a good night's sleep."

Desirée called her friend. Celine was relieved that Desirée wasn't angry, and Desirée was glad Scott had learned her secret. From the bedroom, Scott could hear Desirée reinforce Celine's promise not to discuss the situation with anyone. She'd surely tell Albert, but he was a first-class gentleman, and Scott would bet that the news would go no further. The women said their farewells fondly, without any hard feelings.

Madame de Bellecourt, Desirée, and Scott shared an impromptu dinner of cheese, cold cuts, rustic bread, and wine. After that brief glimpse into her vulnerable side, Madame had resumed her more comfortable role as matriarch, mistress of her domain, and returned to that intimidating straight posture, stiff manner, and Parisian dialect that warded off all but the most secure. As they dined and chatted, Scott hoped there were no new wars on the horizon for these two stubborn women; he'd heard about mothers and daughters wrestling over wedding details. Madame had her own connections in Paris and

Geneva; she was indispensable as an ally, and they couldn't waste any time. Scott envisioned the situation as an hourglass with the sands gradually, but inexorably slipping away.

Catching Desirée out of the side of his eye, Scott realized that she was closely monitoring his attention. Did he harbor any anger? Did he resent her in any way? Was there any hesitancy in his affection? She'd use this as a barometer for his affection, and Scott became determined that his actions would match the love he felt for her.

In bed, he pulled her close, enveloping her with his body. He caressed her, teasing her about the changes in her body to come. Their lovemaking was slow and tender, but there were passionate murmurs of approval. With the last sighs and release came the feeling that, once again, they were together.

DESIRÉE AND HER MOTHER SAT IN THE BREAKFAST ROOM adjacent to the kitchen, the beautiful view from the bay window of the lake and Alps beyond the backdrop to their domestic tableau. As Scott joined them, he noticed with pleasure they were discussing the wedding. He greeted Madame, embraced Desirée, and informed Helena of his request for breakfast.

"My dear, I think it should be a wedding with family and close friends. Not too grand, mind you, but not too small, either," Madame continued.

"Yes, Maman, I agree," Desirée said. "If small, the wedding must appear intentionally private."

Over breakfast, they solidified the essential details: Scott and Desirée would be married at St. Pierre de Chaillot, near the apartment on Avenue Foch, in six weeks, on a Friday, at noon. The reception would be held at Le Pré Catalan in the Bois de Boulogne. Desirée would be eleven or twelve weeks into her pregnancy; with the right dress, all should be concealed. (It would not be the first time, Madame de Bellecourt remarked conspiratorially, that Givenchy camouflaged an early start.)

Scott had news to share. "I heard from Father Kohler," he said.

"It is good news, I hope?" Desirée said, a worried look on her face.

"Provisionally good news. Within two weeks, you and I must appear in Rome for an interview. Monsignor de Pita will accompany us." At Desirée's excited reaction, Scott had to caution, "But there is a complication."

"A complication?" Madame inquired.

"Yes; I must bring a certificate to prove I was baptized in my church. My mother surely has my baptism certificate, and she'll want to know why I need it. The only recourse is to tell her about our impending marriage." Scott managed to look embarrassed under Madame de Bellecourt's incredulous stare. "I haven't told them. My parents haven't the slightest idea I proposed."

"Then you must tell them at once," Madame said. She stood, placed the phone receiver in Scott's hand, and left the room.

He looked at Desirée. "It's only ten o'clock in the morning. I'll call them around one o'clock, before my father goes to work."

As he replaced the phone, Desirée asked softly, "Are you going to tell them I'm pregnant?"

"I think it is preferable. I don't want to deceive them anymore. In the end, they'll know; they can count, you know."

"Will they be angry?" Desirée said.

Scott knew it would be a difficult conversation. "They'll be shocked first, perhaps angry second."

forty-one

ONCE AGAIN, SCOTT WAS DREADING A PHONE CALL TO Charleston. He walked in the garden to clear his mind; when one o'clock came, he steeled himself and reached for the phone. He could see his hand shaking, and his breath was short. *Steady now*, he thought.

His mother answered. "Good morning, Mother," he said.

"Hello, dear. It's nice to hear from you." She sounded so pleased, and Scott immediately felt guilt. "Let me call your father—Edward! It's Scott!" She asked for him to wait a moment until he came to the phone. *Thank God Father is home*, Scott thought.

"Is anything wrong?" she asked, just as he heard the click of the line. "Hello, Son," his father said.

Scott collected himself. "No, Mother, nothing is wrong; I'm fine. But I have news. I know it will come as a shock, but Desirée and I have decided to get married in Paris, six weeks from now, and I hope you will come. You will love her, I'm sure. She's very special, and she means more to me than anything." There—he'd had his say. It was out. Now it was their turn.

There was a long, shocked silence. Would there be an explosion, a hang-up, or a harangue? Anything was possible.

It was his mother who spoke next. "Is she . . . is she . . . pregnant?" his mother asked haltingly. Scott closed his eyes; he knew how hard it was for her to ask. "Yes," he said. Another stretch of nothingness, which was eventually punctuated by an audible sigh.

In a barely restrained shout, his mother let loose. "Scott, this is not the way we raised you! You've acted in a most irresponsible way, and now your entire future is at risk. How are you going to live? Is your father to support you both—the three of you—while you continue school? Did you ever stop to think how this could possibly work?" She gathered her breath, and Scott knew better than to interrupt. Silently, he waited. "No, you don't need to answer that. It's obvious you didn't. If you had, we wouldn't find ourselves in this position. It's so embarrassing."

At this point, his father interrupted. "Mother, it's spilt milk; he's got to marry her."

"It's not like that," Scott said. "I *want* to marry her. I'd proposed before we knew." He heard his mother's gasp. *In for a penny, in for a pound*, he thought. *Might as well come clean all around*. He plunged ahead. "We were going to marry anyway. This just pushed it forward a little."

"How does her family feel about it?" his father asked.

"At first, her mother was angry and reacted as you have, Mother, but now she has adjusted to the idea; she and Desirée are planning the wedding. Sadly, Desirée's father passed away several years ago."

"And how long has her mother, Madame de—de—, oh bother, whatever her name—how long has *she* known?" his mother asked. "Are we the last to find out?"

"Madame de Bellecourt has only know for a day or two," Scott said gently. "Desirée herself hasn't known much longer. I found out just yesterday."

His father, the more practical of the two, wanted nothing more than to put this situation to rest. He said, "So Scott, what do you want from us?"

In the past, Scott had thought his father's rather Spartan ways cruel and uncaring, but in this instance, he welcomed that unvarnished directness. With one question, Edward Stoddard had changed the focus from what and how it had all happened to making plans for the future.

"Mother, I know this will come as a shock, but Desirée is Catholic." His parents were reeling from the pregnancy, he knew, and the

Stoddards had viewed Catholics with distrust. But what could they do? Deeply rooted in their upbringing was a sense of responsibility. Their son had gotten this woman in trouble, and they would see to it that he did the right and honorable thing. With that in mind, Scott secured his mother's promise to send his baptism certificate that very day.

As the shock wore off, his mother began to pepper him with more questions. "Desirée lives in Geneva, doesn't she?" his mother asked. "In your letter, you said she was Swiss and French. And she's a fund-raiser. What else should we know?"

"She was married for a short time—there were no children—and the marriage was annulled four years ago. Desirée has homes in Geneva and Paris."

"Houses in Geneva and Paris?" Scott's father chimed in. "She must be rich."

"She is well off financially," Scott said.

Mr. Stoddard cut to the chase. "Is she going to support you?" he asked.

"Is that what the two of you have planned?" his mother asked. "What about all your future, your studies? A law degree?"

"We've talked about several possibilities," he said. "One of which is that I continue my studies. Another is to change direction toward a more professional degree. We're considering a few other options as well." Scott did not mention that he had been attending precious few classes at the university.

"This is not at all what we agreed on," his mother said. "You're throwing your education away, Scott."

"I'm sorry, but when our romance began, everything seemed so improbable. Then it all happened in a rush."

"Son," his father said patiently, "are you sure she loves you? I mean, she is more experienced—"

"Dad, I'm sure of Desirée's feelings."

Naturally, the Stoddards wanted to ask more questions and get more answers from Scott. His parents would need some time to get over the unexpected reversal of their dreams, and, with their background, some revision of their prejudices to accommodate Scott's

intended. That Desirée was Catholic and the child would be raised—
indoctrinated was the term his mother used—in that faith was a bitter
pill to swallow. Scott had heard his parents make innuendos about
Catholics since he was a child.

Though the Stoddards hadn't learned half of what they wanted to
know, Scott was able to get off the phone with a promise to call again
within the next few days. In the meantime, they would plan to be in
Paris the third week in July. Their goodbyes were not happy, but Scott
reflected that the discussion could have been worse. He had presented
them with a fait accompli. Desirée's pregnancy had the unexpected
(but welcomed) consequence of silencing criticism of and protest
about their marriage from all parental parties.

THE LUNCH TABLE WAS SET WITH THE FINEST SILVER AND
Bernardaud china and Baccarat crystal glasses. Madame de Bellecourt
and Desirée watched Scott as he approached, looking for a sign of victory or defeat and satisfaction or misery—any hint as to how the conversation with his parents had gone. Toying with them, he purposely
kept an impassive stare.

"Oh, my darling," Desirée said breathlessly. "How did it go?"

"As well as could be expected under the circumstances. And I didn't
have to tell them. My mother guessed immediately."

"Ah—we know where you get your intelligence, Monsieur Stoddard," Madame said dryly.

forty-two

D ESIRÉE DECIDED IT WOULD BE BETTER IF HER
mother returned to Paris, where she could handle any
number of wedding details better: invitations engraved
and posted, priest and church engaged, date reserved, menu and wines
selected, flowers ordered, wardrobes selected, hotel for Scott's parents
reserved, and chauffeur and car hired for their use. The list went on and
on. Meanwhile, Desirée and Scott would wait on the baptism certificate to arrive and then proceed to Rome for the interview.

With wardrobes in mind, Madame de Bellecourt wanted Desirée
to return to Paris with her, but she refused to leave Scott again, and he
liked that. Desirée decided she would begin the fittings for her wedding
gown and trousseau at the Geneva outposts of her favorite designers.

And they reminded Scott he needed two witnesses. He should give
some thought as to whom he might choose. Designating two best men
was easy, Scott said; that is, if they would accept. "I would like for Jean
and Albert to stand up for me."

"I think both would be perfect," Desirée said. "Celine will be so
pleased."

"Could you broach the subject with Celine, so Albert will not be
completely surprised when I ask?" Desirée gave Scott a quick kiss to
say yes.

❧

Once Madame de Bellecourt left for Paris, Scott and Desirée were glad to be alone again. The weather in Switzerland can be glorious in June and July, and they took well-worn paths crisscrossing the countryside. Wildflowers of every possible species colored the meadows, popping up among the clumps of luscious green grass in random bouquets as only nature can arrange. They used these carefree days to fall in love all over again. Desirée's pregnancy brought a new level of trust to their relationship. The gravity of their situation was not lost on the couple; Scott and Desirée had matriculated from lovers to fiancés to expectant parents within a two-week period. Scott detected slight changes in Desirée's appearance already; even without makeup, her cheeks were rosier, more peaches and cream. When he looked into her aquamarine eyes, it felt as though he could see forever. Desirée had never seemed so attentive or as tender as these days before their trip to Rome. Neither of them anticipated the petition might be refused—to the contrary, they were proceeding as if it were already a fact. To add to Scott's bliss, the school year had just ended; with no more pressure to study, his conscience could take a rest, and he resolved that after the honeymoon, he would make an appointment with the dean to propose a new arrangement—that is, if the school administration would agree.

At last it came. Scott's certificate of baptism was delivered by registered mail to Desirée's house in Geneva. So much hinged on this single sheet of paper! Though not an impressive document, it was, more importantly, authentic; slightly tattered, blurred by a water stain, the important parts of the text—Scott's full name, the date of baptism, church and officiating pastor, and two signatories—were fully legible.

Before they called to set up the meeting in Rome with Monsignor de Pita, Scott said, "Darling, we should invite Father Kohler to assist in the ceremony in Paris." Desirée was two steps ahead; she and her mother had already discussed the trusted priest's role in their wedding.

When Desirée phoned Father Kohler, they first addressed details pertaining to the Rome meeting. Then, she announced that, if all went well, she and Scott intended to be married in Paris in mid-July. Scott couldn't help but eavesdrop; he gleaned that Father Kohler expressed congratulations and wished them well; then, Desirée asked if he would do them the honor of officiating at the marriage mass. From her happy responses, Scott could tell the priest was deeply touched and had accepted without hesitation. But then, Scott could see Desirée shifting uncomfortably, and there was a decided pause in the conversation. In her most confidential tone, he heard her say, "Father, the seeming speed with which we have decided to move forward is in deference to my mother. As you know, she is very devout and traditional. She persuaded us that, if we love each other, it would be imminently preferable to marry sooner rather than continuing to live together and break the sacraments." He noticed she gave the priest no mention of the coming baby. Scott guessed she felt the omission was a necessary fib.

forty-three

THEY WERE SIX IN ALL: CARDINAL EDUARDO MASSELA, two assisting monsignors, and Desirée and Scott, who were represented by Monsignor de Pita. Dressed in a Chanel suit of navy blue and white in a raw silk with large, dark blue buttons, a small pillbox hat with subtle veil, and a silk white scarf encircling her neck, Desirée presented a picture of demure grace. Scott properly looked the part of her fiancé in an elegant Lanvin navy blue gabardine suit, Charvet white shirt, and blue Hermes tie with a periwinkle flower pattern. All were seated in high-backed chairs surrounding a conference table in an old palace on a side street steps away from St. Peter's Basilica.

The second-story room overlooked a small courtyard piazza where a fountain burbled, surrounded by terra cotta pots of pink geraniums; sounds of laughter and screams from a group of young school children as they played football during recess floated through the open windows. A mural of angels and clouds had been painted on the domed ceiling.

They were now subject to the determination of the Congregation for Divine Worship and the Discipline of the Sacraments. Cardinal Massela was a portly man in his late sixties, balding, with hooded eyes and soft hands that had never experienced manual labor. He wore the formal purple vestments; the two monsignors were dressed in the somber, traditional black with white collar. Scott and Desirée let Monsignor de Pita do the talking. Since the discussion was entirely in

Italian, Scott hoped that Desirée understood what was being said, as he could only grasp a few words.

Scott and Desirée had arrived the day before and booked rooms at the Excelsior hotel on the Via Veneto, next to the American Embassy and one of the most fashionable shopping and dining street of Rome. The monsignor joined them that afternoon; he wanted to prepare them for the interview: how to conduct themselves and answer certain questions that might be posed. He reiterated—the decision had previously been made—yet only last week, he had amended the petition to allow for the new July date. The normal pace would have put the marriage off for six months to a year to provide suitable instruction time for a non-Catholic. Monsignor de Pita noted that the cardinal had been a bit grumpy when this unexpected amendment was sprung, but in the end, the monsignor had persuaded the cardinal by informing him that the bride-to-be's mother had pushed for the new date. Cardinal Massela was in accord with her reasoning and applauded the devout lady's influence. And lastly, Monsignor de Pita gently reminded Scott and Desirée several times that one completely unacceptable answer to any of the interview questions could derail their granted dispensation.

While Cardinal Massela spoke at length to Monsignor de Pita, he would from time to time nod this way and that to Desirée; occasionally, he would gesture toward Scott as well. Then, he began to address them directly, the tone of his voice shifting from that of an official to a kindly priest. In French and English, he asked Desirée and Scott if they loved each other. Did they understand the sanctity of marriage? Were they prepared to follow the sacraments regarding the union of two people in matrimony? There was a list of psychological questions, background review, inquiries as to their promise to raise any children as Catholic. When it seemed he must have reached the end and exhausted all possible questions, Cardinal Massela asked one more.

"My dear children, when a man and woman from different backgrounds approach marriage, sometimes the greatest impediments to their happiness can be those people who should want their happiness the most—their families. Can you assure me that both of your families approve and have given their consent to this marriage, so help you God?"

"Oui," Desirée said. Scott, too, answered in the affirmative.

Desirée and Scott were asked to step outside into the anteroom as the committee deliberated a final time. Less than ten minutes later, Monsignor de Pita asked them to come back inside. Cardinal Massela read from the dispensation document; it was a heavy parchment, featuring calligraphy and illuminated hand-painted initial capital letters adorned with gold leaf. After he finished reading the text, he dipped a quill pen into an antique ink well and signed the document with a flourish. One of the assisting monsignors lit a candle, melted a red glob of wax, and impressed the official seal.

Rising, Cardinal Massela wished Desirée and Scott a bountiful and happy life together, congratulated Monsignor de Pita, and thanked his assistants before calling for a moment of prayer. He implored God to look over these young people and provide them guidance and solace throughout their lives.

When they reached the exit, Scott and Desirée would have broken into a full-tilt run in their excitement and elation, alternating between kisses and hugs, but they showed restraint out of modesty for Monsignor de Pita, who was too dignified for such celebration (though he did agree to join them for lunch at Tre Scalini). One of Rome's most popular restaurants, the Piazza Novona sidewalk café featured darling tablecloths and umbrellas, and traditionally uniformed waiters. The happy party was shown to a fine table, and they ordered a feast: massive artichokes, steamed with garlic, mint, and parsley; grilled scampi with white rice; a bottle of dry, white Frascati; and dessert, lemon sorbet with fresh slices of blood orange from Messina.

Scott lifted his glass in a toast. "Monsignor, Desirée and I can't thank you enough for taking on our petition. It was enormously important to us, and we are certain that you are the only one who could have succeeded," he said.

"My children, you give me too much praise. You had a very worthy (and obviously, correct) premise that made my work easy. The baptism certificate was key."

All modesty aside, Scott and Desirée were convinced that, but for Monsignor de Pita's astute and expert guidance through the maze of Vatican process, their dispensation petition could have languished in some prelate's office ad infinitum. The monsignor deflected their praise with the deference they had come to expect; he had already sent them his fee, and it was as modest as its maker. But Desirée had a surprise up her sleeve.

Handing the monsignor an envelope, she said, "Some time ago, before you took our case, Father Kohler told us of your devotion to Santabono Children's Hospital in Naples. You must allow us to share our happiness and celebrate our good fortune with those children. I have enclosed a check that can be used for the hospital in any manner you prescribe. I hope you will understand that, from our vantage point, a simple thank you is inadequate."

Completely floored—the good man had expected nothing but his modest fee—the monsignor wiped tears from his eyes. "*Cara*, you honor me, and I and the children of Santabono thank you for your generosity," he said in a choked voice.

As they parted, goodbyes were difficult. The usual well wishes were exchanged, as were appeals to be remembered to Father Kohler, and Monsignor de Pita's request to give thanks to Madame de Bellecourt for her assistance with moving the marriage forward. Scott and Desirée effusively thanked their friend again. Back at the hotel, Scott decided to change the gravitas of the mood. He left Desirée at the hotel with instructions to change into some slacks and meet him in half an hour at the entrance.

She was waiting in a pair of camel pants, emerald green blouse, and camel-colored ankle boots when he returned, a matching cardigan thrown over her shoulders. She gave a knowing grin as she watched him enter the hotel's grand *porte cochère*. Scott stopped directly in front of her and asked, "Want a ride, little girl?"

Scott had first seen an Italian two-wheel motor scooter (a Vespa) in *Roman Holiday*, the film starring Gregory Peck and Audrey Hepburn. Mismatched in every way—Hepburn a princess; Peck a reporter—the two characters rode around Rome on a motor scooter. In the space of that afternoon, they'd fallen in love. Desirée adored the film, and Scott wanted to create a similarly romantic afternoon, certain Desirée would enjoy the experience. They could both do with blowing off some steam. Without hesitation, she swung her handbag cross body before straddling the light green Vespa behind Scott.

The light from the southern sky lasted well into the early June evening, casting long shadows across the monuments and antiquities spread across the eternal city. They cruised the Via Veneto to the bottom of the Spanish Steps and then chased the sun along the Via Condotti where, just the day before, Scott had purchased Desirée's engagement ring, a square-cut Bulgari emerald as impressive as his exaggerated allowance could allow. As they rode, Desirée wrapped her arms tightly around his body, her cheek resting against his back; the ride sparking a more playful and romantic state of mind after the serious ordeal they'd experienced. Stopping at a small café in the Piazza del Popolo, they sipped a cappuccino. Next stop—the famous Trevi Fountain, where Scott parked the Vespa so they could admire the multiple statues—Roman gods of the sea and all its creatures—that decorated the splashing bowl. The main pool was illuminated by submerged lights, which cast a shimmering blue green glow. The effect was reminiscent of a grotto.

"Shall we throw a few coins into the fountain to ensure we come back to Rome?"

"Let's throw a lot of them," Desirée said.

As Scott tossed his coins, he kissed her and said, happily, "The next time we come, we'll be three."

forty-four

B ACK IN GENEVA FOR A FEW DAYS, SCOTT HAD A LUNCH rendezvous with Jean, who was still unaware of recent developments. Scott hoped that Jean wouldn't be annoyed with him. Since his romance with Desirée began, he hadn't been a very good friend, particularly considering how Jean had treated Scott when he first arrived in Switzerland, helping him to assimilate.

They met at the Café de la Paix restaurant in the old town. Jean was reading the *Tribune de Genève,* no doubt checking the details from last night's loss (Geneva versus Zurich, 2–1). When Scott entered the restaurant, Jean stood, and they embraced once, then twice more. He seemed the same friendly, jovial, and fun-loving Jean whom Scott always found so enjoyable. After the two men exchanged pleasantries and commiserated on last night's loss, Jean asked, "So, to what do I owe the honor of your presence?"

Scott called the waiter and ordered a bottle of vintage Krug. Jean raised an eyebrow. "We must be celebrating," he said, rubbing his hands together eagerly. "What is it?"

"I have a request, but you must promise to say yes," Scott said.

"Okay, you have it: *yes.* Now, what have I just agreed to?"

"Desirée and I are getting married in Paris, on July 23, a Friday, and I want you to be my witness."

At first, Jean didn't say a word. Then he rose from his chair and embraced Scott in an unabashed fashion, whispering, "My God, it is unbelievable. Yes, my friend, yes. Congratulations! Please convey my best wishes to the countess. Of course, I will be honored to be your witness."

"Jean, you are a better friend to me than I am to you," Scott said with feeling.

"Don't be crazy," Jean replied. "But, my God, what a surprise."

"I guess we surprised everybody," Scott said.

AFTER A WONDERFUL LUNCH WITH JEAN, SCOTT WALKED TO the nearby garage to retrieve his Austin-Healey. On the second lower level in the garage, two men in mechanic's work clothes hovered over his car. Perhaps someone had backed into his fender. Scott approached for a closer look; suddenly, the more heavy-set of the two grabbed his wrist, twisting that arm into a hammer lock. The man's other arm snaked around Scott's neck in a choke hold. His partner stuffed a dirty rag in Scott's mouth, stifling any attempt to shout for help. Though he struggled, Scott couldn't get free. The men slammed him to the ground, where he was pinned between the Austin-Healey and another car. They held him facedown on the pavement.

The burly one said in French, heavy with a thick Sicilian accent, "This is a warning. Leave the countess, or next time we won't be so nice." With that, the other man let loose with two violent kicks to Scott's ribs, and he gasped for air around the gag. Scott rolled in pain on the garage floor; by the time he could see again, they were gone.

Calm, calm, he told himself. Scott pulled the dirty cloth from his mouth and struggled into the car. Reflected in the rearview mirror, his face had all the pallor of a ghost. His first inclination was to report the attack to the police; but on reflection, what would he accomplish by doing so? He could see it now. There would be the business of filing police reports; the newspapers and photographers would follow. There would be no way to trace the two thugs, who were clearly profession- als. Work hats had been pulled down, and collars pulled up, obscuring their faces. What with the dim lighting in the garage, Scott would have difficulty describing their appearance. The attack was so sudden—he couldn't remember anything remarkable about either one, except that they were very strong and surely Italian.

This had to be Stefano's doing.

He must be desperate if he thinks these Mafiosi will scare me off, Scott thought. Had the count known Desirée was pregnant, he doubted Stefano would have bothered. An Italian *macho* such as the count would never want a woman who was pregnant with another man's baby.

&

WHEN SCOTT ARRIVED HOME, HIS SIDE ACHED LIKE HE HAD been shot. Desirée was in the salon upstairs at her writing desk.

"Darling, you look a fright," she exclaimed. "What happened?" Peering closely at him, she gasped. "Why is there blood on your shirt?"

"Two men just threatened me and roughed me up in the garage near the restaurant."

"What do you mean, 'roughed you up'?"

Scott took off his jacket and lifted his shirt so Desirée could see the bruises that were already turning his side purple. And now they both saw the bloody scrape on his forearm. Wincing, Scott said, "Two Sicilians grabbed me; one of them held me down while the other kicked me. They warned me to leave you."

"It's Stefano," Desirée said, beginning to cry. "He's insane with jealousy and possessiveness. We must call the police."

Scott tried to calm her down. She said it was her fault, that he should leave her if it meant they'd hurt him. He told her he wouldn't leave; together, they would work through this. Once they were married, Stefano would see the futility of his actions, and he reminded her that the police would attract the press, and then a scandal would begin. They couldn't afford that right now.

At last, Desirée agreed to drop the idea of notifying the police, but it was harder to dissuade her from confronting Stefano.

Scott tried reasoning. "That's what he wants, to scare us," he said "We can't let him win. Stefano wants attention from you, even negative attention; it's your indifference he can't stand."

But the next morning, Desirée insisted on contacting her attorney, Wilhelm Waldmeister. His first reaction, like any rational person's, was to call the police. Desirée explained the consequences and how futile involving the police would be. She spoke at length on who the likely suspect was—Stefano—though Waldmeister cautioned against jumping to conclusions without proof. "But who else could it be?" she countered.

Scott asked to speak to the attorney; Desirée gave him the phone.

"Scott Stoddard here; I'm Countess de Rovere's fiancé, and I'm sure the count is behind this attack. How do I know this? A few weeks ago, his attorney in Geneva offered me 300,000 Swiss francs to leave the countess." Desirée's face registered something between rage and horror as she gave a muffled gasp of disbelief. "Of course, I refused. And yes, I kept the note and envelope."

With this new evidence, Waldmeister was more adamant that they call the police. In addition, he wanted to contact the count's attorney and warn him to rein in his client. The threat of a lawsuit might help Stefano regain some sanity. But Scott reminded him—while the attorney had offered the bribe, Scott would bet he had no knowledge of the incident in the garage. Had the count made him complicit in the dusting? As Scott posited various scenarios where enlisting the count's attorney could backfire, Waldmeister grunted, and Scott interpreted that as agreement.

At a minimum, Waldmeister insisted they engage a company that provided bodyguards to Geneva's diplomatic corps. Desirée thought hiring security was a good idea; could they be discreet, though? Waldmeister reminded her that one of the primary deterrents of having bodyguards is their visibility; their sheer presence wards off all but the most determined. Scott, realizing that no one who was serious could be completely deterred, hoped that frightening Stefano would be enough. *Although the count was stupid*, Scott thought, *perhaps he was not so stupid as to follow through on the threat.*

They wrapped up the discussion with Waldmeister. Scott hung up the phone and turned to find Desirée with her hands on her hips. "Why didn't you tell me about the bribe?"

"I didn't want you to be upset."

"But now I am upset."

"Look, Desirée, you're frightened. This isn't about the offer." Taking her in his arms, he teased her. "Oh, the offer was very tempting. I figured if things didn't work out, I could circle back and take his money." She slapped at him playfully, the tense mood broken. "You're so mean. I guess you left some on the table, and now you're stuck with me."

They wrestled together. Despite his sore ribs, Scott worked her to the ground, covering Desirée with his body. "No," he growled in her ear. "I'm stuck on you."

forty-five

WALDMEISTER WORKED FAST. THE SECURITY CON-
tingent arrived that afternoon. Scott and Desirée went
out to meet them. The head of the detail was Heinz Bergenheit, a Swiss German, who made Scott feel safer immediately. Bergenheit informed them that one security person would be parked in a
car at the property's entrance, another outside in front of the house, and
another would roam around the back. The men, dressed in unassuming
gray suits, were impressive in size and professionalism. When Scott
asked if they were armed, Bergenheit's quick nod assured him they were.

Two teams of three, in twelve-hour shifts (from six to six) was the
schedule. A separate detail would accompany Scott and Desirée on any
activities outside the home, whether they went together or separately.
Bergenheit urged Scott and Desirée to follow their detail's instructions, even if they believed them nonsensical, reiterating that they
couldn't protect an uncooperative client. When the couple returned to
Paris, the office there would take over security.

Overwhelmed, Scott and Desirée listened without asking any
questions. They went back inside, leaving the security personnel to take
up their positions.

"This is going to cost a fortune," Scott said.

"Should we send Stefano a bill?" Desirée asked sarcastically.

He rubbed the spot on his side that bloomed with painful bruises,
now beginning to turn a sickly green, and clenched his fist. "I'd like to
send him something, but it's not a bill."

"He'll give up when we're married."

Wedding invitations had gone out the week before with an admonition to observe the couple's request for secrecy. Still, friends were calling to congratulate Desirée, and most came with inquisitions about the suddenness of the decision. They'd become quite practiced in dodging questions. Some may have been suspicious; of course, seven months after the wedding, when the birth could well take place, the premature and pregnant-before-married camps would be divided on the answer.

THERE WERE NO MORE ATTACKS, AND SCOTT AND DESIRÉE returned to Paris in July. Their security team adjusted, and when people asked questions, they gave the believable excuse that paparazzi had become overly aggressive since their impending marriage had become common knowledge. The capital was gearing up for July 14, Bastille Day (French Independence Day), and the wedding would take place nine days later. Madame de Bellecourt had worked her will, coordinating, cajoling, and even bribing vendors into seeing things her way. Since her daughter was now an expectant mother, Madame had become even more formidable than before.

The women had things to do, so Scott invited Albert to lunch; he needed to formally ask him to be his second witness. He'd had Desirée pave the way with Celine, and he'd confirmed Albert's invitation, but Scott thought it was important to seal the agreement with a face-to-face meeting. Scott liked Albert very much. Though the doctor wasn't an overly formal person, Albert was serious, and he and Scott were quite similar. With his solid ethics and sense of fair play, he must have been a dedicated student and principled person. Less physically imposing than Scott, he had an intellectual side that appealed to Scott's sense of what really mattered.

Madame de Bellecourt had made a reservation for Scott at Fouquet's on the Champs-Élysées, in the club area, which was reserved for Parisians. The club section wasn't decorated much differently than the public space, but in the warm months, it concealed a sidewalk terrace, beautifully landscaped by containerized boxwoods and other formal, wax-leafed evergreens, and was outfitted with tables covered in delicate ivory linens, and wicker and rattan chairs stuffed with teal cushions. It wasn't that the lucky diners on the terrace were hidden from the public, but that the less-informed never saw the entrance, much less a table. French discretion and reserve were on full display, and Scott was glad his security contingent remained discreetly outside.

Quite naturally, Albert would be on time, if not early. He arrived dressed in a conservative, tweedy suit (more a winter costume, worn past its season of comfort) that demonstrated his focus was on his profession, not fashion. Scott admired Albert's lack of superficiality, his special charm. The two men had always socialized accompanied by Celine and Desirée, so Scott was interested to see if they could form a separate, personal connection.

At first, they struggled with the obligatory pronouncements and greetings, but there was a brief conversational respite as they ordered turbot and steamed potatoes with a Chassagne-Montrachet. After the waiter had left, they seemed to be at a new standstill. Albert's tortured face and nervous manner suggested he had something on his mind, something he was eager to discuss. Scott encouraged him to have a little more wine, which Albert accepted. Shifting slightly in his chair, Albert focused on the pepper mill, using more than necessary, before uncharacteristically blurting, "Scott, tell me; were you certain as to whether Desirée would say yes when you asked her to marry you?"

Oh—Scott knew what this was about; Albert was about to propose to Celine, and he wanted a few pointers. He smiled. *Women overestimate men's self-assurance*, he mused; *if they only knew*. Here was Albert, a leading cardiologist and man of intelligence and character, who was mentally pacing, wondering whether the woman he loved would give a yes or no. He was so uncertain of her answer that he hardly dared to ask the question. Meanwhile, his intended, the sweet Celine, was waiting and longing for him to ask that very question, simply bursting to say yes. Somehow, though, Albert couldn't imagine he was worthy of her approval. *Such is the mystery of love*, Scott thought.

"Of course, I was shaking," Scott said, hoping to give Albert courage. "It took me days to prepare my plea. I wrote it out, rehearsed, and tried to steel myself for the possibility of rejection—or worse, her derisive laughter. Those were difficult days, with sleepless nights, and bouts of indigestion." This got a laugh out of Albert. "But one lovely afternoon, I assumed the stereotypical position, got down on bended knee, and asked her if she would be my wife, half dreading the whole thing. Then, her answer came, easily, without equivocation, unexpectedly, joyously, and emphatically: yes. With that, all the tension and doubt drained away, and I was quite possibly the happiest of men." It hadn't quite gone like that, but how could Scott tell Albert that Desirée had put him off for weeks and that it had taken a baby and canonical dispensation to get to "yes"? No, Albert needed the fairytale version, and Scott happily—if somewhat less than candidly—obliged.

"It sounds so easy when you say it," Albert said. He shifted this way and that in his chair, drinking water and then more wine.

"Albert, listen to me. Celine loves you dearly. All you must do is ask, and she's yours. We all can see it in her eyes. She's just waiting for you."

Albert reached across the table to give Scott's hand a hearty shake, and then he stood up to embrace Scott in the French fashion. Was it Scott's imagination or was Albert standing a bit taller, a more confidant man?

"My dear Scott, may I ask another question?" Albert asked.

"Of course, please do." They resumed their seats, and Scott poured them both more wine.

"It might seem a little impertinent, and if it's none of my business, then please tell me. I will harbor no ill feelings."

"When someone prefaces a question with this much preamble, there is usually cause to worry," Scott said, laughing.

"Okay, here it is. How do you feel about finding yourself day after day in the company of all these wealthy and entitled people?"

"Win the prize, Albert. You can worry about the details of living later."

"I better ask Celine soon before I lose my nerve," Albert said. "And Scott, just to let you know, your secret is safe with me."

Secret? Scott presumed that Celine had confided Desirée's condition to Albert. *So much for the fairytale*, he thought.

THE MUSÉE NISSIM DE CAMONDO IN THE 8TH ARRONDISSE-ment was a residence that had been willed in trust to the French government, to be maintained in its original condition. What made the Musée Nissim de Camondo famous was its exquisite decorative arts, including place settings and silver. Desirée and Celine had conspired to spend a Saturday looking at the antique china collections; they were hoping to have a special pattern made for them at Sèvres. The women invited Scott and Albert to come with them on their expedition. The men lagged behind while Desirée and Celine wandered ahead, chatting about the art pieces.

"Scott, look," Albert said. He held a red box with a gold border and, stamped into the leather, one word: Cartier. Though no further explanation was necessary, he proudly lifted the hinged top and *voila*, Scott saw an emerald-cut diamond (so large it had to be four carats) with two round cut stones on each side. Even in the low light of the museum, it glistened. Scott gave his friend a congratulatory and conspiratorial smile.

"When?" he asked.

"Now," Albert replied. "Keep Desirée busy for a moment, will you?"

Scott sprang into action, moving ahead to ask Desirée to look at a beautiful vase he had seen in another room. Desirée followed him, but Scott could tell she didn't like being interrupted in her quest.

This left Albert and Celine alone in the museum's living room.

Only a minute passed before they both heard a happy squeal from Celine, followed by some nervous laughter, a little bawling, several sniffles, and Albert's voice calling, "You two can come back now."

They found Celine with big tears of joy and Albert with a Cheshire cat grin.

❦

DURING THESE LAST DAYS LEADING UP TO THE WEDDING, Scott managed to reconnect with Andre and Leon. They met at Époque, their usual haunt.

Their first two meetings had taken place during winter and early spring, but it was full summer now, so they took a table outside. In the nice months, tables spilled onto the Champs-Élysées' wide sidewalk and turned the corner onto the intersecting street. Trim evergreens in planters defined the restaurant's boundaries and offered a degree of privacy, while umbrellas shielded guests, food, and wine from too much direct sunlight. The waiters wore traditional black pants, bow ties, vests with a white shirts, and aprons common in brasseries. Still, the red and gold colors so prominent in the interior decoration of the restaurant flowed thematically onto the sidewalk, contributing to the festive atmosphere.

"My dear Scott, you honor us with your presence every three months," Andre said saucily. Jerking his head toward the ever-present security detail, he went on. "Leon has noticed that you have some new friends following," he said.

"Leon is too observant," Scott said. "The paparazzi, you know."

Grinning, Andre replied, "That's how we get our news about you."

"Well, I have news you can't get from them, at least not yet. The countess and I are to be married on July 23 at the Church of St. Pierre de Chaillot. I've come today to pass on the invitation. We hope you will come with your wives, of course."

Andre rose from his seat to wrap Scott in a genuine bear hug. "My God," he shouted, "what does one say, but congratulations *mon ami*; you are so full of surprises."

Leon seconded the well wishes. "Quite, quite stunning," he stammered. "Really stunning. Congratulations. My; you don't waste any time, do you?"

"I must admit I was worried, but this May-December romance has turned out superbly," Andre said.

"And you were worried about what, exactly?" Scott inquired.

"I don't have to tell you that the tabloids will know about this as soon as the invitations go out. That is, if they don't already know from their spies in the couture houses where the wedding trousseau originates. Or from the caterers. Or florists, or . . . you understand, Scott." Andre wasn't telling Scott anything he didn't already know. His friend continued.

"The wedding will be a spectacular story, and they'll play up every angle—if you understand my meaning. You're marrying the Countess de Rovere, and there's no way to keep the paparazzi away. They will know your every move in advance. They will be at the wedding and the reception. I'll bet they're even tracking where you plan to honeymoon. All you can do is limit their access."

"We're dealing with it," Scott huffed, irritated at Andre's warnings.

"Remember, you can't even trust your friends. What about the count?"

"What about him?"

"He's disturbingly possessive. Count de Rovere was incensed when she secured an annulment."

"He's disturbed all right."

"Is that why you have the security?" Scott declined to answer, but his response was unnecessary. Andre said, "He's dangerous, Scott, and likely more dangerous now that you plan to marry."

It was almost as if Andre were privy to the events of the last few weeks. Everything had seemed to be lining up in a most favorable way: the dispensation, the wedding plans, the special friends on board, a minimum of innuendo and gossip.

And then some three weeks ago, a story had appeared about the Countess de Rovere's impending marriage to an unknown university student; Scott was even mentioned by name. The headline, "American Student Captures Countess's Heart and Hoard," painted Scott as a gold digger, a less than complimentary picture of his intentions. Stefano had added to the tasteless speculation, and some of the specifics indicated an informer within the wedding party. Desirée was upset; Madame de Bellecourt had found it necessary to retire to her bedroom for the day, after the story was published. Scott prayed no one discovered that Desirée was pregnant. If the press gained access to that fact, they would show no mercy.

Stefano had been reduced to a naysayer, a prognosticator without credentials, predicting impending and hoped-for doom. According to him, the marriage was an ill-aligned and ill-advised match that would surely spiral into an abyss of blame and discord. He spread his venom at his reputation's expense. Unwilling to accept that he had been replaced, he embarrassed any who sought to temper his outbursts and maintain some decorum. But who could blame him? Once, he had held Desirée, but he had valued that prize so little that, eventually, he'd lost her.

forty-six

ONE MORE MOUNTAIN WAS LEFT TO CLIMB; THE Stoddards were due at Orly Airport, and Scott was worried. This was their first time in Europe; in addition to that adjustment, it was his parents' first meeting with Desirée, whom his mother blamed for Scott's predicament; last, but not least, they would meet Madame de Bellecourt. Desirée's mother couldn't conceal her aristocratic underpinnings, even to prevent alienating her future son-in-law's parents. Oh, she might surprise him, but Scott thought she would find a way to demonstrate her displeasure regarding the marriage. In any case, he knew he couldn't control Madame de Bellecourt, nor could he oversee and supervise his parents' every move. They would already be on the defensive, being in a new place, with new people, and new everything; they would criticize before they could be critiqued. It was a dangerous game, and Scott could hear Cardinal Massela's intuitive words about families and their impact on a couple.

The evening before his parents' arrival, Desirée asked, "Will they be nervous?"

"Nervous would be preferable," Scott replied. "Defensive is what I'm worried about."

"So, we have from the airport to the hotel to get them to relax."

"Do you have a plan?"

"Maybe we could tell them how everyone is looking forward to meeting them."

"Not believable."

"Do you have a better idea?"

"Yes, I was thinking narcotics."

"We could conduct French classes on the way from the airport to the hotel. Maybe by the time we arrived, they could have a kind of *patois* going for them."

"Yes, and after the dinners and festivities, we could conduct seminars on French table manners, the basics of knife and fork, polite conversation (including tone and volume), and gestures of the hands and face, all designed to transform them from this nice American couple into sophisticated and jaded continentals."

Scott and Desirée laughed and carried this absurdity to its limits. They wouldn't be able to ward off every challenge nor protect themselves all the time. If either one made a little (or big) mistake, the lovers agreed: *que sera, sera.*

"But I do hope your mother likes me," Desirée said wistfully.

"She will, my dear. Why wouldn't she?"

"I can think of several reasons, not the least of which is that I am taking her little Scott from her."

Scott agreed, grinning. "You're probably right about that. You know she kept me in the crib until I was eleven," he said.

"It's not a laughing matter," she said, though she did giggle a bit at the image of Scott crammed into a baby's crib.

"I agree, but my mother is a smart lady. She knows how her brioche is buttered."

Desirée insisted on coming to the airport; of course it was the right thing to do, but Scott was nervous, because with them came a phalanx of security and the commensurate increase in interest by the press. His parents were proper, if relatively middle class, people—Scott wasn't worried about their appearance or comportment. They would do fine. But he hadn't seen them since last September, and since his telephone conversations had been crafted more to conceal than reveal, his parents had been denied a chance to adjust to the rapidly progressing circumstances of his romance with Desirée. In a different scenario, Scott could imagine they might be proud of his link to a countess, a woman of wealth, social standing, and prestige. But he knew they felt surprised, taken advantage of, and without options or say-so in the outcome. In the past, they'd always been a part of any decisions affecting Scott. With Desirée's financial means, the Stoddards no longer had any monetary leverage with their son. But emotional? Perhaps Scott didn't require their approval, and maybe their disapproval had lost the impact it had carried before.

They made it through customs before Scott spotted his parents, who were looking everywhere for his face in the crowd. His mother and father were fastidious; they'd disembarked from the plane looking as though they'd been at a spa. His father wore his perennial dark blue pinstripe; his mother, in camel and beige Céline. Scott thought they looked good, even better than ten months ago, when they'd accompanied him to the ship.

He led Desirée toward his parents. His mother saw them first, and Scott reached to embrace her, at the same time shaking his father's hand. After a moment, they separated, and Scott said, "Mother, Father; let me introduce you to my fiancé, the Countess de Rovere. Desirée, my parents, Edward and Sarah Stoddard."

"It's very nice to meet you," his father said. "I don't believe I have ever met a countess. And Scott was right; you are quite beautiful indeed."

"Thank you, Mr. Stoddard. You are most kind," Desirée said graciously. Turning to Scott's mother, she handed her the welcome bouquet she'd brought. "And Mrs. Stoddard—I am so pleased to meet you. Scott has told me all about you both. I'm so glad you are here," Desirée said in her excellent English, caressed ever so slightly by a light French accent.

Mrs. Stoddard, standing at his father's right, and slightly behind him, shyly extended her hand and then, when it was accepted, ventured to embrace Desirée. It was a nice moment. They walked to the car, the luggage was loaded, and Desirée whispered to Scott before climbing into the plush seat, "Oh, your parents are so nice, my darling, just like you."

The photographers and journalists discovered them, and began to press close on all sides of the Mercedes, pushing to get better angles. A look of annoyance spread across Scott's mother's face. Mr. Stoddard remarked, "Isn't there anything that can be done about these people? How in the world do you put up with this?"

On their way to the hotel, Desirée and his father filled the car with unexpected, banal chatter. Scott was surprised his father possessed such charm; the elder Stoddard did not hesitate to ladle it on heavily. Scott's mother, meanwhile, was taking in Desirée, surveying her future daughter-in-law's every minute detail. Her scrutiny wasn't pointed enough to notice unless you knew his mother, but Scott could tell she, too, was taken with Desirée's beauty and elegance. He smiled; today, Desirée's sensitivity to others was so apparent. She'd dressed modestly (well, modestly by Paris' standards) in a simple, white linen pencil skirt with a printed gray and ivory jacket. She looked fabulous in a large bone cuff and ring, encrusted with diamonds, and matching earrings. Scott's mother loved jewelry more than most, and had a substantial collection, so she appreciated the quality and taste of Desirée's accessories.

By the time they reached the hotel, his father had become a convert. Scott expected his mother would be a harder sell (he wondered, did she view Desirée as a rival for his affection? That wouldn't be unusual; Mrs. Stoddard was fiercely and competitively protective of her only child, often measuring herself against every woman she met).

They'd booked the Stoddards at the Plaza-Athenée, one of Paris' grand hotels, all five-plus stars. Madame de Bellecourt had specifically chosen the Plaza-Athenée because of its proximity to the church and prime shopping, which she thought Scott's mother might enjoy. She'd insisted on making the reservations herself, in person, reviewing the specific accommodations with the general manager. The Stoddards would be enjoying a suite of some proportions, decorated with antiques and period furnishings, all enhanced with the brocades and toiles so quintessentially French. Orchids were placed an hour before his parents' arrival. Madame de Bellecourt had supervised their selection as well, voicing her opinion that flowers should not have an annoying or overpowering scent. She suggested orchids, and orchids they were.

They checked into the hotel; tired from the trip, Scott's parents wanted to rest a few hours before dinner. That first evening, Desirée thought it best to have a quiet, easy dinner at the hotel. But before leaving, she said, "There will be a car and driver at your disposition while you are in Paris. Mrs. Stoddard, there is a hairdresser in the hotel, but if you would like, I would be pleased to arrange an appointment with Frederic, my coiffeur at Alexandre de Paris."

Scott worried that Desirée's attention would make his mother feel managed. Too much oversight, however generous, could backfire. But Mrs. Stoddard seemed to accept Desirée's information in the vein in which it was intended, thanking Desirée and telling her she had thought of everything.

THREE DAYS—AMPLE TIME FOR SOMETHING TO GO WRONG before the wedding. Scott was relieved that the initial meeting and ride into the city had gone so well. Since his parents had never been to Paris, Scott was going to show them some of the sights while Desirée and her mother worked with the dressmakers, florists, and caterers; after the tour, they would all meet for lunch at the Club Interalliée.

When Desirée had been present, she regulated the tenor of his parents' questions. Without her, Scott knew they would feel free to ask about anything they could think of, relevant or irrelevant to the situation. He knew how hard they were trying, but the unfettered joy usually found in a wedding was absent. He suspected that would've been different had he traveled a more traditional path—finishing his studies, returning to America, and marrying a Southern girl; they'd have been pleased. He wondered: was his choice of Desirée and Europe, things so foreign to them, seen by his parents as a rejection of them and their way of life?

When he stopped by the hotel the next morning for sightseeing, his parents asked him up to their room. His father met him at the door. Although Madame de Bellecourt had described the suite to Scott, it was more palatial than he'd imagined. The large bed had acres of beautiful Porthault sheets, with silk pillowcases and a fine coverlet. The Eiffel Tower was clearly framed in the floor-to-ceiling French doors that led to a wrap-around terrace. There was Madame de Bellecourt's touch, the orchids, placed in strategic spots in minimalist French fashion.

His mother, impatient to have her say, got right to it. "Scott, do you really know what you're getting into? You realize your child will be raised Catholic. And have you thought about the fact that Desirée has all the money?"

"I know that I want to marry her, and that's all I care about," he said.

"Let me be frank with you," his mother continued (*as though she'd ever be anything else*, Scott thought). "Desirée, of course, is a lovely woman and could not be kinder, but be realistic. She is older, more sophisticated, and considerably experienced in the things a woman knows and uses to manipulate men."

Well, there it was; his mother resented the fact that another woman had seduced her son, and she was suspicious of some of the very wiles she used to manipulate his father.

"Are you suggesting that Desirée has some kind of sexual hold on me? Nothing could be further from the truth. That is not only untrue but also demeaning," Scott said. "Mother, I love her. Even without the baby, I would marry Desirée."

Mrs. Stoddard was rendered speechless by Scott's directness. Her lips pursed into a well-known pout; she didn't like situations where she could neither influence nor control their outcome. His father's facial expression revealed that these were unchartered waters, perhaps too dangerous to navigate. But she recovered quickly. "I'm not suggesting anything of the sort," she said haughtily. "I'm only asking if the two of you have given everything due consideration."

How many times would Scott have to rebuff doubts about their love? He'd had enough; he sat on one of the chairs and toyed with an orchid leaf. "I can't say we've thought of everything, Mother. Desirée and I have been over as many things as we could think of and every-thing well-meaning others—like you—have suggested. Nevertheless, we always come to the same conclusion: we love each other and want to be married." Mr. Stoddard had moved to stand by his son, placing a hand on the younger man's shoulder in an unexpected move of sup-port. Scott continued. "We hope those we love will support us, but if they don't, our feelings for each other won't be jeopardized. Nor will that interfere with our plans. And, if it turns out that we were in error, then Desirée and I will suffer the consequences of our misfortune and bad judgment." His father gave a supportive pat, which Scott appreciated. Yes, he'd been converted all right. His mother, on the other hand, was still working through the details.

"Are you saying we can't register any reservations or ask any questions? Our only role is to accept?" his mother asked.

"I had hoped your role would be to accept our love, hope for the best, and be happy for our future. It's too late for your counsel, however well intentioned. But just to be clear," said Scott firmly, standing to signal an end to the discussion, "I would have ignored any advice that excluded Desirée from my life. I'm very set on what I want."

"There's nothing new to that," his father chuckled. "You were always headstrong and determined."

"I've had good examples," Scott said. He wanted to mend some fences if he could. "You've taught me that was okay, especially when presented with something you wanted me to accomplish. But this marriage is something I want," Scott said, pounding the table with his fist.

"What about all the money your father has spent on your education?" His mother asked, "Has it all been wasted? Are you going to give up school and live on the countess's money? What happened to your plans for a graduate degree and law school?"

How could Scott explain? "Something came up" was the best he could offer.

"Something came up!" His mother snorted disparagingly. "You mean you let Desirée interfere with your plans."

"Don't blame Desirée. The reason has nothing to do with Desirée; it has everything to do with your original plan. The one you approved. The one that I didn't create."

Out of the blue, his father joined in with an uncharacteristic candor. "Son, are you suddenly too good for us? You've become part of the countess's world—my boy, you're young, and there's so much you don't know. I hope you don't get hurt." He took Mrs. Stoddard's hand, patted it briefly in a soothing gesture (though such demonstrative action completely discombobulated his wife), and addressed another issue. "Scott, you don't know the customs, but Mother and I do. While it's the tradition for the bride's parents to 'put up' the groom's parents," his father said, "nobody's paying for me to stay here. I can pay for myself." His mother started to protest, but a firm shake of the head put her in her place.

This is payback, Scott thought harshly. *A way to salvage his pride over my living with a woman who would support me.* Edward Stoddard had begun with nothing; his education limited to a night school college degree pursued after a long day at work. No one had paid his way, and he'd built a substantial business, with multiple locations across several states. Undoubtedly, the older gentleman was disappointed that this new generation was rejecting his life's matrix for a quite different approach to work and money.

"Father, please reconsider paying this time," Scott said. "While I know you can afford these luxuries, and I appreciate how hard you've worked to earn the money to do so, Madame de Bellecourt is a stickler for etiquette. She'll be embarrassed and, by the way, so will you and Mother."

His father didn't answer. Leaving it at that, the three set out to see Paris.

forty-seven

THE TOUR AROUND ONE OF THE WORLD'S MOST BEAUTI-
ful cities was somber and abbreviated. His parents seemed
disinterested and wounded, unable to enjoy what could have
been an amazing experience. Instead of preparing for a celebration, the
Stoddards were on edge, brimming with anger and resentment. Scott
dreaded lunch, worried that the slightest perceived infraction by him
might set them off. And there was Madame de Bellecourt yet to meet.
He sighed.

At the club, the sullen trio was guided to the second-floor grand
dining room where Desirée and her mother waited at a prominent
corner table; joining them was Desirée's paternal uncle, Pierre de
Bellecourt, who would be giving the bride away. Introductions were
exchanged, and the party took seats as the Stoddards exclaimed over
the presiding view of the gardens, which pleased Madame de Bellecourt immensely. She'd taken great care, arranging the luncheon
seating per appropriate etiquette and the guests' language abilities.
Scott had only recently met Desirée's uncle (who was supposedly a
carbon copy of his brother, Desirée's father). Pierre, a man of education, wealth, bonhomie—and, thankfully, proficiency in English—was
seated between Scott's parents; Desirée, next to his mother; and Scott's
father beside Madame de Bellecourt.

A sensitive man of good size in both stature and girth, Pierre possessed a casual agreeableness. Though his suit was expensive, its cut was
not so imposing as to intimidate. His manners and gesticulations were

unstudied, reminding Scott of someone between a banker and a priest. Immediately sizing up the guests, Pierre commandeered the menu, recommending the *sole meuniere* and *filet de boeuf* and evaluating the dishes until he found something pleasing for each of them. He was, as they say in French, *un animateur* (one who gives life to a party), and the ease and humor with which he conversed put the entire party at ease.

From his vantage point directly across the table, Scott enjoyed a front row seat to these interactions. His parents were absent any smile that might have made the situation less brittle, but Pierre was ready to address their uneasiness. Speaking first with Scott's mother, he began a genial conversation. "Mrs. Stoddard, we are lucky that the weather is so wonderful right now; we can only pray that it holds for the wedding on Friday."

"Yes, it is really perfect. I was a little worried when I was packing whether I was bringing the right clothes," she said.

"Well, Madame, you brought the perfect outfit for today; you are quite chic." Pierre's deft compliment brought the smallest of smiles to Mrs. Stoddard's face. (Scott had seen her quickly assess Madame de Bellecourt's ensemble, then Desirée's, as they took their seats.) Next, the suave Frenchman turned to Scott's father. "And Mr. Stoddard," he said. "Perhaps I need to warn you of the Avenue Montaigne, where your hotel is situated. It is known that the shopping on that street can be damaging to one's wallet, even for a man of your considerable means," he said conspiratorially. *Ah,* thought Scott, *brilliant work, Pierre. You are applying some salve to my father's wounded pride.*

"Mr. de Bellecourt, thank you so much for the advice. I will do my best to steer Sarah away from that street, but the woman has a mind all her own," Scott's father said.

"We men are aware of the problem," he laughed, including Scott in the comment. Pierre had ordered several bottles of Krug, and he raised a glass. The group's attention focused on Desirée's uncle, who stood. "Would you allow me a toast?" When each glass was held aloft, Pierre intoned: "To the lovely couple; may they experience untold happiness."

Madame de Bellecourt gave a sweet *à votre santé* while Mrs. Stoddard silently clinked glasses with Scott. His father, not to be outdone, raised his glass and said, "Sarah and I join in that wish, and we thank you all for your hospitality."

Madame de Bellecourt smiled in a rather perfunctory manner. Gazing at the Stoddards, Scott saw in her cool eyes an assessment of what might have been. He knew she had dreamed of a successful marriage for Desirée, some wealthy French family's son, a noble or banker. Scott's Southern background and self-made parents could not compare. But his father was graciously toasting, and ever proper, she found grace enough to smile and incline her glass toward Mr. Stoddard. "I certainly hope that your accommodations are satisfactory and that the hotel staff is answering your needs," she said in her formal way.

Scott's mother replied, "Oh yes, Madame de Bellecourt; the rooms are superb, the flowers exquisite. Edward and I do so thank you for your incredible efforts to ensure that our visit to Paris is lovely. I hope that I'm not saying anything untoward," Scott's eyes shot to his mother—whatever she might say could very well be untoward, "but even though we're familiar with the wedding custom, it's difficult to accept your generosity regarding the suite at the hotel."

"I understand and appreciate your feelings, but you must allow me this pleasure," Madame de Bellecourt said.

"Of course, but it cannot pass unnoticed and without thanks," his mother said.

Overhearing this exchange, Scott was very proud of his mother; not only had she been tactful, but also her recognition would find favor with Madame de Bellecourt, who then lowered her voice to a confidential pitch. Leaning toward his mother, she said, "Mrs. Stoddard, I'm sure you were as shocked as I (or maybe more so, if that is possible) by what our offspring have visited on us." The two women were, as Scott knew, quite united in their opinions on that front. Studiously, he addressed his salad, but his ears were attuned to every comment.

His mother shot him a quick glance. Satisfied that his attention was elsewhere, she replied, "Yes, Madame, I confess we were shocked. Scott had written us about meeting your lovely daughter, but we were surprised to see the *Life* magazine photograph from Cannes." Madame de Bellecourt clutched her napkin to her bosom and closed her eyes.

Gratified at the reaction, Mrs. Stoddard continued. "The photo and caption revealed that Scott had obviously withheld important details about their relationship."

"I can imagine how you felt, my dear." Madame de Bellecourt began to fill her in on the details. "Naturally, being Desirée's mother, I had known of their involvement for some time. Desirée had introduced us at Easter; as you know, Scott is quite a charming and intelligent young man." She leaned closer to Mrs. Stoddard, who was glowing at the praise the elegant woman had just bestowed upon her son. "The young Mr. Stoddard is almost too intelligent, if you know what I mean. I liked everything about him save but one. Each time I saw the two of them, they'd become more and more serious, and Desirée wouldn't listen to any of the important differences I felt they must consider."

Scott struggled to mask his pleasure as his mother placed a hand over Madame de Bellecourt's. What was the saying? *The enemy of my enemy is my friend*, he thought. *Brava, Madame de Bellecourt, on uniting the fronts.* Sarah Stoddard's voice trembled. "I do sympathize, Madame de Bellecourt. Scott can become quite determined when he sets his mind on something. I, too, attempted to voice my concerns, but they fell on deaf ears."

"And my daughter, particularly after her father's death, has become even more headstrong than before."

Desirée, suddenly noting their proximity and intimate conversation, was startled at whatever conspiracy these formidable women might be hatching. Entering the fray, she exclaimed, "Maman, darling, you should see the beautiful suit Mrs. Stoddard is wearing to the ceremony. It is simply perfect in every way." With satisfied smiles, the two matriarchs resumed the meal, but their connection lingered.

As the waiters were clearing the main course plates and silverware in preparation for dessert, Desirée's uncle cleared his throat. "My dear friends and family," he announced. "I would like to say what everyone is thinking but no one has mentioned. Desirée, my always special but often unpredictable niece, you and Scott have taken us by surprise." He bowed in the direction of Madame de Bellecourt. "Naturally, my sister-in-law told me some time ago that you were seeing an American, a graduate student in Geneva, but the situation advanced rather more quickly than any of us could've imagined. But the more I think about your love, it is not as surprising as one might think. My dear brother, Bertrand (God rest his soul), moved to America in the mid-fifties, and if one thing is certain, he loved that country, and he loved Americans. It was part of his *esprit,* as we say in French. So, when I heard the news, I thought, *why not Desirée, too?* She is her father's daughter, through and through, as her mother will surely attest: strong willed, full of joy and love, and optimistic about all life has to offer. Why wouldn't she fall in love with someone who embodies those characteristics that make Americans uniquely, well, *American?*" Scott, moved, saw that there were smiles all around and Desirée's eyes were moist with tears. "I raise my glass to this surprising couple," Pierre concluded.

Madame de Bellecourt and Mrs. Stoddard were the barometers of record; as their sentiments rose and fell, so would those of the entourage. Pierre's speech had worked for the moment. Finally, there seemed a hint of the joy that one expected with a marriage celebration (if not joy, then a happy acceptance that any opposition to the wedding, either in thought or action, was counter to destiny's designs). For better or worse, and in spite of anyone's misgivings, Scott and Desirée would be married.

Scott's father, ever more malleable than his mother, was the first to respond favorably, complimenting Pierre on his well wishes to the couple (and the compliments to his son and country). His mother didn't want to appear to give in to platitudes and sentimentality; even following her friendly conversation with, and approval from, Madame de Bellecourt, her face still retained traces of her intractable streak. Though she was warming, Scott felt certain there was little prospect that his mother would fully embrace the nuptials before she and his father returned to the States, and that could be particularly unfortunate. She was playing a dangerous game; after the wedding and once the baby came, Desirée would hold most of the cards.

forty-eight

IN THE UNITED STATES, A SMALL INTIMATE GATHERING OF the bride's and groom's families, their witnesses, and officiant (in this case, Father Kohler) is called the rehearsal dinner. Scott and Desirée's was held at the Ritz Hotel's private terrace, just off the main room of the hotel's Michelin-awarded, three-star restaurant and bar. The court was enclosed by ivy-covered walls and a series of French doors with mousseline drapes through which the dazzling restaurant and bar were visible. Planted with trees and small hedges and paved with polished stones and tiles in a geometric pattern, the terrace was arranged in intimate groupings, with tables and chairs clustered in the center of the garden. The party's private bar was situated on one flank while hors d'oeuvres were served on the other. Lanterns at various locations illuminated without overpowering the festivities. The staff, in white coats with gold epaulettes, were stationed at strategic points, ensuring no guest went unattended.

Scott, Desirée, his parents, and her mother and uncle arrived together. As they waited for the others, Pierre struck up a conversation. "My dear Scott," he said in his pleasant way, "tomorrow is the big day. Tell me—are you nervous? Excited?"

"I'm all those and more. Mostly, though, I'm very happy," he said.

"My boy, that is the correct answer. You are aware that you're getting quite a prize?" Both men looked at Desirée fondly, who gave them a brief wave from across the room.

"No one is more aware than I. I'm a lucky man," Scott replied.

"By the way, I like your parents very much. It isn't my place to say, but they are very distinguished. Very correct," Pierre said graciously. Scott was touched; the older man clearly didn't offer praise falsely; he meant what he said.

"Thank you. I'm sure they would be pleased to know you think so," he said.

Out of the corner of his eye, Scott saw that his mother had pulled Desirée aside and they were intently engaged, his mother's dark bob contrasting with Desirée's mane of blond hair. Their conversation appeared to be more than an exchange of opinions on the weather. They talked for some time, and Scott was relieved to see their facial expressions remained cordial. Finally, they parted, embracing awkwardly in the French way, with light kisses on each cheek. His mother sought out her husband while Desirée found Scott.

He gave her a quick kiss on her offered cheek. "So, darling; am I to know what that was about?" he asked, inclining his head toward his mother.

"Yes—we had a clearing of the air," she said.

"How so?"

"I've noticed your mother is very tense, so I decided to ask why; had I or my family done anything? And I'm glad I did; like you, your mother is very direct. She said she was having difficulty adjusting to a situation that had been forced on her without consent, and she and your father were disappointed in ways connected to what their dreams for you had been."

Scott sucked in his breath. "I'm surprised she was able to describe what she's feeling. I'm well aware; she and I have had this conversation before, and I'm sorry if those comments hurt you in any way. She is just angry," Scott said. "I am her only child, and they had pinned so much on my academic success."

"I was surprised myself, but this was her chance to voice her opinion to me, and she took it. After all, I did ask her to be frank with me—did she blame me for the circumstances?"

"What did she say?"

"Yes; she could blame me, because I'm older and more sophisticated; but then, she wouldn't blame me because I was to be the mother
of her grandchild and her only son's wife."

"A triumph of pragmatism over personality."

"Then, she acknowledged that everyone had been very kind, kinder
than either of them had expected. That she could see why you fell in
love with me."

"My mother is a woman who knows how to change gears."

"And I told your mother that I admired her honesty. I understood
her anger and her disappointment and hoped that time and our love
would prove we're not making the mistake they all fear." A warm
smile played about Desirée's lips then, and Scott so wanted to kiss
her deeply. "And well, you saw the rest. She thanked me; I thanked
her; and we embraced."

THE FINAL GUESTS ARRIVED, AND FESTIVITIES WERE FULLY
under way. As the bride-to-be, Desirée commanded the room, and
she'd chosen her attire carefully, aware that she'd be the main interest.
She was wearing an exquisite silk chiffon dress in a muted helio-
trope, still tempting fate by choosing an empire waist. Diamonds
were draped modestly (if so many carats on display could ever be
called modest). She always wore her hair up at formal occasions, and
diamond earrings dangled from her lobes; on her finger, her engagement ring, that square-cut emerald, dazzled. Stiletto heels brought
her height even with Scott's and positioned her still sexy figure into
its most feminine silhouette.

There was Andre. He pulled Scott aside and said, "My dear boy, I've
seen the countess in newspaper photographs, and she is beautiful; in
person, however, she is a vision."

When Madame de Bellecourt approached Sarah Stoddard, the
party held its collective breath. The two women had realized their
figurative importance to the families, and their facial expressions and

gestures reflected genial rapport and happy acceptance. If they held unrealized dreams for their offspring, it wasn't visible. Neither would ruin the party by placing a pall over the couple's happiness.

Meanwhile, Uncle Pierre was translating as Mr. Stoddard conversed with Father Kohler. "I believe I may have been among the first to observe the way your son and the Countess de Rovere seemed so much in love and were so temperamentally matched," the priest said. "You probably know of your son's gift of humor, but Desirée, whom I've known since she was small, can hold her own with him. They match wits in a nice way, if you know what I mean. They love each other's humor without being competitive. This bodes well for the future."

The banquet table, ablaze with candles in imposing and gilded candelabra, was decorated with a profusion of white and yellow flowers arranged at intervals and matching linens. As the guests took their seats, the place settings of antique Bernardaud china and Baccarat crystal glasses shone in the soft light; antique Christofle silver with gold filigree in the handles, arranged with military precision, sparkled. Small cards with each individual's name inscribed in decorative calligraphy marked the correct seating.

When all were in place, and a white Chassagne-Montrachet poured, dinner service began. A host of waiters bustled about, serving the first course (a crab salad with Louis dressing and mixture of hearts of palm and artichoke bottoms). The dinner partners warmed to each other and began to talk; the meal passed quickly as the wine and food continued to flow.

After dessert, a St. Honoré cake, Desirée's uncle and Scott's friends, Albert and Jean, made toasts, each wishing in various ways happiness, long life, and health for the couple.

When the toasts had finally concluded, Father Kohler took the lovebirds aside for what they assumed might be a brief prayer or devotion.

"Unfortunately, something of extreme urgency has come up," Father Kohler said. Scott and Desirée, alarmed, felt the warm glow of just moments ago dissipate. "I have been commissioned to relay a desire. His Holiness, Cardinal Giorgio Pignatelli of the Basilica of

San Marco in Venice, has requested a meeting with you this evening, if possible, at your home on Avenue Foch."

"What's this about, Father?" Desirée asked, panic rising in her voice.

Scott felt no panic, only anger. "It's the count, Desirée," he said through clenched teeth. "Venice, San Marco—put the clues together," Scott growled.

"I can't believe it," Desirée gasped.

forty-nine

GUSTAV GUIDED THEIR CAR ALONG AVENUE FOCH, where Scott noted a large black Mercedes idling across the street. Shortly after they entered the apartment, the building's concierge announced Cardinal Pignatelli was in the foyer, and Desirée asked the concierge to escort the cardinal to the elevator.

When the door opened, a frail, older man of sallow complexion stood waiting to be welcomed. Scott was going to have a difficult time controlling his anger. He wasn't Catholic, and he was tired of pious clergy with their clasped hands constantly interfering in their life. He was a nonbeliever—how were these old men the final arbiters of truth? Didn't they have enough to do managing their own affairs? Desirée, however, wouldn't see things as Scott saw them. That, somehow, Desirée might be persuaded to sacrifice her own happiness for her faith had always been a risk. He'd have to be careful.

The cardinal apologized for the late hour and unexpected nature of his visit, thanking Desirée for agreeing to meet on this matter of supreme importance. He ignored Scott, though he did offer to speak in French implicitly for his benefit. Desirée agreed that French would best accommodate all present. They took a seat in the salon.

The cardinal cleared his throat and began. "Tomorrow, Countess, you will take a very dramatic step, a fateful step—a step that cannot be retraced."

"I'm aware of the significance of tomorrow," Desirée said coolly.

"I'm here as your husband's spiritual pastor as well as a representative of his family in Venice."

Desirée squared her shoulders. "Ex-husband, Father. As you are aware, our brief and unfortunate marriage was annulled."

"Yes, Countess, but we are not here to speak of legalities. We are here to address spiritual preferences, ecclesiastical bedrock, and core principles of faith," he replied pompously. Scott glared; he could see where this was leading, and he didn't care for the conversation one bit.

"And what preference would that be?" Desirée asked, pretending that she, too, could not see what the cardinal had planned.

"That marriage is final, forever, and indissoluble."

Scott wanted to choke the old man (or, preferably, Stefano), but he knew it was a moment for control. He remained silent, the cardinal deliberately continuing to ignore him.

"We are well past any consideration of that," Desirée said. "That union ended with the count's infidelities. He had no respect for the sanctity of marriage."

No flicker of feeling crossed the cardinal's countenance. Clearly, he had the upper hand. "It is possible that the dispensation will not be available tomorrow for the ceremony," he said, locking his eyes on Desirée's face.

"It's too late."

"My child, it's never too late to follow God's will."

"I'm pregnant, Father."

Ah, Scott thought; *you didn't see that coming, did you?* For a moment, it appeared the cardinal might faint, but he braced himself at the last second and looked at Desirée with an expression somewhere between disbelief and resignation. "I see," he said. Without another word, he quickly stood, bid them farewell, and retreated the way he had arrived.

Scott and Desirée remained where they were on the couch, pondering what had just happened, the same thoughts, questions, and fears swirling about their minds. Would the cardinal reveal Desirée's pregnancy to Stefano? Tasked as he was, how could he not? And what new stunt would the count pull when he realized his plans were foiled? Could the cardinal still wreck the dispensation and cancel the ceremony, now only some eleven hours away? And would the whole sordid matter be splashed about in the morning's newspapers?

Scott broke their silent reveries. "Will he tell?" he asked.

"I don't know," Desirée said.

It was a fitful night, one they had to endure separately. They'd decided earlier that Scott would sleep in an adjoining guest apartment to honor the tradition of grooms not seeing the bride on the day of the ceremony. No one wanted to tempt fate at this juncture.

fifty

THE EARLY NEWSPAPERS MADE NO MENTION OF Desirée's delicate condition, only that she and Scott were to be married that very day. This didn't necessarily mean anything; perhaps the item had been too late to fit into the morning editions. All was relatively quiet outside, which Scott took as a good sign, reasoning that the paparazzi would be outside their door screaming for verification if they had been provided with any inside information. Maybe the count had something even more humiliating to spring on Desirée now that he was fully aware of his desire's futility. As Scott prepared for the day, it occurred to him that Andre had been right; tradition can be an unrelenting taskmaster.

He left the apartment about an hour ahead of Desirée, bound for the church, and everything seemed normal. His security personnel and the press behaved predictably (at least, for them); the only worrisome sign was another black Mercedes stationed across the street from the church, precisely where Desirée would arrive within the hour.

❧

THE CEREMONY WAS TO BE A HIGH MASS, AND, AS NOON approached, Scott waited at the altar with Monsignor Philippe des Champs (the presiding priest), Father Kohler, and his two best men, Jean and Albert. He had time to admire the church's architecture; the impressive stone edifice, with its stained-glass windows, beautiful murals, and frescoes depicting the trials and life of Jesus and the apostles, dated from the eleventh century. The mighty altar with crucified Christ majestically looming dominated the interior while the organ's mathematically scaled notes rang of Bach and Vivaldi. Scott's mind drifted back to his first vision of Desirée, there on the ship, a singular and unexpected delight. How could he have anticipated that what was love at first sight on his part would result ten months later, here in Paris on the Avenue Marceau in the very church that had, along with many happy occasions, seen the funerals of de Maupassant and Proust?

He stood there, much as he had stood that morning in Le Havre, waiting for and finally catching sight of Desirée as she'd left the ship: her face upturned, her blue-green eyes, searching upward across the decks in the morning mist, looking for him. Then, as now, he was searching for her.

There was a rustling sound beyond the doors. Scott saw Pierre first; next, a flash of white before the mighty organ resounded with the intonations of Wagner's *Bridal Chorus*, and the attendees rose as one to turn toward the aisle. Floating on a cloud of alabaster taffeta and chiffon, Desirée slowly made her way toward the altar on her uncle's arm. A lace train of French *dentelle* trailed behind; in her hands, Desirée clasped a bouquet of lily of the valley and edelweiss in deference to her French as well as Swiss origins. From behind the veil, Scott could see her sparkling eyes and radiant complexion. Watching her regal approach, he glanced at the faces surrounding them; all were, like him, struck by Desirée's exquisite beauty. Madame de Bellecourt's expression rested somewhere between resignation, pride, and peace; his mother's one of strain, curiosity, and love for her son; and his father, beaming with resolve and pride.

As the monsignor and Father Kohler shared duties regarding the wedding sacraments, Desirée and Scott gazed into each other's eyes with love and joy. This day was finally happening. They made the classic vows and promises under the happiest of circumstances, and Scott hoped that none of the specters previously raised would ever test the fortitude of their commitment.

In the exchange of rings, Scott and Desirée placed matching gold bands from Cartier on one another's fingers. Then came *I dos*, the pronouncement that they were now man and wife, and the lifting of her veil. Desirée's siren face shone, and then came the kiss, reserved yet loving, correct to the point that even Madame de Bellecourt would approve.

AFTER THE CEREMONY AND THE OFFICIAL AND THE UNOFFI-cial photographers had exhausted their appetite for pictures (*or*, Scott thought wryly, *run out of film*), the happy couple was finally alone. Ensconced in the rented white Rolls-Royce Cabriolet, Gustav at the wheel, they rested in the back seat on the way to the reception.

Hardly able to contain his happiness, Scott exclaimed, "We made it!"

"We did," his wife agreed.

"But how?" he asked wonderingly. "Doesn't it seem surreal to you, Desirée? Are we truly, finally, going to be happy together—without any impediment?"

With a coy smile, Desirée reached to extract a small envelope tucked in her garter. Handing it to Scott, she explained. "This was delivered at the house only ten minutes before I left for the church."

Scott unfolded the message and read: *Your wedding gift is my silence. S.*

allow him to seduce her, is indicative of the architecture of their relationship. This episode was difficult to write to keep the action elevated but still sexy.

The most challenging sequence in the novel is any encounter that Scott has with Desirée's mother, Madame de Bellecourt. When Scott first meets Madame in Mougins, he learns of the full extent of Madame's displeasure with the relationship, and later, when the pregnancy is reveled, Scott must persuade Madame of the only course possible.

Q: Was there a character in *An Improbable Pairing* that you relate to the most? If so, who and why?

A: I relate most to Scott. In effect, the story itself is an amalgam of my own experiences, fantasies, and imagination. At his age, I admire his cool head, his intelligence, and his flexibility.

Q: Did you have to research in preparation for this book? If so what parts? What kind of research did you do?

A: Very little research was required to write this story. It's one that has been with me in one form or another for some time, and over the years, I have continued to reinforce my memories by continuous visits to the locales and situations that set the scenes in the story.

Q: What do you want readers to take away from this book?

A: I didn't write this book with any great message. Look for no soap-boxes; there's no subtle agenda here. Most of all, I hope readers will find joy in a story about how love and respect between two people of disparate backgrounds can triumph over long odds and determined naysayers. Additionally, perhaps readers can peek into the Europe of the 1960s, the golden years. They can participate voyeuristically in the elegance of the settings and the traditions of

QUESTIONS FOR DISCUSSION

1. At the beginning of *An Improbable Pairing*, Scott is attracted to an unknown woman, somewhat older than he. How does this set the tone of the story to come?

2. Control is a common theme in *An Improbable Pairing*. Discuss the role it plays in Desiree and Scott's relationship. Who had more control in the relationship? Did it work for them, or was it a problem?

3. Tangent to this issue of control is the gender reversal within the Scott/Desirée relationship. As Scott exhibits in the first chapters, he has been brought up as a traditional male of the 1960s, particularly in relation to the opposite sex. Desirée proves that she is not a woman of this period, but rather a woman more resembling a woman of current times. Discuss Scott's ability to adjust to a paradigm so opposite to his nature. Discuss how the two protagonists accommodate each other's needs without losing their individuality.

4. Scott has several different relationships when the story begins. Discuss the role of relationships and its different forms presented throughout the book. How were they similar? How were they different? Were these relationships an advantage for Scott? How did they work to move the plot along?

5. Discuss the role religion plays in this book. Why was it so important to Desiree and her family?

6. Why do you think age is so important to Scott?

7. Discuss Scott's relationships with Marlyse and Desiree. How were they similar? How were they different?

8. How might the book have been different if the roles of Scott and Desiree were reversed? Would there be more or less obstacles?

9. Were the characters easy to relate to? Who did you identify most with? Why?

10. Do you think the time period influenced the events in *An Improbable Pairing*? How? How do you think this story would have differed if it were set in present day?

11. What obstacles do Desiree and Scott face in their relationship? Which do you think was the hardest to overcome?

12. What are your opinions of Desiree? How did her relationship with Stefano differ from her relationship with Scott? Do you think her past relationship had any influence on her current life and choices?

13. Scott's parents always had a plan for Scott's life. What was that plan? Was it ever important to Scott or what he wanted? Was that plan or goal met in the end?

AUTHOR Q & A

Q: What inspired you to write *An Improbable Pairing*? Why did you choose this setting and time period?

A: *An Improbable Pairing* is my first novel, and quite simply I chose to tell a story with the kind of characters and settings that are very familiar to me—one that encapsulates so many of the places that I love.

Q: Do you have a favorite character in the story? If so, what is it about this character that you most appreciate?

A: My favorite character, which I assume comes as no surprise to those who have read the book, is Desirée. Desirée is that impossibly perfect fantasy that possesses all the qualities and more that I admire in a woman: beauty, self-confidence, empathy, romance, social adeptness, and independence.

Q: What was your favorite chapter to write and why? Were there any chapters that were challenging for you to write? If so, why?

A: My favorite chapter to write was the one in which Desirée and Scott finally get together in Gstaad. The interaction between the two of them dictated by their attraction for each other, while each jockeys for position is revealed through their playful repartee and wry innuendo. Desirée's ability to first hold him off, then later courtesy and manners that were present at a time before commercialism and corporate acquisition disrupted the charm, delicacy, and grace of old Europe.

Q: Can you describe your writing process? Did writing energize or exhaust you? Do you have any unusual writing rituals?

A: My writing process is based more on thinking and reflection than sitting before the keyboard. A healthy breakfast, followed by a long walk, allows me to ruminate and argue with myself regarding plot directions and character development. I restrain myself from trying to write anything until I have worked out the next sequences in my head. Only when the story is at the tips of my fingers do I seek out my MacBook.

I've read a lot about various writers' quirks and habits, but I don't observe any preconceived repertoire regarding time of day, word quotas, writer's block, etc. But when I've had a good day, I reward myself and thank my wife for her patience by going out for a nice dinner where we have a good bottle of Burgundy or Bordeaux.

Q: Was there anything you edited out of this book? Or something you wanted to include but didn't? If so, what was it?

A: I've found that in the writing of a novel, many of the trails that seem promising turn out to be box canyons. At that point, there's nothing to do but circle back or hit the delete key. But not all is lost; rather the situation that didn't work goes back into the mental inventory where it might work the next time.

Q: How did you choose the names of the characters? Were any based on real people?

A: Choosing the names of the characters was the most fun of all, except for coming up with a title. I found that both are harder than they might seem. For my characters, I used the names—either first or last—of people I actually know. But the characters in the book have no connection to these real people, their personalities, occupations, or physical characteristics. If my friends read the book, I'm sure they'll be tickled to be included. On the other hand, the names Desirée and Scott were chosen based on my perception of their traits.

Q: What authors do you like to read? Did any of them have any influence over this story?

A: I read when I'm not writing, as much nonfiction as fiction. I'm not aware of any tendency that my writing exhibits, but over the years, I've enjoyed authors such as: Hemingway, Fitzgerald, Roth, Salter, Nabokov, Tolstoy, Dostoevsky, Austen, Fellows, and since I read in French, Flaubert, Gide, Stendhal, Sagan, and de Beauvoir.

Q: Do you have any plans for a future book, or do you perhaps already have something in the works?

A: Shortly after finishing *An Improbable Pairing*, I wrote its sequel, *A Spy With Scruples*, a blend of romance and espionage yet unpublished. Currently I'm writing the sequel to the sequel, which has the working title *St. Sucrose*. I also wrote a novel that deals in mystical circumstances entitled, *An Oddity of Some Consequence*. Additionally, at the suggestion of a friend in Paris, I have written a small book of French poetry based on a loose Alexandrine metre with English translations and supporting recipes which celebrates French food specialties and my acquaintance with same: *La Poesie De Bonne Bouffe* or *The Poetry of Good Eats*.